# Barefoot
# Days

A novel
by Darlene Deluca

*Happy Reading !*

*Darlene
Deluca*

Other titles
by Darlene Deluca

The Storm Within
Book One, Women of Whitfield

Second Wind
(Book Two, Women of Whitfield)

Her Greatest Risk

Something Good

Meetings of Chance

Unexpected Legacy

This is a work of fiction. Names, characters, places and incidents are fictitious products of the author's imagination. Any resemblance to actual persons, living or dead, events or locations is entirely coincidental.

# Barefoot
# Days

## Chapter One

Mary Logan hesitated. And the heavy glass door of The Coffee House smacked her in the backside, pushing her forward and causing the chimes at the top of the door to clang, alerting everyone in the shop to her presence. Heads swiveled in her direction. She blamed Regina Daniels for the sting to her hip, and the inelegant entrance. Mary considered Regina a friend of sorts. But the look the woman had given Mary in response to her jaunty wave was anything but friendly. It was, in fact, an unquestionably icy glare.

Before she could process that outrageous thought, John Sherman turned from the counter. "Hello, John," Mary said. "How are—"

John gave a barely perceptible nod and walked past her.

Confused, Mary stepped to the counter and gave her order while frost settled in her chest. What in the world was going on? She couldn't remember offending anyone – recently. Mentally she ticked through the various committees she served, trying to pinpoint an issue. She came up empty, but she was no stranger to drama. The slightest ember could erupt into flames with but a whisper of hot air.

She surveyed the crowd, surprised to see so many tables filled. Apparently she wasn't the only one who needed a mid-morning pick-me-up. She'd left the house early to work the seven a.m. shift at the food pantry, and settled for a cup of the dark, murky liquid provided there – a bitter brew that fell outside Mary's definition of coffee. She was overdue for some good stuff.

When a young man behind the counter called her name, Mary sensed eyes settling on her. Normally, she might linger and visit with acquaintances. Instead, she took the cup, pasted a smile on her face, and walked to the door with her head held high.

Inside her car, Mary blew out her breath and switched on the radio, almost expecting to hear the notes of the Twilight Zone tune drift from the speakers. She had clearly entered another dimension. Hmm. Whom to call, she wondered, drumming her fingers on the steering wheel as she drove. If only her friend Claire were still in town, she could do reconnaissance for her, sniff out the issue and report back. She'd have to try someone else. Or not, she reconsidered. Most likely she'd catch wind of whatever it was within the hour. Probably should've marched right over to Regina and demanded to know what her snit was all about.

Two pick-up trucks sat in her driveway when Mary turned in. "Now what?" she muttered. Grant hadn't mentioned that he was expecting company this morning.

Mary entered the house through the garage door. She dropped her purse on the counter, then picked up her calendar and sank into a chair at the kitchen table, determined to enjoy her well-earned latte. She heard muffled voices coming from the living room, and considered whether she should play hostess and see if anyone needed anything. The room smelled of coffee, so Grant had obviously taken care of that on his own.

Deciding against interrupting the low din of conversation, she kicked off her shoes – the closed-toe kind. They were cute, and stylish, and appropriate for fall weather, but she'd gone into them kicking and screaming. Early October, and she still mourned the loss of her sandals and flip-flops – and the weather that went along with them. She glanced outside the kitchen window. The cool temperatures were starting to make their mark on the trees. The dogwoods on the shady side of the yard hinted at the vibrant red that would soon follow. Another week or so, and the entire landscape would change hues. If the Kansas winds cooperated, it could be a spectacular couple of weeks. Would've made for some beautiful wedding photos, she couldn't help thinking. Her daughter's choice of dates baffled her. No summer flowers, no autumn leaves, and too early for festive Christmas boughs and berries.

Mary opened her calendar, and checked off the pantry shift. A few more commitments and then she was clearing the calendar. Annie's wedding was only five weeks away. It would be spectacular, Mary reminded herself, even without Mother Nature's help. They'd ordered loads of gorgeous flowers and–

"What are we going to do about it?" A voice thundered from the next room, breaking her train of thought. Automatically, she bounced up from her chair and hurried to the front room, her slippery socks nearly skidding on the hardwood floors as she rounded the staircase. Hanging onto the entryway casing for support, she stared at the three men seated there, taking in the flushed red face of her husband's best friend.

"What is going on in my living room, gentlemen?" she demanded, her voice carrying surprise, humor and a hint of scolding all at the same time. "May I remind you this is my home, not a bar room? So, if there's going to a brawl, might I suggest . . ." her gaze shifted pointedly toward the door.

"It's okay," Grant told her with a slight shake of his head.

Doug Wharton nodded. "Hello, Mary."

The third man was much younger, and Mary recognized him as a former employee, but couldn't come up with his name.

"Sorry, Miz Logan," he said, his voice low, like a chagrined schoolboy.

"Just watch the furniture." She gave a little laugh, but something fluttered inside when she met her husband's eyes. His expression was serious, but there was something else . . . sadness? Had there been some kind of accident, she wondered. "Can I get y'all anything? Something civilized, like a beverage?"

Three heads shook a negative response.

"All right, then."

Retreating, Mary heaved a sigh. Wasn't even noon and this day was skyrocketing on the scale of strange. Instead of resuming her place at the kitchen table, she opened the refrigerator door, and studied the contents. Might as well start thinking about supper. But it was hard to concentrate on anything other then the men's voices, and she found herself straining to make out the conversation.

When she heard the front door close a few minutes later, Mary pushed aside her grocery list, and leaned against the granite-topped island that separated the kitchen from the family room, waiting.

Grant's steps were slow as he made his way toward her. "Hey," he said, stopping just short of the kitchen.

"Hey. What's up?"

He held out a hand, and Mary instantly moved forward. As soon as she put her hand in his, he pulled her against him and nuzzled into her hair. Several long moments passed before he spoke.

"Ah, Mary-me, we've got some trouble."

She took a tiny step back and met his eyes. "Yeah, that didn't sound like a friendly shoot-the-breeze kind of meeting. What's the matter?"

He led her to the kitchen island and helped her onto a chair. Hands on his hips, he faced her. "Essex is laying people off."

"What?" Mary nearly jumped back out of the chair, his words hitting like a jolt of electricity. "You have got to be kidding. You've been gone– what? a month? and already they're having financial trouble? How is that possible?"

Grant shook his head. "They're not having financial trouble. I'm guessing there's pressure to increase profits. Pure and simple."

"Oh, no. Oh, Grant, I can't believe it. They– they *promised* to keep your employees."

He raked a hand through his hair. "They did what they promised as long as I was on the board. One year. Gave 'em all one lousy year."

"So that's it? One year, and they're off the hook? This must've been their plan all along."

"Maybe. With the slow months coming up, I expected there to be some consolidation issues, but I sure thought they'd work everybody in someplace."

She could see where his thoughts were going, feeling responsible, as usual. "You can't take it personally."

"I just wish they'd been straight with me so I could've warned the boys, could've told them to start looking a year ago."

"How many, Grant?"

"About twenty."

"Oh, no." Her stomach dropped. That was a third of what used to be his work force. "Are they getting a severance package?"

"Sure. Based on length of service. Thing is, they're pushing out some of the older guys like Doug. They'll have a harder time finding something else. I'd bet my last dime they'll replace them next spring with younger, cheaper fellas."

"Of course. Happens all the time. That's the way it works." Mary blew out her breath. "Well, that explains the frosty glares I got at The Coffee House this morning."

Grant bristled. "Somebody say something to you?"

"No. But I swear, if looks could kill, you'd be planning my funeral about now."

His jaw hardened. "Who was it? By God, they can come over here and rip me a new one if they think it helps, but they better leave you out of this."

"Whoa. Down, boy," Mary said, grabbing onto his arm. Her husband had a nice, long fuse that was slow to turn into anything more than a low simmer, but on rare occasions, he reached the end. When that happened, the resulting explosion could put Mt. St. Helens to shame. She gave him a wry smile. "You can put your sword away – no one compromised my honor."

"They better not." He hitched a thigh onto a chair, and turned, his eyes going distant, as though he were deep in thought.

"So," Mary said softly. "What do we do? Is there anything you can do?"

"Haven't talked to Joe, yet. Don't see as I have any say unless I want to buy it back." He looked at her then. "And I don't."

God, no, Mary thought. They *could*. They'd invested almost all the money. Guilt washed over her. It was a lot of money. Grant's business was doing well when Joe Thomas, chairman of Essex Industries, had approached him about buying the cement operation. With Grant itching for a change, it'd been perfect timing.

Mary let out a soft groan, and slipped from the chair. "I need an aspirin."

"You got another headache?"

"Love, I think I'll have a headache until this wedding is over."

"Thought you were having fun."

She tossed back the tablet and a drink of water before answering. "Think roller coaster. Extreme bursts of fun and excitement intermixed with head-pounding bouts of stress and anxiety."

"Might have fewer guests."

Mary heard the regret in Grant's voice. She walked back to the counter and ran a hand down his sleeve. "The ones who matter will be there." She swallowed hard, thinking of the wedding guest list. She hated to think of anything casting a shadow on Annie's big day.

"What about Sally?" Mary asked. Sally Connors had been one of his first employees. She and Mary had handled all the bookkeeping, filing, and secretarial duties until the business grew and Mary stepped aside to raise kids. Sally's role had become administrative assistant.

"Out," Grant said.

"Well, shoot," Mary said. "I'm sure she's bummed, but maybe it'll be good for her. It'd be nice if she could have a life before she dies, you know." Mary meant that in a good way. Sally was older than Grant, had lost her husband early in life, and had no children. She lived with several dogs, and was a workaholic. Retirement was a notion that never seemed to cross her mind.

"She'll be all right, but people are upset."

"I'm sure."

"Maybe we should get out for a while. Go somewhere until this dies down."

"Oh, Grant, we can't leave now, not with the wedding a few weeks away. Besides, we live here. We can't hide from this." She took hold of his arm. "You didn't do anything wrong. It's not your fault."

"A month," he said, his voice low and weary. "I've had one month of retirement." Grant shoved his hands into his pockets and shook his head. "People just don't understand. They don't get how much pressure there is. How hard it is to be responsible for other people, for their paycheck and livelihood. I don't want to do it anymore."

"You don't have to. You aren't responsible for this. Yes, it sucks, but these people are adults. They know the economy, how business works."

"Bad timing. Some of them just got their houses put back together after the tornado. Money's already tight." A deadly tornado had ripped through Whitfield just over a year ago, and a chunk of the town was still in recovery mode.

"So let's think of something we can do," Mary said. Once again, she felt a wince of guilt. She and Grant lived the good life. They had a beautiful home with a pool, drove nice cars, and had sent each of their children to college. Some people, the ones who weren't personal friends, might be resentful. What could they do that wouldn't look like charity? "What about setting up a fund for financial planning or job placement? Anonymous gift cards to everyone? Just to help out a little?"

"Maybe," Grant said, his tone non-committal. "Don't worry. I'll talk to Joe and some of the guys. Give me some time to make sure I've got all the facts." He leaned in and planted a quick kiss on her lips. "I've got some calls to make."

"Sure." She watched him head toward his office, her heart aching. He didn't deserve to be yelled at or blamed for this. He'd always worked hard. Had been a good and fair boss. He'd built that business from nothing. The man had earned every cent the company made – and the right to retire. She took a deep breath, willing herself to stay calm and think rationally, but at the same time a fierce loyalty burned inside her. Her husband would not take the fall for this.

## Chapter Two

Mary tapped her phone against her palm, trying to remember Jane's schedule. As a good friend, Mary felt compelled to touch base with her. Jane worked at the Whitfield High School office part time, but never knew where she would end up on any given day. Today she might be reeling from the news of Doug's layoff. With a lump in her throat, Mary hesitated. Would Jane need more time to process? Or be too busy to talk? Sometimes she was out front dealing with visitors and students, and sometimes–

*Oh, no.* Mary's thoughts collided with concerns about the day's unwelcome news. Would Jane be able to get health insurance for herself and Doug through the school district? Mary knew Jane loved the flexibility of working part time. Would she have to increase her hours to qualify for insurance? Work full time for a number of years to get retirement benefits? Would Doug be able to continue insurance through Essex?

Sucking in a deep breath, Mary hit the call button. She needed answers to those questions whether it meant interrupting Jane at work or not. In her mind, this counted as an emergency.

"Hey, Mare." Jane picked up on the second ring.

Mary let out a sigh of relief. Jane's tone sounded perfectly normal. "Hi, there. Hey, are you working? Can you talk?"

9

Jane sputtered a humorless laugh. "I'm at work, but I can't say I'm actually working. My phone is ringing nonstop."

"About Essex?"

"Yeah. Doug called me this morning. The announcement was at eight o'clock, as soon as everyone got in. They dropped the bomb then told everyone who was let go they could take the rest of the day off – if they wanted to. As if anyone would stick around after that."

"Oh, Janie, I'm so sorry. We never expected–"

"You didn't know, right?"

"Not a clue. I can't believe they–"

"Some people are wondering, you know."

"Wondering?" Mary echoed.

"If you and Grant knew this was coming. If Grant was part–"

"Not a word." Mary couldn't keep the emotion at bay as her voice hardened. "He hasn't been in the office for a month. We're just as surprised as anyone. And furious, I might add. Grant says the financials looked good when he left the board. Greedy bastards."

"It was definitely a surprise," Jane agreed. "A big one."

"Listen, hon, I'm not trying to pry into your business, but are you guys going to be all right? Doug still gets retirement and insurance benefits?" She heard Jane's deep breath.

"He's still studying the packet they gave him, but yeah, it looks like he'll get coverage. It'll be more expensive, though."

"Thank God it's available, at least. I was having visions – very ugly visions – of you chained to a desk at that school for the rest of your life."

"Oh, I don't think it will come to that. You know Doug, Mr. Frugal. We've got savings and investments. We'll be fine."

"I knew that, but the insurance thing can bite."

"You don't need to worry about us."

That statement should have been reassuring, but something in Jane's voice triggered an alarm. Was there someone they *did* need to worry about?

"What do you–"

"Listen, Mare, I better get going. Really, I've been dealing with this all morning, and have accomplished absolutely zilch. If I'm not careful, I'll be getting the boot, too."

"Okay, but let's go to lunch. When's your next day off? Or dinner out, the four of us. Maybe tonight? I don't want to hide from this."

"I get it. I'll talk to Doug, and we'll be in touch."

An hour and three phone calls later, and Mary commiserated with Jane. She hadn't gotten anything accomplished, either. The trip to the grocery store still hadn't happened. Maybe they'd have to eat out tonight. She was reconsidering the options when her cell phone rang again. Mary checked the caller ID, surprised to see her youngest daughter's photo pop up. She usually tried the land line first.

"Mother Knows Best at your service. Go ahead, please."

"Hi, Mom," Sara answered in a dry, indulgent tone.

"Hey, sweetie, how you doing?"

"Pretty good."

"Working a lot of hours? Haven't heard from you much lately."

"Yeah, been busy. What's going on there?"

"Oh, my. It's a crazy day around here."

"Really? What's up?"

Tired of that conversation already, Mary gave her the Reader's Digest condensed version. "I'm sure it'll all blow over in a couple of months when people find new jobs and realize it's not the end of the world. Dad feels bad, though."

"I bet. He always takes things so hard."

"I'm glad we have the wedding coming up. It'll take his mind off Essex and their troubles. At least, it better." She gave a short laugh. She expected to have her husband's full attention for the wedding of their eldest daughter.

"So I was just thinking about the wedding. That's why I called. Do you have my dress?"

Mary glanced toward the hall closet where all the bridesmaid dresses hung, including Sara's shimmery apple green maid-of-honor gown. "Yes. They're all here, ready to go. Why?"

"I thought I might pick mine up. I haven't decided on jewelry and shoes for sure."

"What about the shoes you wore to the fitting?"

"I have some others I think might be more comfortable."

"Sarie, I'd really rather keep them all together. They've been steamed, and they're hanging up in plastic where they won't get creased or dirty. And you know we talked about Annie giving all the bridesmaids those pearl and sea-glass necklaces as gifts. I'm sure you don't need to think any more about it."

"Well, maybe I'll come down this weekend and bring the shoes with me."

"As in tomorrow?"

"Yeah, is that okay?"

"Of course. We'd love it. But you're not making a special trip for the dress, are you?" Mary shook her head. How odd. It wasn't Sara's nature to be so concerned with clothes. Annie had always been the fashion queen in their house while Sara was content with jeans and sweatpants.

"No, but at least I could try it on again while I'm there."

"I'm sure it's fine. It fit beautifully when you tried it on at Vickie's shop."

"But, Mom, that was two months ago."

"Well, you haven't changed dress sizes in the last two months, have you?" Mary laughed. Her daughter had always been enviously thin. Had even managed to avoid the freshman fifteen when she went to college. She certainly couldn't afford to lose weight. At that thought, mama bear radar went up. "Sweetie, you're not losing weight, are you? Are you eating enough?"

Sara worked a lot of hours, and Mary had no idea whether she ever had a decent meal or had been reduced to eating junk on the run. "Are they running you ragged at work?"

"No, Mom. Don't worry. I eat and sleep."

"Well, then—"

"Never mind," Sara broke in. "I'm sure it'll be fine."

In which case the original concern made no sense. "Well, unless the shoes are much higher or shorter, the dress is perfect." She tried to remember the specific style of Sara's dress. Fairly snug, she thought. Oh. Could Sara be eating too much? Dealing with stress by eating, and putting on weight? If she'd gained a few pounds, she might not want to mention that. Mary groped for a tactful approach.

"Are you worried that your dress was a little snug?"

"It did fit awfully close," Sara said.

Bingo! "Let me take a look at the design. Maybe I could let it out a bit. Sweetie, are you gaining weight?" Again, Mary wondered if something were wrong. Given a choice, Sara had always gone for healthy foods, wasn't one to overindulge in sweets or— Mary sucked in her breath as an idea popped into her head out of nowhere. There was one other reason Sara could have put on enough weight to make a difference in her dress size. Where in the world had that come from? That was crazy, wasn't it? The gears clicked inside Mary's brain, and she stood still clutching the phone, while her heart pounded.

"Sara," she said slowly, "are you sure everything is okay?"

Heavy silence filled the air.

Hardly daring to breath, Mary asked, "Anything you want to talk about?" She heard the reluctant sigh from across the line. "Cuz I just had the craziest thought. That you—" Mary let out a nervous laugh, wishing Sara would give her a hand, some clue as to what was going on. "Oh, my gosh. There for a minute, I wondered if you were pregnant."

The sound Mary heard could only be described as a squeak.

"Sara? Talk to me."

"Well, shoot, I messed that up, didn't I? I wasn't going to tell you until after the wedding, but I'm afraid the dress could be too tight by then."

"Oh, Sara." Mary scrambled to keep up. "Are you serious? You're pregnant?"

"I am."

"How far along are you? You think it'll be obvious?"

"Only a couple of months. If we let the side seams out a little bit, it should be good."

"Oh, my God. I can't believe this. You're pregnant?! I'm going to be a grandmother?"

"Mom, keep it down. Can anyone hear you?"

"No. I'm home alone."

"Okay, so don't tell anyone."

"Sweetheart, I can't keep it from your dad."

"Fine, but nobody else for now. I don't want to steal Annie's thunder."

"Right. We don't need a big announcement before the wedding. But, um, let's talk about weddings, toots. Is there one in your future?"

"I think so." Excitement crept into Sara's voice.

"You think so?"

"We're going out for a nice dinner tonight. I– I think he's going to propose."

"Does he know about the baby?"

"Not yet. I'll tell him tonight."

An uneasy feeling settled in Mary's chest. This didn't seem exactly right. "Well, I sure wish we'd had a chance to meet him before all of this."

"I know. Me, too. But he's coming with me to Annie's wedding, and we already talked about being there for Thanksgiving. You'll love him. I promise."

"And I'm assuming you do, too. You want this baby?"

14

"Yeah," Sara replied softly. "I do."

"All right, then, sweetie. I have to say it's awfully sudden, but I'm happy for you, and can't wait to see you. Are you feeling good?"

"I feel fine. Just hungry. It's so weird."

"Oh, just wait. You don't know weird yet."

"I'm sure."

"What time will you be here tomorrow?" She did some quick math. It was only a couple of hours from Kansas City. "Maybe we should plan on lunch? A big one?"

"Very funny. But, yes, I can be there around noon. And you can feed me."

"Deal. See you then. Be careful, and I love you."

"Love you, too. Bye."

Mary ended the call, and collapsed into an armchair. Was this for real? She was finally going to be a grandmother? The thought almost made her whoop out loud. Her first inclination was to get right back on her phone and call Claire. But she'd been sworn to secrecy. A cruel twist of fate. How was she supposed to keep this a secret for five weeks? No cards? No sweet little gifts? *Ack*. She'd better buy a big ol' roll of duct tape. This wasn't going to be easy.

Somehow, she'd have to keep her focus on Annie's wedding. With that in mind, she marched to the hallway closet and pulled out Sara's dress. Fingering the fabric, she wondered how well the soft folds could hide a small baby bump. If there was one.

\*\*

With supreme effort, Mary pushed away thoughts of a new baby while she and Grant drove the short distance to Bailey's for dinner. Telling him would have to wait until afterward. He wouldn't be excited that Sara was pregnant and not married, but if she showed up tomorrow with an engagement ring on her finger, it wouldn't matter. And it just might be welcome news after dealing with the Essex debacle.

She glanced his direction. Since he'd been gone all afternoon, they hadn't had time to catch up. Mary rested a hand on his thigh. "So fill me in, quick," she said. "Anything I need to know before dinner? Doug was angry this morning."

"He's okay. Was just hot about how it was handled. He never clicked with Joe."

"What about the others?"

"Little bit of everything. Twenty's the right number, though." He shot her a look, his eyebrows raised. "Surprised you wanted to go out tonight."

"Of course I do. Like I said, we can't hide from this. If we see anyone, I want to let them know we care, that we're upset, too. Plus, Doug and Jane are good friends. People need to see there are no hard feelings. Jane said her phone was ringing all morning."

"People calling her about Essex?"

"Uh-huh. She's caught in the middle."

"She upset?" Grant pulled the car into the crowded parking lot.

"No. She's fine."

"I've set up time with Joe on Monday, but from what I can tell, the terms are pretty standard."

Outside the car Mary took Grant's arm. "Hmm. Standard doesn't sound the same as good."

His only reply was a grunt.

Mary spotted Doug and Jane immediately. They already had a table – and visitors who'd stopped to chat. As Mary and Grant approached, the others scattered like cockroaches in the light. Though disappointment pooled in her stomach, Mary smiled and tightened her grip on Grant's arm. "Just act natural," she whispered under her breath. Grace under pressure was her mantra.

But as she sank into the chair Grant pulled out, it occurred to her that she hadn't faced a lot of external pressures in her life. In fact, the only thing that came to mind was the time in high school when a rumor had been started that she was a two-timing slut stringing Grant along while he was away at college. The ensuing drama could've been a Mean Girls mini-series. She'd survived that by staying cool and true to herself. Exactly what she planned to do now.

As usual, the Friday night crowd at Bailey's was loud, and nearly every seat in the bar and restaurant was taken. Maybe it was her imagination, but Mary felt tension wrap around her. Like this morning, she sensed hostile eyes staring at her – confirming that the layoff of twenty people in a small town impacted a lot of others. Every person laid off had friends and family. The chain reaction could cause a significant ripple effect. And then there were the other forty who hadn't been let go. The situation had to be awkward for them, too.

She tried to shut out the noise in her brain as well as the booming music and hollering around her. She nodded toward Jane's glass of wine. "How's that going down, girlfriend?"

Jane lifted her glass. "Just what the doctor ordered."

"I bet. I think I'll join you."

When Mary's glass arrived, she quietly took a sip. Normally, she would've raised it in the air and toasted their friends, or the weekend, or something. As much as she wanted to behave naturally, normal wasn't appropriate right now.

"Did the afternoon get any better?" Mary asked Jane.

She shrugged. "Stopped answering my phone."

"So what's the deal? Everyone just venting or are they expecting you to do something?"

"Oh, venting, mostly."

Mary arched her brows. "And the not-mostly?"

"A few are trying to figure out whose side I'm on, you know. Since Doug got sacked, too, am I one of them? Some want to know if I have any inside intel since we're friends with you guys."

"Bobby Daniels is an ass."

Doug's words whipped Mary's head around. She dropped the french fry she was about to eat, and gave the men her full attention.

"Sure, it hit him hard," Doug continued, his voice low. "Hurts worse because he had some damn notion in his head that he was going to be promoted."

"Regina called twice today," Jane added. "I haven't called her back yet." Jane took a long drink from her glass. "Not sure I'm up for that conversation."

"She gave me the cold shoulder at The Coffee House this morning. I guess—" Mary broke off when a hand slid across her back. She looked up to see Dana Gerard and her fiancé, Kent Donovan. One of Mary's closest friends, Dana had recently been promoted from head nurse to administrator at the Whitfield hospital.

"Hey, y'all! Pull up a chair." Mary surveyed the nearby tables for open chairs as Grant stood to put her invitation into action.

"Oh, we don't want to interrupt," Dana told her.

"Come on, we'd love it. There's a wait, right?"

"About twenty minutes."

"So do you want to stand around for twenty minutes or take a load off and have a drink?"

Mary scooted to the end of the table so that Dana could squeeze in by the girls, and still sit beside Kent.

"What's everybody doing this weekend?" Dana asked.

"Putting out fires as near as I can tell," Mary said.

"Oh. Essex?"

"Doug and nineteen others were laid off this morning."

Dana nodded, a sympathetic look flashing across her face. "I know. Sorry to hear that, Jane. You know Jeanie Thresher, one of my nurses, right? Her husband got a pink slip, too."

"Ohhh," Mary wailed. "Scott, too? He's the nicest guy. I cannot believe they're willing to let these people go. It makes me sick."

They fell into conversation divided by gender, as usually happened. Though Kent Donovan, part of an insurance disaster team, had arrived in Whitfield only as a result of the devastating tornado, he fit in without a hitch. Mary had liked him even before his fiancée did, and she was thrilled that her friend had found love at this stage in her life.

"Man, it stinks in here," someone hollered from the bar, turning every head in the restaurant.

"Yeah, but they think their shit don't stink."

Mary caught her breath, and glanced at Grant. Was that comment directed at them?

"You boys about finished up here?" the bartender addressed a motley crowd of men at the bar.

"No," one of them answered. He stood and glared toward Grant, an arrogant challenge in his eyes. "We're about to get started." Mary didn't recognize the young man in jeans and hooded sweatshirt who swaggered a few steps in their direction. A second later, the owner and another bartender flanked the man.

"Look, we're not having any trouble in here tonight. It's time for you to pay your tab and hit the road."

"Pay my tab?" the man shouted, wrestling to free his arms. "Hey, man, guess what? I can't pay my tab. You want to know why? 'Cause I don't have a job anymore, man. Thanks to that jerk-off right there."

With another shove, the two managed to turn the man around and head the opposite direction. Thank God.

"Hey, I got an idea," another one of the guys shouted. "Let's give the tab to team hot-shot there. A whole table full of big shots."

"You guys cool it or get out of here," Tim, one of the owners, shouted back toward the bar. "Take your troubles somewhere else."

"Yeah, thanks for nothing. I'll take my business somewhere else." He followed after his buddy, but a few of the others remained. Mary figured they didn't want to be on Tim's bad side. There weren't that many places to go for a beer on a Friday night without leaving town.

Tim approached the table. "Sorry about that folks. We'll take care of it."

Grant waved a hand, and spoke quietly. "I'll take that tab, Tim."

19

"Nah. Forget it." He strode back to the bar and shook a finger at the smaller group. "No. More."

Mary couldn't eat another bite. Her fingers shook when she picked up her glass and attempted to finish her wine. All conversation at their table had come to an abrupt halt.

Dana put a hand on Mary's sleeve. "Oh, Mare. You've been dealing with this all day?"

"Yeah. I thought getting out and facing people would be better than holing up at the house. Now, I'm not so sure. I wish someone would give me an idea of how to help."

"If you ask me, it was pretty stupid of Essex to let people go this morning instead of the end of the day. I bet those idiots have been drinking all afternoon."

An hour later, after they'd paid their own bill, Grant pushed back his chair. "Be right back." Mary watched him walk calmly to the bar while he fished his wallet out of his back pocket. He handed some bills to the bartender, then gave a curt nod to the wide-eyed, but silent group still nursing their beers. She glanced around the restaurant, hoping everyone could see what a class act her husband was.

"You about ready to go?" he asked, back at their table.

"Absolutely." Mary pushed back her chair, then grabbed for the table as her ankle gave way.

Grant caught her arm. "You okay?"

She wiggled her foot in front of her. "Oh, fiddle, my foot's gone to sleep again." Great timing. All she needed was to land in a heap in the middle of Bailey's. Everyone would assume *she'd* been drinking all afternoon.

"After I get through this wedding and the holidays, I have to sign up for one of those Zumba or Pilates classes at the community center. Something to get the circulation going, I guess."

"Hey, make sure it's on one of my days off, and I'll join you," Jane told her.

"Yeah? That'd be great. I'll keep you posted." She glanced at Dana – the career girl who often got left out. Mary gave Dana a nudge. "We can go with an evening or Saturday if you're in."

Dana shook her head. "Thanks, Mare, but I'll pass." She jerked a thumb toward Kent. "This task master is keeping us both on a rigorous walking schedule."

Mary smiled in Kent's direction, and hugged Dana's arm as they walked to the exit. "Mostly likely he just wants to keep you all to himself."

In the parking lot, only a few steps from their car, Grant stopped short. "Well, hell," he said under his breath.

"What?"

He nodded toward the car. "Guess I shouldn't be surprised." He moved forward, and ran his hand across the car door.

Mary crouched down for a closer look. "Oh, no!" Even in the dim light of the parking lot, she could see a thin line scarring the length of the metallic gold Acura, ruining the smooth paint job. Last year, Grant had finally relented and agreed to buy something other than a Ford since so many parts and assembly plants operated in the United States these days. Mary had quickly adjusted to the bells and whistles and luxuries the newer car provided.

"Damn it! I cannot believe this." Mary exploded, her eyes searching the parking lot for the culprits. "Vandalizing my car! What is the point—"

Interrupting her tirade, Grant pulled her close before taking her arm, and steering her to the passenger side of the car. She inspected the finish. As far as she could tell, there was no damage. As soon as they climbed inside the car, Grant blew out his breath. "It's just a car."

Unused to being a target of hostility, tears stung Mary's eyes. Sure. But it was *her* car. She waited a moment before answering. "I suppose it could've been worse. At least no one threw any punches inside."

"You all right?" Grant reached for her hand, and gave it a squeeze.

"I'm fine. Bummed about the car, though. And it's exhausting to be on pins and needles around people."

"Yeah, I'm about ready to crash."

Mary pushed aside her irritation over the damaged car during the short drive home. The night wasn't over. "Well, don't crash in front of the TV. I have something to tell you."

His head turned. "What?"

"I'll tell you inside. Don't worry. It's good." At least it would be after he got used to the idea. And after Sara had that ring on her finger.

Ten minutes later, she handed him a cold beer and dropped onto the sofa facing him.

"What's the good news, darlin'?"

"Now this is a secret—"

"You're telling secrets?"

"This one is for us." Mary gave a nervous smile, keeping her own feelings in check. "You're going to be a grandpa."

Good thing she'd let him swallow the gulp of beer he'd just taken because his jaw dropped as his eyes widened. Mary held her breath, her stomach fluttering. She knew Grant loved their kids as much as she did. But she also knew that her husband was on the old-fashioned side. He believed in the proper order of things. You don't "shack up" with your boyfriend or girlfriend before getting married. And you don't get pregnant before you get married.

After a long moment of silence, he stretched an arm along the sofa and lifted his brows. "A grandpa? Huh. We have three kids, and as far as I know, none of them are married."

Mary rested her arm along his. "True that. But Sara has never been one to follow all the rules," Mary reminded him.

"Sara?"

"Mm-hmm."

"Well, hell. I would've thought Annie."

Mary shook her head. "No. Think about their personalities. Sara's always been the one to push the boundaries and do her own thing."

Grant sat up straighter. "Right. So what's the plan?"

Mary reached down to massage her foot while she talked. Immediately, Grant took over. "She's coming home tomorrow. Should be here about lunchtime. And she just might be wearing an engagement ring. When she called this afternoon, she said they were going out for a nice dinner tonight, and she thought he might pop the question."

"She bringing him with her?"

"No. Just her."

"So I'm going to be a grandpa. Am I ever going to meet this kid's father?"

"Relax. She's bringing him to the wedding. And if they get engaged first, maybe she'll bring him for a visit. Or, we could do a quick weekend in Kansas City."

"Hell, yes. I'm all for that."

In Kansas City, they could shop. She could buy Sara a few maternity items and get away with picking up a cute blanket or pair of booties to stash at her apartment. With that hurdle cleared, Mary leaned in for a kiss. A short hiatus from the tension around Whitfield might be best for everyone.

## Chapter Three

The image reflected in the mirror hid its secret well. Sara surveyed her figure with a critical eye. The little black dress with a band of sequins at the waist was perfect. Dressing up wasn't her thing. It always made her feel self-conscious, but over the years she'd begun to subscribe to her mother's philosophy of letting the occasion dictate the dress. This might be a special occasion worthy of a little extra effort.

Her heart fluttered as she smoothed her hands over the front of the dress. She held up her bare left hand, envisioning a diamond ring sparkling there. Would Todd pick something out for her, or would they go to a jeweler together? She'd always thought a simple solitaire would be lovely.

With anticipation building inside her, she slipped into the high-heeled black pumps, hoping she wouldn't teeter and twist an ankle. She'd only worn them a few times. With a last fluff of her hair, she carefully made her way to the front room, and was waiting near the door when Todd arrived. Before he could ring the bell, she stepped outside, and lifted her face for his kiss.

"Hey." His lips briefly met hers, and he took her arm. "You ready?"

"Oh. Um, sure." She quickly pulled the door closed. As he steered her toward the parking lot, the October breeze floated over Sara's bare shoulders, and she stopped to shrug into her sweater. Todd moved ahead and opened the car door for her before climbing in the driver's side. Sara looked at her watch, wondering if they were running late. Seemed like they had plenty of time, but maybe Todd was in need of a Friday evening cocktail. It'd been a hectic week.

She settled into the leather seat of Todd's sleek gray Jetta and leaned her head back. "Ahhhh," she said. "Happy Friday."

"Yeah."

"How did the budget meeting go? You guys get everything straightened out?"

He nodded. "Yeah, it's good. We cut out a couple of print ads, though."

"Oh, okay. That doesn't sound too bad." Sara's marketing team handled a chunk of advertising and public relations for Todd's company, which had recently asked its departments to tighten the belts a little.

Driving along Brush Creek Boulevard, Sara surveyed the night life. They'd miss the lighting ceremony this year. Last year, on one of their early outings, she and Todd had joined thousands of other people on a cool but clear Thanksgiving night to watch the spectacular flipping of the switch – the moment when bright, colorful lights suddenly outlined the Plaza buildings and illuminated the entire area. How different things would be this year. For the first time ever she'd be taking a boyfriend – or fiancé – home for a holiday.

Todd pulled up to the valet station in front of the restaurant, handed the valet his key, then ushered Sara inside. They checked in with the hostess, but instead of heading for the bar, Todd hovered near the front. "I made reservations, so we should get right in," he told her.

Sara stifled a giggle. Poor guy was so tense. Maybe she should pop the question herself and put him out of his misery so they could enjoy dinner. They were seated after a few minutes in one of the quieter sections of the restaurant.

"This is good," Todd commented, glancing around.

"Sure," she murmured.

"Evening folks, can I get you something other than water to drink?" their waiter asked. "Cocktail? Glass of wine?"

A flash of panic swept through Sara. Would Todd think it was strange if she didn't order a glass of wine? That's what she usually had. She licked her lips. "Um, you know, I think alcohol might put me to sleep. Could I get an iced tea, please?"

Todd didn't seem to notice. He ordered a gin and tonic then excused himself, leaving Sara to wonder if he was arranging something with the kitchen or waiter. She opened her menu and considered the options.

When Todd returned a few minutes later, he silently did the same.

Peeking over the menu, she watched him. He was fidgeting, and gulping down water as if he'd just finished running a marathon. Nervous, she supposed. After they placed their order and the waiter left the table, Sara leaned in expectantly.

Todd shifted in his seat, and glanced away, tapping his fingers against his glass.

Okay, maybe he wasn't ready. She sat back and took a sip of her iced tea, belatedly wondering if the caffeine was any better than wine. They chatted about work and the restaurant, and pretty much nothing for several minutes. So odd, she thought. She'd never felt awkward with Todd before. Attempting to push past the tension, Sara lifted her water glass to his. "We should toast to the weekend. And, hey, since you've got stuff going on tomorrow, I think I'll run down and visit my parents."

"Sounds good."

"They can't wait to meet you."

Surprised when he didn't echo the sentiment, Sara turned her attention to the waiter and the plate he delivered, her thoughts drifting. This didn't seem to be going well. No way would she tell him about the baby in his current mood. Something was obviously bothering him. Not the right time to spring that kind of announcement on him.

The evening wore on, and Sara picked at her lemon chicken with glazed vegetables, hardly tasting them. By the time they'd finished dinner, the conversation had gone from stilted to non-existent. Finally, she couldn't stand it any more. "Todd, what's the matter? You seem—"

"Look, there's no easy way to do this, so I'm just going to say it."

Taken aback, Sara stared across the table. Ice filled her veins. This was all wrong. His tone, his fidgeting, the look in his eyes. This was not going to be a marriage proposal. Something was wrong. She pasted on a rigid smile, and fought to stay calm. "What do you mean?"

He reached for her hand, and grazed his thumb across it. "Look, Sara. I don't want to hurt you."

"What is it, Todd? Just tell me." Damn. It sounded more serious than another delay in the divorce proceedings. She was so tired of the stupid games and legal maneuvers.

"Alyssa and I are getting back together."

Sara blinked, her mouth gaping, unable to make sense of that statement. He and Alyssa? Ex-wife Alyssa? No. Not ex. Not yet. Oh, God. This could not be happening.

"What?" Her voice pitched to a high squeak. "You have got to be kidding."

But the truth was in his eyes. His fake, pleading, lying eyes. He was serious.

Sara squeezed her eyes closed, and he squeezed her hand, which she promptly yanked from his grasp. "I cannot believe this," she hissed. "After all this time? You've been stringing me along? You lied to me. You said—"

He leaned across the table. "I know. I know what I said, and I'm sorry."

"I'm sorry, too," Sara told him, her voice clipped. "I'm sorry I believed you. I'm sorry I didn't run away the second you told me your divorce was *pending*. I trusted you. Tell me, was it bullshit all along?"

"No. I swear, I thought we were through. But things are different now."

"Different? Yeah, they are different. You have me. She's your past. That's what you keep saying."

"She's pregnant."

"So what? That is no longer your concern. You don't owe–" Oh, no. *What?* The guilt on his face churned Sara's stomach. Horrified, she stared at him while alarm bells clanged in her head. "It's not– You did not–" She couldn't form the words.

He looked at the table for a moment before glancing back at her. "It's mine."

A sharp gasp escaped before she covered her mouth with her hand, her head shaking back and forth. In denial. "Oh, my God. That means you've been together. You've been with her. While we . . . at the same time–" Her voice quivered as her throat tightened and tears threatened.

"We– We've been talking."

*"Excuse me?"* The silverware bounced when her hand hit the table. "Talking? You don't get pregnant talking, Todd."

"I'm sorry. It just happened. I guess– I guess I still have feelings for her."

Hot, burning pain and anger replaced the chill inside Sara, and she stood. "Yeah? Well, that's great. Feel this." In a flash, before she could consider her actions, she leaned forward, and her hand connected square on his cheek, exactly where she'd aimed. "You. Are. So. Lame." She ground out every syllable then picked up her purse and sweater, and fled from the table.

Pregnant. *Pregnant.* The word beat against her skull like a hammer. Oh, God. Two pregnancies. And neither one should have happened. With tears blurring her vision, Sara stumbled to the Plaza Hotel half a block away. Inside the lobby, she sank into a chair, rocking back and forth.

"Miss?"

Sara vaguely heard the distant voice, but deep in her misery, ignored it.

"Miss?"

She looked up to find the concierge only inches from her face.

"Please go away."

28

"Can I help you? Can I get you something?"

Get her something? She shook her head, tears falling harder. Like what? A husband? A daddy for her baby? A new life?

**

At five in the morning, Sara pressed a warm washcloth to her swollen, bloodshot eyes, debating whether to make the trip to Whitfield after all. And wishing she'd kept her big mouth shut. God, not only had she spilled the beans about the baby, her mother was expecting her to show up with a ring on her finger. Or at least a plan for a wedding.

How quickly plans had changed.

She wouldn't marry him now if he broke down, crawled on his hands and knees through fire and begged her. It was over. She could never stay with someone she couldn't trust. So now what? That question had haunted her for the past eight hours. And she still didn't have an answer.

Five hours was all she had to come up with something. Pushing off from the counter, she slid her glasses onto her nose. It'd be impossible to get her contacts in. Besides, the glasses would help hide the physical evidence of her all-night crying fest. Not that her mother would miss any clues.

Padding into the kitchen, Sara started coffee, careful to be quiet and not wake her roommate, Natalie. The apartment was the perfect set-up, with a private bedroom and bath on either side of the shared living areas. She'd be sorry to leave it. She sucked in her breath, clutching the cupboard door handle. Where had that come from? Leaving? Would she have to leave? *Well, of course, dummy.* Even though she wasn't getting married, no one wanted to room with someone who had a new baby. She'd have to find a new place. A place of her own.

Sara accidentally slammed the mug onto the counter as a thought occurred to her. Hell, yes. Leaving was the best scenario. There was nothing keeping her in Kansas City now. She liked the city well enough, but she didn't love the weather. This would be the perfect opportunity to fly south. Dallas. There'd be plenty of job possibilities there. A couple of friends had moved there after graduation and loved it. Her heart thumped. It was an excellent idea. She'd give her two weeks' notice on Monday and hit the road as soon as possible. Todd Riley would never know about this pregnancy. She'd never see him again.

She managed to kill time until nine o'clock. Then she snatched up her overnight case and purse, and headed for her car. She spent the next two hours alone with her thoughts, contemplating her new life. By the time she reached the Whitfield city limits, she was sure moving and having the baby on her own was not only the right thing to do, but the only real option – the best solution for everyone involved.

Mary heard a car door, and glanced at the clock on the microwave. Sara already? It wasn't like her to arrive early. Maybe she was super excited – or really hungry. Mary quickly rinsed her hands, and hurried to the front door.

A blustery, cool wind met her when she opened the door and stepped onto the cushioned welcome mat outside. Trying to keep from jumping up and down, she watched Sara lift a small suitcase from the hatch of her bright blue Ford Focus. When Sara came around the car, Mary's heart clenched. She immediately noticed two things – no rock sparkled on her daughter's left hand, and she was not glowing with happiness. Drawing a deep breath, Mary leaned against the door. Those were two things she'd have to ignore for the time being.

"Hey, Leadfoot," she called out. "You made good time!"

Sara shrugged. "Got out early."

As soon she reached the porch, Mary pulled Sara into her arms, and squeezed. "Hi, sweetie. It's so good to see you." She nudged the door open, and slid an arm around Sara's shoulders. "I just finished making some chicken salad for lunch. How's that sound?"

"Good." Sara dropped the suitcase near the stairway.

"And I've got fresh fruit. The Honeycrisp apples are amazing this year."

"Sounds great."

"Why don't you freshen up, and I'll pour some drinks. You want Coke or iced tea?"

Sara started up the stairs. "Water's fine."

That last short response was laced with a definite "whatever" tone. Mary turned back toward the kitchen, sensing that all was not well. *Proceed with caution*, she told herself.

Mary poured water for Sara and an iced tea for herself, then sliced a lemon while she waited with mounting concern. What the hell had happened last night? She glanced outside, wondering where Grant was, and hoping for a little time alone with Sara to get the scoop.

What seemed like ages later, Sara ventured into the kitchen. "Here you go," Mary said, handing her the glass. "Now let me look at you." Her eyes went straight to Sara's middle. "You aren't showing one teensy bit." A pale face looked back at her, and Mary lifted a lock of Sara's cinnamon-brown hair. "Are you feeling okay, honey?"

"Mom." Sara's voice caught as her face crumpled.

In a flash, Mary took the glass and set it down then pulled her daughter into a fierce hug. "Shhhh, sweetie. It's all right," she murmured, smoothing Sara's hair while her thin shoulders shook, the tears coming hard. "It's all going to be fine." She could only assume that the baby's father had not been happy about Sara's announcement, and a protective outrage began to simmer inside.

"Hey, I think I'm feeling some sunshine in here," Grant's voice boomed from the hallway. "Where's—"

Eyes bulging, Mary gave a slight shake of her head when Grant appeared in the family room, stopping him in his tracks. Concern immediately clouded his features, but he stepped back and sank into an armchair, his folded hands bouncing against his lips.

Mary continued patting her daughter's back and making soothing sounds for a few more long moments. Finally, when she felt Sara's body slacken, she pulled back and gently cupped Sara's face with her hands. "What's the matter, sweetheart?"

Watery eyes met hers. Sara's bottom lip trembled. "I'm— I'm not getting married."

The tears spilled down her cheeks again, and Mary drew her forward once more, rocking her, and meeting Grant's eyes over their daughter's head. "It's all right," Mary said again. "You don't have to get married. The worst thing you could do is marry the wrong person."

Sara broke free, her arms flailing. "He *is* the wrong person. Completely wrong." She put her head in her heads. "God, I can't believe I was so stupid."

Grant quietly stood and approached the kitchen.

Mary faced Sara. "What do you mean, honey? Tell us what happened."

Sara swiveled Grant's direction.

"Hi, Daddy."

"Hey, Sunshine." Grant moved forward and folded her into his arms. After a few moments, he took her hand and helped her onto a bar stool, then slid the glass of water toward her. "Why don't you take a minute to calm down, then we can talk."

"Are you hungry?" Mary asked. "Do you want to talk while we eat?"

"Sure," Sara said, letting out an audible sigh. Still sniffling, she hopped off the chair and followed Mary into the kitchen.

Mary handed her a bowl of fruit, trying to ignore the pang of hurt to her own heart at seeing the gloom on her daughter's face. "Let's sit at the table."

Grant wordlessly filled a mug with the morning's leftover coffee and heated it in the microwave.

When they were all seated, Mary passed around the chicken salad, but she was not one to ignore problems with small talk or work around an elephant in the living room. She let Sara take a few bites, then turned to her. "So what's going on?"

Sara's glance shifted to Grant then back to Mary. "Does Daddy—"

"He knows about the baby." Mary told her. "And we both know you thought your dinner last night might lead to an engagement announcement. I gather that did not happen."

Eyes on her plate, Sara shook her head. "Not even close."

"Why?" Mary asked. "Was he upset about the baby?"

Sara swallowed hard before answering. "I didn't tell him about the baby."

Mary arched her brows, but waited for more.

"He's getting back together with his ex-wife. Wife. And she's pregnant."

Mary stared at her daughter. That statement made no sense at all. "Wife?" she repeated softly. She stole a glance at Grant, whose face had gone blank.

"Yes. They've been in the process of getting a divorce forever. He—"

Grant interrupted, his fork stopped midway between mouth and plate. "Wait a minute. This Todd guy is married? You've been messing around with a married man?"

"Grant," Mary said, censure in her voice.

His eyes darkened as they turned on her. "Did you know he was married?"

Mary shook her head. "Of course not."

"Well, neither did I," Sara cried. "Not at first. No one at the office said anything like that. He had his own place, and he didn't wear a ring. How would I know? They were split up and getting divorced."

"But that didn't happen, either," Mary said, a heavy thud settling in her stomach.

"No." Sara swiped at her eyes then took a deep breath. "He told me it was complicated because they owned property together and his parents had died while they were married, so there were inheritance issues." She spread her hands. "I mean, it sounded logical to me."

Mary caught Sara's hand. "No one's blaming you, honey."

"No," Grant agreed. "But there's a hell of a problem to deal with. What about the baby?"

His question hung in the silence. A number of thoughts hit Mary's brain in rapid succession but the one that stuck was that her daughter was going to be a single mother. And even for a college-educated woman making decent money that was never easy.

"Sarie, can you take some time–"

"I have a plan," Sara announced at the same time Mary found her voice.

Mary blinked. "You do?"

"Yes. I'm moving to Dallas and having the baby there."

Silence descended again as Mary and Grant stared at Sara.

"Dallas?" Mary echoed while Grant voiced her immediate thought.

"Why Dallas?" he asked. "What's Dallas got to do with anything?"

"First, it's a big place so lots of job opportunities," Sara said, her eyes brightening. "Second, it's warm, which I like. Plus, I already have friends there."

"And it happens to be seven hours away," Mary added. "What about a support network? Your friends will be busy working. If you want to leave Kansas City, why not move closer to home? You know I'd love to–"

"There's nothing here, Mom. It could take months to find a decent job even in Paxton or Wichita. Besides, Aunt Gretchen and Uncle Wes are there."

Mary blanched. They hadn't seen her brother and his wife in a couple of years. When the kids were young they used to visit regularly, but their lives got busy, and now it seemed that only a wedding or funeral brought them together. She wouldn't count on them, but decided against mentioning it. Maybe they could chat at Annie's wedding.

"It's going to be hard to interview for jobs in Dallas while you're in Kansas City," Grant said.

"I'm not going to, Daddy. I'll give my notice on Monday." She shot Mary a quick glance then looked down, pushing the lettuce around on her plate. "I want to be out of there before it shows that I'm pregnant," she added softly. "I don't want anyone there to know."

Mary received that message loud and clear. "Oh, honey. Are you sure?"

Sara took a long drink then turned hard eyes on Mary. "A hundred percent positive. I'm not going to share time with someone who doesn't want or love my kid. His wife would hate me and my baby."

Swallowing hard, Mary leaned in and spoke in a quiet voice. "You know, sweetie, you don't have to keep this baby."

Tears flooded Sara's eyes. "I'm not having an abortion, Mom, and I'm not giving her or him away to someone else to raise. I can't. I just can't do that. I'd rather do it all by myself."

"Shhh. It's okay. I understand. And, hey, you aren't going to be by yourself. We'll do everything we can to help you." She glanced at Grant for confirmation, but his jaw was set, and he remained silent.

Needing to move, Mary got up and refilled drinks, then began clearing plates. "I made some of those raspberry brownies you like. Want one?" she asked Sara.

"Not right now. Thanks, though. Maybe later."

"You up for some shopping in Paxton? Or we could go to a movie." She sensed that they all needed a break from the emotional conversation. They had plenty of time to talk about details later.

"Shopping would be fine, I guess," Sara said. "I don't really need anything, especially—"

"You will," Mary told her. "Come on. It'll be good to get out, anyway. Our nice days are numbered, you know."

She grabbed a beer out of the fridge and handed it to Grant. His eyebrows shot up, but he took the cold bottle without comment. She had the feeling he'd have more to say on the subject later. "We'll be back before supper," she told him. "How 'bout we pick up a pizza or something?"

"Sure."

Mary knew from experience that keeping everyone fed was one way to reduce tension and calm tempers.

**

Shopping gave them something to do, but it was clouded by a veil of tension. Both she and Sara were still mentally absorbing the life-altering changes before them. Mary did her best to behave normally and curb her enthusiasm about becoming a grandmother. She could tell Sara hadn't quite reached the stage of excitement about the pregnancy. Probably in shock – one shock on top of another.

They purchased some stretchy leggings, a couple of tunic tops, and a few maternity essentials, but no baby items. No sense buying baby stuff that would just have to be moved to Dallas.

After a couple of hours, Mary took Sara's arm and guided her to a chair in the food court. "You sit. I'll get some drinks." She dumped the packages into another chair and found the lemonade line. It was one of their favorite places.

With a flourish, she handed Sara a bright yellow plastic cup. "Here you go. If this doesn't cheer you up, well, I'm afraid it's hopeless."

When Sara cracked a reluctant smile, Mary grinned and squeezed her hand. "No worries, doll." Mary watched Sara sip the lemonade and visibly relax.

"You know what's really fun about being a mom?" she asked a few moments later.

"What?"

"Just watching your kids. Seeing them discover new things, laugh, enjoy life. It's going to be fun watching you be an amazing mom."

Watery eyes met hers. "What about Dad? He doesn't seem too excited."

Mary let out a heavy sigh. "Obviously it's not what we expected or wanted for you. We want you to find a man who will love and cherish you the way we do. The way you deserve. And we don't want you to settle for anything less than that. Dad might be disappointed, but I promise, it's not going to last. He loves you and he's going to love that little baby."

\*\*

It wasn't until after dinner and what seemed like hours of exhausting discussion that Sara went up to bed and Mary and Grant had a moment alone.

Mary reheated her cup of tea and sank onto the sofa opposite Grant's chair. She looked at him, and blew out her breath. "What a day, huh?"

He ran a hand over his jaw. "The boyfriend is already married. Good Christ."

"I feel so bad for her. Talk about being sideswiped."

"Sounded like you were encouraging her."

Surprised by what sounded like criticism, she stared at him. "Well, yeah, Grant. I do that. I try to take every opportunity I can to encourage our children."

"That's not what I mean. You were encouraging her to have this baby."

"Did you not hear the same conversation I did? She's already made up her mind. Now it's our job to support her."

"Maybe it's our job to give her some direction. Advice. That's what I'm saying."

"Oh, Grant, my advice is for her to follow her heart. I don't want to see her make a decision she might regret for the rest of her life. I think there's a way bigger chance she'd regret an abortion or giving her baby away than keeping it. Come on, we've had kids. You love them the second you lay eyes on them."

"And you want a grandbaby."

Mary gaped at him, his words stinging as though he'd slapped her. "Seriously? Is that what you think? What has gotten into you? You think this is about me? That I want Sara to have a baby so that I can play Grandma? That is a rotten thing to say." She knew it was the wrong approach, but she punched back. "Are you worried I won't want to travel as much? That this baby might cramp your retirement style? Well, guess what, love? It's not about you, either. It's her decision, Grant. And she's made up her mind. Of course I would love to have a grandchild, but most of all I want our kids to be happy. That's all I've ever wanted."

Practically shaking, Mary stood and left the room. No need to make things worse by adding fuel to the fire.

For more than an hour the house was quiet except for the yammering of the television. Mary went through her usual bedtime routine then tried to read, but her mind kept bouncing back and forth between the harsh words with Grant and her daughter's future. Finally, she tossed the book aside and slid her feet into her slippers. Taking a deep breath, Mary padded into the living room and perched a hip on the arm of Grant's chair. When his arm went around her waist, she rested her head on his, and he pulled her onto his lap. They might not agree on how Sara should handle her pregnancy, but one thing they'd always agreed on was that they'd never go to bed angry. And in thirty-five years of marriage, they hadn't. She wasn't about to start now.

"Hey," she said. "You have any commitments at church tomorrow?"

"Don't think so," he said into her hair.

"I'm thinking a nice, quiet, lazy morning sounds good."

"Works for me, but that means we won't be seen. Last night you wanted to go out."

Last night? What did that– Oh, right. All of the turmoil of yesterday came flooding back. Was that really just yesterday? With a heavy sigh, she straightened. "Wow. I forgot about that. Doesn't seem possible so much could happen in two short days. What do you think?"

Indecision gnawed at her – and she didn't like it. How had life become so crazy? In general, Mary felt as though she had a handle on doing "the right thing" in most situations. But this one had her stumped. A giggle welled up in her throat.

Grant nudged her. "What's so funny?"

"I think I just asked you for advice in a social situation."

A slow grin spread across his face. "Have you lost your mind?"

Laughing, she fell back against his chest. "Apparently. To be fair, though, this one does have a business aspect."

38

"Right." He scooched out from under her and gently pulled her up with him. "How 'bout we give it a rest for a couple of days?"

She nodded. A little rest sounded good. Maybe after a decent night's sleep she'd have a better perspective. Or some fresh ideas. Then again, she conceded, she might have to throw her chips in the air on this one and see where they landed.

Even as she thought it, though, she knew that fading into the background wasn't her style. She wanted to turn this thing around and see these people land on their feet. She wanted to *do* something. But what?

## Chapter Four

Quiet Sunday mornings were a rare treat. Most of the time, they were rushed – filled with meal prep and church activities that went right up to lunchtime. As longtime active members of Whitfield Presbyterian, going to church was part of the normal routine for both Mary and Grant. Their absence would, without a doubt, be noticed. Would it be interpreted as a sign of guilt? More than once, Mary almost changed her mind about staying home. She'd miss cuddling with the babies in the nursery, but the idea of pampering her daughter, and therefore her grandchild-to-be, was strong enough to win the mental tug-of-war. At least when someone asked, she could say Sara had been home. It'd be considered a good excuse, Mary told herself as she refilled her coffee. Of course plenty of people would have loved to see Sara this morning, too.

Mary glanced at the clock, wondering if *she*'d see Sara this morning. Maybe it was a sign that she'd been able to sleep soundly.

Only moments later, her daughter strolled into the kitchen still in her pajamas. "Hey, there," Mary said. "Did you get some sleep?"

Pushing back her hair, Sara gave a brief smile. "A little. It felt good to be in my old bed, anyway."

Mary pulled her close for a moment. "I'm glad. Coffee?"

"Sure."

"You still adding about a cup of sugar?"

40

Sara screwed up her face. "A teaspoon would be fine. Where's Dad?"

"Went outside with his coffee and newspaper a while ago, and I haven't seen him since. Puttering around, I suppose."

"Okay, I don't want to miss telling him goodbye, and I can't forget to try on the dress."

"Right. Let's do that before you get dressed. You don't need to get back right away, do you?"

"No. Thought I'd leave around two."

Her voice was matter of fact, but Mary didn't miss the distant look on Sara's face. Her daughter may be rested, may have worked out the perfect plan in theory, but Mary knew there was still some deep hurt to work through. It would take some time.

Just thinking about all the details Sara had in front of her made Mary's head spin. A move, a job search, and a baby on the way was more than enough to overwhelm anyone even without adding the emotional trauma of what she'd just experienced.

In her head, Mary mapped out the weeks ahead. So much to do. "Hey, I've been looking at my calendar," she told Sara. "I could probably run down to Dallas with you for a few days the week before the wedding and help you look for apartments."

"Oh, Mom, you don't need to do that. I'm sure I won't be ready. I'll stay with my friends until I find a place. I can couch hop for a while if I need to."

"What are you going to do with your things?"

"I don't know. Maybe I leave the big stuff in Kanas City for an extra month. I doubt Natalie will mind."

"And pay the rent?"

"I'll have to pay through the end of the year, anyway. She's not going to find another roommate that fast, and our lease is up in January. It'll be fine."

"Okay, but don't sign anything until Dad or I can take a look. We want to make sure–"

"I'm not going to get a place in the 'hood," Sara said, not quite rolling her eyes, but the tone of her voice conveyed the same message.

"Oh, that's good to know."

"Mom, I'm going to have to take this one thing at a time and see what happens. I can't plan it all out and schedule it, and neither can you."

Mary took a deep breath. It was the same old argument she always had with Sara. Mary wanted to plan and Sara wanted to go with the flow. Wait and see what happened. She could never understand the purpose of waiting. Why wait when you could possibly have some input and direct the course of events in your favor?

"Fine. But you know I've got the wedding, then Dad and I are going to Phoenix, then the holidays. Things will get crazy around–"

Sara held up a hand. "I know. I'm not asking you to do anything."

Mary went quiet for a minute. The last thing she wanted was to make the weekend even worse. Sara obviously wasn't ready to deal with practicalities. And clearly *didn't* get enough sleep. "Listen, sweetie, I've been pregnant before. You might start getting morning sickness. You'll get tired more easily. You won't be able to do lifting and moving after a few more months. You might need some help."

"I'll let you know. Just don't try to manage me, okay? That doesn't help."

Neither would any retort that came to mind, Mary reminded herself. Instead of responding, she busied herself in the kitchen while Sara sipped her coffee. With a little luck it would improve her mood.

When Mary refilled Sara's cup for the second time, she said in a much-too-cheery voice, "I'm ready when you are."

Sara eyed her suspiciously. "Ready for what?"

A nap, Mary thought, suddenly feeling worn out. *Not even noon, but I could go for a nap.* "Trying on the dress," she said.

"Oh. Right." Sara pushed back her chair. "Yeah, I'm ready. Where is it?"

"It's in the hall closet. You go on up. I'll get it."

She'd been careful to keep each dress hanging smoothly inside its own plastic bag. She lifted Sara's from the bar and headed toward the stairs. Though she held the top of the hanger above her head, the plastic dragged along the floor, and a moment later Mary and the dress crashed in a heap. Her elbow slammed against the wall as her hip connected with the hardwood.

She let out a sharp yelp, and Sara clambered down the stairs.

"Mom! Oh, my gosh, are you all right?"

Mary winced, rubbing her still-stinging elbow. "I'm okay, I think."

"What happened?"

Pushing off from the floor, Mary righted herself and wiggled her foot, unsure whether she'd simply tripped or her foot had given way. She kicked off the shoe and stroked her foot. "I guess my shoe caught the plastic," she murmured. "Pretty graceful, huh? I'm thinking my hip is going to match the color of your dress in the next day or two."

"Do you need some ice?"

"No, no. I'm fine."

"Jeez, you scared me."

"Thanks for coming to the rescue." Mary handed her the dress. "Here. Without further ado, let's see how this looks, shall we?"

Sara started up the stairs with a glance back at Mary. "Might want to use the handrail."

Mary swatted at her. "Go." Still, she did as Sara suggested, just in case. In case what? she wondered. She couldn't shake the feeling that it hadn't been an innocent stumble. She'd never been such a klutz before.

Inside her room, Sara faced the full-length mirror, and stepped into the shimmering dress. Mary zipped the back, pausing only a second to pay tribute to the sharp curve of her daughter's waist, which was about to disappear – possibly forever. "Positively gorgeous," Mary said, looking in the mirror. She pinched the sides of the dress. "Looks to me like you have plenty of room, but I can let the seams out a smidge if you want. I'm sure you

43

won't be showing a bump by the wedding, but you might be losing your waist."

"Can *you* do it?" Sara asked.

"I wouldn't want to do any more, but I think I can manage a straight seam. I just hope the previous stitch marks won't show."

"It'll be fine. No one's going to be examining it. Besides, all the attention will be on Annie."

Mary met Sara's eyes in the mirror. "Sure you don't want to let her in on the secret? She'll be happy for you, you know."

"No, Mom. There's too much to tell. She can be happy for me after her honeymoon."

"I feel kind of bad that we didn't call or stop and see her when we were in Paxton yesterday."

"I know. Me, too. But I talked to her a couple of times last week. It's not a big deal."

Good to know they were talking regularly, at least. Mary had always wanted her kids to be close. Two miscarriages in two years had kept them farther apart in years than she'd planned. The five-year age difference made it almost impossible for them to be close when they were young. Now that they were older, the family bond seemed to have blossomed into a friendship. Mary had almost wondered if Annie had chosen Sara as maid of honor simply out of convenience. It was easier than choosing one friend over another.

Her thoughts drifted back to the wedding. "You know, there'll be toasts and drinking at the wedding and rehearsal dinner. Don't you think Annie's going to notice that you aren't having big-girl beverages?"

"I'll tell her I got wasted a few nights before and can't stand the idea of alcohol or something."

"Oh, good, we're making up lies now." Mary shook her head. "I'm not so sure about this."

"Well, I'm not going to worry about it. If it turns out I have to tell her, then I guess I will."

The old wait-and-see-what-happens philosophy again. "You can have a couple of sips of champagne for a toast. That won't hurt the baby." And then it struck Mary that

Sara wouldn't be the only one unable to drink. She sank onto Sara's bed. How could she have missed that detail? "You know what? Claire can't drink, either. I'd better get some sparkling cider or something as an alternative. I completely forgot about that." The death of her son and subsequent surprise divorce request from her cheating husband had left Mary's best friend vulnerable, and she'd turned to alcohol for comfort. The past year had taken its toll, but she'd battled back. But she was, and always would be, on the wagon.

"She's probably used to it by now. And it's not going to matter to me, Mom. Will it just be Claire and Elise or is Elise bringing the kids?"

"Her whole family. It'll be fun to see her kids and Brian. And all of Dana's—" She stopped, and put a hand to her chest. "Oh, wow."

"What?"

"This is going to be hard on Claire," Mary said softly. "I think this will be the first time we've all been together since . . . since Ben's funeral."

Sara stepped out of the dress, and handed it to Mary. "I can't imagine Evan or Maddie coming since neither one lives here."

Mary looked at her in surprise. "They *are* coming. Why wouldn't they? A wedding is a big deal. It'll be like a reunion. Besides, it'll be a good reason for them to come home and see their mom and each other." Dana's kids had scattered, just as Mary's had. Only Chase, Dana's youngest, still lived in Whitfield.

"Is Evan still in Tulsa?"

"Yes. Don't you keep in touch?"

"Nope."

"Oh. That's too bad. The three of you used to be so close."

"That was a long time ago, Mom. We pretty much lost touch after high school." She shot Mary a questioning look. "You know that. Evan just didn't—"

"What?"

"Didn't want to be social."

"When was the last time you saw him?"

"Ben's funeral."

"Well let me tell you, he's matured and filled out since then. I saw him a couple of months ago when he was home, and he had that facial hair that all the models seems to have now, and was full-throttle handsome."

"Really? Well, he was always cute."

"Hmm," Mary murmured. "This could get interesting. Just wait. You might like what you see."

Sara's mouth dropped open. "Motherrrrr," she groaned. "Get real. We've got too much going on to start match-making. Besides, that'd be weird."

"Why weird? You've known each other forever."

"Exactly. Too much history. We were practically like brother and sister."

"Which means you know each other well, and have a lot in common." Surely in light of recent circumstances Sara would figure out there was a lot to be said for knowing someone's family and background. Mary shook her head. "Poor Evan. He had such a crush on you, and you always had an eye for Ben."

"Mom, you do realize that until two days ago I thought I was in love with someone else, right?" She pulled a top over her head and reached for her jeans.

Mary moved forward, and ran a hand down Sara's shoulder-length hair. "I do. I'm sorry. I'm not making light of that. But . . . well, maybe the best thing for getting over him is finding the real Mr. Right, hmm?"

"I have no idea what Evan is doing now, Mom. Heck, he could be married. I told you, we don't talk anymore."

"You *would* know, because I would know."

"Whatever. Give it a rest, okay?"

"Fine, but for the record, I don't think he's dating anyone." She leaned in, meeting Sara's eyes in the mirror. "And I know he isn't bringing anyone with him to the wedding."

\*\*

Mary watched the tail lights on Sara's car disappear around the corner, then sank against the door frame, a nap on her mind once again. She'd get to that, but there was one thing she wanted more. She pushed the hair back from her face, and headed for the phone. "I'm going to be on the phone for at least an hour," she hollered to Grant.

He looked at his watch, and followed her. "Guess that's my cue. Meeting Doug to watch some football." He pressed a quick kiss to her lips.

"Okay. Bye, love." As soon as the door shut behind him Mary punched Claire's number. Once neighbors, they were now separated by the two-hour drive between Whitfield and Wichita. Still, Claire remained Mary's closest confidante aside from Grant.

"Well, hi, stranger. What's–"

"Guess what?" Mary interrupted.

"Oh, I love these guessing games," Claire drawled. "Let's see . . . you've fallen and you can't get up?"

For a split second Mary thought of her undignified trip to the floor that morning, and it unnerved her. "That's not funny," she said.

"Is too, but I give up. What's going on?"

"I'm going to be a grandmamma!"

Claire let out a soft squeal. "Are you really? Oh, Mare, that's big news. Which kid is crowning you with this title?"

"Sara."

"Yeah? Ah, sweet Sara. She'll be the coolest mom ever."

"No doubt. She did have an excellent role model."

"Or two," Claire added.

Mary laughed. It was true. As neighbors and close friends, they'd been like second moms to each other's kids. "Exactly. She's only a couple of months along. Was here this weekend to try on her maid-of-honor dress again."

"Oh, good thinking. Will it be okay?"

"I think so, but I'm going to let out the side seams a tiny bit to be sure." Mary grabbed a sweater, and wandered out to the patio, feeling the familiar pang of missing her friend as she talked. Hard to believe it'd been almost a year and a half since Claire had divorced and moved to Wichita to be closer to her daughter and two grandkids.

"And, um. Not to be indelicate, but . . . what about daddy? The mystery guy that no one's met? Are they getting married?"

Trust Claire to get right to the issue. Claire was the one friend who knew everything about Mary's life. Of course she knew Sara had been dating someone.

"Oh, Claire. You won't believe this."

For the next forty-five minutes Mary filled Claire in on Sara's situation and decision. "I sure would like to be closer to that baby, but I know Dallas is probably better for her. At least she can meet people there."

"She's so laid-back, though. Somehow, I don't see her enjoying the big-city life and traffic."

"True. Maybe after she tries it she'll realize it's not a good fit."

"You know I'd always hoped that she and Ben . . ." Claire's wistful voice trailed off.

And Mary knew exactly where her thoughts had gone. "I know, hon. Me, too. It would've been so much fun."

Claire gave a dry laugh. "Well, maybe. Think how jealous you'd be if I was the favorite granny."

"Ha! As if." But visions of the two of them duking it out over a baby's affections had Mary chuckling, too. "Girlfriend, you sure do know how to spoil a Hallmark moment."

"Anyway, you'll probably have more than one grandkid underfoot soon enough. And Annie's close enough for frequent grandmamma time."

"I hope so. I'd love for their kids to be close. Hey, speaking of Annie, we're not telling her about the baby yet, so zip your lips. You can't tell anyone, especially not Elise."

Claire's daughter was one of Annie's four bridesmaids. The two girls had been friends growing up and had reconnected after Claire's divorce and subsequent fight with alcoholism. As awful as that time was, it had brought them all closer together.

"I won't say a word, I promise. Listen, what can I do for Sara? Other than host a shower later, of course."

Mary blew out her breath. "I honestly don't know. I think she's going to have to take care of things in Kansas City and wrap up her job before she can switch gears and get excited about the baby."

"Why don't you get me her current address? I'm going to send her something."

Tears pricked Mary's eyes. More than anything she hoped for a friend like Claire – someone who always had her back, always stepped in to help, and was always real – for each of her daughters. "You don't have to–"

"Oh, stars and stripes," Claire whooped. "I have an idea. How 'bout this. I'll send flowers, a huge bouquet of roses, to her at work. Then all her co-workers will be talking about it, and maybe Jackass will hear. I could even tell the florist to say it's a delivery from Dallas. That way people will assume she's already got something good cooking down there. How's that?"

Mary choked out a laugh. "Claire, you are priceless. Go for it, lady."

**

While gas pumped into her car, Sara glanced at her cell phone, again. No messages. No new emails. Nothing. She hadn't told anyone other than Todd and Natalie she was leaving town for the weekend, but you'd think she'd left the planet. She tossed the phone into the passenger seat. First thing she'd do when she got home would be to email her friends in Dallas that she'd be joining them soon. That'd create some buzz.

She considered calling Morgan, her best college friend, but Morgan knew about Todd. And she'd ask too many questions. The hard ones. Probably not a good conversation to have while driving. Even though she'd cut Todd out of her life, she couldn't seem to keep from crying when she thought about the breakup. That was normal, she supposed. After all, she'd been dumped. Dumped and duped. The weasel.

As she swung the car onto the highway, Sara replayed the weekend in her mind. Her parents had taken the news as well as could be expected. No yelling or blaming. No big freak-out. She took a long drink of her Diet Coke, remembering the disappointment in her father's eyes. That might haunt her for a while. At least she could depend on her mother defending and supporting her. She smiled. Her mom would always defend her ducklings.

Sara couldn't explain why she'd gotten irritated with her mother that morning. It just happened sometimes – okay, that wasn't true. It happened when her mom was trying to plan and control and put everything in a neat little box like the squares on her calendar.

Of course she'd need her parents' help, but Sara couldn't stand to have someone hovering over her, breathing down her neck. And she wasn't about to cave to pressure and move back to Whitfield. Sure, it'd be great to have her mom and sister handy to babysit and help out, but Sara didn't even know anyone in Whitfield anymore. All of her friends had left.

She remembered her mother's needling about Evan, and her thoughts turned to those days when she and Evan and Ben and all the siblings of the three families had been friends – or like one big extended family, overlapping and mixing into each other.

She and Evan had been in the same grade while Ben had been a year ahead, and always seemed older and more sophisticated. He'd been popular, and fun, always a leader. Yeah, she'd had a crush on him. As did every girl in school.

She swiped at the tears that threatened. The idea here was not to cry while driving, after all. They'd all scattered after college – or after her freshman year. After the disastrous spring break trip. They'd tried to mix Whitfield high school friends with new college friends on a ski trip to Winter Park. Did. Not. Work. Ben didn't want to be responsible for anything. One of his friends started drinking first thing every morning. And he wanted to be their driver. Evan was totally uptight. At the time, she'd been annoyed with him for not loosening up a little. For being such a baby.

An unexpected wave of guilt rolled over her. Evan was probably the reason they'd all survived the trip.

50

Afterward, they drifted apart. And then Ben died. Shot in Iraq. The night of his funeral they'd been together with some other friends. It was awkward. She barely remembered that day. Everyone was in shock, didn't know what to say or do, so they'd gotten high. Then went their separate ways the next day. She and Evan had never spoken about the trip or Ben privately.

Would they talk at Annie's wedding? Should they? What would be the point? So much time had passed. She gripped the steering wheel hard, the truth squeezing her lungs. The truth was, she'd lost two friends.

If she were honest about it, she'd pushed Evan away. Ben had, too. And it started in high school – when they'd become aware of their differences. And had started treating him differently. He had to do more things at home to help his mom. He didn't have as much free time or money. Didn't live in as nice a house. What he did have was a deadbeat dad.

Sara checked the rearview mirror then quickly moved into the next exit lane. She had to get off the highway. She pulled into the closest gas station and stopped the car. Then let the tears come.

A deadbeat dad. Exactly what her baby would have. After several minutes, maybe more, she drew in a huge gulp of air, shuddering and sniffling. She had to admit Todd wasn't a total deadbeat. He was smart in the business environment. Had his MBA. Was neat and fun to be with. Good looking. He'd always been a gentleman on dates. At least her baby would have those genes – just not the person they belonged to.

Questions hammered her brain. Would it matter? Would people treat her child differently because she or he didn't have a father? Could she compensate for that? For the first time, Sara felt a connection with Evan's mom.

How many times had Sara heard her mother say how much she admired Dana? How she'd kept her family together, worked hard and raised good kids? Of course, her mother had helped out. So had Claire, and Dana's mom and sister before their accident. Dana had done all of that and was a cool mom. She was fun and pretty, and had a career.

Sara swiped at the tears again. Evan's mom had been on her own a long time. Sara couldn't even remember his dad. And now Dana was engaged. After all these years she was finally getting married again. Would Sara have to wait that long to find someone? Wait until her child was grown up? She flopped back against the headrest feeling a new sense of respect for Evan's mom, for what she'd accomplished. And more than a little fear. Dana had done it. But could she?

## Chapter Five

"It's business, Grant. You know that." Joe Thomas, chairman of Essex Corporation, pushed a piece of paper across the table. "Here's the list. You can see we didn't target your employees. Almost twice that many are people who were on our payroll before the buyout or who work in other divisions. You've got to remember, we're a bigger corporation, and we have to look at the health of the entire company."

Grant studied the paper. Some of the names he recognized, but many he didn't. It was the confirmation he wanted. Clearing his throat, he nodded. "That's a lot of people, Joe."

"With oil prices bottoming out, the petroleum division is taking a hit. Market's down and investors are skittish." Leaning forward, Joe tapped the document. "Every one of those names was chosen for a reason. We gave it a lot of thought. The people on that list either weren't pulling their weight, or they were in areas where we had some duplication. A few of them are close enough to retirement that they should be all right. They got generous severance packages."

"Why didn't I know about this before it happened?"

Joe ran a hand over his face. "I'll be honest with you, Grant. We considered it. I wasn't a hundred percent comfortable keeping it from you, but come on, you probably would've given yourself an ulcer. You were too close to it. Don and I agreed this was the best way. I'm sorry it caught you by surprise. I really am. But this way you can honestly tell people you had nothing to do with it. You are guilt-free, my friend."

When he put it like that, it made sense, Grant supposed. Knowing about the lay-offs wouldn't have stopped them. Finally, Grant stood, and extended his hand. "Thanks for taking the time to see me."

"Always good to see you, Grant. Go enjoy your retirement," Joe told him. "Do all the things you've been talking about. And stay in touch. I'd like to hear about your trip to South America. Maybe we'll get involved in something like that one of these days."

"That'd be great," Grant agreed. "Just remember, people won't take kindly to you doing charity work in another country while you're laying people off in your own community."

Joe nodded. "Point taken. Might have to get you back on the payroll as a consultant one of these days, too."

"No time soon," Grant told him. "Got a busy year coming up."

It had been shaping up to be busy even before Sara's announcement. Adding her move and a new baby to the agenda might crunch the calendar. He wouldn't be taking on any business-related projects.

Joe slapped him on the back. "You take care."

Grant left the Essex offices feeling better, if not exactly guilt-free. Joe was right. It was better that he hadn't known. At least he hadn't misread Joe. The guy was decent and had been fair. With that off his chest, Grant could think about other things – like the upcoming opportunity to walk his eldest daughter down the aisle, traveling with his wife, and now, looking forward to being a grandpa. Not just busy – momentous.

Finalizing plans for going to Bolivia on the Building Neighbors project was next on his list. The final payment was due, and an online meeting was scheduled for Nov. 1 for those who committed. He'd never been away from Mary for that long, but he had a feeling the time would fly by – at least for her. While he was building roads and bridges in foreign lands, she'd probably spend some time with Claire, and of course, Sara and the baby. She'd enjoy the girl time. Wouldn't be too long after he got back before they left on their Alaskan cruise. That one was on the bucket list – part of the plan to visit all fifty states. Payoff for years of hard work.

He found Mary at her computer, scribbling notes on a pad of paper, deep in concentration. Grant tapped softly on the door. "Hey."

Mary looked up, and removed her reading glasses. Her face lit up with a bright smile. "Hi, there. How'd it go?"

Grant entered the room and propped himself against the desk. "Good. He showed me the numbers. I still don't like people being let go, but it looks like they were fair. Folks need to move on."

"Exactly!" Mary said. "And we can help with that. I've already got a couple of agencies interested in doing an employment workshop in Whitfield. They'll help people with resumes and interviewing skills, and how to work with headhunters. They can–"

"I'm not sure it's necessary," Grant cut in.

Mary's eyes widened. "I'm sure it's not *necessary*, but maybe a nice thing to do. Shows some goodwill."

Grant nodded, wondering how her idea might be received. "Babe, how's it going to generate goodwill if people don't even know we're doing it?"

"That doesn't matter," she told him. "The point is that someone is thinking of them and offering them some assistance. No one wants to feel cast aside and forgotten. Jane seems to think it's a good idea."

Grant held up his hands surrender style. "I don't have a problem with it if you can get it pulled together in the next couple of weeks. Folks'll already be starting to look."

"I know." She grinned up at Grant. "Don't worry, love. I can make this happen."

He planted a kiss on her cheek. "Did I ever say I doubted it?"

When she rolled her head, he put both hands on her shoulders and began massaging them. "Stiff neck?"

"Yeah. I could hardly turn my head this morning. It's better now, though." She smiled up at him. "Thanks."

"My pleasure," he said, brushing his lips to hers. "Mmm. You about done here?"

"Getting close," she said.

"No meetings?"

"Not today."

"No cleaning lady?"

"Nooo. Why?"

The laughter in her voice told Grant she knew exactly the reason behind his questions. He slid a hand under her hair, stroking the base of her neck. "I'm thinking there are certain benefits to being retired . . ."

"Uh-huh. Like being home in the middle of the day?"

Taking hold of her hand, he pulled her up from the chair and against his chest. "Like both of us being home in the middle of the day."

"I suppose I could use a diversion," Mary said, a soft smile playing around her lips.

\*\*

Glancing at the clock, Mary settled back into her office chair, ready to pick up where she'd left off. Grant was right – the workshop needed to happen fast. Nailing down some details would help her face any hostility she might encounter around town this week. She wasn't sure her husband fully understood how important camaraderie and the feeling of we're-all-in-this-together was in her world of philanthropy and community spirit. Besides, it was good for her to keep busy, though she admitted, with so many things going on at once, she was having trouble focusing. She figured she had to wait until at least six o'clock before checking in with Sara to see how her announcement had been received. Maybe if she gave it enough time, Sara would do the checking in.

Mary opened her email and found what she was hoping for – a list of potential dates and times available at the community center. Looked as though there were plenty of options. She was just about to hit send with the times she wanted when she saw the part about the online

56

form. *Ugh.* She hated online reservations. With a heavy sigh, she filled in the form and hit send. And the screen went blank.

Groaning, Mary picked up the phone. "Should've called in the first place," she grumbled. When a female voice came on the line, Mary explained the situation.

"Oh, I'm so sorry," the receptionist said. "We've been having some computer problems. Let me take that information for you."

Mary gave her name and the dates.

"And what is the event, again?" the woman asked.

"An employment seminar."

"Right."

"I've been working with Elaine to set this up. The client is actually On Track Employment Services. They'll be handling all the event details. Elaine has their information."

"Great. I'll get this to her. Thanks for calling."

Mary had made her decision on the agency, going with her gut reaction to the two representatives she'd spoken with earlier. She hoped the woman was as competent as she seemed on the phone. "Let's say seven to nine on Thursday evening, and then two to four on Saturday," she told Wendy Miles, director at On Track. "That gives people a choice."

"Absolutely. That's a good idea. We'll plan for the first session to focus on résumé writing and job research. The second session can focus more on interviewing and presentation."

"I want it to be casual, but nice. Let's provide coffee and water and some soft drinks. And some snacks."

"Sure. We can do that."

"And what about a goodie bag? Maybe some office supplies, a flash drive or USB charger and a couple of pens?"

"That would be very nice," Wendy agreed. "But it would significantly add to the cost."

"Yes. We'll cover the costs."

"All right. We can make those purchases for you wholesale. And, of course, everyone who attends will get our packet with sample résumés, tips and resource materials."

"Perfect. This sounds wonderful."

"Let me write all of this up, and I'll email you a contract tomorrow. How's that?"

"Thank you, Wendy. I'll look forward to that. And I'll get you the names and addresses of people who should receive paper invitations."

Mary hung up the phone and twirled around, the accomplishment infusing her with a little rush of adrenaline. She had to admit that, like a junkie, she enjoyed the high. It was tempting to keep going, to put together a flyer and contact the newspaper for some publicity, but if she wanted to remain anonymous, she'd have to rely on Wendy for all of that. Instead, she called Jane.

"Hey, I've been nailing down the details for the job workshop," Mary told her.

"Yeah, how's that coming?"

"It's going to be fabulous. I can't believe how it's all falling into place. Here's the deal. It'll be open to the whole community, for anyone who wants to attend. But the agency will mail invitations to the people laid off from Essex. That way it doesn't look like we're sponsoring it, and there's no mention of Essex. What do you think?"

"Sure. Sounds great, Mare."

"Do you think Doug will come?"

"Oh, I don't know about Doug. Corey, maybe. He's been talking about looking for a new job. Would that be okay?"

"Well, of course. Your husband, your son, your dog . . . the more, the merrier. I'm hoping the people laid off will come, but who knows?"

"I'm sure they will, Mare. It sounds wonderful. You and Grant are going above and beyond with this."

"I don't want kudos, I just want to help. Listen, Jane. I'd really like to keep this under wraps. Can we keep it between us? Don't tell anyone that Grant and I are involved, okay?"

"Lips are sealed."

"Thanks. I'll talk to you later." Mary ended the call with slightly less enthusiasm. Another secret. She wanted to make the workshop happen, but the number of things she was keeping from people was starting to add up. And it made her nervous.

That brought her thoughts right back to her daughter. With super willpower, Mary shoved the phone aside and turned her attention to the agenda for this week's women's auxiliary meeting. It was her final volunteer commitment until after Annie's wedding. She was anxious to check it off the list.

\*\*

Evening meetings were always harder to get motivated for. The days were getting shorter and colder, and curling up at home in front of the television sounded better and better. At least people were usually in a good mood for this one. Even if they'd had a rough week, everyone would be looking forward to Friday – a sure-fire mood-lifter. Mary shrugged into her denim jacket, said goodbye to Grant, and backed the Acura out of the garage. She considered switching on the seat heater, but figured the warmth could easily lull her to sleep.

Climbing out of the car, Mary took a moment to let the cool night air blow against her face. Then, heels tapping against the tiled floors, she walked into the meeting at the Legion Hall – and looked straight into the icy stare of Regina Daniels. Caught off guard, Mary froze in the doorway. Was it her imagination, or had the room gone silent? Mary sucked in a deep breath. This had to end. She'd speak to Regina tonight and settle this if it killed her. The chairs on either side of Regina were already taken, so Mary smiled and took a seat across the table. But when Regina got up to refill her coffee, Mary made a beeline for the coffee station.

"Regina," she said, her voice low. "Listen, I want to tell you how sorry I am, Grant and I both are, about Bobby losing his job.

Regina turned, eyebrows raised. "Why are you sorry? Was it your fault?"

Taken aback, Mary faltered. "Well, no. Of course not. We had no idea this was coming. Still, we feel bad about–"

"I hear you're planning some kind of pity session for everyone. Helping people write resumes or something."

Mary's face flushed hot, and it took a moment to find her voice. "Excuse me? A *pity* session? What are you talking about? I– I'm helping the community center organize a job search event. It's for the whole community. We hope people laid off from Essex will take advantage of it, but–"

"Feeling guilty? Is that it?"

"Since when does someone have to be guilty to want to do something good, Regina? I don't understand. What's bad about trying to help out?" And how the hell had she found out about the workshop?

"Right. This is so typical. You sit up there in your fancy house – like kings in your castle, and you want everyone to love you for tossing out a bone to the rest of us. Well, get over yourself. No one wants your help."

Someone cleared her throat, and they both turned toward the conference table. "Ladies, I think it's about time to get started." A wide-eyed Gloria Swanson, president of the auxiliary, stared at them.

With a shaking hand, Mary lifted her cup and returned to her chair. She picked up the papers in front of her and looked at them without seeing a thing. She heard almost nothing of the meeting, and contributed the same. They sometimes got into debates about programs and procedures or something as trivial as a menu item, but never had Mary been publicly attacked like this. She didn't move her head until Kelly Jessup, also a member of her book club, nudged her arm and pushed a tablet toward her.

*Don't worry about her*, the note read. Mary almost smiled. Passing notes at their age. She drew in a calming breath and turned her attention to their VP of finance. When Gloria declared the meeting adjourned what seemed like hours later, Mary gave Kelly's arm a squeeze. "Thanks," she whispered. She hurried around the table, determined to have a last word with her adversary.

60

"Regina, wait."

Regina stopped and sent Mary a long-suffering look.

"Listen, I just want to clear the air," Mary said. "I understand you're upset. I— we don't want to make things worse. We want to help however we can."

"Haven't you done enough, already? You can't just butt out, can you? Good God, you want to run the whole damn town. The City Council. Every committee. Every event. What's next, running for mayor?"

*Not a bad idea*, was the first thing that popped into Mary's head. Thankfully, it didn't come out her mouth as well. Grant had, in fact, been approached about running for mayor a few years back. He'd considered it, and had tucked the notion in his back pocket for possible retirement. And Mary had been appointed to the council when Simon Pritchett and his family had moved after the tornado. She was simply finishing his term. It certainly wasn't a control thing. They loved Whitfield, wanted to be involved. Wanted to see it thrive, and be a part of that. That was the fun of living in a small town.

With all the poise she could muster, Mary spoke quietly. "Losing a job is never an easy thing to deal with," she said, doing her best to keep her voice from quivering. "I hope Bobby finds an even better job and discovers some new opportunities that—"

Regina gave a harsh scoff, and turned away. "Oh, he will."

Mary headed for her car with much less pep in her step than when she'd arrived. Inside, she rolled her neck, and ignored the buzzing of her phone. In the short distance back home, she mulled Regina's words. Of course the woman was angry. Mary could understand that. What she didn't understand was the need some people had to cast blame when something bad happened. For whatever reason, they couldn't accept that bad things just . . . happened.

Anyway, she refused to take it personally. She'd do what she could to help, and she and Grant would go on with their lives, participating and being contributing members of the community.

Still, the idea of having an enemy didn't set well.

## Chapter Six

Sara stared at the cardboard box, and it stared right back as if taunting her. *Now what, huh? What about me?* All of the other boxes were sealed and labeled with their destination – going to Whitfield or Dallas. This box would not be making the trip to either place.

Her first inclination was to simply pitch it in the dumpster and move on. But Todd had delivered a box of her belongings to her front door. Of course he'd done it when he knew she'd be in Whitfield. Still, was it a kind gesture? Should she do the same? And risk running into his wife? She had no idea whether Alyssa had moved into his place or whether he'd moved into hers. For that matter, Sara had no idea whether Alyssa even knew that Sara existed. Part of her would love to shove the collection of Todd's personal belongings at the woman. But the rational part of her said there was no point.

Maybe the best alternative was to leave the box outside the apartment door then text Todd to come and get it if he wanted the contents. Or leave it at the dumpster. She rather liked that idea – dump and dash.

She'd have to decide before her parents arrived, which could happen any minute. Even though she'd offered to hire a moving van, her dad insisted on doing it himself. Made more sense, she supposed. Everything she owned would easily fit in her car and her dad's pickup. The big stuff and – *yippee* – her winter clothes would park in her parents' basement until she found a place in Dallas.

Until then, she was traveling lightly while she imposed on friends' couches.

Sara pulled packing tape across the box flaps, then shoved it aside, and picked up the shopping bag from her dresser. She'd promised payment-by-beverage in exchange for her roommate's help with packing and cleaning.

"Here you go," she sang out, entering the kitchen and pulling a bottle of wine from the bag.

Natalie grinned. "Thanks. I might need to indulge this weekend."

"There's plenty for you and a guest."

Snorting, Natalie dropped into a chair at the kitchen table. "Sure. One can dream."

"Boulevard Pale Ale, hard cider and some chardonnay. And here's a little something that you absolutely cannot share." With a flourish, Sara slid a box of Christopher Elbow artisan chocolates across the table.

"Oh, my gosh!" Natalie gaped at her and pulled the chocolates close. "Not a problem. Mine. All mine."

Sara laughed, but her throat tightened. This was it. She was really leaving. "Hey, thanks for everything," she said softly. "I won't have a roommate, but I hope I can find a neighbor just like you in Dallas."

"Not going to happen, so you might as well stay put."

A knock at the door reminded them it was too late for that. The wheels were in motion. Sara regretted that she couldn't tell Natalie – or anyone in Kansas City – about her pregnancy. But it was the only way to ensure her secret was safe, that no one would slip up. That Todd would not find out.

As far as people there knew, Sara was leaving to join friends, and maybe a special friend, thanks to Claire's thoughtful floral delivery. She almost chuckled at the memory. The stunning bouquet of fuchsia roses had been delivered with perfect timing – only hours after she'd announced her resignation. Confusion had been her first reaction to the man's claim that the flowers were from someone in Dallas, but that had quickly changed to delight when she read the attached card. Her mother and friends were quite a team. Thankfully, Sara and Todd had been careful to keep things cool and undercover at the office, so few people even knew they'd gone out together.

On that positive note, Sara took a deep breath and opened the door, greeting her parents with a smile.

Two hours later, her bedroom was empty, and her car was stuffed. She gave Natalie a last goodbye-hug, dumped Todd's package on the small covered porch, and headed for her car. Her plan was to stay one night in Whitfield and then hit the road again – the road that would take her to a new destination and her new life. Somewhere beyond the yellow brick roads of Kansas.

**

A few miles outside of Whitfield Mary glanced at her watch again. The second session of the On Track seminar should be under way. She swallowed hard, debating whether to drive by the community center. Since most of the routine classes and events were held on Saturday mornings, the number of cars in the parking lot might give her an indication of the turn out. The Thursday evening session had been a dismal failure. According to Jane, only two people had attended – her son and one former Essex employee.

Mary had confirmed the numbers with Wendy from On Track who had tried to convince her that the low turnout may have simply been bad timing. Saturday might be more convenient for busy families. Mary wanted to believe it, but the knot in her stomach sent a different message.

She lifted her purse from the floor in front of her, about to fish for an aspirin. But then she remembered that Grant seemed to be charting her intake. She retrieved her nail file instead.

With another nervous glance at her watch, she touched Grant's arm. "Hey, love, let's swing by the community center before we head to the house." She felt his eyes on her, but refused to meet them.

"Mary. Are you sure? Maybe it's best to let it go. Nothing you can do about it at this point, and Sara's right behind us."

"She knows the way," Mary said dryly, pulling out her cell phone. "I'll call her."

Mary told Sara to go on in, then tucked the phone back in her purse. She looked over at Grant. "Just humor me on this, okay? I want to know."

He made no comment or objection, but passed by the turnoff to their house and continued toward downtown Whitfield. As they neared the community center, Mary leaned forward, eyes straining, fists clenched. "Slow down."

Grant reduced his speed, and turned the truck down Ash Street.

Mary gasped. Seriously? A total of three vehicles dotted the parking lot. She swiveled around. "Maybe the side–" She broke off, her face burning as the reality of what she was seeing hit her full force. The side street was clear. Almost no one had come. A free and beneficial service, and they hadn't taken advantage of it. After all her efforts. She blinked back the tears that threatened.

"Mary-me," Grant said softly.

He stopped the truck at the curb, and slid an arm around her shoulder, pulling her toward him. She let him hold her for a moment, but drew back, too frustrated to be consoled. Swiping at the tears that escaped, she flopped against her seat. "I can't believe it. Why? Why would they turn their back on this opportunity? Just to spite me? It doesn't make sense."

"Can't take it personally, darlin'. It's not–"

"Oh, I think it *is* personal," Mary interrupted. "But I don't understand why." In a shaky voice, she told him of her recent encounter with Regina Daniels. "I had no idea people felt that way, did you? Have I just been blind to it?"

She had her circle of friends, enjoyed her social life and activities, and had always considered herself to be genuinely liked. Did she really come off as controlling and snobbish? And did Regina Daniels really have enough pull to turn others against her? What about Jane? Surely Jane had as much influence as Regina, if not more. Mary's breath caught as an unwelcome, unpleasant thought intruded. Had Jane not been completely straight with her?

"Mary, come on. You know there will always be people who are jealous of the success of others. It goes with the territory. Doesn't matter how much you do or how nice you are. Some people will resent that. You don't need to worry about what Regina Daniels or anyone else thinks. Hell with 'em. You did something worthwhile, and if they're too stupid or stubborn to see it, it's their tough luck."

Mary sputtered a laugh. His words sounded exactly like something she'd say. He was right, of course. Basically, it was the ol' 'You can lead a horse to water' adage personified. Against the headrest she closed her eyes. What a waste of money. What would she do with all of those freebies and flash drives? Maybe Wendy could return them.

How embarrassing. Mary's face warmed again. She must look like a complete fool to the On Track director.

You don't need to worry about what anyone thinks, she reminded herself. What she did need was that aspirin. And a heart-to-heart with Claire. Head pounding, she hopped out of the truck as soon as it came to a stop, and hurried into the house.

She stopped short at the sight of Sara in the kitchen. Oh, man, schlepping boxes inside sounded like more effort than Mary could handle right now. "Hey, sweets. Can we wait a bit to start unloading? I want to lie down for a while. Give me an hour, okay?"

"Sure," Sara said, her eyes tracking her mother's already retreating figure. *That was weird.* At the sound of her father's footsteps in the garage, Sara turned, surprised to find his face missing its normal easy smile.

"What's the matter with Mom?" Sara hadn't missed the tired, pained look on her mother's face.

His brows rose. "What do you mean?"

"She seemed upset. Went to lie down." She jerked a thumb toward the hallway.

A heavy sigh escaped her dad's lips before he answered. "Let's give her some time. We can get started on your things."

"Okay." Sara set down the can of sparkling water she'd just opened wondering what had happened. Oh. *Oh, no.* As realization dawned, her stomach clenched. Her parents had had a fight. And she'd bet it was her fault.

That's why they'd needed a "quick detour" before coming home. They'd been arguing and needed to cool down before facing her. That's why her mother had practically sprinted toward her bedroom. Sara felt physically ill. The last thing she wanted was for her baby to be a wedge between her parents. She could probably count on one hand the number of times she'd witnessed her parents at odds with each other.

"You get the little things," he told her brusquely. "I'll take care of everything else."

With tears threatening, Sara slipped past her dad and headed for her car. Most of the boxes there could stay. She lifted her small overnight bag from the back seat, then sank down in its place, wishing she'd gone on to Dallas without stopping in Whitfield. How could she convince her parents that she was going to be fine? That they didn't need to get uptight – with her or each other – over her situation? She could handle it.

What was the big hang-up, anyway? Did they think she wasn't smart enough to raise a child? Annie had always been known as the smart one. The over-achiever. Or were they embarrassed that she wasn't married? Her dad could be, she supposed. That didn't sound like her mom, though. Maybe that's what caused the argument. Or it could be they were afraid they'd have to support her forever. Of course Annie had a great job as an attorney. Plus, she was marrying Mr. Perfect, an engineer who apparently already pulled down a six-figure income. At least they wouldn't have to worry about Annie.

And her younger brother was well on his way to becoming *Doctor* Jason Logan. So maybe she was the failure, the place where they'd gone wrong. The middle child. Different from the others. The problem child . . . who couldn't possibly be ready to raise her own child.

But they were wrong. In the two weeks since she'd given notice at work she'd spent almost every evening online, reading about pregnancy and babies. She'd read inspirational stories about single moms and motherhood. Everything she read made her more sure, more determined. She was looking forward to being a mother, to bringing a tiny creature into the world, nurturing it, and sharing an amazing bond. This little baby would be her family. Her legacy to the world. And her joy, she was sure of that. She was ready to feel that depth of love and emotion.

The clang of the tailgate lowering on her dad's pickup brought her back to the present, and she realized it had turned chilly, and her exposed arms were sprinkled with goose bumps. The sun had disappeared behind flat gray clouds. Sara climbed out of the car with her bag and made for the house.

How quickly the day had changed. Just like her life. She hadn't meant to get pregnant. She hadn't planned to be a single mom. But that's what kept things interesting. How boring life would be if every detail was planned out and went according to that plan with no surprises. That was not the life for her. Sara smiled up at the darkening clouds. Behind every storm cloud was a silver lining – and she'd found hers. Her independence. Her new adventure. Her child.

"Pop your trunk when you come back," her dad hollered as she wandered past.

"Sure," Sara said absently.

At the door, Sara stopped, and considered turning back and confronting her dad. But her dad was notoriously non-confrontational. No matter what, he'd put on a good face. A wave of guilt rolled over her. Was her mother taking the brunt of Dad's ire? He rarely even raised his

69

voice, especially at her mother. He was too much of a gentleman for that. But he did have a quiet way of making his disappointment known.

The thing was, it'd eat at her if she didn't know.

"Hey, Dad?"

"Yeah?"

"Is everything all right? I mean, with you and Mom?"

He turned and stared. "What?"

She blew out a deep breath. "Did you guys have a fight because of me? Because of the baby?"

With a shake of his head, her dad moved toward her. "Sarie, let me tell you something. Your mom and I are fine. We've got a lot on our minds, but believe it or not, some of it has nothing to do with you, or any of you kids."

As tears filled her eyes, Sara swiped them away. She was obviously becoming too emotional. But what else was going on to upset her mother? His response didn't answer that question.

He slid an arm across her shoulder, and kissed the top of her head. "Come on. You don't need to start imagining new problems. Let's get this job done, okay?"

"Okay." Got it. They had their own lives. She knew that. Her mother had always been the queen of multi-tasking. Always involved, always busy. All the more reason to go to Dallas and not impose on her parents any more than necessary.

After three more trips up the stairs, Sara surveyed the mess of boxes and bags in her room – and realized it'd been more than an hour since her mother had bailed on unloading. Way more.

Quietly, Sara tiptoed down the hallway toward her parents' bedroom, stopping when she heard her mother's voice.

"No worries, honey, everything is in great shape."

Sounded like her mom was talking to Annie.

"Oh, I think we'll have dinner here tonight. I've got a pork roast in the crock pot."

Ah-ha. That's what smelled so good coming from the kitchen. That sounded–

"Sara's here. I'll ask her, but she has a long drive ahead of her tomorrow."

"I know. It's a long way. I wish she'd look at Paxton or Wichita."

"Well, yes, but—"

Sara listened harder. She wouldn't normally eavesdrop on her mother, but it was obvious the conversation had turned to her. Too bad she couldn't hear the other side as well.

"Oh, Annie. Of course she wasn't fired. Why would you think that?"

Fired? *Fired!* That's what Annie thought? Sara groaned inside. Figured. She took a step closer.

"Yes, it was sudden, but I don't think it was anything that drastic. Maybe she was tired of a person or project and something happened to tip the scales. She's been there three years. Maybe it's just time to move on. Anyway, she has friends in Dallas."

At least her mother was covering for her.

"All right. Well—"

Uh-oh. Her mother's voice took on that I'm-ready-to-wrap-this-up tone. As quietly as she could go, Sara hurried back down the hallway. In the kitchen, she turned when she heard her mother's steps on the hardwood.

"Hey, I was about to come check on you," Sara said. "You feel—"

"Where's Dad?"

Sara shrugged. "Not sure." She reached into the refrigerator and grabbed a Diet Coke, then caught herself. Too much caffeine. Replacing it, she took a Sprite instead.

"Has he started unloading?" her mother asked.

"We're done."

Her mother's eyes widened. "All done already? I was going to— You didn't lift anything heavy, did you?"

Sara resisted rolling her eyes. If she heard one more comment that proved how stupid everyone thought she was, she'd scream. "Of course not." Toggling between irritation and concern for her mother Sara struggled for a normal tone. "That smells good," she said, nodding toward the counter and deliberately changing the subject. So far, she'd had some morning queasiness but no particular foods turned her stomach.

"Oh, I just talked to Annie. She asked if we want to join her and Blake for dinner."

"Isn't this dinner?" Sara asked, gesturing at the steaming crockpot.

"Well, it can be. But doesn't have to be. It's pulled pork. Does that sound good?"

"Sounds great. There's no sense driving to Paxton when you already have this. Besides, the less time I have to spend pretending around Annie, the better. I'll see her soon, you know."

Her mother gave a wan smile. "True. Why don't you text her back for me?"

Sara pulled her phone out of her pocket and sent her sister a brief message while her mother poked at the meat inside the cooker.

"I might need to get all of your crockpot recipes," Sara said, thinking out loud. It might be a convenient way to prepare meals-for-one while she was dealing with a demanding newborn.

"Sure. I bet I have extra cards, or you can type them into your computer." She turned. "Do you have a crockpot?"

Oh. Small problem. She actually didn't. "No, but–"

"What you need is a bridal shower. That's where–"

Sara stared at her mother. "Well, I don't happen to have any of those scheduled right now," Sara told her, sarcasm creeping into her voice. *Get over it*, she thought.

Slumping against the counter, her mother held up a hand. "I'm sorry. That– that was just a brain cramp." She rubbed her temples. "Let's run down to the hardware store and get you one." Before Sara could even think, her mother had grabbed her purse, and Sara's arm. Then she stopped, causing Sara to nearly stumble.

"What?"

Her mother glanced at her watch. "Rats. They close in a few minutes. Maybe tomorr—" She let out a heavy sigh. "They aren't open on Sundays."

"Mom, it's not a big deal. I'm sure I can manage to get my own crockpot. And I bet they sell them in Dallas."

Her mother waved a hand. "Oh, don't bother. You can take one of mine."

"What? Mom, come on. I'm not taking your things." After all, she'd been living on her own for almost four years, and had enough essentials to get by.

"Sarie, I've got three, for cryin' out loud." She knelt in front of the cupboards and began pushing things around. "Here we go. This one is probably the right size."

She pulled it out and set it on the island. "There. Take it."

"Okay, if you're sure."

"Of course."

"I was thinking it might be a good way to make several meals at once. Especially when I'm rushing from work to day care then home. It might simplify things."

"Definitely," her mother agreed. "That's a smart way to do it."

Ha! Imagine that. In her head, Sara patted herself on the back. Score one for her. Okay, so it was a small victory about her ability to feed herself, but she felt ridiculously pleased at her mother's comment. Many other smart moves to come. She'd just have to prove it.

## Chapter Seven

"Doug and I are helping Johnston tear down that old barn on his parents' land this week, so I won't be around much. Not for lunch, anyway," Grant told Mary over Monday morning coffee.

"Now there's something that could've benefited from a good tornado."

"Got that right. At least it gives us something to do, and keeps me out of your hair."

"Did I say I was having an issue with my hair?"

Standing, he brushed a kiss across her lips. "I know a few things without being told." He refilled his mug.

"Hey, take the rest of that in a Thermos if you want. Might be chilly out there."

"Good idea."

When he began opening cupboards as if he had no idea where she'd kept that sort of thing forever, Mary got up from the table and handed him a small insulated jug.

"Love you."

"Love you, too. Bye." As soon as Grant closed the garage door, Mary turned back to the coffee pot and refilled the canister, knowing she'd need more. Eight hours of sleep apparently hadn't cleared her head or cured the stiffness in her lower back. Next thing on her shopping list might be a new mattress.

But it was her to-do list that begged for her immediate attention. She reached for the file folder she'd left on the kitchen island.

Normally she loved that moment when she was in the house alone, and all was quiet, and she could start planning her day. Today was too quiet. Probably had something to do with Sara being gone, starting her new life – that had taken a dramatic new direction.

What Mary had to look forward to was several phone calls, a couple she didn't want to make. It took all the energy she had to open the folder – and not go back to bed.

Mary toyed with the pen in her hand. She wished she could've gone with Sara to help her get a feel for Dallas, help her get her feet on the ground. Friends could only do so much. They'd be busy with their own lives. Mary considered calling her sister-in-law to get some ideas, but Sara hadn't minced words when she told Mary not to try and manage her move. Or her life.

Mary jumped when her phone pealed.

"Hello?"

"Hi, Mary, this is Wendy. From On Track."

All right, then. Might as well get this out of the way. "Good morning, Wendy," Mary said in the cheeriest voice she could muster.

"You've probably heard by now that we didn't get the turnout we were hoping for."

"Yes. I did." The whole county had probably heard about it by now.

"I'm wondering if you'd like to choose some other dates. Maybe wait a few weeks until people have had time to realize they do need some professional help. We'd be glad to hold onto–"

Absolutely not. She was done with that project. And her give-a-damn was at an all-time low. "Oh, thank you, Wendy, but I'm afraid I've spent all the time I can give on the seminars. I'm so sorry it didn't work out."

"It's really a shame. Such a missed opportunity for the community."

"It is, but we can't force it down their throats. Please send me the bill for the remainder of the expenses. I'll get it taken care of right away. Do you think you could get a refund on the giveaway items you bought?"

"I'll look into it. There may be a restocking fee that doesn't make it worthwhile. If that's the case, shall I ship them to you?"

Sure, because she'd need them hanging around to remind her of– *Enough!* She shook her head, trying to clear the negative thoughts. What was done, was done. If nothing else, she could give them as prizes at the library opening or some other event. They wouldn't go to waste.

"That'd be great, Wendy. Thanks, again, for all your efforts. It's been a pleasure working with you."

Mary ended the call, took a couple of sips of coffee, then punched in Jane's number. Maybe while their husbands were laboring, they could have a leisurely lunch – and she could put to rest the niggling question about Jane's support. Surely if Jane had accidentally slipped and mentioned Mary's involvement in the career workshop, she'd fess up.

She heard the heavy sigh before she heard Jane's voice. "Hey, Mare."

Mary's response died in her throat. Why the sigh? Was that directed at her or had Jane been talking to someone else as she answered the call?

"Hello?" Jane asked. "You called? Mary, are you butt-dialing–"

She came-to. "Hey. I'm here. Sorry, I was, uh, distracted."

"Yeah? What's up?"

"Thought we could play ladies-of-leisure and grab lunch today since we don't have to feed the guys. You free?"

"Oh, sorry, Mare. I can't. I've got a dental appointment and some errands to run."

"That sounds like a jolly good time."

"Doesn't it, though? Just how I like to spend my days off."

Mary chuckled. "I'm sure. Hey, I'll let you get to it, but I have a quick question. Did Corey make it to the workshop on Saturday?"

"He did. He said it was great, that the people running it were really sharp and–"

"Did he tell you how many people were – or weren't – there?"

Another deep sigh.

"Yeah, I'm afraid so. It's too bad."

"I just can't figure it out. Do you think people didn't go because Grant and I sponsored it? No one was supposed to know that, but Regina Daniels somehow got wind of it. Is she on some kind of bashing campaign?"

"I don't know, Mare. She didn't hear it from me. I'm really trying to stay out of the fray, you know?"

Mary chewed on that for a moment, relieved that Jane hadn't given her away, but thinking that staying out of the fray didn't sound like trumpeting support, either. Then again, she could hardly blame Jane for her feelings. Being caught in the middle was stressful, and Doug's layoff was enough to deal with.

"The gal from On Track called and asked if I wanted to choose some new dates and try again, but–"

"Don't do it," Jane said, her words short and sharp. "Honestly, Mary, I think you need to stop. Let it go."

Mary blanched. "I didn't say–"

"It was a nice gesture, and I'm sorry it wasn't successful," Jane continued, her voice more even, but still firm. "But you can't fix this. It's out of your control."

Mary swallowed hard. While the words were different, to her ears they sounded very much like Regina's telling her to butt out.

And they stung.

Closing her eyes, Mary took some time to collect her thoughts and regroup. "Okay," she murmured. "I guess there's nothing more I can do."

"Look Mare, I don't want to hurt your feelings, but–"

"No. I get it. I'm sorry I brought it up again. You don't need anything else to deal with."

"And neither do you," Jane told her.

"Right. Over and done. I'm shoving this is the bullshit file." She picked up the black marker on the counter, and wrote the sentiment in bold letters on the folder, then shoved it aside.

After ending the call, Mary considered opening the folder that held the agenda for the next City Council meeting and accompanying documents that she needed to read. But it seemed too much like work – too much like dealing with other people's problems. She pushed it away, too. For the next week and a half, her family would get her undivided attention.

**

Claire arrived first. Mary couldn't contain a grin from the moment Claire stepped out of her car dressed in a soft pistachio green sweater with signature scarf to the instant she was wrapped in her friend's arms.

"Come in, come in," Mary told her. "It's so good to see you. Wow. You look gorgeous. That's a great color on you."

They automatically wandered toward the kitchen.

"Thanks. How's everything going? You about ready to do this?"

"Absolutely. Annie will be here by noon. I figure we can eat a quick lunch then get busy on the bags and favors."

"Sounds good. How many?"

"Only about twenty-five gift bags, but a hundred-and-fifty table favors. We've got every room at the lodge booked."

Claire threw her hands in the air. "Put me to work."

"Nah. We can wait for Annie. Let's talk. What do you want to drink? I've got coffee and tea, and every kind of juice."

"Plain old coffee is fine. I'm a little chilly."

"Oh, I was afraid it'd turn cold. The girls will freeze in their dresses."

"As long as it doesn't sno—"

"Stop," Mary commanded. "Don't say it. Don't even think it. There's nothing in the forecast, and I want to keep it that way."

"Right, because you can totally control the weather."

"Staying positive. Thinking good juju, you know? Feel free to join in."

Claire reached for the cup of coffee. "Fine. I'll play along." She dropped into a chair at the table. "Your house looks perfect, as usual."

"More thanks to Rita than me," Mary told her.

"Your style," Claire countered. "So, what do you hear from Sara?"

Mary screwed up her face. "About as much as I'd hear if I tried whispering at a rock concert. I may have to rent a drone to keep up with that girl."

"Maybe she doesn't have a lot to tell yet."

"Guess we'll find out soon enough. She should be here around three o'clock."

"Oh, good. I want to spend some time with her."

Mary held up a finger. "Just remember, no baby talk. Annie doesn't know. And you aren't supposed to know, either, so try not to get my ass in trouble, will you?"

"I got it. Speaking of trouble, did you talk to Jane?"

Studying the liquid in her cup, Mary debated whether she wanted to get into this conversation. She'd promised to let it go.

"Mare?" The concern on Claire's face welcomed a heart-to-heart.

"I did." Mary blew out her breath. "It wasn't her. But it's obvious she's hearing stuff that I'm not. People are getting ugly and hateful. And–" She broke off, swallowing hard. "And I think a lot of it is directed at me. I don't get it. Tell me the truth, do people think I'm a rich bitch who wants to run everyone's life?"

"What?" Claire's voice pitched as she reached out and squeezed Mary's arm. "Mary, come on. People love you. Think how many friends you have. Don't let the noise of a few discontents drown out the sound of good sense. We've had so much fun in book club, PTA, the library board, because of teamwork and friendship and camaraderie. Think of everything you do for this town, and—"

"But that's what I mean. Is it over the top? Do I come off as a control freak? Do people put up with me because I have money while they secretly resent me? I'm telling you, I'm picking up some bad vibes."

Claire leaned forward. "And I'm telling you that you're being paranoid. Snap out of it!"

Mary managed a smile. "Maybe I'm losing my mind."

"Maybe you need a break. Listen, I've talked to Susie and Dana and Kent this week, and no one has mentioned anything about the Essex mess. Think about this – in two days you're going to be surrounded by friends and family, tons of people who love you."

"God, Claire, I know you're right. I *hope* you're right. But the thought of people boycotting Annie's wedding the way they did the career workshops is keeping me up at night."

Claire scoffed. "Girlfriend, maybe you *are* losing your mind. That's ridiculous. Quit thinking like that because you're just going to be proven wrong, and I know how much you hate being wrong."

Pushing off from the table, Mary grabbed Claire's mug. "Thanks for the therapy. Let me warm that up."

"Will work for coffee," Claire told her, with a grin.

Annie's arrival put an end to the therapy session – and lightened the mood. Annie's bright smiles and obvious excitement were contagious.

\*\*

They'd just finished wrapping the bridesmaids' gifts when Sara arrived.

It'd only been a week and a half since Mary had seen her. Still, her eyes went to Sara's middle. In black leggings and a long sweater, she looked cute and stylish – and not pregnant.

"So what are we working on?" Sara asked.

Annie shoved the gorgeous packages aside. She'd give those to her attendants at their Saturday morning brunch. "Welcome bags and favors," she said.

"I've got all the stuff separated into trays," Mary added. "We need to assemble, then add the ribbon." She gestured to the dining room table, laden with locally made soaps, honey and other goodies for out-of-town guests.

As they started the assembly line, Claire spoke up. "Sara, tell us about Dallas. How's that going?"

Mary held her breath a moment when Annie stopped moving and stared at Sara.

"Yeah. What's the scoop? I still can't believe you just up and moved to Dallas."

Sara popped a chocolate-covered almond in her mouth and kept working. "You know, it's kind of fun to up and do something spontaneously every once in a while." She gave Annie a pointed look. "You should try it sometime."

Mary glanced at Claire, and saw the smile before she managed to hide it. Ah . . . sisters. "What about apartments?" Mary asked.

"Mmm. Still looking. Single places are pretty expensive."

Annie stopped again. "Why don't you want a roommate?"

"I've had roommates since college. If I can swing it financially, I'd like to have a place of my own."

"What about the job search?" Mary asked. She was ready to hear something she didn't already know.

Sara met her eyes, and smiled. "I've sent out a bunch of résumés to head hunters and individual companies. And . . ." She paused for a beat. "I've already had one interview, and have two more set up for next week."

"You do?" Mary asked. "Well, sweetie, that's great. Wow. That was fast." Hooray, she said to herself. Sara needed to land something within the next few weeks to avoid having her secret detected. Mary's stomach fluttered. It seemed awfully optimistic.

"Yeah. And I have an appointment with one of the headhunters. I'm sure I'll have something by the end of the year."

"And you're going to camp out with friends until you find something?" Annie asked, her eyes widening. "That could still be several weeks. Hope you don't wear out your welcome."

"Hey," Claire cut in. "If this Dallas thing doesn't work out, you come on up to Wichita. We'd love to have you, and you can camp out at my place for as long as you like."

Mary gave Claire a smile, but made no comment. If only. Maybe that suggestion coming from someone else would have more impact. Not only was Wichita much closer for grandmothering, it'd be cheaper. She studied Sara for a moment, and wondered just how expensive the apartments were. Was this Dallas thing really do-able? Spontaneity might be fun, but in this case there could be serious consequences. The clock was ticking.

## Chapter Eight

Sheer excitement pushed Mary out of bed Saturday morning. Arching her back, she rolled her neck one way and then the other. If she had to pop Advil all day long, she would not allow her aches and pains to have a place in this day.

She stopped on her way to the shower for a quick peek outside, taking a quiet moment to simply feel grateful. There would be so much emotion today, and she didn't want to let this pass without notice. A clear golden-pink sky with the promise of abundant sunshine greeted her. Such a relief. No snow. No travel difficulties. Friends and family safely gathered.

Which reminded her, she had a house full of guests. Better snap to it.

Thirty minutes later, the smell of fresh coffee beckoned to her from the kitchen, and she was also thankful she'd thought to hire Rita, her housekeeper, to be there all day to keep up with food and drinks in addition to ongoing kitchen cleanup.

"Good morning, Rita," Mary said reaching for the mug the older woman held out to her.

"Morning, dear. Where's all your company? Been here an hour, and I haven't seen a soul."

Mary shook her head, and glanced around the empty rooms. Apparently no one else was in any hurry to get the day started. "It's called the calm before the storm, Rita. Enjoy it."

Soon enough, Mary expected Blake and all the groomsmen to show up. Grant and Jason would be in charge of keeping the men occupied with pool, video games and any sightseeing requests. There wasn't much to see, especially in November, but sometimes city folks enjoyed a tour of the farmland and small-town charm. Too bad the charm was out of season. In the summer, overflowing flower baskets hung from the street lanterns. And in the holiday season colorful banners and lights gave a festive feel to the quaint downtown area. Oh, well. The guys might not even notice such things.

The girls would spend the day being pampered and prepped at the salon. Sherry, the salon owner, and Mary's longtime stylist, had promised they'd have the whole place to themselves. But that was after brunch at Hannah's– The sight of Sara's fuzzy pink slippers on the stairs broke Mary's train of thought.

"Morning, sweetie."

"Morning, Mom. Got any decaf?"

"Coming right up, Miss Sara," Rita sang out.

Sara turned. "Hey, Rita. Thanks."

Automatically, Mary glanced toward the stairs to see if Annie had appeared. Maybe Sara had deliberately come down before Annie. Decaffeinated coffee would be a red flag for sure. No one in their family drank decaf in the morning. For that matter, did anyone drink decaffeinated coffee in the morning? What would be the point? If anyone commented, she'd just have to say she wanted to have it available for guests.

"Brunch is at ten-thirty," Mary told Sara. "Do you need something before then?"

"Are you kidding? I'm starving. I'd pass out if I didn't eat something now."

Mary waved her arm toward the kitchen counter. "We have enough food to feed all of China. I guarantee you will not go hungry."

She'd hardly spoken the words when Grant appeared at the same time Jason stumbled up from the basement. A minute later, as if the dinner bell had rung, the guys swarmed in through the front door, and the house was suddenly crowded.

Grinning, Mary got up to help Rita. *Let the fun begin.*

**

Hand at her chest, Mary looked at her daughter, and fought back tears, taking in the lovely picture – beautiful hair in an elegant up-do intertwined with sparkling crystals, stunning white gown, and a gorgeous smile that radiated happiness.

Mary's throat tightened, clogged with emotion. She moved in close for one last hug as the wedding party assembled in the church foyer. Guests were seated, and soft music filtered out of the sanctuary.

"Oh, sweetheart, I'm so happy for you," Mary whispered, squeezing Annie's hand. Turning, she pulled Sara close, too, and the photographer snapped yet another photo of the three of them. They'd taken hundreds – no, thousands – of photos already, but Mary knew these last few moments were precious. She beckoned to Grant, and when he moved forward and slid an arm around her waist, she almost lost it. Then Jason joined in, and she knew this would be one of her all-time favorite family portraits.

Blinking rapidly, she stepped back. "Okay, this is it. I'll see you inside." She took her son's arm and they began their walk down the aisle. Her presence would signal the guests that the wedding ceremony was about to start.

Mary wore a knee-length dress in a deep rosy coral raw silk with a matching lace jacket that was only about seven inches shorter than the dress. The jeweled clasp at the center added just the right amount of bling for the mother of the bride. She smiled, careful to look at both sides of the aisle, and move slowly. Familiar faces beamed back at her from all directions. Relief rushed through her as she approached the front pew, and realized the church was packed. She glanced at Claire in the row behind her, and grinned, happy to be proven wrong. Claire smiled with an I-told-you-so wink.

As soon as Mary was seated, Blake and Reverend Pauls took their place at the front of the church, and then the procession began. The bridesmaids floated down the aisle, their dresses shimmering in varying shades of sea glass. Sara could not have looked more radiant – no evidence of her recent trauma. And then came Claire's adorable granddaughter, Olivia, spreading coral-colored rose petals along the path. At the end of the aisle, she tossed the last of the petals, then skipped back to join her father and grandmother, leaving the entire crowd chuckling.

A moment later, the music changed. That was Mary's cue. Her full heart pounding, she stood and watched her daughter step into the spotlight on Grant's arm, ready to begin a new chapter in her life.

**

Self-consciously, Sara smoothed the soft folds of her dress as she entered the reception with the rest of the wedding party. Given the design of the dress, she couldn't imagine anyone would suspect her pregnancy, but she felt more exposed without the bridesmaid bouquet in front of her. Those had been snatched away and were now decorating the long table where they would soon be seated.

She held the arm of Blake's brother, and smiled at the audience's applause, then took her place beside Annie. Once the entire party was introduced, they scattered throughout the room. Rather than have a reception line, Annie and Blake planned to visit each table individually, giving guests time to get drinks and mingle.

Sara was talking to Maddie, Dana's daughter, when she noticed Annie and her new husband laughing with a good-looking guy sporting a trim dark beard – and who nicely filled out his charcoal gray suit.

"Whoa, who is that?"

"Where?"

Maddie turned, and Sara gestured toward Annie. "Must be a friend of Blake's." She gave a little laugh. "Mmm. I might need an introduction."

Maddie gave her a puzzled look. "Are you talking about—"

86

Sara sucked in her breath. "Oh, my gosh. Wait. Is that—"

"Sara, that's Evan."

Sara's face flushed hot, and she wanted to drop through the floor. Not only had she not recognized Evan, she'd practically drooled over him in front of his sister. There was no chance that wouldn't get back around to him. He obviously realized they were looking at him, because he stepped away from Annie and was heading straight toward Sara and Maddie.

Sara tried to cover by addressing Evan before Maddie had a chance to open her mouth. "Hey, Evan."

His smile widened as he reached them.

"Well, hi there," he said, his eyes on Sara. "I was wondering if I'd ever get a chance to talk to you." He moved forward, and wrapped her in a hug.

Brief though it was, Sara felt the muscular contours of his arms. The unexpected contact rattled her, and the subtle scent of his cologne clogged her brain. While Sara stood tongue-tied, she felt a sharp jab to her side.

"So, do you two need an introduction or what?" Maddie asked, her voice full of teasing laughter. She took Evan's arm. "Sara, I'd like you to meet my big brother, Evan. Evan, may I present Sara Logan? You may remember we used to—"

Evan held up a hand. "Thanks, Mad. I think we've got this."

Finally, Sara came-to, and laughed at herself. Shaking her head, she touched Evan's arm. "How are you?"

He nodded. "Doing great. How 'bout yourself? You look beautiful."

"Thanks."

"All right," Maddie said. "I can see you two have a lot of catching up to do, so I'll, uh, see you later." As she turned to make her exit, Maddie leaned toward Sara and whispered, "Jeez, get a drink or something."

Sara wished she had. If nothing else, it would give her something to do with her hands.

"It's good to see you," Evan said. "It's been a while."

"Yeah." Oh, some spiked punch would be nice right about now, Sara thought. Why was talking with someone she'd known forever so awkward? She moistened her lips. "I'm kind of surprised to see you, actually."

His brows pulled together. "Why's that?"

Maybe it was her imagination, but she'd swear his smile had tightened. "Oh, I don't know. It's been—"

Evan shrugged. "It's like a wedding in the family. Why wouldn't I be here?"

Aha. That said a lot. So he thought of Annie like a sister – which would mean the same for her. Except that– except he wasn't looking at her as if she were his sister. His eyes looked deeply into hers. As if searching for a deeper connection. The connection of an old friend who knew her well, who could read her thoughts and feelings . . . Oh, God, she hoped not.

"Uh-oh. I think you're wanted." His gaze shifted past her.

Sara turned only a second before Elise grabbed hold of her. "Come on. We need you." Sara flashed Evan an apologetic smile. "Sorry. Maid of honor duties. Clap after my toast, okay?"

With a nod, he raised his glass to her.

As she made her way to the bridal party's table, the DJ announced that it was time for Annie and Blake to begin the dinner buffet, so she made a detour, and fell into line behind them. A short reprieve from her duties.

By the time everyone was served, the wedding party was finished, and there was no escaping. The DJ, sticking to his well-choreographed script, put her on center stage.

Sara stood, and smiled at the crowd then gestured toward Annie and Blake. "Wow. They look pretty happy, don't they?"

Cheers and clapping erupted, and Sara waited until the noise died down to continue. "So this is where I get to tell you about my big sister. I'll try to keep it short and sweet. But remember, we're sisters. I've got stories." She paused for the murmur of chuckles. "Honestly, almost all of my stories end with Annie as the hero. Because my sister is one of the nicest, most thoughtful people I know.

When I visited her in college and was underage, she ditched her friends to hang out with me. When she saw a teenaged girl bored to death with her family at the bowling alley, Annie invited her to join the two of us, and we had a blast. She finds little ways to brighten someone else's day. The truth is, Annie has always been my role model. Some of you may ask yourselves when facing a tough decision, 'what would Jesus do'? I do that, too. But I often find myself thinking what would Annie do? I'm not even kidding. She's an excellent role model." She stopped, and gestured toward Blake. "And she obviously makes good choices. Okay, so maybe she doesn't quite walk on water, but she's the best sister a person could ask for, and I'm so happy to see her so happy today marrying the love of her life." She lifted her glass. "To Annie and Blake."

After a few more toasts and cheers, the dancing began, with Blake and Annie taking the spotlight. A hush fell over the crowd as the lights dimmed, and all eyes turned toward the couple floating across the floor. Seeing the two of them together, was proof positive to Sara that she hadn't been in love with Todd. He'd never looked at her the way Blake looked at Annie. And the opposite was true as well. Thank you, Alyssa.

When the lights brightened, Blake let go of Annie's hand, and Sara watched her father pull her sister into his arms. And in a split second, tears filled her eyes. Her dad's love shone on his face, and her sister's radiated happiness. Sara fought the envy that wrapped around, threatening to choke her. Would she miss out on the magic of this moment? Did her choices mean she'd never get her own daddy/daughter dance?

A moment later, a warm arm slid around her shoulders, and her mother was at her side, pulling her close. "That was a lovely toast you gave, sweetie. Well done."

Sara gave her a soft "thanks."

Her mother rested her forehead against Sara's. "Now don't you start crying, or I will, too."

If that wasn't like turning on the faucet. Tears streamed down Sara's face.

Her mom snatched a napkin off of the table nearby and dabbed at Sara's cheeks. "You're next," her mother murmured. Sara wasn't sure whether she meant to dance or get married, but as soon as the music waned, and clapping erupted, her dad spun their direction. He pulled her mother onto the dance floor.

"I'll be back for you," he called, winking at Sara. Her mother's arm was replaced by Claire's.

"Look at that cute couple out there. So sweet, I think I might puke."

Sara laughed. Apparently her parents had made up. Or things had cleared up. Either way, they looked happy. Adorable even. The crowd cheered as the two dancers twirled in perfect rhythm and then her father dipped her mother almost to the floor with a sexy flourish. *Ugh*. She was with Claire on this one.

At her mother's gesturing, a few other couples moved onto the floor. And then something happened. It was so fast Sara couldn't be sure whether her mother had stumbled or what, but she suddenly lost her balance, and clutched at her dad. Sara could see him practically lift her mother up. Then, as if it were part of their dance move, he whisked her into his arms and off the floor. When he set her down near one of the tables, her mother didn't sit, but pulled out a chair and rested a knee against it. Pretending nothing had happened?

Sara exchanged glances with Claire. "What was that all about, I wonder." She started to move forward, but Claire gently stopped her.

"Let's wait a minute, shall we? You know how much your mother likes a fuss."

A moment later, Dana sidled up to them. "What do you make of that?" she asked, jerking her head in the direction of Sara's mother. "Grace over there."

"Tipsy?" Claire suggested.

"Hmmm. Maybe." Dana turned to Sara. "Has your mom been feeling all right?"

Surprised at the question, Sara stared at Dana. "I– I think so." And then she remembered a few things. Little things. Anything worth mentioning? "She's been kind of tired, I guess. You know, the wedding and all."

"Right."

"She did fall when I was home a while back."

Dana's brows arched. "She fell?"

"Well, tripped. She was fine, though."

"What made her fall?"

Claire nudged Dana. "Why the interrogation? What's up?"

"Oh, probably nothing. Call me Nurse Paranoid."

In unspoken agreement, the three of them started walking – their destination clear.

"Sara, did you have a chance to catch up with Evan?" Dana asked. "I know he was looking forward to seeing you."

Sara eyed her suspiciously. Had she not heard of Sara's earlier faux pas? "Yes, I saw him for a minute, but we didn't really have time to talk."

"Oh, that's too bad."

Sara gave a light laugh. "Well, I've been busy with wedding duties, you know."

As they approached her mother's table, she smiled and waved. And immediately attempted to shoo them away. "Why aren't you girls out there dancing?" she demanded. "Go! Have fun. Hey, Grant?"

Sara's dad hadn't moved more than a foot or so from her mom. "Dance with Sara. I want some pictures of you two dancing. I mean it. Go!"

They did as ordered, but it wasn't the same. Both of them kept looking back to the spot where they'd left her mother. Besides, the music was wrong for couples dancing.

"So what happened? Did you step on Mom's toes?" Sara teased.

"I guess we're out of practice," he hollered over the music.

The tune changed again, and a line dance formed, forcing them to the edge of the floor. That's when her dad deliberately pulled her in front of one of the photographers, and posed for a shot. Probably not what her mother had in mind.

He bent down. "Sorry, sweetie. I can't dance to this. You go have fun with your friends." Her dad kissed her cheek, then ushered her off the dance floor.

She didn't bother to tell him that she didn't have any friends there. All the guests were friends of theirs, or Annie's and Blake's. Didn't matter, though. She was quickly pulled into the group dance by Annie. It had to be at least an hour later before Sara could catch her breath and take a break. She hurried to the bar, hoping to order a non-alcoholic drink without an audience.

About three steps later, Evan intercepted her. "Want to dance?" he asked.

Sara sagged. "Not really."

"Kind of figured," he said, looking down at her shoes. "Want to go sit in front of the fire and talk about the people drunk-dancing?"

She laughed out loud. "Yes! That sounds much more appealing."

He grinned as he took hold of her arm. "That's what I thought. Wait. Did you want a fresh drink?"

"You know what sounds really good?"

"What?"

"A cup of coffee. It's kind of chilly in here."

His glance dropped to her bare shoulders. "I can see why. Let's get the lady what she wants." He stopped one of the wait staff. "Any chance you could bring us a cup of coffee?"

"Of course, sir."

Sara chimed in, "Decaf, with a little sugar, please."

The woman returned only moments later with a mug and saucer. Clutching her warm mug, Sara turned toward the lobby, and Evan fell into step beside her.

Evan tossed his jacket on one of the sofas, and they both sat on the hearth bench in front of the fire.

"I hear you're moving to Dallas."

"Just did."

"Better job?"

She gave him a wry smile. "No job."

He sent her a curious look. "How's that?"

She let out a long sigh, unsure whether she wanted to have this conversation – which would surely mean lying. Stalling, she took a sip of coffee. "Good timing. Lease was about up, and the job had gotten pretty routine."

"Prospects are good in Dallas?"

"I hope so. I've sent out a couple dozen resumes, had one interview on Monday, a couple more set up for next week." Ready to change the subject, she asked, "How are things in Tulsa?"

"No complaints," he said.

"I talked to your mom a while ago. She looks amazing tonight."

"She does. She's happy. Happier than I've seen her in a long time."

"That's great. So you like Kent?"

"I do. He's a good guy. He'll take care of her." Evan stood, and loosened his tie as he took a couple of steps back from the fire.

"When's the wedding?"

"End of January. In Hawaii."

"That's awesome. A destination wedding."

"It's more of a vacation. Just a few of us. Mom's always wanted to go, and we never had many vacations growing up."

"So you three kids are going?"

"Yeah, and Poppa. Kent doesn't have much family. I think his brother and sister-in-law are going. Should be fun."

"Sounds like. How will that work with your grandpa, though?"

"Mom's got it all figured out. She's found a place that has nice gardens and paths onto the beach. She really wants him to be there. He missed Maddie's graduation last year, and Mom's felt guilty about it ever since. We'll make it work."

Sara heard the determination in his voice, and realized with a lump in her throat that Evan was mature beyond his years. And he was a nice guy.

"You don't seem to come home often." Or was it that he came home but didn't seek her out over holidays when there was a good chance she'd be in town? The silence was just long enough to be awkward.

Evan studied his hands as though thinking hard about his answer. Then he shrugged. "Holidays, mostly. It's been harder since the tornado. No home."

"Yeah. What a nightmare. How's the new house coming along?"

"Good. Mom's planning to be in by Christmas. Believe it or not, I hosted Christmas last year."

"Oh, my. That's impressive."

A smile spread across his face. "That means everyone came to Tulsa, and Mom cooked at my apartment."

"Oh. Well, that counts."

His eyes met hers, and again she felt as though he were searching for something. "You coming home this Christmas?" he asked.

"I hope so. Guess it depends on whether I have a new job, and what day it falls on."

He nodded. "Yeah, definitely harder when you're just starting out, and having to watch vacation days. It'd be fun if the families got together like we used to."

"Yeah," Sara said. "It'd be so different, though. Elise has her kids, and now there are husbands and significant others . . ." Her voice trailed off.

"You have one of those significant others?"

Sara caught her breath. This was getting awfully personal. She shook her head. "No. Do you?"

"Nope." He pulled his wallet from his back pocket. "Even if the families don't get together, that doesn't mean we can't. If we're both in town, let's go for a drink." He held a business card out to her.

Sara held up her free hand. "I don't have my purse."

He reached back for his jacket, and produced a pen. "Here. Write your email on the back."

She wrote her email address and her cell phone number, and handed the card back to him.

"You know, I've missed talking to you." He said it in a tone that sounded as though he'd only just realized it.

94

There was only one answer she could politely give. "Me, too," she said. Was it true? They used to talk all the time – about school and teachers and homework. They traded notes and studied together, and discussed who liked whom. They'd helped each other decide where to go to college. But that was all a long time ago.

"You keep in touch with anyone around here?" he asked.

"Not too much. Seems like the whole class scattered. What about you?"

"Couple of people. It's easier with Chase still around."

Of all the kids in the three families, Chase, Evan's younger brother, was the only one still living in Whitfield. Annie was the next closest in Paxton. "Yeah, I suppose–" She broke off when a group of wedding guests descended on them.

"Well, isn't this cozy," Mrs. Haskins said, reaching for Sara. "Why didn't I think of coming out here? How are you Miss Sara?"

Sara stood, but before she could answer, the woman shook her arm. "Your parents sure do put on a nice wedding."

"Mighty nice," her husband chimed in, with a wink for Sara. "I can see now why your dad needed to sell his business. Sure hope he's got some money left when it's your turn." He gave a hearty laugh as though he'd told a hilarious joke.

Okay, folks, time to go. Sara smiled, and inched toward the door with them.

"My parents were certainly generous with the alcohol," Sara whispered to Evan before saying goodbyes to a few others who were crossing through the seating area, whooping and cackling on their way out. Apparently the older crowd had decided to call it a night. When the room cleared, Sara and Evan looked at each other, and burst out laughing.

"Ouch, my eyes," Evan said. "Did I just see Delores Inkle shaking her booty?"

"Don't worry, the image should fade in twenty years or so," Sara said, still chuckling as she resumed her place by the fire. "I have a feeling some people won't remember much of the wedding in the morning."

"I bet they'll remember it was a good time, though."

Sara met his eyes, and once again registered a little jolt of surprise. He seemed so confident, secure in his own skin, and happy. She couldn't help letting her gaze linger. Her mom was right. Evan Gerard all grown up was . . . interesting.

\*\*

"Where is your fiancé?" Mary asked Dana. She and Claire had been hovering way too long. Mary noticed the crowd beginning to thin, but she wasn't ready for the party to be over. They'd reserved the space until midnight, and she wasn't leaving a minute before then.

"Around. He doesn't need to be at my side every minute."

"I do like that in a man," Claire commented.

Mary sent her a droll glance before addressing Dana again. "You two should be out there dancing."

"We were, but now it's the kids' time. So, you feeling all right?"

"Of course. I'm having a blast. This mother-of-the-bride thing is pretty fun."

"That's not what I meant. What happened to your foot?"

"Nothing. I just slipped. I should've known better than to try dancing in these heels."

"Nice that Grant happened to be at your side at the time," Claire said.

"True that."

"Sara said you fell a while back." Dana pushed.

"Fell?" Mary echoed.

"Yeah, you know, ass on floor. Did you?"

Taken aback, Mary's eyes widened. "So?"

"Mare, almost every time I've looked at you tonight, you've been wiggling your foot, or rolling your neck, or stretching your back. This foot thing also happened the night Kent and I met you with Doug and Jane at Bailey's. Remember?"

"Yeah, it's happened a couple of times, but—"

"When was the last time you had a physical?"

"I don't know. I go every year."

"Get in and get this checked out, okay?"

"I will, I will. I promise. Just as soon as I get a spare minute."

"Uh-uh. Not good enough, girlfriend. Make time for it. Do you have a regular appointment already scheduled?"

"Not yet, Mother, but I'll get to it." Mary scowled at both of them. "Now can we get back to the fun at hand?"

"You see Diane Bates, right?"

Mary let out an exasperated sigh. "I do." Diane was a women's health specialist who kept offices in Whitfield and Paxton. Mary liked that the woman was exposed to more medical procedures in the larger city, and probably more up to date than the few doctors who only practiced locally.

"Tell her you want a full blood work-up. If she can't get you in soon, come to the clinic."

"All right, already." Mary reached for her glass and chugged what was left of her room-temperature wine.

"Let me get a fresh round of drinks. You want another wine?"

"Sure," Mary told her, grateful for the offer. She wasn't quite ready to test the stability of her foot just yet.

"Claire?"

"Ginger Ale with a slice of orange if they've got it."

"Coming right up."

As soon as Dana turned, Claire leaned in. Mary held a hand up. "Do not start with me."

Grinning, Claire took her arm. "I was going to say, aren't you glad she's gone?"

Mary couldn't help but crack a smile. Another look at her friend, and they were both laughing uncontrollably.

"But you better do what she says," Claire warned. "Or we'll gang up on you."

And they'd be relentless, Mary knew. But call a doctor because her foot was falling asleep? She'd probably be referred to a psychiatrist.

## Chapter Nine

"You popping pills again, darlin'?"

Mary visibly jumped, and whirled around, small brown tablets spilling onto the counter and floor.

She put a hand to her chest, and the other on her hip. "What are you doing sneaking up on me like that?"

Grant moved forward and knelt down, picking the tablets off the floor. He dumped them into Mary's outstretched hand. "Why so jumpy? Headache?"

"Just ache."

He crossed his arms. "You need to call your doctor."

She picked up the cup of water and a tablet. "That's what Dana said. And I'm going to, but come on, you know as well as I do, the doctor is going to tell me to take a pain pill, or get a cortisone shot. She's the one who told me to start carrying Tylenol in my purse when I hit fifty, remember?"

Grant smiled. He remembered how offended Mary had been by the cavalier advice. Seeing her now, it was hard to believe she'd passed that milestone seven years ago. She was still beautiful and youthful. She'd been every bit as stunning as their daughters at the wedding.

Looking closer at her eyes, she appeared a little tired, he supposed. No surprise there. An event like that was a huge undertaking. He ran his hands along her arms. "Hey, did I tell you how beautiful you looked Saturday?"

Cocking her head, she smiled up at him, her eyes brightening. And his chest thumped. The way it always did for Mary.

"Maybe once or twice, but I don't mind a little repetition."

"You going to be ready to get out of here on Friday?"

"Absolutely. Can't wait. Pretty sure they've got a lounge chair by the pool with my name on it."

"I guarantee it," Grant said, kneading her shoulders.

"By the way, I'm going to call the hotel and see if I can get an appointment at the spa. I think I've earned about a three-hour massage. Care to join me?"

"Nah. You schedule that, and I'll see if I can get a tee time about then." He stepped back, and leaned against the counter. "What do we need to do to before we go?"

Mary let out a long sigh. "Mostly laundry and packing. The house is in good shape, thanks to Rita."

"Why can't Rita do the laundry?"

Mary's eyes widened. "That's not her job. I've never—"

"Might be time to ask," Grant cut in. "All the aches and pains? Maybe you're doing too much. Tell you what, you get things sorted, and I'll haul it down here."

"Not much to sort. It's mostly sheets and towels. The good thing is we won't need any of the clothes we've been wearing around here. I'm packing crop pants, summer dresses, and sandals. I cannot wait to get out of these boots."

"That should make packing easier. Listen, I'm going to take my truck in for an oil change. I'll deal with laundry when I get back. How's that?"

"Sure. Maybe I'll toss a few things in a suitcase."

The oil change took longer than he expected, and when Grant returned home an hour and a half later, he climbed the stairs to get a load of towels, but it looked as though none of the kids' bathrooms had been touched. Back downstairs, he found Mary asleep in their bed. Quietly, he peeked inside the bathroom, and their walk-in closet. No piles of laundry, and no luggage.

He ran a hand through his hair, staring at the figure on the bed, wondering if he should be worried. At what point did headaches and backaches and being tired add up to more than the stress of a busy schedule? And now that he thought more about their earlier conversation, what made Dana suggest that Mary call her doctor? Had she noticed something?

He had half a mind to lie down beside her, and pull her close, but that would disrupt her sleep, which she obviously needed. Hell, she'd earned it – a nap every day this week, and some time in that lounge chair in Phoenix.

If that didn't revive her energy level, they might have to talk about that doctor's visit. He wanted her healthy. Wanted her beside him to get away and enjoy retirement. With their kids grown and out of the house, it was their time.

Stepping as softly as he could, Grant turned back to the bathroom and began gathering towels from the racks. He couldn't explain why wanderlust had taken hold of him over the past couple of years, why he felt such an urge to get out of Whitfield and explore the world. Age probably had something to do with it. And the fact that he'd lived his entire life in the small town. But then, so had Mary. Yet, she seemed perfectly content with life in Whitfield and only an occasional girls' trip or vacation. He knew she liked having the flexibility and means to pick up and go if she wanted to, though.

He snatched up towels from the other bathrooms, then made his way back downstairs, dumping his load into an empty basket. If there was a positive outcome from the Essex mess, maybe it was to encourage Mary to pull back from civic duties and all the volunteer projects, and get out of town more often. It just might be the spark that made her jump on board and let go for a while. He hoped so.

\*\*

On Wednesday morning, Mary sat up and swung her legs to the side of the bed, testing her foot against the carpeting before pushing herself up. She let out a long sigh. Yes, the fact that she'd gone to testing the foot

101

before putting any weight on it was a sign that she should have a chat with her doctor. It wasn't normal.

And it was a nuisance. Dr. Bates had no openings this week in Whitfield, so Mary would have to make the drive over to Paxton if she wanted to get in before leaving for Phoenix on Friday. She didn't want to go see her doctor at all, but figured she might as well get it over with. She said a quick prayer that she'd end up with a prescription for a pill and a couple of exercises, then showered and dressed before heading downstairs for coffee.

Grant had left a note on the table telling her that he'd be gone until mid-afternoon. That was fine because she hadn't mentioned the appointment to him. Didn't need more questions she didn't have answers to.

Halfway into the drive, she regretted taking the Paxton appointment. Her head felt foggy, and she had to force her eyes to stay open. She slipped her sunglasses on to help ward off the cloudy glare, and pumped her foot back and forth to ward off any numbness.

She fought a sudden wave of panic as the absurdity of the situation hit her. Clearly, something was not right. Uneasiness settled in her stomach as she walked slowly into the medical building. What had Dana said? Blood work. Request a full workup. The timing was good at least. Mary would be basking in the sun poolside not sitting around the house waiting for lab results. That thought cheered her, and she greeted the receptionist with a smile.

"Please have a seat, and we'll call you soon," the woman at the desk told her.

Mary settled into a floral-printed armchair, and picked at the selection of magazines on the table in front of her. Many of them featured young pregnant women, while others touted fabulous flat abs and what looked like body builders to her. Ugh. She reached for the one with an attractive woman sporting stylish silver hair and more than a few laugh lines.

But only moments later, she found herself re-reading the same paragraph. Unable to concentrate, Mary tossed the magazine onto the table and simply waited until the door opened and a nurse called her name.

Inside the small examination room, Mary traded her warm sweater for a flimsy cotton wrap. The nurse checked Mary's weight and blood pressure, and asked a few standard questions. The questions got tougher when Dr. Bates arrived.

"How long have you experienced this numbness?" She asked when Mary described her symptoms.

"Oh, a few months, I guess."

"The headaches?"

"About the same, I suppose."

"Do they come at a certain time of day?"

Mary thought a moment, but couldn't come up with specifics. "They develop through the day."

"How many Advil a day?"

"A couple."

Nodding, Dr. Bates studied her. "The pain in your joints. Tell me more about that. Is it constant? Does it come and go? Is it worse when you're active or after you've rested?"

"Seems pretty constant these days."

"Describe the pain on a scale of one to ten, ten being the worst you could stand."

Mary shook her head. "It's just a dull ache. I'd have to say one or two. Nothing severe."

"Okay. That's good. We can manage that with over the counter meds for now."

"But—"

Dr. Bates raised her brows. "What?"

"Sometimes I'm so achy that I feel like curling up in a ball. I'm not in pain, but sore or maybe cramped. Does that make sense?"

"Sure. What about sleep?"

Mary squirmed. "I'm sleeping fine, I guess. But . . ."

"Yes?"

"Well, the thing is, it seems like I'm sleeping, but I still feel tired. By noon I'm already looking forward to a nap."

"Okay, so fatigue, and you mentioned some stress. Those could be related."

The doctor made some notes on her keyboard. When she looked up, intense eyes met Mary's.

"Listen Mary, I don't want to scare you, but I do want to take this seriously. Let's do some tests and get some lab work done."

"The fact that you say that doesn't exactly reassure me," Mary told her doctor. "What are you looking for?"

"Anything that gives us a clue. Let's do a complete workup. It's been a few years since you had a routine profile done."

"Uh-huh, but this isn't routine, right?"

"Well, obviously something is going on or you wouldn't be here. Let's check it out. We'll look at your overall health, your blood sugar and cholesterol, thyroid and liver function, and hormone levels."

Mary heaved a sigh.

"I will say this thing with your foot bothers me, especially since you've had no accident to account for it. That kind of numbness isn't normal, and would indicate a neurological connection and can sometimes," she gave Mary a pointed look, "*sometimes* be a sign of a serious condition."

"Like what?"

"I'm not about to speculate without some more information."

"You know if you don't tell me, I can always do some online research."

"Mary, that's a really bad idea. Try to be patient and–"

"No sugar coating. Tell me what kinds of things."

"If I do, will you promise to wait until we get labs done before you start trying to diagnose online?"

"I promise."

Her doctor heaved a great sigh. "Lots of conditions have similar symptoms. There's    fibromyalgia, Lyme disease, a blood clot or even ALS or MS."

"ALS?" Mary gasped as her heart fluttered. She couldn't possibly–

"Mary," Dr. Bates warned. "Relax. I am not saying you have ALS. In fact, that's a very uncommon diagnosis.

But something is going on, and it's important that we figure out what it is."

Mary swallowed hard, the first real inkling of concern taking root as she watched Dr. Bates tap furiously into her keyboard.

She moistened her lips. "Can everything be done here?"

"Not in the office. I'm sending you over to the lab at the hospital. They'll draw the blood samples and send a report in a few days. In the meantime, I want you to start keeping a journal. Write down how you feel in the mornings, how well you slept and for how long. Note whenever you have a headache or feel any numbness or tingling sensations. Record anything that doesn't feel normal. It'll help us track frequency and we'll see if there are any patterns."

"Hmmmm. How I spent my winter vacation. This sounds an awful lot like homework, Doc," Mary said, wiping clammy hands across her cotton cover-up.

"It is. And I'm a stickler for detail. And just like a teacher, I've heard every excuse in the book. Don't blow it off."

*All right, already.*

Standing, Dr. Bates closed her laptop. "I'll be right back. I want to get you some papers."

Papers? Mary had no idea what that meant. She nodded and pulled a magazine from the rack on the wall of the examination room. None of the headlines or stories caught her attention, though. All she could think about was whether her body was turning against her. She didn't have time to be sick. There was too much to do. In her mind, that poolside lounge chair beckoned once again. As did her empty suitcase.

Dr. Bates breezed back into the room, and shoved several pieces of paper Mary's direction. "Here you go. This is the lab order. They're expecting you. These illustrate some exercises I want you to start. Some are for tension in your head and neck, and there's one for strengthening that might help with your feet."

More homework. Mary glanced at the papers, but couldn't help wondering if it made sense to start a program before they even knew what they were dealing with.

"Regardless of what the lab results show, these will be good for you," Dr. Bates added, as though reading Mary's mind.

Resigned, Mary blew out a breath. "Yes, ma'am."

**

After the lab technician drained five vials of blood from her arm, Mary trudged across the hospital parking lot, and sank into her car. Drained, period. But not finished with the errands she needed to do in Paxton. She wasn't going to miss this opportunity to run by Annie's new place and leave a little surprise for their return from their honeymoon.

She'd strung tiny white lights around a three-foot, potted Alberta Spruce. Normally, it'd be no big deal, but now she wondered if she'd have the strength to haul it out of her car and up the steps to their porch. She guzzled the bottle of water the nurse had given her, hoping it'd revive her, and fast. Leaning against the headrest, she closed her eyes.

Startled, Mary lurched upright, and looked around. Someone knocked on the window beside her. Blinking, she fought to clear her head. She turned the key in the ignition, and let the window down about half-way.

"Are you all right?" a young woman carrying a toddler peered in at her.

"Excuse me?"

The woman put a hand to her chest. "Sorry to bother you. I just– I saw you sitting here and thought you might need some help. I was afraid you were having a heart attack or something."

Mary glanced at the clock illuminated on the dashboard. Oh. She'd fallen asleep in her car. Running a hand through her hair, she smiled at the stranger. "Oh, no. I'm fine. Thanks for checking, though. I was kind of tired after my appointment." *After they bled me dry.*

"All right, then. You take care."

Mary gave a little wave. "Thanks, again." Oh, brother. Thank goodness the woman had knocked before flagging down an ambulance and causing a scene. Time to get moving. She started the car, and drove the short distance to Annie's house, determined to wrestle the potted tree onto the porch. At least the hatchback design allowed for easy grabbing without bending over. Opening the back, she scooted the pot up against her hip, then lifted it. *Please do not give out on me now*, she implored all of her limbs.

On step number three, she eased herself down to a sitting position so that the pot was almost level with the floor of the porch. Gingerly, she leaned out, gave a little shove, then let go of the pot. It remained upright, and Mary sagged against the stair rail. So far, so good. She glanced around, hoping none of Annie's neighbors were watching. After another moment's rest, she climbed the remaining stairs, and dragged the pot into place by the front door. *Whew!* Mission accomplished.

Back in her car, she gulped a couple of swallows of water. She didn't want to arrive home looking as if she'd walked to Paxton and back – and have Grant worry that they should postpone their trip until the test results were in. She was about to start the car when her phone buzzed. She fished it out of her purse and looked at the screen. Her stomach fluttered. A new Snapchat from Sara. Good news?

Two more taps to the screen and a full-length image of Sara appeared. Besides a huge smile, she wore a copper colored long jacket with large black buttons up the front. It was paired with black leggings and dressy black pumps. She looked stunning. Definite management material, Mary thought, smiling as the final two seconds of the image played then disappeared.

She set the water bottle in the cup holder and tapped Sara's number. "Wow, Sarie. Model much?" Mary said when Sara picked up.

"You like?" Sara asked.

"Oh, sweetheart, that jacket is gorgeous. You're a knockout. Was this before or after your interview?"

"Before. I'm getting ready to head out now. I love the jacket. I think it looks arty and professional at the same time, don't you?"

"Absolutely, and the color is perfect. Great choice." She decided not to state the obvious and comment on the fact that it also perfectly disguised her expanding midsection. "How'd the meeting with the headhunter go?"

"It was okay, but I think I'll contact a few more. These people weren't real positive."

"Hmm. About you or the market?" Mama bear instinct flared instantly.

"Both, honestly. They kept telling me how I'm competing in a tough market with a bunch of people who have MBAs."

"Oh. That's interesting."

"They weren't a good fit for me, anyway, Mom. Who knows, I may not even need them. I think I'd really like this job I'm going for today. It's a small up-and-coming agency."

Small made Mary wonder about benefits. Sometimes smaller companies offered fewer benefits at a higher price than a big firm. But she heard the ever-present optimism in Sara's voice, and wasn't about to say anything discouraging. "They should hire you on the spot," she said. "You look like you could be interviewing for a seat on the board."

Sara's light laughter rang out. "Aw, thanks, Mom. But I'll settle for assistant manager or team leader."

"I have complete confidence. Now remember, Dad and I are leaving for Phoenix on Friday, but I still want updates."

"Well, I won't bother you unless something really exciting happens."

"You won't be bothering me. The only two things on my agenda are a massage and chilling by the pool. I could actually get bored."

With a little luck, they could stick to that agenda.

## Chapter Ten

"And you're available to start right away?"

*Ahhhhh!* Sara squealed inside. Oh, yeah. They were interested. And so was she. This was no time to be coy or play hard to get. She laced her fingers on the table, and smiled at her three interviewers, each high-level decision-makers at Imagine Media. "Absolutely. You name the date."

Smiles and nods greeted her.

Parker Jones, the creative director, slid a business card across the table to her. Sara looked at both sides of the card, and ran a thumb across the soft matte finish. "Who did your design?"

Parker grinned at his two colleagues before meeting Sara's eyes. "I did."

"It's very nice."

"That fact that you know good design along with the principles of marketing and communication is a great asset." Parker told her. "We like hybrids around here."

"That's right," Carolyn Reyes, one of the partners, added. "We don't work in silos. We work in teams. There's a lot of brainstorming and collaboration."

Exactly what Sara was looking for. And why she didn't need an MBA. She didn't want to be locked into a single track or concentration. At a place like this, she could contribute in multiple ways. She wished she could ask about flexibility of hours and day care, but she didn't dare. Raising red flags at this point would be plain stupid.

And just when Sara thought the interview was wrapping up, the conversation took off again. They talked for twenty more minutes, until Carolyn glanced at her watch. "Hey, guys, I'm going to have to break this up. We've got the Westside strategy  presentation in a few minutes."

Parker glanced from Sara to Carolyn, and opened his mouth as if he were about to say something. Looking discreetly away, Sara gathered her things, aware of some non-verbal communication among the three. She wondered if they might invite her to the presentation. That'd be great, but she desperately needed to find the ladies room. She'd had a large iced tea at lunch, then a bottle of water during the interview, which was going on almost two hours now.

"Sara, thanks so much for coming in today. It's been a pleasure." Carolyn extended her hand, and Sara shook hands with each of them.

Sensing that these people liked direct communication, she flashed a smile and asked the question most on her mind. "Any idea when you might make a decision?" Wouldn't bother her a bit if she had to cancel the other interviews she had scheduled or remove her resume from the big online employment sites.

"Shouldn't be long," Carolyn said. "Couple of weeks at the most."

"Perfect," Sara said, though in her heart, she'd been hoping for an on-the-spot offer. They'd clearly clicked. Oh, well. Proper procedures, and all. "I'll look forward to hearing from you."

She tucked the business card into her slim leather satchel, and made a beeline for the restrooms she'd seen in the office lobby.

Since it was close to four o'clock, and that meant rush-hour traffic, Sara checked her GPS for a back-roads route to Morgan's apartment. It'd take longer to get there, but that was preferable over the jockeying for position, tailgating and pressure from other drivers.

She'd rather meander the roads while her mind returned to the interview she'd just nailed. The phone buzzed in her hand, and Sara grinned at the text from Morgan. Meeting for an early dinner would be great. She could stop at a coffee shop, spend an hour at her laptop, and avoid rush hour all together. *You're on*, she texted back. *Where to?*

They settled on a Thai place still about fifteen minutes from Sara. She put the car in gear, and drove the short distance to a Starbucks in the next strip center.

With a decaf Mocha in hand, Sara connected to the Wi-Fi and watched dozens of emails load. She scrolled through. Most of them simply acknowledged receiving her résumé and application. Ah, this one wanted to set up an interview. She blew out her breath, and closed her eyes for a moment. On one hand, it was flattering to receive so many requests. On the other hand, she'd love to be done – and politely decline all other interviews. She'd forgotten how emotionally draining the ups and downs of interviewing and job hunting were. The frequent restroom breaks and need to eat only added to the stress. And her short window of opportunity. With each day that passed, her abdomen grew while her chances of being hired diminished.

A few more sips of coffee revived her as she continued scrolling through the emails. She blinked. And did a double-take. This must have been buried earlier. A message had come at one a.m. from Evan. In the subject line was a simple 'hello.' She toyed with her napkin, folding and twisting it while she wrestled with conflicting thoughts and feelings. Did she want to rekindle the friendship? There'd definitely been a connection at the wedding. She couldn't help but wonder what his reaction would be if – no, *when* – he found out she was pregnant. Of course he'd find out because Dana would find out. No way could her mother keep it a secret from Dana, one of her best friends. Besides, Whitfield was a small town. Once people knew her mom was a grandmother, the jig was up.

Did it even matter? She couldn't go through her pregnancy being ashamed of it. Really, the only reason she needed to keep it under wraps right now was to get a job.

After that, it was simply part of who she was. Friends would support her – or they wouldn't be friends.

She clicked on the email.

*Hey, there. Just thought I'd check in and see how Dallas is treating you. Any luck on the job search?*

Short and simple. Testing the waters? Well, perfect timing on his part. She was dying to tell someone about her interview with Imagine Media. Smiling inside, her fingers tapped the keyboard.

*Hey, just got out of an interview. I think they liked me. I'd love to get this one. Keep your fingers crossed for me. What's happening there?* She hit send, wondering how long it would take for him to see her response. She didn't know much about his job, but figured he spent a fair amount of time at a computer. Sure enough. Less than a minute later, a new reply popped up.

*Hi. You caught me watching the clock today. Playing a little basketball with some guys after work. I may have to uncross my fingers. Temporarily. Hope you get the job. Who's it with?*

*A small agency called Imagine Media. They seem smart and fun. Lots of good energy.*

*Cool. Sounds perfect for you.*

Really? Interesting. He thought he knew what was perfect for her.

*You think?*

*Sure. Never did see you in corporate America.*

She couldn't argue with that. Maybe they hadn't changed that much since high school after all. Basic personality and style had been set by then, she supposed. And what about Evan? She had to smile. Banking seemed to fit. Not boring accounting, and not risky investing, but a solid, steady institution. A stable career with standard hours and a good paycheck. She could see how that would be attractive to him. Of course, good looking, smart and personable would be attractive to a bank. Evan was probably their poster child – maybe even featured in their advertising. If only every company she worked with could be lucky enough to have someone like him on staff.

That thought brought her abruptly to Todd Riley. *Ugh.* She honestly hadn't thought about him in days. He was handsome enough to be in ads, but didn't have the easy-going manner that Evan did. In fact, Todd tended to come across as harsh or tense in photos. Not that she'd seen many – only a few selfies they'd taken during the time they'd dated, and a small collection of family photos at his place. Just as well. The fewer images she had to purge from her head, the better.

A new email brought her attention back to her computer. *Oops.* She hadn't responded to Evan's last comment, and now he was out of time.

*You still there? I gotta go for now, but let's talk later.*

Sure. Why not? Wasn't as if she had a full agenda. She'd probably be on the computer, anyway, looking at websites about pregnancy and caring for newborns.

*Sounds good,* she wrote. *Have fun.*

She answered a couple of other messages, and then packed up her things and headed for the restaurant, ready for an appetizer – or two.

Climbing out of her car, Sara wished she'd thought to toss in black flats when she left for the interview. Her feet were beginning to protest the tall heels. A stiletto girl she'd never be. At least the leggings and jacket would look just as cute with some ballet flats, and would be perfect office attire for a place like Imagine.

Inside the restaurant, Morgan waved. She slid out of the booth as Sara approached the table. Her mouth practically gaped.

"Oh, my gosh. Look at you. This is sassy." She lifted a chunk of Sara's hair. "Wow. You should wear your hair down more often. Looks fab."

"Thanks."

"I didn't order you a drink. Wasn't sure if you'd had any caffeine today."

Sara sank into the booth. "Yeah, I decided I needed it before my interview, so I guess it's just water now."

"You're being so diligent. Are you getting headaches from withdrawal?"

"No. I'm getting hunger pangs from being pregnant."

"Okay, let's order food. Then I have something to tell you."

"Not fair," Sara said. "But stomach pulls rank. Let's get a couple of appetizers."

They ordered edamame and pan fried dumplings, then Sara leaned in. "So what's up?"

Morgan's sheepish smile turned into a wide grin.

"What?"

"Sam and I are moving in together."

Sara's mouth dropped open. "Seriously?"

Morgan's head bobbed. "Yeah, we've been talking about it for a while, and well–" she shrugged. "Last night we just decided to do it."

A couple of what-about-me thoughts crashed into Sara's head, but she pushed them back, trying to focus on what this meant for her friend. For now.

"Aw, that's great," Sara told her. Wasn't hard to see the happiness on Morgan's face. "Are we a little bit excited?"

"And scared," Morgan added. "We've been dating a long time, but living together will be different."

"For sure," Sara agreed. She'd met Sam several times, the first when he'd accompanied Morgan to a mutual friend's wedding in St. Louis a couple of years ago. On first impression, he'd been friendly and fun – and pretty hot. The few encounters she'd had with him since crashing in Dallas were just as positive. Seemed like a great guy. She hoped she wasn't wrong. Her confidence in judging character – in men, at least – had taken a beating.

"Have you talked about getting married?"

"Why yes, we have as a matter of fact. And we turned twenty-one about six years ago, by the way."

Morgan's voice dripped with sarcasm, and water dribbled down Sara's chin as she choked on a laugh. "Oh, my God. I'm sorry. You know that's not how I meant it. If he asks, will you say yes?"

"Yeah. I think so. Ask me again after I've lived with him for a few months, though."

"Ah, so this is a trial run?"

"I suppose so. He thinks it'd be weird to get married while he's still in law school. Says it'll feel more like starting real life after he graduates. I get that."

"Sure. Makes sense."

Conversation suspended while their waiter delivered their entrees. Sara immediately reached for the steaming Pad Se Eu noodle dish. "I can't believe I haven't gained fifty pounds already," she said. "It seems like all I want to do is eat."

"Hey, no big deal. You're eating for two."

"I'd rather not give birth to the Michelin Man."

"Don't worry. It's good for you."

"Hope so."

"Hey, this is good for you, too," Morgan said.

"What?"

"My move. This way, you can stop worrying about where to live while you're job hunting. You can just take over my lease."

Sara chewed while she processed Morgan's offer. Sounded as though she thought she was doing Sara a favor. Maybe she was, but Sara had some doubts. Morgan's place wouldn't be the ideal location if Sara got the Imagine job. At least a thirty-minute commute – twice as long as Sara wanted.

"I'll think about it," Sara said, finally.

Morgan's eyebrows rose. "You get along all right with Leah, don't you?"

Leah was Morgan's official roommate. Sara didn't know her well, but had no issues with her, either. "Oh, sure. It's just that I really want to get an apartment close to where I end up working. I'd love to get the one I interviewed for today, but it's a pretty long drive."

"Oh." Morgan's face fell. Obviously she was hoping Sara could solve the sub-let dilemma for her. "Well, maybe for a few months, anyway? Until you're sure? I can leave all my furniture for now."

"Yeah, maybe. I don't want to commit to anything long term yet." Could be a decent temporary solution, she supposed. Sara took a deep breath. She should be grateful. It could be that things were falling into place. "When are you moving?" she asked.

Morgan grinned around her lettuce wraps. "Soon."

"Okay. The gal at Imagine said they'd make a decision soon, too."

"Perfect. So you like that one best so far?"

Slowly, Sara nodded, wondering if she were putting too much weight on the one interview. "Yeah. But I can't stop looking. I have three interviews next week, and one is with a headhunter, so you never know what will come up."

"Well, Sam and I will figure out the details this weekend. He's got a court case they're following in Austin on Friday, so he'll be home late. I'm getting a few people together to go out Friday night. Leah, and Jess, and maybe a few others. I want you to come with us."

"Yeah, sounds fun. Where we going?"

"I'm thinking West Village."

"But, Morgan, isn't that mostly a bunch of bars? What about a movie?"

"But then you can't talk. You've got to get out and meet people while you can, you know."

Sara groaned inside. Even in college, bar-hopping had never been her thing. She'd much rather go to an event – a gallery open house, movie or concert.

"Once this baby comes, you'll be stuck at home all the time," Morgan told her.

"I don't think I'll be stuck. But I won't be bar-hopping." Sara tried to keep the edge out of her voice. Truth was, Sara didn't love crowds. Staying home and watching a movie or reading a book sounded like a good time to her. Morgan knew that. While they'd become friends in the sorority, Morgan was more like Annie – thriving on going and doing with a pack of friends. Sara preferred having a few close friends. Maybe that made her boring. Or a nerd. But she didn't care. That's who she was.

Morgan blew out a heavy sigh. "You know, you are the perfect person to do this single mom thing. I mean it. You'll probably be completely happy being at home every night and won't miss the rest of us at all."

"Not true," Sara told her. "Well, only a little bit true. I'll miss you, but not the bar scene. You'll just have to come visit. I can manage to use a corkscrew and pour a glass of wine, you know. And I like to cook."

Now there was an idea for a baby shower – instead of buying booties and equipment for the baby, bring a home entertainment item for the mom-to-be. Her friends could come to her. The opportunities to meet new people would take care of themselves. Or would have to wait.

## Chapter Eleven

Mary jumped when a thud of some sort jarred her from her sleep. Blinking, it took a moment to realize the plane's wheels had touched down.

"Wow. We're here already?"

"Nah. Emergency landing," Grant said.

Her mouth dropped open, and she sat up straight, coming instantly alert. "*What?* Are you serio–" One look at her husband, and she knew he had her. His lips twitched, and a second later, he broke into laughter.

Her elbow connected with his, pushing it from the armrest between them. "Not funny, you arse."

"That was quite a nap."

"Well, we did leave the house before the crack of dawn, you know." The early morning drive to Kansas City International Airport had left her feeling groggy. Probably should've gone ahead and driven up last night. Of course their plans had changed when Sara's did. Normally, they would've spent the night in Kansas City, taken Sara to dinner, and left their car at her apartment complex while they were away.

Mary gave a lion-sized yawn, and checked her watch. The landing was right on time. With the time difference, they still had the whole afternoon ahead of them.

"So, you ditching me straight away for the pool?" Grant asked.

"Of course not. I'm going to let you feed me first. I'm starving."

"My pleasure. Want to stop on the way or go to the hotel?"

"Hotel is fine. I don't want to waste time driving around looking for something."

"You mean you didn't plan this out?"

She playfully curled her fingers as if to show her claws. "You are asking for it, Mister. You really want to mess with me on an empty stomach?"

His hands shot up surrender-style. "Reconsidering . . ."

A flight attendant interrupted with instructions for exiting the plane. While other passengers began the frenzy of collecting bags, Mary stretched as best she could, and bounced her legs up and down to make sure nothing had gone to sleep, hating that she didn't automatically trust that particular body part as a matter of course.

Forty-five minutes later, Grant pulled the rental car into the hotel's beautifully landscaped circle drive, the entrance almost hidden by the lush gardens that were still a vivid green. Mary opened the car door, and stood in the drive a moment, enjoying the blast of warm air that hit her face. Oh, yes. Eighty degrees in November.

"You all right?" Grant asked, coming around the back of the car, where a bellman stepped forward to retrieve their bags.

"Perfect." The grin that spread ear-to-ear across her husband's face reminded Mary that he'd looked forward to this as much as she had. Maybe for different reasons, but he'd earned his getaway. When he lifted the trunk handle, she put out a hand to stop him from assisting with the luggage. "Hey, you're on vacation now. Why don't you let the valet and bellman take care of this, while we find the patio?"

"You sure?" Grant asked.

"Of course. Let's get checked in." She waited while he gave the valet the key and a tip, then she took Grant's arm, and nudged him toward the door.

Once they'd checked in, they headed directly to the terrace café. Mary settled into a bright green cushioned chair on the shaded side of the patio dining area, and ordered an iced tea. "Ahhhh." She let her head fall back. "This is gorgeous."

"Pretty swanky," Grant said. "So, pool for you. What's on the rest of the agenda?"

"Well, I have some dinner recommendations. We talked about the arboretum or that nature park for tomorrow." Mary watched for Grant's reaction, as apprehension washed over her. Could she manage a hike? What if she got in then couldn't get back out?

"That hiking trail sounds good, if you're up for it."

"We can check it out," she murmured, turning her attention to the menu. She ordered a fresh market salad with grilled chicken, then rested her arms on the table. "Hey, the hotel does this fun thing where you can order a picnic or a cheese board with a bottle of wine. Why don't we do that for the walk tomorrow, and go late afternoon?"

That way, if she wussed out, they could salvage the experience and enjoy the beautiful vistas with a glass of wine.

"Works for me," Grant said. "I'll head over to the driving range while you're working on your tan."

Mary's phone pealed from inside her purse, and she checked the screen. "Oh, it's Claire." She turned the phone so that Grant could see the photo of a smiley-face sun sporting sunglasses. "Just wishing us fun in the sun."

She sent a quick "thanks," and tucked the phone back in her purse. "I was hoping to hear from Sara today. She was so excited about that interview she had on Wednesday."

"Takes more time than that."

Mary reached out and put a hand over Grant's. "Why don't you text her, or give her a call while I'm at the pool? She'd love to hear from you."

Grant was quiet, his gaze moving from Mary to somewhere beyond her.

"You know she thinks you're disappointed in her."

His brows rose as his glance snapped back to Mary's face. "I am disappointed in her."

"But you love her to pieces, right? You'd do anything for her."

"Just not sure what to say to her. If I'm honest, she'll hear the disappointment in my voice. Probably not what she wants to hear."

Definitely not what she needed to hear, either. "True, but I'm not sure silence is any better. With no communication, you leave it up to her imagination. In times of stress and tension, that leaves things wide open. You can relieve some of that by just telling her you love her and you're thinking of her." When Grant didn't respond, Mary rested a hand on his arm. "Let's don't make things worse by withholding support, Grant. Or making her feel bad about herself. That never works out well."

She saw him tense.

"She's making things hard on herself. There's all kinds of ways this could go bad."

"Exactly. She has enough to worry about already. Give her a call and let her know she doesn't have to worry about letting you down."

He blew out his breath before nodding. "Yeah. Maybe I'll do that."

Mary sat back, smiling inside and out – and hoping Sara would be free to talk when her dad called. "Annie and Blake will be home tomorrow. Did you see that last picture she posted?" Mary retrieved the phone again. "Look at this. So darn cute."

They spent the rest of lunch time talking about the kids. No surprise there, Mary thought. The three of them always gave her and Grant plenty of material, whether it was good for their digestion or not.

In their room, Mary quickly changed into her swimsuit and cover up while Grant contacted the golf pro shop. She'd purchased a new suit for the trip, liking both the design and the fit, which almost constituted a miracle as far as she was concerned. The pink ombré suit started out a dark rose at the bottom and gradually shifted into lighter shades of pink until it hit her shoulders. Gathered lightly along the side, it had a slimming effect across the front. A definite plus. She tossed a bottle of sunscreen into her bag. She could take care of that at the pool. She just needed to get down there before the fatigue beginning in her head enveloped her.

With a little wave to Grant, she grabbed the bag, then headed for the elevator. Fortunately, it was a solo ride, and she leaned against the side and closed her eyes until the sharp ding signaled her arrival. Intense sunshine greeted Mary when she stepped into the pool area, and she had to stop, squinting as her eyes tried to adjust. To her relief, an eager-to-please pool attendant hurried to her side with a towel and glass of water.

"Lounge chair, ma'am?"

"Yes, please. One of these will be fine," she told him, gesturing to a line of chairs within a few steps. Slipping her sunglasses on, she was finally able to look around. She put a hand to her chest. Oh, my. Crystal clear water shimmered in the pool as sunlight danced over the light ripples, and colorful umbrellas dotted the bright blue sky like a game of Twister.

Mary wasn't sure whether she felt lightheaded or simply giddy over the sunshine and stunning pool before her. Did it matter? She dropped her bag, and sank into her lounge chair. Bring on the vitamin D. Perhaps a deficiency in that area accounted for her sluggishness. She waited a short few minutes before a server arrived. "Can I get you something else to drink?"

"Absolutely. I'll have one of those Hawaiian sunset frozen margaritas." Hopefully that would take the edge off and she could skip the next dose of Advil. By the time the waitress returned with the drink, Mary had slathered herself head to toe with sunscreen and was ready to settle in for the long haul. Grinning, she reached for the drink, hoping it tasted as good as it looked. The skewer of fresh pineapple, orange and cherry did not disappoint.

After one sip, she found her phone and snapped a photo of the drink and sent it to Grant. "You're missing out. Join me when you're done there." She was about to replace the phone when she noticed a missed call from

Jane. Odd. Jane knew they'd left for vacation. Mary intended to unplug, but curiosity won out, and she pushed redial.

"You rang?" she asked when Jane's voice came on the line.

"I did. I hope you didn't pick up because you were in the pool."

"Working on it. Enjoying a frozen libation as we speak. First things, first. What's up?"

"Well. I want to run something by you. Allison Young called. Said she'd heard that Corey had gone to the employment workshop at the community center, and wanted to know if I could copy the materials for her."

The big gulp Mary took gave her brain freeze, and she grimaced while she wrapped her head around that request. *Some nerve*, was her initial reaction. She slipped her foot in and out of her sandal, and took a smaller sip of her drink, considering the implications. Apparently people were beginning to realize that landing a new job required more than filling out a few applications these days.

"Really. That's interesting," she said, for lack of anything more intelligent to say, and aware that she'd left Jane dangling on the line.

"I told her I wasn't sure if there were any copyright issues, and I'd have to clear it with the agency. But I really meant you."

Mary snorted. "I paid for fifty copies, and only used a few, so I'd say they owe me." She hadn't thought to keep some of the kits for herself. Hadn't expected anyone to reject the workshop and then come asking for the information. Closing her eyes, she let out a heavy sigh. The petty part of her said too bad, too late. But the rational side knew that response was petty. The objective, after all, had been to help people find a new job. She pushed her hurt feelings aside. It wasn't about her. It'd probably been hard for Allison to make that call to Jane. Probably cost her some pride. Maybe a friendship.

"I'm fine with it," Mary told Jane. "The thing is, there was an online component, with some videos and role-playing. I don't know if the code was individual to each packet, or to our event."

"I could try it on my computer," Jane offered.

"Sure. That's a good idea. Let me know if it doesn't work, and I'll contact the gal at On Track and see if we can get a few codes in case we get any other requests."

"Sounds good. Hey, Mare?"

"Mm-hmm?"

"That's– it's really nice of you to let Allison and Rick have this stuff."

Her throat tight, Mary brushed off the compliment. "I guess you caught me in a moment of weakness."

"Have fun out there. Remember those of us shivering in coats and sweaters while you're basking in your bikini."

"Oh, right." Mary chuckled. At this point in her life she vowed only Grant or the coroner would gaze upon the white flesh of her tummy.

Ending the call, she switched the phone to vibrate, and closed her eyes, basking in her not-so-sexy, but classy, one-piece as the sun warmed and soothed her aching muscles. Her pool bag held her Kindle reader and a stack of magazines, but she chose to ignore them for now. Even reading sounded like too much effort. Lifting the margarita glass to her lips was the only physical activity she cared to engage in for the next thirty minutes, at least.

As she became aware that her skin felt warm, Mary shifted onto her stomach and continued dozing until a dip in the pool became necessary. She wanted to enjoy her time in the sun, not cook. Swinging her legs to the side of the chair, she pushed off. And nearly lost her balance. What in the world was going on? Her foot wasn't asleep, but felt funny. She stepped forward gingerly, and found herself dragging her left foot, as though a weight held it back. Concentrating on each step, Mary made her way across the concrete surface to the pool. Clutching the handrail, she lowered herself to the steps, and blew out her breath. With her elbows on her knees, she let her head fall into her hands. This was ridiculous. How could seven steps be so difficult? Swallowing hard, her thoughts went to the blood tests. When would the results be in, and what would they reveal? Her breath caught in her throat. Oh, God. She couldn't be sick. There was too much–

"How's the water, gorgeous?"

Mary jumped, her head snapping up to see Grant crouching at the side of the pool, a grin covering his face. Quickly, she straightened, and flashed him a smile. "Hey, didn't expect to see you so soon. How'd you do at the range?"

"Think I'm ready for the tour." He gestured around the pool. "Everything good here?"

"Perfect. Did you talk to Sara?"

Grant sat down, and let his feet dangle in the cool blue water. "Sure did."

"Can I get you something to drink, sir?" The pool waitress interrupted.

Grant looked at Mary. "We got time for a beer?"

"Of course. And I'll have an iced tea, please," Mary told the young woman. "What'd Sara say? Did she sound all right?"

"Yeah. Says she feels good. 'Course she's not getting up at six o'clock and working eight hours every day."

When their drinks arrived, Mary floated to the side of the pool next to Grant. "Actually, it's good that she'll be past the first trimester before she has to do that. She should have more energy and be over any morning sickness. I think she's working hard at job-hunting, though, don't you?"

He nodded. "Sounds like she has her heart set on this one job. Might make it harder to get excited about other ones. Did you know her friend is moving out and wants Sara to sublease her space?"

"Oh. No, I didn't. Did she say she would?"

"Not yet."

"Hmm. That would leave her there with a roommate who's not really a friend. I was hoping she could get through the pregnancy with some friends to help her."

"Help her what?"

"Just to be there for her. You know, be the one to take out the trash, or grab her a blanket or something to drink without her having to get up. Little things like that." Her voice trailed off, and once again she considered a trip to Dallas. Even if Sara's friends were there, they might not know that much about pregnancy. Maybe they wouldn't think to help her out. Truth was, Mary wanted to be there to pamper her daughter. But could she manage it? What about this ridiculous thing with her foot? Would she even be able to shop or look at apartments? Maybe on Monday Dr. Bates would have some answers, and Mary would have a prescription and be on the mend by the end of the week. That thought bolstered her spirits.

"Hey, I'm having second thoughts about our Thanksgiving plan. Maybe we should go see Sara instead." Since they'd all gathered for Annie's wedding, they'd decided that everyone would stay put for Thanksgiving, and come to Whitfield for Christmas. That way, Annie and Blake could see his parents for Thanksgiving, but be home for Christmas. At the time, it had seemed like a good idea.

"And ditch Kent and Dana?"

Mary screwed up her face. "Well, I don't think I would put it quite like that." The current plan was to help serve the noon dinner at church while Dana and her son Chase had Thanksgiving lunch with Dana's dad at the senior center, then meet up late afternoon for cocktails, football and supper. Easy and low-key. If they changed the plan, Dana would understand.

"We could still have Sara come home," Mary said, thinking out loud. "Or what about going down on Friday and staying the weekend?"

"Darlin' I'm game for whatever. You and Sara figure it out, and let me know."

Mary let out a long sigh. Of course she couldn't back out on her commitments. Going to Dallas on Friday made the most sense. She'd rather be on the road than in the stores on Black Friday for sure.

"I'll talk to her in a day or two. Who knows, maybe she'll be invited to dinner with a friend."

126

"She didn't mention anything," Grant said.

Mary linked an arm around Grant's leg. "I'm glad you talked to her. I bet that made her day. You're the role model for what she's looking for, you know." She flashed Grant a smile. "Mr. Good Guy."

"Huh. And I thought you married me for my looks."

Laughing, Mary, let her fingers drift up his leg. "It was the whole package, love."

Grant slid into the water, tossed an arm around her shoulders, and leaned in close. "You think you can say something like that and not have me want to haul you out of here and up to our room?"

She looked at his plastic beer cup, and smiled. A few more gulps, and the beer would be gone. "Looks to me like we're almost done here, anyway."

And hauling her might not be far from the truth.

Grant took her hand, and helped her up the pool steps, allowing her to test the waters, so to speak. Her foot took the weight, but still felt sluggish. "Go slow," she told him as they made their way to the lounge chair.

His brows shot up. "What do you mean?"

"My foot's bothering me, so let's not sprint up to the room, okay?"

"What's wrong with your foot?"

"I don't know for sure. Grab my bag, would you?"

About half-way to the lobby, Grant stopped. "Mary-me, you're limping."

She took a step forward, tugging on his arm. "I'm aware."

"Does it hurt?"

She shook her head. "Doesn't hurt, just feels unsteady. This is the foot that's been falling asleep."

They ambled to the elevator, where Grant let out a heavy – audible – sigh. "Get this checked out when we get home."

"Yes, yes. But for now, let's just take it easy and enjoy the trip."

He pulled her close, nuzzling his face in her hair. "That's the plan."

**

Mary woke to find Grant dressed again and standing in the doorway of their balcony, a slight breeze moving the curtains. She propped herself up on one elbow. "Hey."

He turned, his brows pulled together in a frown. "You feel all right?"

She ran a hand through her hair, coming more fully awake. "Yeah. You ready for dinner?"

"Whenever you are. Where we going?"

Mary plopped back onto her pillow. "Not sure. It's written on my list." She closed her eyes again. Was she even hungry? It was tempting to snuggle back into the covers.

"Sure you want to go out?"

She forced her eyes open, and sat up. "Of course. Let me hop in the shower real quick." Hopping was a stretch, she thought, pushing off from the bed, her muscles aching in protest. How many silly verbs people used for doing ordinary stuff. She was going to take a shower, not jump or hop or run or dash.

Grant tossed her one of the plush robes from the closet. She shrugged into it, and glanced at the clock on the bedside table. Wait. Was there a time change? She looked at Grant. "What time is it, love? This can't be right."

With a slow nod, he confirmed the time. "It's right. You've been asleep awhile."

Mary's face warmed. Apparently she'd fallen asleep at the pool and again after their late afternoon tangle in the sheets. Ignoring the implication of that, she flashed him a saucy grin. "Whose fault is that, I wonder?"

She slipped past him and the half-hearted smile that didn't quite make it to his eyes. "Be right out," she told him in a sing-song voice.

Ten minutes later, Mary wrapped a bath towel around her, and sank onto the lid of the toilet to rest a moment. She rubbed her temples, trying to find the energy to move again. Finally, she pushed off and faced the mirror, giving her hair a quick fluff. *Get going.*

She slipped into the red-and-white maxi dress she'd planned for tonight, but decided to go with the beaded black flats instead of the strappy heels. Hopefully she wouldn't trip on her dress.

"Ready?" She asked, perching a hip on the armchair where Grant was waiting.

She was rewarded with a true smile. Standing, he grazed a hand across her shoulder, then pulled her up. His lips met hers in a long, slow kiss that had her spine tingling. "Why didn't you tell me you didn't want to go out?" Mary asked against his lips.

Chuckling, he pulled back. "I do. I'm starving."

"Apparently."

He gave her a light swat, and nudged her toward the door.

The sun had already dipped beyond the horizon by the time they arrived at the upscale Agave Bistro, making the patio too chilly for Mary's bare shoulders. They took a table near the window where they could see the twinkling lights outside as well as the distant lights of downtown Phoenix.

They were well into dinner before Grant broached the subject of the next day's walk. He took Mary's hand. "Want to make a new plan for tomorrow?"

Mary took a sip of wine. She knew exactly what he meant. And it was probably the smart thing to do, but she couldn't bring herself to cancel. The nature preserve had been high on Grant's list of things to do. Smoothing the tablecloth, she shook her head. "No. Let's give it a try. Besides, I've already ordered the wine and cheese cooler."

She looked up to see his clear blue eyes leveled on her. She swallowed past the lump in her throat. Of course he'd understand if she cancelled. He wouldn't be resentful or make her feel bad. Instead, he'd do everything he could to make sure *she* was happy and comfortable. She squeezed his hand. "I'm game, as long as you realize you might have to carry me out."

He shot her a wry smile. "I appreciate that you think I could manage that, but babe, does it make sense to push when we don't really know what's going on with your foot? Or why you're so tired?"

"Are you kidding? Isn't more exercise the cure for everything? Look, how 'bout a compromise? When we get back to the hotel let's get online and take another look at the preserve areas. Let's make sure we go to one that has good access by car and the easier trails. How's that sound?"

"Sounds like you've made up your mind."

"I'm sure it'll be fine. I've got my visor and sunscreen, and I brought my little yellow backpack, so we can take plenty of water and–"

"The real question is did you bring proper shoes?"

Mary sputtered a laugh. Ah, the man knew her well. Of course he was remembering the time she'd been caught wearing sport sandals in a too-close-for-comfort encounter with a copperhead on a walking trail. As if she'd ever forget that mistake – or anyone else would, either. "Checked, and double-checked." She picked up her glass, and sat back with a smile on her face. "Stop worrying."

**

At three-thirty the next day, they pulled into the entrance of the Lookout Mountain Preserve, which claimed to have breathtaking vistas without the crowds or steep elevations of the northern mountains. Already the views were magnificent, with one peak casting shadows against the other, and tall saguaros standing like soldiers among the assorted boulders and brush.

"Beautiful," Mary said, squelching the apprehension that flared in her chest, as she peered at the rocky landscape. She hoped the trails would be solid, worn dirt without a lot of loose rock and gravel on the ground.

"Where to?" Grant asked.

"Let's drive as far as we can and get a feel for it, then choose where we want to walk, and where we want to be later." The winding road took them above the city. Mary strained to see the walking areas, also keeping an eye out for rock formations with easy access that would make a good perch for watching the sunset. "Oooh, that looks good," she said, pointing to a large flat boulder that extended outward, but didn't look like it would require much climbing.

"Okay. This place could work. Want to park here for now and look around?"

"Sure." Grant brought the car to a stop, and Mary reached for her backpack. Rolling her neck, she opened the door, and stretched her legs, willing them to cooperate. Was that too much to ask? Was it? She reminded herself that she'd asked before. She'd put off dealing with whatever the hell was wrong with her foot until after the wedding. Just a few more weeks. Just this one more trip. She slammed the car door harder than she intended, and ignored Grant's questioning eyes.

The stiffness in her muscles was harder to ignore, but Mary slid her sun visor into place, and scanned the trail ahead. Hopefully the Advil she'd taken before they set out would kick in soon. "Hey, hon," she called to Grant. "Can you grab the camera?"

"Sure thing. Want me to take that backpack, too?"

"Nope. I got it." She tucked her cell phone into the front pocket of her pack to take a few fun photos. The bigger, "real" camera was for the scenic shots Grant had in mind. Another reason for hiking in the late afternoon – more dramatic light for better pictures.

As they started along the trail, Mary recalled her impatience with Grant's photo-taking on previous hikes – his determination to get the right shot slowing them down. He'd wait for the sun to hit his subject at just the right angle or sit still for what seemed like hours for an animal to poke its head out of a hole or from under some rock so that he could capture its image. She had a feeling she'd be grateful for such dilly-dallying today.

A few minutes later, when Grant stopped for a close-up of a cactus, Mary plopped onto a large rock nearby, taking advantage of the opportunity to rest. The trail was gentle, but still an uphill climb. "Hey," she called when Grant lowered the camera. "Come here. We should be in some pictures, too. Show the kids that old empty-nesters can still have fun."

Grant knelt beside her, and Mary stretched her arm as far as she could in front of them for a selfie. "Smile!" She pushed the button a couple of times, then handed the phone to Grant. "Okay, you try. Maybe we can get some scenery in the background."

He took a few more, then Mary positioned herself in front of a cactus so that she appeared to have a crown of needles. "How's that look?"

Grant chuckled. "Painful."

She took the phone from him and thumbed through the images. "Haha. I have to post that one. Looks like an encounter with a porcupine gone bad." At least it looked like they were having fun. No one would know the smile was forced, or they'd stopped for any reason other than a funny photo.

"We done here or do you want more pictures?" Mary asked.

"We can move on," Grant told her. "As long as you're doing all right."

"Sure. But you go ahead and take pictures so I don't slow you down."

He turned with a grin. "You slowing me down? That's got to be a first."

As Mary began to feel the effects of the walk in her legs, she took a keen interest in the boulders along the way. Another thirty minutes, and she felt as if she were furniture shopping – sitting on each rock she encountered as though sampling the feel and fit of a new chair.

"Looks like I've got a couple of bars of service, so I'm going to post these," she said, dropping onto a boulder with a smooth indention in the center. She'd bet she wasn't the first to have a little rest here. "You go ahead and shoot while the sun is hitting this side." The towering rock formations were impressive, and the light enhanced the deep red coloring. She removed her visor, and swiped at the perspiration beading her forehead. The sun was into its early evening descent, but still plenty intense.

After several more minutes, Grant joined her. "You about ready to find that outcropping we passed?"

"Sure," Mary said a little too brightly.

"We can follow the trail on around and see if that puts us close, or go back out to the road."

"Up to you," she said. "Going back is more of the same. Do you think there's anything different to shoot up ahead?"

He grinned at her. "Won't know until we try. I could go back and get the cooler out of the car, but I hate to leave you up here by yourself."

Mary glanced around. They'd only passed one other couple on the trail so far, which gave them a nice, quiet hike, but she didn't love the idea of being alone, either. "Oh, let's keep going," she said. Surely if they kept moving that direction, they'd have to come to both the rocks and the car, since they'd parked nearby. Standing, Mary stretched her back, which brought Grant up behind her.

He kneaded her shoulders, each squeeze sending a lovely feel-good kind of ache from her spine to her head.

"I think we're pretty close," he said.

Good, she thought, stepping away from his hands. Much more of that, and she'd collapse into a limp heap at his feet. As they moved forward, Mary's right leg began to tremble, and it took more effort to lift her foot. Grant noticed immediately.

He took hold of her arm. "What's wrong?"

"Ah, this leg's getting weak." She stopped, and propped herself against a boulder. "Why don't you go ahead a bit and see what's around this curve. I'll stay right here."

Indecision clouded Grant's features as he looked around them.

"I'll be fine," Mary assured him. "Go take a look."

"Okay," he said, with a resigned sigh. "Be right back."

It was only a few minutes before he returned, wearing a smile. "Almost there, babe."

He moved in close beside her. "I can carry you."

Mary gave a shaky laugh, and pushed at him. "You will not. If it's close, I can manage."

He held out his arm instead, and she clutched it. Relief whooshed through her only minutes later when the ledge of rocks she'd seen earlier appeared before them. "There it is! Woo-hoo! We did it." *Thank God.* She could perch there in the shade and send Grant to the car, which might even be visible from her vantage point.

But as they got closer, she realized it was more of a climb than she'd originally thought. Hands on her hips, she turned toward Grant. "Well, big guy," she said grimly, "do you want to push or pull?"

"You go up. I'll spot you then go to the car."

With a shake of her head, Mary climbed onto the first rock. "You're going to get a view, that's for sure," she muttered.

Laughing, Grant hopped up behind her. His arms circled her as he pulled her against him. "I love the view."

He helped her onto the next rock, following once again, and then he braced her feet as she made the next two steps and practically crawled onto the flat rock at the top. Breathing hard, Mary dusted the sand from her jeans. Not exactly graceful, but she made it.

"Stay here. I'll be back in a minute," Grant said. He left the camera beside Mary's backpack, and retreated the same way they'd come up.

Uh, yeah. "Not going anywhere." Mary pulled her knees up to her chin, curled her back against the rock behind, and closed her eyes. A nap sounded good. Oh. Wait. She forced her eyes open. They were here for the view. Her eyes scanned the dusky sky, just starting to take on some gold tones. Movement below caught her eye, and she peered forward. Grant was already heading toward her. The trail must've followed the road more closely than they thought. That meant only a short walk in the dim light after their sunset picnic – a thought that cheered her immensely.

"Here you go," Grant said, clambering up the rocks. He sat beside Mary and set the soft-sided cooler in front of her.

Mary smoothed the paper placemat on the ground between them, then lifted the platter of cheeses with grapes and dried fruit. "This looks fabulous," she said. "Such a great idea." She handed the bottle of wine to Grant. "You can pour."

In less than five minutes, they had a spread of food, and glass of chardonnay each.

"This is the life," Grant said, holding his glass toward Mary.

She clinked her glass against his. "To us."

The sunset met all expectations, and Mary sipped her wine with a satisfied sigh. "Absolutely gorgeous."

As the bands of blue, orange and pink intensified, she dumped the remnants of the picnic into the cooler, and scooched in front of Grant. Then she noticed the camera on the ground. "Oh, hon. Don't you want to get some shots of this?"

"Nah. I can remember." He pulled her against his chest, and a peaceful stillness enveloped them, the rest of the world disappearing along with the sun.

Mary didn't stir again until Grant whispered against her hair. "We probably better get going before it's completely dark."

"Oh, but that means I have to move."

Grant landed a quick kiss on the top of her head. "'Fraid so, darlin'. Why don't I run all this stuff to the car then come back for you? It's not far."

"That's not necessary," Mary told him, even though her muscles contradicted her as she attempted a standing position. "Assuming I can get up," she added with a chuckle.

Grant helped her to her feet then gathered up the cooler and camera. Mary grabbed her backpack and took a few steps toward their access to the trail.

"Let me go first," Grant told her.

Her brain agreed, and she intended to step back. But her leg buckled. It happened so fast. The next thing she knew, she was slipping. Almost in slow motion she felt herself falling, heard Grant shout her name, and vaguely heard the camera slam against the rocks. Her thigh hit first, then the underside of her left arm, her exposed skin scraping against the side of the ledge. And then strong fingers wrapped around her right arm like a vise. With a fierce yank, Grant pulled her to safety.

Mary trembled against him. "Damn, damn, damn," she said into his shoulder.

"Shhh," he murmured, though he'd let loose a few expletives himself. He bent to meet her eyes, pushing the hair from her face. "You all right?"

She nodded. "I think so."

"Okay. Let's get out of here."

Grant practically carried her down the stair-stepped boulders. She felt the soreness in her thigh and the sting of raw skin with each step, but she managed to get to the car.

At the hotel she considered a hot bath, knew she should at least clean the abrasion on her arm, but all she wanted was to climb into bed and feel the cool sheets around her.

\*\*

Mary awoke to some rustling sound behind her. Rolling over, she let out a soft groan, and Grant's kiss brushed her cheek.

"Hey, I'm going for coffee while you sleep a little longer."

"Okay," she murmured. Pulling the sheet around her, she curled into a ball.

"It's eight o'clock," Grant said. "Another hour?"

"Mm-hmm." Didn't really matter, she thought, drifting between consciousness and going back to sleep.

"Mary?" A voice whispered in her ear.

"Hmm?"

"It's nine-thirty. You ready to get up?"

136

She attempted to stretch out her legs, but pulled them up again. She held up a hand. "Five more minutes."

A moment later, his heavy arm circled her waist, and Grant nestled her against his chest. "Mmmm." Mary let out a soft sigh.

"What time is your massage?"

Oh. She'd forgotten about her appointment. She tried to clear her head enough to think. "Ten-thirty."

"Do you still want to go?"

Yes, but did she want to get out of bed? Every muscle screamed in protest at every move she made. It would be the perfect time for a massage, right?

"Yeah. I'll get up."

Grant stood, and Mary attempted a sitting position.

"You feel okay?"

Mary ran a hand through her hair. "I think—"

"Oh, Christ. Baby, your arm is all scraped up. We should've got that cleaned up last night."

Mary waved him off, and swung her legs to the side of the bed. "It's fine. Aren't you supposed to be playing golf?"

"No. Remember, they couldn't get me in this morning, so I decided on tomorrow morning instead of afternoon."

"Oh. Right. It'll be cooler then." Ugh. She didn't really want him hanging out in the room while she hobbled around like an old woman.

"Hey. Why don't I run a warm bath for you?"

She let out a choked laugh. Maybe she did want him hanging around after all. "Yeah. That'd be great."

When she was done, Grant met her with a robe and a fresh cup of coffee. Her smile was automatic. "Thanks, sweetie."

Seemed kind of silly to dress simply to go to the spa where she'd slip into another robe, but she pulled on some exercise capris and a soft tunic. When she ventured back into the bedroom, she stopped short. Taking in the scene, she stared at Grant. "What are you doing?"

137

Troubled eyes met hers. He dropped the pair of slacks he'd been folding into the suitcase in front of him. "Mary-me, let's go home. There's a three o'clock flight out this afternoon. We can be home by ten, and first thing in the morning you can call your doctor. Or go to the clinic. Something."

"Oh. But– No. You're supposed to play golf tomorrow morning."

His face softened. "I can play golf another time."

She swiped at unexpected tears. "But–"

"Mary. It's done. I cancelled my tee-time, and I rebooked our flights."

Her mouth dropped open. "Well," she said, finally. "You've been busy."

Grant came around the bed and gently placed his hands on her shoulders. "I had some time last night to look into it while you were sleeping. I think it's the right thing to do. Let's get you downstairs for your massage. We can have lunch by the pool, and then call it done."

Mary swallowed hard, and nodded. Her voice came out a hoarse whisper. "Okay."

He was probably right, she conceded. But in truth, the thought of going home – and facing reality – filled her with dread. What news was waiting for her at home?

## Chapter Twelve

Grant bolted upright. What the–? He listened intently, thinking he heard something outside. Voices? He glanced over at Mary, who was still sleeping soundly, her breathing soft and even. Huh. Maybe a dream had woken him. He rolled toward the window, and re-adjusted, his body still on high-alert.

There. Footsteps. Someone running. He was sure of it.

He pushed aside the covers, careful not to disturb Mary. Crouching, Grant moved forward, intending to have a look outside the bedroom window. But in the next instant, he ducked as the window shattered, showering him and the room with glass fragments.

"Son of a bitch!" He sprang forward, wincing as shards cut into his feet, but needing to get to the window.

The light behind him suddenly illuminated the room. Immediately, tires squealed and the acrid smell of burning rubber burst through the now-missing panes. He was in time to see a small red pickup jump the curb and speed away from the house. His jaw clenched. Grant knew exactly who owned that vehicle.

Chest pounding, he lunged to the bedside table, snatched up his cell phone and dialed 9-1-1. Sleepy eyes frowned at him from the bed. "What are you doing?" Mary mumbled. "Grant? What's going on?"

"Don't move!" he shouted.

Her eyes widened.

While Grant spoke to the police dispatcher, he surveyed the room, and got a sharp punch to the gut. A red brick lay not two feet from the bed. A hot rage burned through him. At another angle, that brick could've landed in their bed. Could've hit – he swallowed hard – *Mary*.

"Grant! What is it?"

He jerked his head toward the gaping hole now letting in a cold breeze. "Busted window."

"Oh, my gosh." Sitting upright, she swung her legs over the side of the bed.

"No. Stay there a minute. I'll pick you up. There's glass everywhere." He rolled across the bed, then tiptoed to the bathroom, and rinsed his punctured feet. Ignoring the scratches on his arm, he yanked on a pair of jeans and shirt, then grabbed shoes for both of them from the closet.

"How the hell did the window break?"

Grant blew out a heavy breath. "A brick."

Mary's hand covered her mouth. "Are you kidding me? Someone threw a brick in our window? That doesn't–"

Returning to the bed, Grant helped her into the pink fuzzy robe that had been hanging in the bathroom. Then he lifted Mary in his arms. "Just a window. Let's get you out of here."

"Just a window, Grant?" Her voice quivered. "Isn't that a lot like just a car? What's next?"

He set her down in the hallway. He never imagined anything more would happen than the keyed car the night at Bailey's. "I don't know, but the police are on their way. I need to call Doug and get some boards. Why don't you lie down in the guest room?"

"No. I'm already awake. I'll start some coffee."

He helped her to the kitchen, then grabbed a coat from the hall closet. Cold air coming from the living room stopped him in his tracks. The curtains billowed, and broken glass shimmered in the light from the front porch. Grant braced a hand against the framework between the two rooms. Another brick. This window had gone first, he realized. It's what had initially woken him up. Shaking his head, he yanked open the front door, and met the police car outside.

Officer Tim Gleason and another man Grant didn't know, approached the house.

Tim extended his hand and introduced his partner, Randy Winston.

"So, we've got some vandalism?" Tim asked.

"Right. Two bricks through the windows."

Randy scribbled in a notebook.

"Cold night for missing windows," Tim said. He clapped Grant on the shoulder. "Everybody okay?"

Grant grimaced, but nodded. "Yeah."

"Glad to hear it. Let's have a look."

Grant led the officers toward the front room. Gleason took some measurements and photographs, then they all traipsed to the bedroom.

"You can see the brick right there," Grant said. "I haven't moved anything."

"You and your wife were asleep at the time?"

"That's right."

"Got any idea who'd do this or why?"

Grant clenched the doorknob with one hand and shoved the other in his pocket. "I know exactly who did it and why."

The officer's brows shot up. "You do?"

"Mary's got a pot of coffee, why don't we go sit down and talk," Grant told him. The absurdity of that spiked Grant's blood pressure. After one o'clock in the morning, when she should be sound asleep after a long day of travel, Mary was waiting in the kitchen to serve the police coffee. Unbelievable.

She looked up as they shuffled back down the hallway, and unfolded herself from the chair in which she'd been curled up.

Tim nodded. "ma'am."

"Coffee?" she asked.

Grant strode to the kitchen. "I'll get it." He filled three mugs then ushered the men to the family room.

"So what's the story here?" Tim asked.

Raking a hand through his hair, Grant explained the situation with Essex. "Bobby Daniels was one of the men let go. I've heard rumors of tension on the home front. His boy did this."

"You got proof?"

"Saw his truck leave my driveway. There's probably a tire track in the yard where he went over the curb."

They talked a while longer with both officers taking notes, and Grant growing impatient. He needed to get covering over the windows and get Mary back to bed.

"I'd like to take a look at those tracks," Tim said.

The men thanked Mary for the coffee then headed back outside.

As Grant suspected, the latest snow had melted, leaving the ground soft and muddy. It created a perfect mold of Rob's tire treads.

Rising from his crouched position, Tim snapped his notebook shut. "Okay, Grant. We'll take it from here. We'll file the report, and be in touch."

"Now, listen," Grant said. "I don't want to press charges. But I want you to talk some sense into this kid." He held up a finger. "And I want it to stop. Period."

"No charges?" Tim echoed. "You sure about that?"

Grant took a deep breath. "We aren't hurt. It's just windows," he said, as much to remind himself as to explain his reasoning to Tim. "I don't want to make things worse."

"Uh-huh. Well, let's file the report and see how it goes up the chain of command."

"How 'bout making the kid do some community service? Or pay for the repairs?"

"Can't be a penalty if there's no charge," Tim said.

"All right, then. Tell them I won't press charges if the kid agrees to community service?"

"We'll be in touch," was Tim's only response.

Fine. Grant would talk it over with the chief later. He gave the officers a curt nod, and took out his cell phone. He hated to disturb anyone else at this hour, but he needed help with the windows. He punched Doug's number.

Doug was always building something, and sure to have enough lumber on hand to get the job done.

"Be there as soon as I can get it loaded," Doug told him, when Grant explained the situation.

"I'll meet you at your place," Grant offered.

"No. You stay put."

"Six sheets ought to do it," Grant said, surveying the gaping hole in the front of his home.

"Won't take long," Doug told him.

Still swearing under his breath, Grant strode back to the house to update Mary. He stopped short when he found her huddled inside a blanket on the family room sofa. Wide eyes met his. Her face was pale. "Mary? You okay?"

"Look at this." She lifted a bag of frozen corn from under the blanket. "I– I think I broke my wrist." Her words were soft and strained. "Tried to catch myself."

"What?" In two great strides, Grant knelt beside her. "What happened?"

"Oh, you know. Thought I'd grab those mugs and clean up."

"Couldn't have waited until morning, huh?"

Her lips turned in an attempted smile. "It *is* morning."

"Right." Gently, he touched her swollen arm as she tried to extend it. He could see pain in her pinched lips. "Oh, baby. That's surely broken. We've got to get you to the hospital." He slid his arm under her knees, ready to pick her up, then let go. It'd be hard to get her into the car without banging into things in the garage. "Let me pull the car around. Don't move."

He ran back to the bedroom to get his keys, then headed for the car. A minute later, he jogged back inside the house. "Okay, sweetheart, this might hurt a bit, but I've got to get you in the car."

She nodded.

"Mary? Hang in there." The glazed look in her eyes sent his heart pounding, and he put his face in front of hers. "Come on. Don't pass out on me." He pressed the frozen bag to her arm, then cradled her against his chest. She let out only one soft gasp as he wrestled her into the seat and fastened the seatbelt around her.

"I'll be right back." He hurried back to the house and slammed the front door shut.

"What about the house?" Mary asked when Grant slid in beside her.

"Not going to worry about that now. Doug will take care of it. He's got some boards for the windows."

"Oh."

Grant made another call to Doug as he drove the short distance to Whitfield Community Hospital. With that under control, he glanced at Mary. "How'd this happen, darlin'?"

She turned toward the window. "I just fell."

Grant pulled the car into the circle drive of the hospital, and once again lifted Mary into his arms. The receptionist inside stepped from behind the counter and pushed a wheelchair toward them.

"Hi, folks. What's going on here?"

Grant deposited Mary into the chair and once again explained what had happened, though skipping most of the details about the vandalism. "Looks like a broken wrist."

"Yeah. Let's get you checked in, and I'll call a nurse."

Ten minutes later, a nurse appeared. "Come on back." She motioned them into a small examination room.

"Is there a doctor here?"

The woman smiled, and shook her head. "On call. He can be here in a few minutes."

"Is Dana here?" Mary asked.

"Dana Gerard? She comes in at eight."

"Mary, it's three in the morning," Grant reminded her.

"Oh, yeah."

"Let's make you more comfortable, Mary," the nurse said. "Sir, can you help me?"

They lifted Mary onto the reclining table. "Sit tight. The doctor will be in shortly."

Grant immediately recognized Dr. Greg Talisman when he entered the room twenty minutes later. As head physician, he was well-known in town. Wasn't in Grant's immediate circle of friends, but certainly respected as a leader in the community. Grant extended his hand, and received a hearty shake in return. Once more, Grant explained the mishap.

"Just clumsy," Mary added with a wan smile.

"That happens," Dr. Talisman said. "Don't worry. We're going to get it fixed up." He settled onto the rolling stool and examined Mary's arm. "Looks like a clean break. Good job keeping that frozen pack on it. Still a little swollen, though. May need to let the swelling go down before we can set a cast. We'll go ahead and get some X-rays, though."

While Talisman and the nurse tended to Mary, Grant stepped into the hall to respond to Doug's text message. He reported that the windows were sealed, and asked if Jane should come up and keep Mary company.

*Thanks, buddy. Negative on company. Maybe tomorrow.* Which, of course, was really today. Grant raked a hand through his hair and leaned against the wall, replaying the whole incident in his head. Grant hadn't had a chance to ask the doctor about looking at her foot. With Mary in and out of sleep, he doubted she'd thought to mention it.

It was nearly seven-thirty by the time the cast was finally set.

"We'll have you folks on your way soon," Dr. Talisman said. "I can write a script for pain meds, but—"

Grant held up a hand. "Hang on a sec, doctor. We've got to figure out why she's falling. What's going on with her foot? We came home early from Phoenix so that she could try and get in to see her doctor. There's a problem with her left leg. Keeps giving out on her. She's achy and tired, and—"

"Hey, Grant. What in the world are you two doing here?" Dana breezed into the room, and moved toward him, but her glance went from Mary to the doctor. She took Grant's hand, and he pulled her into a quick hug. Her presence was a relief. Maybe she'd have some ideas, or be able to make some things happen. Grant leaned over the bed. "Hey, sweetheart, Dana's here." Mary didn't stir.

"What's going on?" Dana asked again.

"Couple of things."

"Yeah?" She raised her brows at the doctor. "Greg?"

"We've set her broken wrist, but Mr. Logan says she's had some other issues recently. I'm looking at some lab results now. Just came through."

"Lab results?" Grant asked. "From what?" Mary hadn't mentioned any lab work to him.

"Oh, my gosh," Dana exclaimed. "What happened here?" She leaned in and touched the bruises on Mary's upper arm, then swiveled toward Grant.

He shook his head, hating that his hand had marred Mary's skin. "I had to catch her to keep her from falling in Phoenix yesterday."

"Oh, Grant. So she's had two falls?" Dana asked.

Dr. Talisman interrupted. "Looks like she was in last week for an exam, and Dr. Bates ordered a complete analysis."

"Good," Dana said. "That's exactly what I recommended."

"Last week?" Grant echoed.

Dana cocked her head at him. "What's wrong, Grant?"

He shook his head. "Nothing. What's the report say?"

Dr. Talisman shot him a cool glance then continued to study the screen of the Ipad in his hands. "Let's see . . . not finding a release form. Not sure I can discuss—"

Dana held out her hand. "May I see it?"

Grant drew in a deep breath, trying to keep from losing patience. He watched Dana's face for any clue while she flicked a finger over the screen. "Looks like Dr. Bates hasn't made any notes about the report yet."

"What does the report say?" Grant asked again. "What are we dealing with here?"

Dana pressed her lips together and her eyes met his. "I'm sorry, Grant. Dr. Bates hasn't made any assessment."

Dana turned to Dr. Talisman. "Is she sedated?"

"Some pain meds, but—"

"For God's sake she doesn't need to be sedated," Grant said, his voice rising. "All she's done for the past week is sleep. She's tired all the time. She's having headaches, and can hardly lift her foot. I don't—"

Dana took his arm. "Hey. Don't worry. We'll figure it out. Why don't we try to wake her up?"

"It's not going to matter," Dr. Talisman said. "I can't interpret the data without discussing it with Dr. Bates."

"Have you contacted her?" Dana asked.

"No. This report just came through."

"Okay, let's have one of the nurses send a message."

"I was about to send them home," Talisman said. "Really no reason to keep her any longer."

"Can we wait until we hear from Dr. Bates? Since Mary's asleep, anyway? We don't need the room, do we?"

"No. But we do need to start morning rounds."

"Right. Why don't you get started? We can let Mary sleep a little longer while we wait to hear from Dr. Bates. How's that sound?"

Talisman nodded, and moved toward the door. "Could I talk to you a minute?" he asked Dana.

"Sure."

Grant watched as the doctor took Dana's arm and steered her into the hallway, then he sank into the chair next to the bed. What the hell was Mary thinking? She'd gone to the doctor last week and not told him? The whole time they were in Phoenix she'd known that lab work was under way? And she hadn't said a word.

Nervous energy sent him out of the chair, and pacing the floor. At Mary's side again, Grant ran a finger over the purple smudges on her upper arm. An ugly reminder of a scary moment. He couldn't help but wonder if there were more to come.

Dana returned, and moved to the other side of Mary. She spoke softly. "Hey, Grant? We've put a call into Dr. Bates. Try to take it easy, okay?" She pushed the hair back

147

from Mary's forehead. "Poor thing. She's really wiped out."

**

Mary opened her eyes. She blinked, trying to clear her head. This wasn't– Oh, right. They were in Phoenix. No, wait. They'd come home. She lifted her hand, and memory flooded in. What a night. Another fall. A broken wrist. She let out a heavy sigh, and Grant turned from the window.

"Hey," she said softly.

"Hey. How do you feel?" he asked, walking toward her.

Mary looked around, as if the answer was out there somewhere. "I don't know. Okay, I guess. Except for this." She held up the heavy arm, which now sported an ever-so-attractive clunky cast. What a nuisance that was going to be. "I can't believe I–"

"Since when do we keep secrets from each other, darlin'?"

She stared at him. Admittedly, her brain was a bit sluggish, but that question made no sense. "What? What are you talking about?"

"Blood tests?"

Oh. She closed her eyes. Damn. How did he find out about those? She drew in a deep breath and met the hurt eyes leveled on her. "How do you know about the tests? Is Dr. Bates here?"

"No. We're waiting to hear from her."

"Then how do–"

"Apparently the lab results are part of your medical file."

Mary attempted to sit up, struggling without the use of her left arm, Grant pushed a button, and the back of the bed lifted her to a sitting position. "Thanks." She bit her lip, almost afraid to ask the next question. "What do they say?"

"No idea. They won't tell me a damned thing without the doctor's notes."

"Oh, Grant." She held out her hand to him. He took it, but she could see the disappointment lingering in his eyes. "I'm sorry. I– I just didn't want you to worry while we were gone."

"Were you worried?"

"A little."

He brushed a hand across her forehead. "Is it better to worry alone?"

Mary choked, half laughing, half crying, and Grant bundled her into his arms.

"Don't ever do that again."

Nodding, Mary swiped at the tears that escaped. Crying wasn't her thing. Wasn't pretty. But the thought of what those tests could reveal . . . her doctor's list of potential outcomes echoed in her ears. Her stomach fluttered, and she clutched Grant's shirt. "I could be really sick, Grant."

He pulled back to look at her, his eyes wide. "Why would you think that?"

"Dr. Bates said . . . well, she said my symptoms *could* be serious. Bad stuff."

His eyes narrowed. "She told you that before the tests?"

"I pushed her. Threatened her."

"You threatened your doctor?" Grant shook his head, and crossed his arms over his chest.

"Don't act so surprised," Mary said with a wry smile. "I told her if she didn't tell me what she was thinking I'd get online and do some research. Funny thing, doctors don't like website medicine."

"Can't imagine why," Grant said. "So did you?"

"What?"

"Do online research."

"No. I promised not to, and I didn't want to ruin our trip. So much for that."

Grant squeezed her hand. "Listen, let's wait and see what she has to say. Apparently the results were sent, but she hadn't had a chance to process them. I'll go find out if they've heard anything."

Grant returned a few minutes later with Dana in tow, and Jane following behind.

"Oh, Jane. Thanks for coming up. I hope you got a little sleep last night."

"No problem. Sorry to hear the news, though."

"Speaking of news," Dana said. "I just got off the phone with Dr. Bates. She can come now if you want to stick around another hour, or you can go home, and she'll work you in at ten-fifteen tomorrow at the clinic. What's your pleasure?"

Pleasure? Hmmm. How about getting right back on an airplane and heading south again?

Grant answered before Mary could. "Let's stay put. I don't want to wait until tomorrow if we can talk to her today."

Mary nodded, suddenly ready to have it over with. Surely knowing would be better than wondering – and worrying.

An hour later, almost to the minute, a light tap on the door interrupted the conversation. Without warning, Mary's chest thumped when Dr. Bates stepped inside the room.

Jane made a hasty exit. "We'll see you later, hon. I'll bring dinner."

Dana handed Dr. Bates the Ipad. "Call the nurses' station if you need anything," she told them before she, too, headed for the door. "I'll be in my office."

Mary made introductions, and then waited in silence while Dr. Bates scanned the tablet in her hands.

"Well," she said, finally, with a heavy sigh. "I'm afraid I don't have a lot of answers for you. The tests overall look quite normal."

"How is that possible?" Grant asked, an unusual impatience in his voice.

"Many of the conditions associated with Mary's symptoms don't show up in a simple blood test. These tests are a starting point to give us baseline data." She turned a sympathetic grimace on Mary. "It looks like we're going to have to do some additional testing."

150

Mary kept her eyes focused on the doctor. She couldn't look at Grant. Didn't want to look at Grant.

"But first," Dr. Bates continued. "Tell me what's been happening and how you ended up in here."

Mary and Grant took turns, each filling in the blanks where the other left off or left something out.

"So the numbness in your foot may have worsened a bit."

"Maybe, but either way, I don't trust it. Every time I get up now, I have to test it. I'm afraid I'll fall again."

"Me, too," Dr. Bates said. "You need to start using a simple cane or a claw-foot. You don't want to end up back in here with a concussion or worse. I want you to see a neurologist, and I'm ordering an MRI. We need to start narrowing things down and ruling out as many conditions as possible." She glanced from Mary to Grant, and back again. "I hate to tell you, but this could dominate your life for the next several weeks."

Grant squeezed Mary's hand. "Probably good timing," he said. "At least we got past the wedding. You can slow down now. Not much goes on between Thanksgiving and New Year's."

Mary stared at him. Was he crazy? It might typically be a slow time for him, but not for her. "Yeah, just that little thing called Christmas."

"The girls can help."

Help what? Fix Christmas dinner? Mary almost laughed. That was one tiny sliver of the Christmas pie – a blip on the calendar. In her world, the holidays were the busiest time of year. Next week was the combined November/December council meeting. Right after that was the Mayor's Christmas tree lighting ceremony, and the council always hosted a holiday party for city employees. Mary always took some bell-ringing shifts, and helped with the fundraising gift wrap table at the bank. She always–

"Mary?" Dr. Bates cleared her throat. "You okay?"

"Oh, sure." Swallowing hard, Mary forced her attention back to her doctor. "An MRI?"

"Yes. We can do it in Paxton, but you might consider having it done in Wichita or Kansas City. I know good neurologists either place. They might prefer to take care of it there. Do you have a preference?"

"Kansas City," Grant said firmly. "They have better specialists and facilities there. Chances are we could mess around here for weeks and then end up going there, anyway. Let's cut to the chase."

"Want to tell us what you really think, hon?" Mary asked.

Dr. Bates stood. "I'll get some names for you. Call right away. If you can't get in soon, let me know and we can at least go ahead and do the MRI in Paxton."

Mary licked her lips before she spoke. "What exactly is the MRI going to tell us?"

Dr. Bates turned a consoling smile on Mary. "Hopefully it's going to show us what's going on inside your brain, and then we'll know what we're dealing with. It will rule out a brain tumor and maybe MS. If there are lesions that indicate MS, the neurologist will probably do a spinal tap to confirm." She held up a hand as she met Mary's eyes. "Remember, there are a number of conditions that have similar symptoms. It might take some time to pin down an exact diagnosis."

"Based on what you know, you're leaning toward MS?" Grant asked.

Mary held her breath, waiting for a response.

The doctor's features clouded. "I just can't say right now. I'm sorry."

## Chapter Thirteen

"Here comes your ride," Grant told Mary as they lingered by the door waiting for the all-clear.

Mary peeked into the hallway. Then froze. The wheelchair Dana pushed toward her advanced like some stealthy beast ready to attack. A wheelchair? That was ridiculous. What the hell had happened to the cane suggestion? Wheelchairs were for the disabled, the immobile, and she did not qualify. She breathed a sigh of relief when Dana stepped around the chair, and shoved it against the wall.

"Leaving us so soon?" Dana asked.

Mary attempted a smile. "Nice place you've got Madam Administrator, but I'm outta here."

"What's the news?"

"More tests."

"Oh, Mare. What kind of tests?"

"Starting with an MRI. Checking out the old brain function. Hopefully they'll see a wave or two."

"Come on. What are they looking for?"

"At this point, I think they're looking for anything."

"So, no diagnosis?"

"No, ma'am. I'll have to get back to you on that."

Dana moved in and wrapped her arms around Mary. "Please do. And take care of yourself."

"That's the plan. Hey, we have a question for you. Think Kent might have any recommendations for cleanup companies? Both of the rooms that now have smashed windows also have carpeting. How will we ever get all that glass out?"

"Might have to replace the carpet," Grant chimed in.

"But what a hassle to try and get that done before Christmas."

"I'll ask him, and let you know," Dana said. "Listen, do you want to take a rain check on Thanksgiving?"

"Absolutely not. We're looking forward to it." Mary realized the weak leg combined with a bum wrist was probably a recipe for disaster if she were to attempt serving at the church dinner, so she'd have to bail out of that. A trip to Dallas also seemed unlikely now. She wasn't giving up Dana and Kent, too. "Our place. Any time after four."

"Okay. We'll talk. What a crazy night you've had. Let's get you in this wheelchair, and let you get home."

Uh, no. A cane was going to be bad enough. Besides, she had Grant. Mary waved her hand. "Not necessary."

"Hospital policy, my dear."

She was about to protest when Grant nudged her. "Just play along, babe." Resisting a retort, Mary sank into the chair feeling ridiculous. She had a feeling she'd be doing a lot of "playing along," in the next few weeks. It wasn't her strong suit.

By the time Grant pulled the car into their driveway, it was almost eleven o'clock. Though she'd slept at the hospital, Mary wanted nothing more than to lose herself in a set of sheets and drift off to la-la land. Unfortunately, her rumbling stomach screamed for attention, and her doctor's to-do list loomed large in her mind.

"I'll come around," Grant told her as he opened the car door.

Mary paused. "I wonder if the neighbors will like what we've done to the place," she said, referring to the plywood-covered windows. "Pretty classy."

"I'll call Crane and get new windows ordered this afternoon. Maybe we can get them in before Christmas."

"Yeah, guess I'll make some calls, too," Mary murmured, stepping inside the house. It was like walking into a time warp. Didn't seem possible they'd been in Phoenix yesterday.

"You want me to help with the calls?" Grant asked.

"No. You deal with the windows, and I'll call the doctors. Are you sure about Kansas City, though? If I went to Wichita, I could stay with Claire."

"It's *we*, darlin' and, yes, I think Kansas City is going to have better doctors and facilities." He drew her into his arms. "Like I said, I don't want to mess around."

Play along, she repeated in her head.

Thirty minutes later, Mary curled up on the guest room bed with a warm cup of chai tea, her phone, laptop, and the papers from Dr. Bates. Scheduling an MRI was no problem, but getting in to see the doctor proved more of a challenge. And it would take two trips to Kansas City. The MRI should be done several days ahead of the doctor visit to allow the doctor to review it, the scheduling nurse told her. And just in case the MRI was inconclusive, the doctor may want a lumbar puncture, so she should allow plenty of time. That meant being prepared for an overnight stay. Reluctantly, she scheduled the MRI for Monday, before the council meeting, and the doctor appointment for Thursday. Then she closed the tab for the University of Kansas Hospital, and did what she'd been putting off – a search for the potential causes behind her symptoms.

The sheer number of results was staggering. Forcing her eyes to remain open, Mary started a Word document to begin making notes and copying website addresses for future reference. This could take days.

Words like neuropathy and vasculitis needed more investigation. But words like fatigue, pain, numbness and chronic flashed like warning bells again and again, showing up page after page until Mary wondered just how many different diseases she could have.

When the doorbell rang, Mary flopped back against her pillow, listening for signs that she needed to put in an appearance. She strained to hear the voices at the door. Sounded like their closest neighbor, whose house sat about half a city block down the street. Probably curious about the windows. Nothing that required her presence.

A few minutes later Grant appeared at the bedroom door. "How you feeling?"

"Fine. Ready for a nap."

Grant took the laptop from her, and closed it. "Probably a good idea. Looks like three to four weeks on the windows."

Mary groaned, though it was what she expected. Whatever. Just windows, right? She didn't have the mental energy to worry about it.

"I'll wake you up in a couple of hours," Grant told her, switching off the lamp, and landing a kiss on her forehead. "You get some rest."

By the time the doorbell rang again at six, Mary had managed a nap, waking with enough energy to fix her hair and dust on a little make-up.

She smiled as Doug and Jane come through the door.

"Thought I'd better check my handiwork, make sure it cuts the muster."

"Yes, thank you," Mary said. "I'm always quite particular about the plywood application on my house."

Grinning, Doug leaned in with a peck on her cheek. "I knew it." He set a box on the island counter. "And here's dinner."

Jane peeked around a vase of cheery flowers. "How about I put these in the dining room?"

"Perfect," Mary told her. She should probably play hostess, and offer a drink or go into the family room, but she didn't want to budge. The hot pink and leopard-print cane that Dana and Grant had picked out was tucked under the counter, but she couldn't bring herself to pull it out. Not yet. Jane would talk to Claire, and an automatic chain reaction would begin. Claire would talk to Elise. Elise would talk to Annie. Then Claire and Annie would swoop in, bombarding her with questions. Who needed that?

The men had wandered into the living room when Jane returned, a curious expression on her face.

"So, what goodies are in here?" Mary asked, lifting the covering from the box on the counter. "Oooo. Smells delish."

"Roast and potatoes. And a salad. The best part is a small lemon meringue from Hannah's. Do you have any idea how intimidating it is to take food to one of the best cooks in town?"

Mary grinned. "That should keep you from making a habit of it."

"As would you staying away from the hospital."

Mary's throat clogged. The natural retort would be that she didn't plan to make a habit of being around the hospital. But that might actually be a lie. She brushed off the comment. "Still, I have to say the free food and flowers are pretty sweet. Thanks so much for all you've done, my friend."

"Yeah. I have something to tell you about the flowers." The dry tone of Jane's voice told Mary something was up.

Raising her brows, Mary stared at Jane. "Do tell."

Jane took a seat. "I ordered the flowers from Tina, who it turns out has hired some extra seasonal help.

"Uh-huh."

"Guess who she hired?"

Oh, no. Eyes bulging, Mary clapped a hand over her mouth. She knew 'who' immediately. "Regina." Tina Mansfield owned one of two floral shops in town, and sometimes hired Regina Daniels to help with events. Since Bobby's layoff, Mary had heard Tina had been offering Regina more work.

"So, Regina answered my call, and when I said who they were for, she told me the shop was too busy. Tina called me a few minutes later. Apparently, Regina had a huge conniption fit and stormed out of the shop."

Mary shook her head. "That's just great. So now in her mind I'm responsible for her losing work, too. Where is this going to end?" She paused, unsure whether the other fact of the story had circulated. "You know it was Rob, their oldest, who broke our windows, right?"

"Doug told me, but I haven't mentioned it to anyone. There's been talk at school that things aren't good on the home front, that Bobby and Regina have been fighting. Supposedly someone called Bobby a loser, and that set Rob off."

"Figures. Grant wants to let him off with community service. Try not to talk about it, okay? Spreading the word could make things worse."

Could they get worse? Mary certainly hoped not. She felt bad for Bobby and the family but what else could she do about it? "Oh, man. I can just imagine Regina's face when she found out the flowers were for me. She's been so nasty since Bobby lost his job."

"Kind of serves her right," Jane said.

Mary shook her head with a rueful smile. "That karma thing sure can be a bitch."

"For sure. Listen, we'd better get going. You two enjoy dinner, and take it easy. I'll catch up with you in a day or so," Jane told her, heading toward the door.

Mary gave a last wave, then grimaced as she turned and passed her boarded-up living room. In her mind, she understood that the loss of a job affected the whole family, and that kids could behave erratically. Though she couldn't imagine any of her kids resorting to vandalism, she was grateful none of them had ever had to experience anything that traumatic.

In fact, the biggest "mistake" one of her kids had made was going to be a blessing.

**\*\***

The end of the workday meant Sara could stop watching the clock, stop waiting for her phone to ring. There would be no more interviews scheduled. No job offers extended. She could put another X on her calendar.

She forced herself to chug the rest of the milk in her glass. It was one of her least favorite beverages, but she'd committed to two glasses a day. It would be followed momentarily by a handful of dried cranberries and almonds. That should get her by until supper.

Treats in hand, she wandered into the bedroom that had become hers over the weekend. The apartment was quiet without Morgan, but Sara was happy to have her own space, and a place to put her clothes. Living out of a suitcase got old in a hurry. She grabbed a light fleece vest from the closet, thinking a walk around the complex sounded good. She needed the exercise, and also needed to clear her head – to stop thinking about Imagine Media and get ready for her interview with the employment agency tomorrow. It was the last of the headhunters she'd connected with. If nothing came through in the next week, she'd have to dig deeper. No need to panic, though. Even with the Cobra insurance premiums, her checking account could go a little while longer before it felt the sting of the missing paycheck, and she calculated another month of easily camouflaging her pregnancy.

Tucking her phone in her pocket, she made her way to the sidewalk that looped around the apartments, figuring she had almost an hour before dusk. Funny how her concerns had shifted in the last few weeks – uneven sidewalks in the dark now presented a hazard she wouldn't have thought about before.

She'd taken about five steps when her phone buzzed, and her pulse jumped. Perhaps an end-of-the-work-day decision? Not even close. Her sister's face appeared on the screen. Back from Belize.

"Hi there!" Sara said. "Is this Mrs. Oliver?"

Annie laughed. "Definitely not used to that yet."

"So, how was the honeymoon?"

"Absolutely fabulous," she crooned.

As if there could be any other answer. "Did you get back last night?"

"Saturday night. Dealt with some jet lag yesterday, and went to work today."

"Wow. That's hitting the ground running."

"I knoooooow," Annie groaned. "I'm so glad we decided not to try and rush around to see both families for Thanksgiving. We need some down time to get things put away and start on thank-you notes."

"I bet. It's going to be weird, though, not going home for Thanksgiving."

"I'm sure Mom and Dad would love to have you if you wanted to go to Whitfield."

"Oh, I know. But it's a lot of driving. And I think they've already made other plans. It'll be fine."

"Have you heard from them? I got a text from Mom yesterday."

"Yeah. Talked to Dad on Friday. Sounds like they're having fun. Did you see the goofy pictures they posted on Facebook?"

"Yes. Oh, my gosh."

"The one you posted of you and Blake on the beach was adorable. When do you think you'll get some pics from the photographer?"

"She sent a few, but I haven't had a chance to do anything with them. I can't wait to see them all."

"It was gorgeous."

"It was." Annie's voice went soft and dreamy, and Sara could easily picture the big, dopey smile on her sister's face. "I can't believe it's already been more than a week."

"What do you remember most about the wedding? What was your favorite part?"

"Oh, wow. Walking down the aisle and seeing Blake standing there waiting for me. I just wanted to run and shout and throw my arms around him. Really, the bride should skip and dance down the aisle not walk those slow, painful steps."

"Oh, good idea," Sara said, laughter in her voice. "I think that's what I'll do." Never mind that the only aisle she'd be walking down any time soon was at the food market.

"You know what else was super cool? Dancing with Dad. He said something I'll never forget."

Sara caught her breath. "Yeah?"

"He asked if I felt beautiful. Because when Blake and I first got engaged, Dad sat down with me one night, and we had this awesome talk. He asked me if I was sure, and then he asked, 'When he looks at you, do you feel beautiful? Can you see it in his eyes? Do you feel it?'" She paused for a beat, presumably for dramatic effect. Sara's throat was tight with sudden tears when Annie continued. "Then he said, 'When I look at your mom, I want her to know I'm looking at the most beautiful thing in my life. And I want that for you and Sara.' Isn't that sweet?"

The tears came hard, gushing down Sara's cheeks.

"Sara? Sara! What's wrong?"

She sniffled, and swiped at her eyes, but couldn't talk. She dropped onto a bench near the clubhouse. Her dad had never said anything like that to her. Their last conversation had been . . . polite. He'd asked about her job search, and how she was feeling, but nothing deeper. At the time, Sara had thought it was nice of him to call. But she understood now that the call had lacked some emotion.

"Didn't mean to get you so choked up," Annie said. "Are you going to make it?"

Finally, Sara let out a muffled laugh. "Yes, that was sweet. Yes, I'm fine." Maybe her dad had been caught up in the whole wedding atmosphere and it made him more emotional. She tried to remember the details of his call on Friday, but her sister's voice interrupted her thoughts again.

"Anyway, what's going on with you? Any good prospects?"

"I assume we're changing the subject and talking about jobs?" Sara asked.

Annie laughed. "Well, I was, but if there are any other interesting prospects, then spill."

"No. Not much to tell. One interview tomorrow, and then that's it for the week. Everyone's taking off for the holiday. I'm sure I won't hear from anyone until next week."

Sara pushed off from the bench and began walking again. Of course the biggest thing "going on" with her was the fact that she was on her way to becoming a mommy. Sara had told her mother she'd share the news with Annie after the wedding. So, it was after the wedding. She could tell her now, but it didn't feel right. Annie was still very much caught up in being a newlywed. Waiting until Christmas when everyone would be together seemed to make more sense. By then, she'd have a new job, and–

"Did you find a place to live?"

"Oh, here's some news. Morgan moved in with her boyfriend, so I'm going to sublet for a few months."

"Ah, too bad. I thought Blake and I might visit you in January or February when it's still cold and nasty here."

"Well, we'll see. If I get a job that's in another part of town, I'll go ahead and move. You can still visit, though."

"Maybe. Okay, I better get going. Keep me posted on things."

"Sure." Sara told her sister goodbye and picked up her pace, determined not to dwell on her sister's call or her dad's call from Phoenix. It was nice that he'd phoned. No point trying to read anything else into it.

The fact that it was near the end of November and she was outside walking with only a light vest was enough to cheer her. No coat. No gloves. No frigid cold or biting wind. No snow. To keep her mind occupied while she walked, Sara tossed around baby names and room décor ideas, trying to imagine what it would be like having a boy or a girl. She couldn't quite bring herself to hope for one over the other, though she couldn't help think that it might be best if the baby was a girl.

By the time she returned to the apartment, Sara's stomach had resumed its nagging. She opened the refrigerator and debated her meal options. She could thaw a chicken breast and add it to a salad or some pasta and brocc– No. French fries. She wanted french fries. For the past few weeks she'd craved salty foods. Had gone so far as to add salt to her cucumber-and-tomato salad and a slice of watermelon. Unfortunately, most salty things seemed to be junk food like pretzels and chips and, *sigh*, french fries. The burger place a few blocks away made good hamburgers and the best fries she'd found in Dallas so far – thin and cooked to perfection with a light, crunchy outside.

Decision made. She grabbed her purse and keys, and headed to her car. But before she started the engine, her cell phone chimed again. Hmmm. Few calls trumped food these days. She checked the screen. Evan. They'd talked every couple of days since Annie's wedding. The early conversations were tentative emails. Then they became more immediate texts and some funny Snapchats – sharing silly things that happened during the day. Lately, they'd been longer phone calls. Sara preferred talking to typing. She could keep her hands free and do other things while she talked. Plus, she discovered she liked the sound of Evan's voice. Deep and soothing, it was easy to listen to.

She tapped the screen. "Hi."

"Hey, what are you up to?"

"I was about to bust my diet and go for a burger and fries. What about you?"

"Diet? Are you kidding? If I'm talking to the same girl I saw a couple of weeks ago, I'd say that's completely unnecessary."

Good answer, Sara thought. "Thanks, but I don't mean a diet to lose weight. I'm just trying to eat well. You know, cut out some of the junk." She gave a little laugh. "Or be more selective, anyway." At least that wasn't a lie. She didn't have to give him all the details. "It's hard here. Since the weather is nicer, I'm eating as if it's summer. Ice cream is a problem."

"Impossible. Ice cream is never a problem."

"Well, I'm trading it for fries today. And pie soon. You know it's pumpkin pie season."

"Yes. I'm aware of that. You going to Whitfield for Thanksgiving?"

"Nope. Staying put until Christmas. What about you?"

"Same. Everybody thinks bankers have cushy hours, but we're open for business on Friday, and I gotta be here."

"So what will you do for Thanksgiving dinner?"

"One of the guys in the office feels like it's his duty to invite all the singles to his place. His wife does a huge spread, and it's a decent group of people."

"That's nice. At least you won't be home alone. Or eating at Denny's."

"I hope those aren't *your* options. If that's the case, you're coming to Tulsa."

Sara laughed out loud. Nice that he was concerned about her options. "Thanks for the invite, but we're doing something low-key here. It's fun to be with friends and family, but I don't need the big, fancy ordeal that my mother does. Waaaay too much effort. She works on it for days, and it's over in thirty minutes."

"True. Makes it special, though. Hey, am I keeping you from those fries?"

He was indeed, but she couldn't quite bring herself to end the call. Her stomach could wait. "No. It's okay." Unbuckling the seatbelt, she twisted around and stretched her legs to the passenger seat.

"What are you doing the rest of the weekend?" he asked.

"Probably absolutely nothing. Movies, books, waiting around to hear from all the people who want to hire me."

Evan chuckled. "No doubt there are dozens. And you know they'll all call at the same time, right?"

"Of course."

"Just thinking out loud here. Would a little company make the time pass faster?"

Sara's heart skipped a beat, and she held her breath. Was he suggesting a visit? Would he drive all that way just to hang out with her for a while? It definitely would make the time pass more quickly, but it'd also add some stress. She'd be in pregnancy cover-up mode. Still, a boring weekend yawned before her.

"Well, I– Yeah, that would be–" God, she was stammering like an idiot. "Not sure if– Let me check with my roommate. We've got a sofa–"

"Sara, I'm not inviting myself to stay at your place. I'm sure there's a hotel somewhere close by. It's four hours here to there. I can be there by ten Friday night."

"Umm . . ." Her mind went completely blank. A hotel?

"Give me your address, and I'll Google it."

She managed to remember that.

"Okay, I'll look into it and get back to you. If you're sure you want company."

"Of course. Yeah, that'd be fun." This time she said it like she meant it. And she did. "Not sure what we'll do, but—"

"We can find things to do. Obviously, we can put going for ice cream on the agenda. Or we can do nothing. It'll be good either way."

Sara couldn't help laughing. "Okay." It definitely beat the big fat nothing she had planned before. "But, Evan?"

"Yeah?"

"Don't mention it to your mom, okay?"

"Our secret," he told her, the humor in his voice telling her that he understood the direction her thoughts had gone – grapevine city. "Everything under control with them? Mom told me about the house."

"The house? What do you mean?"

"Talked to my mom over lunch today, and she said your house had been vandalized last night."

"Last night?" Sara sat upright. "Oh, my gosh. Did she call my parents? They're out of town."

"Really? I got the impression they were home when it happened."

"No. They're in Phoenix. Supposed to be home late tomorrow night." Sara shook her head, remembering her mother's comments about the things she'd know about Evan due to the mom network. Still going strong, apparently.

"Huh. Don't know what to tell you, angel. I've got to trust my source on this one."

"Right. Good grief. I guess I need to check in with my parents."

"Parents. Can't let 'em out of your sight for a minute."

"Crazy, isn't it?"

"Sounds like I better let you go. Call me later if you feel like it. I'll probably just be watching TV."

Maybe she would, if she wanted to spend the entire evening on the phone. Might be time to try Skyping. Readjusting in her seat, Sara started the car. Food first, then she'd check in with her mother.

A few moments later, Sara laughed at herself. There, right behind the restaurant was a strip center, and right behind that was a Hilton Garden Inn. She hadn't noticed it before, but it was the perfect location. She'd give Evan a call later.

**

Back at the apartment, Sara practically inhaled the burger and fries. She licked the last of the salt from her fingers then tossed the wrappers in the trash, feeling satisfied. Behind her, Leah opened the oven door, and the air was suddenly filled with the scent of baking bread.

Sara took a giant whiff. "Oh, my. That smells amazing," she told her roommate. "What kind is it?"

"Pumpkin," Leah said, grinning. "Tomorrow is cranberry walnut, my specialty."

"Mmmm. My nose and my tummy thank you. Who needs turkey, anyway?"

"I do," she said. "I want the works. Morgan says we're supposed to start the turkey at seven o'clock. She and Sam will be here about ten-thirty. Everyone else around eleven-thirty."

"Sounds good to me." Sara was fine with being handed her marching orders and letting the others take charge. Too many cooks was, well, too many. She retreated to her room and punched in her mother's cell number.

"Hey, Sarie!" Her mother's cheery voice came on the line. "What are you up to?"

"Mom! I just heard some weird news. Are you at home?" She heard the deep sigh from the other end.

166

"We are. I–"

"What happened?"

"Oh, nothing terrible. I took a little spill and we decided to come back early."

"A spill? Are you hurt?"

"Broken wrist. No big deal. Hope you don't mind all your Christmas presents will be tossed in bags this year."

Sara smiled. Sounded trivial enough, but she knew that would take some fun out of Christmas for her mother, who loved to create packages that could put Martha Stewart to shame.

"I'll try not to be too disappointed. Left or right wrist?"

"Left. So I'm not completely non-functioning."

"That's good. Did something happen at the house?"

Another heavy sigh. "*Who* have you been talking to?"

Sara rolled her eyes. She didn't want to divulge that information. "Mom, seriously? Does that matter? What happened? I can't believe you didn't call."

"Oh, honey, it's a crazy, tedious story, and I don't want it blown out of proportion. We had a little vandalism. A couple of windows broken is all. Nothing to worry about. How are things with you? Do you have something to do for Thanksgiving?"

Sara couldn't help grinning. As of about an hour ago, her weekend plan got a whole lot more interesting. "Yes. We're having a few people over here. Low key."

"Nice. Have you told your friends you're pregnant?"

"Only Morgan. Everyone else can wait."

"Everyone?"

Sara knew where her mother's thoughts had landed. She absolutely could not start spreading the word. Not with Evan coming to visit. "Yes. Everyone. Including Annie and Jason and everyone in Whitfield, Mom. I've decided to wait until Christmas."

"Why?"

"Because no one needs to know yet."

"I don't understand why you want to keep it a secret. Are you having second thoughts?"

How to answer that? The last thing Sara wanted was to let her mother know that her change of plans had anything to do with Evan. "I just need some time to get settled. Another month isn't going to matter."

"I'd love to hang a sweet little extra stocking on the mantel, Sarie. Would that work?"

That visual nearly took Sara's breath away. A Christmas stocking for her baby. That would be sweet. It might be a cute way to make the announcement to the family. "I'll think about it," she said. But in her mind, it still seemed too soon.

She rested a hand on her abdomen. That was still a month away. By then, she'd have her first sonogram. Might even know the gender. And then it would be so . . . real.

## Chapter Fourteen

"This guy is just a friend?" Morgan asked Sara Thursday afternoon when they had a few moments alone in the kitchen. Keen eyes studied her, and Sara tried not to squirm as if she were in trouble. Morgan was the only person who knew about the recent breakup with Todd, and understood that Evan's appearance was sudden.

The answer lodged in Sara's throat. It was the same question that had kept her tossing and turning much of the night. Had her relationship with Evan shifted? Of course they were friends. They always had been. Was his visit any different from any of her other friends coming to see her? She hadn't planned to spread the news of his visit, but he was the reason she'd declined going out Friday and Saturday. Way too early to introduce him to her gal pals. And too little time, anyway. She needed some time alone with Evan to sort out her feelings and the implications of them in her own mind.

Shrugging, she handed Morgan one of the glasses that hadn't fit in the dishwasher. Some of the other guests had filtered out by mid-afternoon, but Morgan had insisted on staying until things were cleaned up and put away. Sam seemed comfortable in front of the TV.

Sara leaned against the counter, keeping her attention on the soapy water in the sink. "Yeah, let's stick with that for now."

"Uh-huh," Morgan said, the tone of her voice conveying her disbelief. "How many guys do you know who will drive four hours to hang out with a girl who's just a friend?" She reached for the next glass. "Unless he's a pimple-faced nerd who smells bad, I'm guessing there's a little more to the story."

Laughing, Sara shook her head as the image of Evan at Annie's wedding in his tailored charcoal suit came to mind. Not even close. Not even close to close. "As a matter of fact," she drawled, pausing to keep Morgan in suspense. "He's pretty hot."

"Who's hot?" Leah asked, coming into the room at the same time Morgan let out a sharp whoop.

"Sara's weekend guest."

Sara's cheeks warmed. That implied more than it was – for now anyway. She'd have to see how the weekend played out. She wasn't ruling out new possibilities. After all, how many "friends" would she describe as hot?

Leah put a hand on her hip. "Well, I hope so. That's the only kind we allow around here, you know."

"Okay. Good to know I'm not breaking any rules," Sara said. At least not that one. She gave them some general background on Evan, and let the boy-next-door teasing roll off her shoulders.

But later, alone with her thoughts, the question gnawed at her. If something developed with Evan, it would complicate an already complicated situation. Intuitively, she trusted Evan, and sensed that he trusted her. She didn't know where this was going, but knew she didn't want to screw it up. Being able to trust someone was a very big deal. Call her a fool, but she was inclined to trust people, to give them the benefit of a doubt. She didn't want to be gullible, but she didn't want to be suspicious and standoffish, either. She'd rather believe the best of people. Unfortunately, as she knew from recent experience, that came at a price.

All day Friday, between naps and reading, she wondered whether she should tell Evan her secret and be done with it. She read whole pages without comprehending any of the words while her thoughts drifted back to Evan. Part of her would love to know his reaction, but another part was afraid. Would their

170

"relationship" end before they had a chance to see where it might go? Would he think less of her? She'd never been bothered much by the opinions of others. Most of the time it didn't matter. Evan, she conceded, was different. She wanted his respect and high opinion.

By the time the doorbell announced Evan's arrival Friday night, Sara had decided to wait and see how the weekend unfolded. Let things take their course. She wasn't about to leap to any conclusions this time around. If it turned out he was "just a friend" she wouldn't mind getting a male perspective on her situation. But if it was possible that he could become more, well . . . telling was a risk.

When she opened the door and saw him standing on the steps, her heart gave a funny lurch. The wide, easy smile that lit up his eyes both delighted and flustered her. "Hi," she breathed, hardly capable of speech – especially when he moved in close and placed a light kiss on her cheek. The brush of his lips and heat of his breath sent unexpected tingles to her spine. She didn't have time to analyze her body's automatic reaction to Evan, but it was duly noted.

"Good to see you," he said.

"You, too," she murmured, stepping back to allow him inside. "Come in. How was the drive?"

"I managed to avoid radar."

"That's always good. Were you speeding?"

He grinned at her. "Little bit."

"In a big hurry to get to that ice cream, huh?" As soon as the words were out of her mouth, she groaned inside, wanting to take them back. Sounded as if she were fishing for some kind of declaration that he couldn't wait to see her.

"Something like that," he said, with a curious expression on his face, as if he were trying to read her mood. His glanced moved behind her. "Nice place," he said.

The kitchen and living room of the apartment blended into each other, making the main living area seem more spacious. Sara had tidied up, so everything was neat

171

and clean, but the neutral décor lacked some personality in her opinion. When she went to Whitfield for Christmas she'd probably bring back some of the pillows and other decorative items she'd left there.

"Thanks. Hey, can I get you a beer or something?" Sara asked.

"Sure. That sounds good."

"Coming right up. The bathroom's first door on the left if you want to wash up."

"Great. Be right back."

She pointed Evan in the direction of the bathroom, and took a moment to appreciate the waffle-weave gray shirt that hugged the contours of his broad shoulders and muscular arms. It was a nice view. Smiling to herself, she headed to the kitchen, where she was startled by a loud whisper.

"Is he here?" Leah asked.

Sara cocked her head toward the hallway. "Pit stop." She opened the fridge, and realized she didn't know which beer he'd prefer. It was a small stash, but still, they had three kinds to choose from. Maybe the IPA . . .

Before she had a chance to select one, Evan reappeared, and Leah lingered, apparently wanting an introduction. Playing hostess, Sara went through the formalities, and watched Leah give Evan the once-over, aware that a report would be transmitted to Morgan as soon as possible. Wouldn't surprise her if Leah managed to sneak an undercover photo with her cell phone.

Sara gestured toward the refrigerator. "Hey, wasn't sure what you'd like, so take a look." She glanced toward Leah, who hadn't budged. What the heck? Was she planning to hang around all night?

Sara shifted her weight. "Would you rather go out?" she asked, since Evan hadn't selected a beer. She knew she should give him some time to stretch and regroup after four hours on the road, but she'd been waiting all day to see him, and didn't want to spend their short amount of time tonight in idle chit-chat with Leah in the picture.

He leaned against the counter. "Totally up to you."

172

Oh, no, she groaned silently. They could use up the rest of the evening politely acquiescing to each other.

"Well—" They spoke at the same time.

"Going out sound good to you?"

Absolutely, she thought. "Sure. I'll drive since you've been driving a while. Let me grab a jacket."

Leah was still in the front room chatting with Evan when Sara returned. "We're heading out," Sara told her.

Leah smiled and threw Sara a speculative look, a little smirk playing around her lips. "Sounds good. You guys have fun."

Inside the car, Sara turned toward Evan. "Do you especially want to go to a bar? There's a little coffee shop close by that's open until midnight on weekends. It'd be quieter."

"Works for me."

She put the car in gear and turned out of the parking lot with a slight hesitation before getting up to speed.

"That doesn't feel quite right," Evan said.

"What?"

"Your car. Sounds like your transmission might be slipping."

"Really?" She thought she'd noticed some sluggishness a couple of days ago. What she didn't need was a car problem. "I hope not."

"Might have it checked out the next time you have service."

"Yeah. I'll ask about it."

Ten minutes later, drink in hand, Sara curled up on a small sofa. Evan settled in beside her, stretching his legs in front of him. Comfortable and relaxed, they slipped into easy conversation.

"So guess what?" she said, facing Evan. "You were right. My parents flew home early, somebody threw bricks through a couple of windows, and now Mom has a broken wrist."

"Oh, wow. That's crazy."

"Isn't it? In sweet little Whitfield. Fall out from all those layoffs, I guess."

"Too bad. You'd think they could catch a break after that tornado."

"No kidding. How's construction going at your mom's place?"

"She's still saying it's going to be ready by Christmas. They start painting inside on Monday, then all the tile and carpet will go down."

"Very cool. I can't wait to see it."

"Yeah. You'll have to come out over Christmas."

"How much time will you have off?" Sara asked, wondering if her time would still be as flexible. Unless she got a job offer soon, she figured it'd be after New Year's before she officially started somewhere.

"Only taking a few days for Christmas since I'm taking off a week for Hawaii."

"Oh, of course. And you'll just go to Whitfield, right? You don't spend any time with your dad?"

"Hell, no."

"Do you ever see him?" Sara knew her mother had a number of unflattering words to describe Evan's dad, but she wasn't a hundred percent sure that his kids felt the same way. Or whether the man had ever tried to make amends and establish any kind of relationship with them now that they were all adults.

Evan's eyes turned hard inside a heavy scowl. "Haven't seen his sorry ass in probably fifteen years."

"Ah. Things haven't changed, then."

"Doubt they ever will. Can't rewrite history, you know. The guy was a sperm donor. He never was, and never will be a dad."

"Oh, Evan."

"Uh-uh. No pity. His leaving was the best thing for my mom and us kids. Mom was a lot better when he wasn't around."

"Your mom is great," Sara said.

"Wasn't easy, and I'm not saying being a single parent is ideal. But doing it by yourself is way better than having someone around who just makes things harder."

His words sent a jolt through Sara's system. She wanted to laugh. Or cry. Or throw her arms around Evan

174

for supporting her without even knowing it. She nudged his arm, and forced a smile to keep her lips from trembling. "I think she did a pretty good job."

He shot her that boyish smile – the one that made her heart slam against her ribs.

"Thanks."

Sara blew out her breath. "Guess not everyone is meant to be a parent."

"For sure. Any idiot can make a baby, but that doesn't make him a parent."

Sara nodded, and as casually as she could, asked the question that was now top of mind. "So has he ruined the whole parenting thing for you, or do you think you want kids some day?"

"Sure. I'd like to have a couple of my own. And the chance to do it right."

"I'm sure you will. And you'll be a great dad," Sara said softly. That he had a perfect example of what not to do would only make him more determined.

"I used to envy you and Ben for having complete families with dads who seemed to be interested in your lives."

A lump formed in Sara's throat. While Evan's voice didn't show any envy or bitterness, she saw a trace of sadness flicker across his face. "I'm sorry. I shouldn't have said anything about your dad."

His face immediately cleared, and he spread his hands in the air. "Nah. It's fine. That's just the way it was for us." He shot her a smile. "We adjusted and moved on. No therapy."

"Glad to hear it," Sara told him.

"Besides, we had Poppa."

"That's right. How's he doing?" Sara asked. "He was always so much fun. I remember diving for his loose change. Jeez, we were so excited about scoring a quarter." Evan's grandpa used to ask them trivia questions, such as who was the president of the United States, or who was the first man on the moon. After someone answered, or he gave the answer, he'd empty the change in his pocket and toss it up in the air, then they'd all scramble for it.

"He's pretty good. Mom had a ramp built into the porch at the new place so it's easy to get a wheelchair inside. He can't live there, but should be able to visit."

As they talked, it occurred to Sara that Evan was up to date on everything happening in Whitfield, and with his mother. "You're close to your mom, aren't you?"

Evan straightened, and sent her a thoughtful look. "I am. I admire her. She's been through a lot and has always kept it together. She's the strongest person I know."

Sara couldn't help but smile. It was cool, and somehow endearing, that he wasn't too macho to admit that he had a close relationship with his mom. She shifted, and reluctantly finished the last swallow of tepid liquid in her cup. An hour and a half had passed quickly. "Any ideas on what to do tomorrow?"

"Going on memory here. Not too early?"

She gave him her best wide-eyed innocent look. "I do manage to get up and get myself to work on time on a regular basis."

"Sure. But it's the weekend."

"How does nine o'clock sound?"

"Guess that depends on what we're doing. Breakfast?"

Ah, he was speaking her language. "Sure. That's a good place to start."

"I figure we can eat our way through the day. Fit everything else around that."

She tossed her empty cup in the wastebasket, and slipped past Evan when he opened the door. Tomorrow promised to be interesting.

**

Saturday dawned gray and cloudy. Though Sara preferred sunshine and warmer weather, she thanked the skies for a cool day that allowed her to add an extra concealing layer. The navy blue vest had become one of her most important articles of clothing. Not too heavy, she could easily pull it over her long, yellow blouse and casual denim leggings.

176

Evan picked her up, and they started the day at a café known for its omelets and pastries. Sara had no trouble finishing both, but resisted a vanilla pinwheel to go. Sharing sections of the newspaper, they talked about everything from the day's headlines to the upcoming holiday movie releases and current best-selling books, lingering long after the waitress brought their check – and stopped refilling their drinks.

"I think the waitress is ignoring us now," Sara said, picking up the paper ticket the woman had left on the table at least forty-five minutes ago. "We should probably give her a double tip for taking up the table for so long."

"Good idea," Evan said, pulling the check from Sara's hand. "I'll take care of it."

Shaking her head, Sara reached for her purse. "No, Evan. That's not necessary. In fact, I'm getting this. You're my guest." After all, he was paying for gas and hotel.

"You know, it'd save a lot of time if you'd just agree with me."

His teasing tone matched the smile on his face.

Sara laughed. "I'm sure it would, but I wouldn't get my hopes up if I were you."

His grin widened as he leaned toward her. "Rock, paper, scissors? Coin toss? Arm wrestling? You know I'll win."

She grabbed his arm, and squeezed. It was true. He always did. No matter how they'd agreed to settle squabbles or reach consensus as kids, Evan somehow managed to come out on top.

"Besides," he said. "I'd be a total schmuck to let a lady with your current employment status pick up the tab."

"Oh, thanks. You had to bring that up." Conceding defeat, she let him place his credit card on the table. "Now that we're stuffed, what do you think about finding a park and taking a walk?"

"An excellent idea," he said. "Got one in mind?"

"I do. I haven't ventured too far from Morgan's place, but she mentioned one a few miles away that's supposed to be nice."

"I've got a Frisbee in my car."

"You do?" She hadn't thrown a Frisbee since college, but the suggestion brought back all kinds of memories. When they were in high school, going to the small lake just outside of Whitfield on weekends and tossing a Frisbee was one of their favorite things to do. "Remember playing at Crawford Lake?"

"Sure. I wonder how many Frisbees are lining the bottom of that place. I know it's got a few of mine."

"Oh, my gosh, Evan, I remember when we lost Ben's brand new glow-in-the-dark. He was so mad."

"Yeah, because he was screwing around and showing off, and he'd had it for less than twenty-four hours. Was his own fault."

Sara gave a chuckle, remembering the incident that had sent them all into the cold water – and Ben into a bad mood. "But he wanted you to pay for losing it. Did you?"

"No way."

She eyed him suspiciously. "And you just happen to have a Frisbee in your car now? Does that mean you play a lot? Frisbee semi-pro, disc golf expert? Anything like that I need to know about?"

"I think you just said you don't trust me."

A giggled escaped Sara's lips. "You catch on fast."

"I'm deeply offended," he said, amusement – and challenge – in his voice and eyes.

Keeping a lighthearted tone, she returned the challenge. "Prove me wrong."

Driving through the park, they found a wide expanse of open grass adjacent to a play area, but not so close that they'd put small children in danger. Sara admitted to being a little rusty.

As they moved apart, she hollered at Evan. "Not too far. Let's start nice and easy."

He took a few steps closer and tossed the Frisbee from only about six feet away. "How's that?"

"Okay, wise guy. Go!"

Instead of throwing the disc to him, she wound up and released it into the sky beyond him in a straight, solid glide. Evan took off at a run, snatching the disc from the air seconds before he tumbled to the ground. He bounced up with the Frisbee still in hand.

Laughing, Sara clapped. "Nice moves," she shouted.

The disc came gliding smoothly back to her. Sometimes she caught it. Other times, it bounced off of her hand, or she miscalculated the speed or trajectory. Didn't matter. She was having fun. Again, and again, she tossed the Frisbee back and enjoyed the view as Evan ran, jumped and dove for the thing.

When he stumbled, then caught the Frisbee between his legs and turned around and threw it back to her in one fluid movement, she was laughing too hard to even try to catch it.

He retrieved it himself and jogged toward her. "Ready for a break?" he asked, catching up to her. He rested his arm across her shoulders as if it were the most natural thing in the world.

"Sure." Sara sank onto the bench only a couple of feet away, and immediately missed the warmth of Evan's arm.

"I've got a blanket in the car if you want to stretch out."

"Are you kidding me? I think I want to explore your car. Is there anything you don't have in there?"

"I like to be prepared. Be right back."

He returned with a gold and dirt-brown plaid comforter.

Sara couldn't help but laugh as he unfolded it, not entirely sure the blanket was an improvement over the bare grass. "Oh, my gosh, Evan. How old is that thing, and where did it come from?"

His grin told her he was aware the blanket would never pass for fashionable home décor.

"You won't believe it. Mom got this in a bunch of stuff donated for tornado victims last year."

Sara's mouth dropped open. "No. Way. That's hideous."

He turned it over to the solid brown backing. "Don't worry. Mom washed it. I think it's found its calling, don't you?"

"Saved from the dumpster, clearly." Still chuckling, she stretched out on her back.

"That was fun," she said. More fun than going to the gym. More fun than she'd ever had with– she stopped herself. She didn't want to think about him, especially in the presence of Evan. But her brain wouldn't let it go. Memories churned inside. Truth was, she and Todd had done a lot of things together, but looking back, it seemed like their relationship revolved around the things – the parties, the concerts, the movies. She couldn't remember ever having silly, spontaneous fun just enjoying each other's company.

Sara swallowed hard, conscious of Evan's solid body stretched out next to her. Not touching, but close enough if she wanted to. If he wanted to . . . she jumped when he nudged her arm. A guilty flush warmed her face, and she willed herself not to turn all shades of pink.

"Check that out," Evan said, pointing toward the children's play area. "We never had equipment like that."

Reining in her thoughts, she propped herself on her elbows, and glanced at the playground area with its brightly colored tunnels, slides and monkey bars. Definitely more elaborate than anything they'd had at Whitfield Elementary. "Oh, poor baby," she crooned.

"Man, look at that climbing wall. How cool is that?"

"Way cool."

"I seriously might have to give that a try."

"You are such a kid."

"That must be why I always seem to get put in charge of kid stuff on family days at the bank."

Sara turned to face Evan. "Family days? What does that mean?"

"Means we're family friendly."

When she gave him a "try again" look, he elaborated. "Part of our marketing plan."

She perked up. "Oh, yeah?"

"The idea is to get parents to come in and start thinking about IRAs and college saving options. And we want to get kids set up on savings accounts. So far, it's working pretty well."

180

Sara laughed. "Wow. And here I thought you were just a banker, crunching numbers and making loans. You're really a marketing master. I should be taking lessons from you."

A lazy grin spread across Evan's face. "Well, when you get fed up with all the people and traffic in Dallas let me know, and I'll get you an interview in our marketing department. Tulsa would be happy to have you."

She sucked in her breath. Was that an actual offer? A hint?

"Some of the stuff we do is pretty cool," Evan continued. "Like the money machine."

"And what is the money machine?" She was trying to keep up, but her thoughts were back on Tulsa. She didn't know much about the city. But she knew it'd be hard to keep up a long-distance relationship. A four-hour drive would get old fast. She certainly wouldn't be doing that as a single pregnant woman or a single woman with a newborn. Their timing could have been better. Then again, once Evan learned she was having a baby, it might be a moot point.

"It's this glass box, kind of like an old phone booth. We stock it with money, mostly ones, of course. Then, when we flip the switch, air blows the money all around inside. A kid has about ten seconds to catch as much money as they can. It's harder than you think, but it's a ton of fun."

"Huh. I've never heard of that. I remember we used to want to go to the bank with Mom just to get a sucker."

Evan gave a snort. "If I had to guess, I'd say things haven't changed much there. Sometimes I think it'd be interesting to go back and shake things up a little. Move Whitfield ahead a couple of decades."

"To go back to Whitfield? Live there?"

He shot her a well-duh look. "I suppose if I went to work for the bank I'd want to live there."

"But would you really want to? It sounds so claustrophobic. Everybody in everyone else's business all the time. And nothing to do. Wouldn't you get bored?" Whoa. She'd just moved from Kansas City to Dallas. A minute ago she was contemplating what life in Tulsa might be like, and now Evan was talking about living in Whitfield? Talk about a culture shock.

"Maybe. I'm anxious to see how the recovery goes. So far, it seems like things are back up and running. People rebuilt. Nicer houses. A couple of new businesses have opened. It's got some growth potential. I've always liked Whitfield. It was a good place to grow up, don't you think?"

Sara's head was spinning with all the revelations she wanted to think about. She'd have to tuck them aside to ponder later. "I suppose," she said. She'd always considered Whitfield a kind of safety net. Liked that it never changed. It gave her a sense of security to go back and find that people and places were familiar. But to move back and live there as an adult? She wasn't seeing the potential. Not in her line of work, anyway.

"I don't know many people there anymore," she told him.

"Probably more than you realize."

While Evan filled her in on a few people from high school days and what he knew of life in Whitfield, the sun made an appearance directly overhead, peeking from behind the clouds that were finally breaking up.

"Hey," Evan said. "Looks like it might be about time for our next meal."

He'd get no argument from her. "How's Mexican sound?"

"Lead the way."

A couple of tacos and a "bottomless" basket of chips later, they wandered through an up-and-coming arts area not far from downtown. It was busy, but not crowded, with an eclectic array of people moving in and out of the shops, listening to musicians on the sidewalks, and hanging out on restaurant patios. Sara had been there only once with Morgan and some other friends, but so far, it was one of her favorite places in Dallas. Laid-back, casual. They stopped and watched for several minutes while an artist created a city skyline mural on the side of a building.

"Guess what's ahead in the next block," Sara said as they left the artist to his work.

"I am seriously hoping you're talking ice cream."

Her grin was automatic. Could the guy read her mind? "Nailed it. Let's go."

They picked up their leisurely pace, and moments later stood before a long counter, facing a difficult decision.

Sara requested Snicker's ice cream with caramel sauce in a waffle cup.

"Well done," Evan told her, eyeing her choice.

She burst out laughing when he asked for chocolate Oreo with gummy bears. "What are you, three?"

"Hey, now. Judge much?"

She handed him a napkin. "You just enjoy that."

"Yes, ma'am. I plan to."

They found a small table outside, and settled in.

"You know what I haven't had in a while?" Evan asked.

A number of things crossed Sara's brain in an instant, and she nearly choked. She couldn't keep her mind from going exactly where it shouldn't, and wondered when he'd last had a girlfriend or dated someone.

"No, what?" she managed to ask, hoping she hadn't turned beet red.

"A Fudgsicle."

"A Fudgsicle? Oh, man. Me either."

"You ask me about summer in Whitfield, and that's what comes to mind. Your mom handing out Fudgsicles on the front porch or around the pool." Evan laughed at the memory. "Those were good times. I used to love going to your house."

"And Mom was quick to bribe everyone with treats to make our house the place to be. Believe me, it was a fierce competition between her and Claire."

"Really? Guess I didn't pick up on that."

"No. You'd have to hear them still razzing each other about it now."

"Convenient that they lived next door. Seemed to me that we all took over both places."

"Yeah," Sara agreed, a bit of wistfulness in her voice. "We all kind of blended together, didn't we?" Things changed when they moved to the new house during high school. It'd been a hard decision for her mother, Sara recalled.

When she looked up, Evan's deep blue eyes locked onto hers.

"Good times," he said softly.

Her throat clogged. True. Good times then. And now. The world had changed. The two of them had changed. But somehow, they still clicked.

**

It was closing in on one a.m. when Sara began to feel the length of the day. When she attempted to cover a yawn, Evan took her hand and pulled her up from the sofa. "Looks like you're on your way out, so I should be, too."

Sara was torn. Her eyes were drooping, but she hated to let him go, knowing that tomorrow he'd head home. Just the thought of Sunday made her sad. Weekends were so short. Long emails and phone conversations were a poor substitute for the real thing. Their carefree day had confirmed one thing – she wouldn't mind spending more time with Evan. Reluctantly, she followed him to the door and onto the small stoop outside.

Leaning against the door, she offered a soft smile. "I had a fun time today," she told him. The day had left her feeling melancholy and content. She hadn't realized before how growing up together had created such a strong bond between them. The shared background and values created a sense of comfortable intimacy.

"Me, too. I think I'll come back tomorrow."

Her smile widened. "You'd better."

"I'd better let you get some sleep."

"Yeah. I'll see you in the morning. We can figure out a plan." Though they were saying goodbye neither of them actually moved.

"I've been thinking about something," Evan said.

Sara raised her brows. "Something you want to do?"

"Yeah."

"What is it?"

"This." His gazed lowered, and in one smooth motion, he slid a hand to the small of her back as his lips met hers.

The assault on her senses was immediate. Blood pounded in her ears as fire swept through her. She twined her arms around his neck, and he tightened his grip, pressing her closer.

In a flash, she knew the answer to Morgan's earlier question, and it rocked her world like an earthquake.

## Chapter Fifteen

"I'm not going." Mary avoided Grant's eyes. She'd already made up her mind, and didn't want to debate it.

"You're not going to the council meeting?"

The censure she detected in Grant's tone irked her. It wasn't as if that's what she wanted. She didn't enjoy reneging on commitments. He knew that.

"Right."

"Why not?"

She pushed the hair back from her face and shot him an impatient glance. "Love, really. Isn't it obvious? The cane. My wrist. It's just . . . it's too much."

Grant sat down across from her, and rubbed a hand over his chin. "Too much what?"

"Too much to explain," she said, her voice rising. "Can't you imagine all the questions? People will want to know what happened, what's wrong." Her lips trembled, as tears welled in her eyes, making her all the more agitated. She wasn't a crier. And not a whiner. She didn't want to stay at home and sulk, but the thought of fielding all the questions, being under scrutiny, made her head pound. "How the hell can I tell people what's going on when I don't even know?"

She'd already had a taste of it in the days since she broke her wrist. The phone rang almost non-stop. She appreciated the outpouring of concern and good wishes. In fact, the stream of flowers and cards cheered her immensely, and helped her get past the disappointment that had still been gnawing at her over the failure of the career workshop. But she'd grown weary of laughing off the fall as a clumsy mishap. As her appointment loomed, it rang more and more false to her ears.

Grant rose from the chair and stepped behind her, his hands lightly kneading her shoulders. "I'm just surprised. Thought you planned the appointments in Kansas City around this meeting."

Mary let her head fall forward. She had. She'd planned to go to the meeting. But she hadn't expected to be so tired. Thanksgiving with Dana and Kent had been low-key and fun, but it still took energy to be social. It was ridiculous how much mental energy it had taken to simply play a game of gin rummy. And the trip to Kansas City, the hospital visit and MRI had worn her out – and shaken her more than she cared to admit. All those nurses and technicians wore a kind of soft, sympathetic smile like a uniform. They knew something was wrong with her or she wouldn't have been there. It was possible they'd seen something in the images, that they already had information about her illness that she didn't. That in itself annoyed her.

And then a nurse had called to schedule another test – a lumbar puncture, or spinal tap. With little to no explanation other than the doctor had ordered it. That was to happen Thursday morning, before she saw the doctor – before she knew the results of the MRI. As far as she could tell from her online research, the spinal tap was fairly common in this situation, and would confirm whether or not she had MS. That was not reassuring.

It'd be a lot easier to put it out of her mind if she could go about her usual routine. But she could hardly even take a shower by herself. With the cane, the cast, and a cart, going to the grocery store would become a juggling act. The irony of it was that she could hardly do anything except talk – the one thing she didn't want to do. Funny how curling up with a good book or in front of the TV sounded good until those were your only choices. She felt trapped, unable to be herself.

And now she faced another trip to Kansas City. More tests. More waiting. More wondering. If she could just get

187

some concrete information, she could get her head around it, and get a plan of action. She needed some answers.

**

Just when Mary was about to lose patience, Dr. Gray entered the small office-like room without apology or explanation for the wait. A tall, thin man with glasses and a full head of coarse salt-and-pepper hair, he was the quintessential neurologist. Looked to her as though they'd both acquired a few more gray hairs since they'd met the previous week to go over her symptoms and discuss the MRI.

"Morning, folks. Good to see you." He extended his hand first to Mary and then Grant.

He tapped the keyboard of the computer on the small desk beside him, then looked at Mary. She appreciated that he looked her squarely in the eye, made her feel that whatever he had to say was the honest truth. She didn't want sugar coating or coddling.

"We've got the MRI results here."

Colorful pictures of Mary's brain sprang to life on the computer screen. She stared at the images. Her brain. In vivid color. Bizarre.

Dr. Gray leaned forward. "The reason I ordered the lumbar procedure is that the MRI doesn't show the kind of lesions that would typically be consistent with a diagnosis of Multiple Sclerosis."

Mary nodded, and glanced at Grant. He linked his fingers with hers, and gave a gentle squeeze.

The doctor pointed to various areas on the images, explaining what the different colors represented, and where the lesions would have shown up. Then he tapped the keyboard, and a different image popped up. A chart of some sort.

"These are the preliminary results of the lumbar puncture," the doctor continued. "We'll have a more detailed analysis by the end of the week, but so far, they also don't show the proteins we'd expect to see in a patient with MS. Therefore, at this time I think we should rule out

MS as a diagnosis. We can revisit later if necessary. These things don't always show up right away."

That sounded like good news to Mary, but the doctor's tone didn't seem encouraging. She raised her brows, needing more. "Isn't that good?" she asked.

"I can't say for sure. We need to explore further. We can back up and send you to a rheumatologist, though that doesn't seem right to me. And you don't seem to have the tender points typical of fibromyalgia. From what you describe, we're seeing a neurological situation, not a muscle or joint problem." He paused, and looked at Grant for a moment, then back to Mary. "I'm sorry, but I think we're going to have to consider ALS as a possibility. Loss of function in limbs is a key component."

Mary gasped, and Grant squeezed her hand again. ALS had certainly come up in her online research, but she'd avoided in-depth reading. Didn't want to go there. Still, she'd read enough to know it was bad. Probably worst-case scenario. The disease had no cure. It was degenerative. Your muscles basically wasted away until you couldn't eat or breathe any more.

"I don't mean to scare you," Dr. Gray continued. "But I want to be honest. You may know it as Lou Gehrig's disease. The medical term is amyotrophic lateral sclerosis."

Nodding, Mary swallowed hard, and kept her eyes fixed on the doctor. Could not look at Grant. Before she could respond, Grant spoke up, his voice strained but calm.

"What's the next step? How can we know for sure?"

The doctor rubbed the back of his neck. "I have to tell you, it's tough. There isn't a definitive test for ALS. It's something we watch, see if the symptoms progress. At this point, it's mostly a process of elimination. The next test we need is an EMG."

The doctor's voice was foggy, distant, and Mary fought to comprehend his words. This alphabet soup was getting tedious. "What– What does it do?" she managed. She pressed her lips together hard, forcing herself to breathe.

"It's an important part of the diagnostic procedure. Unfortunately, this one isn't as comfortable as the MRI. Small electric shocks are sent through the nerves to measure how fast they conduct electricity and to find out whether there is any nerve damage. The shocks tend to feel like the kind you get from static electricity, maybe a little stronger. That will tell us if you have any "nerve block," and whether the nerves that communicate sensation are affected, which could indicate a disease other than ALS."

"Okaaay," she said. Sounded like no fun at all. But if it could prove she didn't have ALS, she was all for it.

"The second part of the EMG tests the electrical activity of selected muscles. This is done by inserting a fine needle into your muscles and using it to "listen" to the pattern of electrical activity in the muscles. If we find that your motor nerves aren't functioning, but the sensory nerves are normal, it's generally a sign of ALS."

"Can you do it now?" Grant asked.

The doctor looked as his watch. "I doubt it, but let me get one of the nurses to call over to the hospital and see. Is tomorrow a possibility? Or, we can wait and schedule it for when we have the rest of the lumbar results, and go over everything at once."

Mary wet her lips. If they could avoid another trip to Kansas City this week, she'd prefer that. But what would they do in Kansas City all day? They'd already seen the Plaza lights, and she didn't have the stamina for shopping. She let out a heavy sigh. The waiting around was the worst.

"Do we necessarily need to be here to get the results?" Mary asked. "Would a phone conversation work?"

"We could try that," Dr. Gray agreed. "Let me see what I can do."

As soon as the doctor left the room, Grant put an arm around Mary's shoulder. His other hand rested gently against her cheek. "You all right?"

She attempted a smile, though the concern in his eyes tugged at her heart. She refused to feed the fear. "Yeah, except for this tornado spinning in my head, I'm great."

Grant pulled her closer. "Don't worry. We're going to figure this out."

Dr. Gray returned. "Jenna will let us know about the schedule in a few minutes. Now, what questions do you have for me?"

"What do we do in the meantime?" Grant asked. "Until we know for sure what we're dealing with, is there anything you can start her on to make her feel better?"

Blowing out a deep breath, Dr. Gray turned to Mary. "I see you're using a cane. That's good." He frowned, looking down at her feet. "You might want some sturdier shoes. Something with a little more support."

Mary also stared at her feet, covered by her cute and comfortable red slip-ons. What did he expect? Clunky tennis shoes or hideous orthopedics like the women in the nursing home wore? She'd never understood that. If a woman was just sitting in a wheelchair all day, why couldn't she still wear cute shoes?

"Here's the biggest problem right now," the doctor said.

Mary's head snapped up, her attention back on target.

"Without a diagnosis, I can't treat. I've got to code for a specific situation and treat for that, or chances are your insurance won't pay for it. We're walking a fine line."

He went back to her chart. "We clearly have fatigue and numbness. But you've not had slurred speech? Any difficulty swallowing?"

Mary shook her head, though she felt as if she'd choke simply talking at the moment.

"We've still got a lot of ground to explore. Even if turns out to be ALS, we won't know right away. We'll need to monitor your motor skills, re-test periodically, and track any new symptoms. I'm going to be as vague as I can on the charts. We'll call it an autoimmune disorder and at least get you started on some meds to help you sleep and manage muscle spasms. Also, you should feel free to visit your primary care physician again, and get a second opinion, perhaps see a neuromuscular doctor. If we get any more confirmation that ALS is likely, I would recommend an evaluation at Mayo Clinic."

Mayo Clinic? That was– Mary's head spun with the implications. More tests, more doctors, and medication. This wasn't going to consume their lives for a little while. It was going to consume their lives. Period. Possibly the rest of her life. *Stop, stop, stop,* she told herself. She drew in a deep breath, vowing that she would not panic. Whatever it was, she'd give it her best kick in the ass.

"And, of course," the doctor continued, "physical therapy is going to be very important to strengthen and monitor your muscles and motor skills."

"What about driving?" Mary asked.

"As long as you feel you have the control and reflexes to drive, it's fine for now. But, obviously, the more you can limit it, the better. If your muscle control in your leg worsens over time, you may want to consider a car with hand controls, but I think we're a long way from that."

A nurse interrupted, handing Dr. Gray a note. He nodded, and smiled at Mary. "How about tomorrow at ten-thirty for the EMG?"

"That's fine."

"All right. I'm sending a report, and a recommendation for physical therapy to your primary care doctor. Work with her to get something set up at a facility near you. I know it's a lot to take in, and you may be feeling overwhelmed. Feel free to call with questions. If you see another doctor, please make sure I'm copied on all results so that we can work together for the best possible diagnosis and treatment."

"Yes. Of course," Mary murmured.

When Dr. Gray stood, so did Grant, and Mary followed his lead. Apparently that was it.

"Jenna will be in with some literature and directions for your procedure tomorrow. And a couple of scripts. Let's see if we can increase your energy level."

That would be something at least. She had so much to think about, so much to process and learn. But all she wanted to do was curl into a ball and go to sleep.

\*\*

On Monday morning Mary crawled out of bed and braced herself for a new form of torture – physical therapy. The current plan called for three days – two at the community center in Whitfield, and one day at the hospital in Paxton. She'd be lucky to even make it there. Her back still ached from the lumbar puncture and she had bruises from the poking, prodding and needle sticks. Barely moving, how could she possibly do an exercise?

She had new empathy for people dealing with chronic illness. With a hand to her chest, Mary leaned against the dresser. It still sent shock waves through her to think that she might be joining those ranks. Could that really be her future? Constant therapy, doctor's appointments, treatments, and medications just to get through the day?

Or worse. What if her number of days was reduced? Or she lost her mobility and independence. What if–

Mary didn't indulge in self-pity, but she couldn't help the quiet tears that rolled down her cheek when a horrible thought slammed into her brain. What if she didn't get to see her grandchild grow up? She expected to hear final results of the lumbar puncture and EMG in the next day or two. Swiping at her eyes, she had to admit that phone call scared her. If the news was bad, there would be no more denial. She'd have to face a new reality.

It took about thirty minutes longer than usual to shower and get herself put together these days. Sometimes closer to an hour. Today she left herself plenty of time to get out the door and to the community center.

In Whitfield, the strengthening class was a joint project between the clinic and the senior center. *Mary and the senior society*, she grumbled under her breath as she smiled politely at the other attendees, and took her place against the wall. In the sea of white, gray and blue-tinted heads, Mary was the lone brunette.

She did as many of the routines and stretches as she could, but the cast was definitely a handicap. Star of the class she was not. "Don't worry," the instructor told her. "There's no prize for completing the exercises. Just do what you can."

193

Most of the stretches she could manage as long as she was on the floor, but the equipment kicked her butt. Gratefully, she hung onto the bar along the wall when her legs began to tremble. Sweating, she rested while the others moved to weights.

By Friday, she figured if her condition didn't kill her, physical therapy would.

Still lacking a definitive diagnosis, she'd taken to calling her illness a "condition," though disorder seemed more appropriate, considering the havoc it was wreaking in her life.

She'd managed to get herself to the classes in Whitfield, but Grant was acting chauffeur for the trip to Paxton. For this session, she'd be working one-on-one with a physical therapist. One look at Jeremy, and she considered running for the door. Never mind that she couldn't run if her life depended on it. Jeremy was a bear of a man – thick and solid with strong hands that she was sure could snap a bone in half.

Turned out those hands could also hold her up, and massage deep into her muscles. One hour, and she was smitten. She thanked him profusely as he helped her into the car.

"You take care, Miz Mary, and I'll see you next week."

Mary lifted her hand with a final wave, and sank into the seat, smiling at Grant. "Wow. I feel drugged." Her entire body tingled. Of course she knew the workover meant she might not be able to move tomorrow.

"Think you can come out of your high for lunch and Christmas tree shopping?"

She wasn't entirely sure, but that was the plan. "You might have to drag me."

"As you wish."

Mary snorted a laugh. "Let's hit the little diner downtown." It was usually a quick in and out.

After lunch, they stopped at the 4-H lot on the outskirts of town.

Grant turned to Mary. "Why don't you sit tight, and I'll surprise you?"

194

Her mouth dropped open. "Surprise me? I don't think so."

"You know, I've done this a time or two. I'm pretty confident I could pick out one you'll like."

"No. I'm okay. Besides, I've seen the kind of tree you like, Charlie Brown."

"How about I pick out a couple and bring them over for your decision?"

It was a sweet offer, but her confidence was not high. "Grant, I want to do this." Sheer willpower forced her upright. Choosing a tree was one of her favorite Christmas traditions, and she was determined to participate.

"Not too tall," Mary reminded him as they slowly meandered the fragrant rows of pines and firs. "No one's getting on a ladder." Dana and Claire were coming to help decorate the tree. One of them could probably be persuaded to use a step stool if necessary. Claire had offered to help with the decorating, and they decided to invite Dana as well. It would be the first holiday gathering of the season, and Mary could hardly wait to get the party started. She'd missed the mayor's tree lighting, and she hadn't seen Claire since Annie's wedding. Time for some holiday cheer.

"You can leave the star for me," Grant told her.

"Will do. I hate for you to miss out on the whole decorating thing." Her voice dripped with sarcasm. With the kids out of the house, she practically had to hold a gun to Grant's head to get him to help trim the tree.

"I'm hurting, let me tell you."

Mary stopped, and pointed to a Fraser Fir with a perfect cone shape and full from base to top. "Want to stand next to this one?" Grant stepped into place, and Mary evaluated the tree with a critical eye. Hmmm. About even with Grant's six-foot frame – and at least a foot shorter than what they usually chose. Wouldn't be as dramatic, but it seemed manageable.

"Let's take this one," Mary said.

"Looks good to me," Grant said. "What time is Claire coming?"

"I told her not before five o'clock. I'm going to need to work in a nap this afternoon."

"I'll bring up the boxes while you do that."

Mary's throat tightened, and she sent him a soft smile. "Thanks, love." She couldn't help but note that his response was proof how much her condition had changed things. At one time, an announcement that she was going to bed in the middle of the afternoon would have prompted a teasing gleam in his eyes – at the least. And sadly, by the time she actually got there, sleep would be the only thing on her mind. Already the afternoon fog was settling in her brain. It was that, more than anything, that had Mary agreeing with the doctor's assessment of a neurological problem. How could the fog that overcame her be muscular?

She gestured around the lot. "And could you ask them to gather up a couple of armloads of loose branches, too?" Those would go on the front porch. She'd have to skip the pinecones this year, unless she found some in last year's boxes.

Mary retreated to the car and let Grant and the strapping 4-H helpers take care of the details. At home, she helped Grant wrestle the tree into the stand as best she could, then crawled into bed. Two hours should do it. Then she'd start the pot of potato soup she'd promised her guests for supper.

**\*\***

When she heard a car on the drive, Mary glanced at her watch, and smiled. About a minute after five o'clock. Blowing out her breath, Mary picked up the cane, and met Claire at the door. Might as well get this part out of the way so they could move on to the fun.

A wide grin covered Claire's face, and she waved all the way up the walk. On the top stair, she stepped back with an obvious look at the leopard print cane. With a hand on her hip, Claire shook her head. "You always have the best accessories."

Laughing, she drew Mary into her arms. They clung to each other for a long moment, until Mary's bare hand became cold on the hard handle of the cane.

"Inside," she said. Mary let Claire hold the door while she stepped up to the entryway.

Claire took off her coat and hung it in the closet, then walked back to Mary. "On second thought, my dear, you may be a little over-accessorized." She grazed a hand over the cast. "When do we get rid of this lovely arm candy?"

Mary sank into a chair. "Not soon enough. Looks like first week of January."

"Good. How'd therapy go?"

"Ah, well, Jeremy was incredible today. He has good hands."

Claire raised her brows. "That's a good start. So you don't mind him touching you. Can you stand to look at him?"

Mary chuckled. "He's a large forty-something-year-old man with a nice smile. Not exactly sexy, but not too hard on the eyes, either."

"That's something, at least."

"Strengthening class at the community center is a different story, however."

"I'm sure."

"I bring the average age down a couple of decades, and I'm no spring chicken."

"Do you think it's helping?"

"Oh, not yet. Especially with this cast. I can't do all the moves. But, hey, they assure me it doesn't matter because there's no prize."

"Well, why not?"

"That's what I want to know. What the hell? For that much effort, I want a prize."

"I should think so. Hey, I'm going to help myself to a drink."

"Sure. You want hot or cold?"

"How about I put on some coffee?"

"Be my guest."

"The wind sure picked up right before I breezed into town," Claire said from the kitchen. "I think the temps are supposed to drop tonight."

"I know. We might get a little snow. Nothing major, though."

Claire shrugged. "I could think of worse places to be stranded. When did Grant leave?"

"About thirty minutes before you got here. I'm so glad this worked for you, or I'm sure he would've cancelled." Grant and a couple of buddies had tickets to a car show and a Kansas City Chiefs game, and planned to eat as much barbecue as possible in a two-day period. Mary figured it was good timing – Grant needed time to decompress, a break from worrying about her, and she loved having time with her friends.

Mary and Claire fell into easy conversation, catching up on all the kids, as usual. They visited for about an hour before the doorbell rang and the door opened.

"Helloooo," Dana hollered.

"Come on in," Mary said. "Go ahead and lock the door behind you."

Dana shed her gloves, then rubbed her hands together. "It's freezing out there."

"Toasty in here," Claire said, standing to hug Dana.

"Don't get up," Dana told Mary, squeezing her shoulder. "How are you doing?"

"Hanging in there," Mary said, aware it was an answer that said nothing really. "You have no idea how much Grant praises you two for doing this. The man simply does not comprehend the finer details of holiday décor."

"Shocking," Claire said, laughter in her voice.

"Hey, let's get drinks and munchies before we start working," Mary said. They all gravitated toward the kitchen, and Mary put extra effort into walking as smoothly as possible.

"Work? Are you kidding? This is fun," Dana told her. "I just did that scrawny table-top tree last year, remember? And this year, a big tree would be in the way, so I'll have to wait until next year for a nice one."

"She needs a Christmas tree fix," Claire said.

"What about a beverage fix? I've got flavored waters, tea, and hot cider."

"The cider smells amazing," Claire said, reaching for mugs. "Dana?"

"I agree."

"Make it three," Mary told her. "And I've got sliced oranges in the fridge."

Claire placed three mugs on the bamboo tray on Mary's counter, filled them, and headed back to the family room. "Starting to smell a lot like Christmas in here," she said.

"Come on," Dana said. "It's about to look like Christmas, too."

With the three of them spaced around the tree, they began winding yards and yards of tiny white lights into the branches.

"When are the kids arriving?" Dana asked.

"Oh, they're all coming about the same time this year. I thought Sara might come a few days early, but it looks like they're getting in Friday. Sara's driving, but Grant's picking Jason up at the airport in Kansas City. I wanted him to fly to Dallas and drive in with Sara, but they couldn't get the times to work out." Normally, as traffic coordinator, Mary would've jumped in and figured out the flights and schedules herself, but she'd left it to the kids. And it didn't happen.

"What about Evan and Maddie?" Mary asked, trying to steer away from negative thoughts.

"Everybody in on Saturday. I keep wondering if Evan might announce that he's bringing a guest. I get the feeling he's dating someone, but he hasn't mentioned it."

Brows arched, Mary peeked around the tree, and met Dana's eyes. "That's interesting. Isn't he the one who usually shares?"

"Exactly. But lately, I ask a simple question like 'what'd you do this weekend?' and get a really vague response. Then he changes the subject. Makes me wonder."

"Hmm. You'll have to keep us posted," Mary said. "It's your turn for a wedding, you know."

Dana grinned. "Ahem. Perhaps you've forgotten. It is *my* turn for a wedding."

Laughing, Mary smacked her palm against her forehead. "Oh, good grief, maybe I should be tested for Alzheimer's. Tell us about Hawaii. Is everything all set?"

"I think so. Flights are scheduled two days before the wedding in case of any weather issues. You won't believe what I did. *I* don't believe it."

The excitement in Dana's voice was obvious, and Mary stared at her friend. "I'm dying here. What did you do?!"

"I bought all new clothes. Swim suit, sun dresses, shoes . . . everything. I can't wait to wear it all."

"Good for you," Mary said, handing her a spool of ribbon. "I can't wait to see the pictures." Splurging on herself was something Dana rarely had the opportunity to do. Until now, money had always been tight, and she'd always been afraid she'd run short for her kids, or her ex would somehow get his hands on what little she had.

"Sounds wonderful," Claire said. "But I'm still miffed about the tiny guest list." She nudged Mary, who, fortunately, had propped her bum knee on a footstool, and remained upright. "I don't see why we couldn't book flights that just happen to coincide . . ."

Mary sucked in her breath. She and Grant were supposed to go to Hawaii at the end of February before the spring break crowds hit. Could she go? The cast would be off by then, but if she felt the way she did in Phoenix, it would be a complete waste of time and money. Then again, a little "vitamin sea" might be therapeutic.

"I'm in," she said brightly, knowing there wasn't a chance. But it was a good segue into the topic she hadn't yet broached. "That'd be a great way to thaw out after I spend a few days in Minnesota in January. Doesn't that sound fun?"

"Minnesota?" Claire screeched. "In the winter? Why in the world—"

Dana's arm stopped, and the ribbon unfurled to the floor. The look of dismay on her face told Mary she knew what a trip to Minnesota meant.

200

"Oh, Mare. Are you going to Mayo?"

Claire turned wide, shocked eyes on her, and Mary felt like a deer caught in the headlights.

The look turned to accusation. Mary hadn't told Claire everything. And didn't intend to. What was the point of worrying everyone until they knew for sure what was going on? Claire was her dearest girlfriend. Had been for years. Yes, sharing the good and the bad was important. That's what friends were for. But Mary refused to burden her friend with too much information.

"You're going to Mayo Clinic?" Claire demanded. "Why?"

"Because they have a lot of experts all in one place, and the doctors here and in Kansas City can't seem to figure out what's wrong."

Claire turned to the tree, and placed an ornament on a branch, dusted her hands on her jeans, and reached for another. Mary knew Claire was processing, probably counting to ten to neutralize before she spoke again. She was good at that.

"So, they think it's something serious?"

Mary shook her head. "That's the problem. We just don't know. But it's possible. I mean, there's something wrong. I can't put my full weight on my leg. I'm dragging my foot. And I'm tired all the time. I feel like I've had the flu for a month, and it isn't getting better."

Claire stared. "Do you feel bad now?"

Mary attempted a smile. "I'm pacing myself. I'm achy, but I took some meds, and I should be able to stay awake for a couple more hours. But then, I swear, I will drop like a deflated balloon."

In a second, Claire was beside her, arms wrapped around her. "You are ridiculous," she said in a violent whisper. "*Arthritis?* Why didn't you tell me how bad it's gotten?"

She handed Mary the cane, and then took her other arm. "All right, you're taking a load off." She brandished the cane. "This is a multi-purpose tool. You point. We'll place. Enjoy while you can. You know how much I love to take orders."

She practically pushed Mary into the nearby chair, then lifted Mary's cider mug. "I'm going to freshen this up for you."

When Claire headed to the kitchen, Mary sensed Dana's eyes on her.

"Do you know what tests they're doing, or what they're looking for?" Dana asked, her voice quiet and tentative.

"Not sure what all they're planning to do. I've already had a complete alphabet of tests, and so far, nothing is conclusive."

"For what?"

"It's a process of elimination game."

Dana nodded, but didn't push for more. "Well, you're going to the right place. Best doctors anywhere. I'm glad you're going."

Claire returned, and set the mug on the side table.

"Hey," Mary said. "As long as you're doing my bidding, want to push play on the stereo? It's hooked to my iTunes, and I've got a Christmas playlist ready to start. We need some jolly."

"I'm on it."

Mary rested a few minutes before the toe-tapping music of Mannheim Steamroller compelled her to get moving. She pushed herself from the chair and picked up a box of ornaments, large sparkly gold balls. "Let's do these next," she said, handing one box to Claire, and another to Dana.

"Glitter?" Claire asked. "Oh, boy, these are going to make a mess. I hope Rita gets a hefty Christmas bonus."

"Glitter. Definitely," Mary said. "I love these." She placed one front and center. They made the whole tree sparkle. In the evenings, she and Grant would dim the lights in the house, light a fire, then curl up on the sofa, and watch all the ornaments twinkle and dance. One of the simple pleasures of Christmas.

They broke for soup and cornbread, then put the finishing touches on the tree.

"Girls, you get a gold star," Mary said. "It's absolutely gorgeous, and I couldn't have done it without you."

202

"Oh, Mare. It really is spectacular," Dana said. "Next year, I'm copying you."

"Next year, we'll help you," Mary said brightly. "It'll technically be your first Christmas together, married, that is." Mary said a quick prayer that next year would be a blissful new normal for Dana, and one of the best holidays ever for Mary – with the worrisome medical mystery behind them, and a new grandbaby to love and spoil.

Then Mary blinked, and the weekend was over. She and Claire, in their pajamas from morning until bedtime, hadn't left the house all day Saturday, and declined church in favor of a lazy morning on Sunday. That, of course, had lit up the phone this afternoon. Mary ignored the calls with a mixture of guilt and glee.

At two o'clock Claire dropped her suitcase near the front door. "Just need to get the sheets and towels I used out of the dryer. I'll get the bed made before I leave," she said.

Mary rolled her eyes. "Oh, please. Rita can do that."

"Uh, no. I'm not creating more work for Saint Rita. Have you seen the glitter on the floor?"

"I call that holiday cheer."

"Not sure she'd agree," Claire said, her boot heels clacking against the hardwood floors as she headed toward the laundry room.

Mary shook her head. That was the problem with someone who knew everything about your house down to the cupboard that stores your laundry detergent. Unfortunately, she didn't have the strength or mobility to put up a fight.

When Claire returned, she glanced around the room. "Looks good." Then she put her hands on her hips and turned to Mary. "You sure you're okay with this? I can stay."

"And watch me sleep?"

"I have a book."

"No. I want you off the road by dark. I'm going to take a nap, and Grant will be here by the time I wake up." She jerked her head toward the door. "Be careful."

Claire's eyes zoomed in on her like a telephoto lens, and Mary braced herself for what was coming. Claire had been way too accommodating. Too quiet. The butt chew Mary had anticipated ever since mentioning Mayo Clinic Friday night, was about to be delivered.

"Before I leave, we need to get one thing straight," Claire said, her voice low and firm. "I know you don't want to play the woe-is-me card, and I know you have good-guy Grant to take care of you. But you and I have been friends a long time, and we've been through a lot together. Whatever this is, you're not doing it without me."

Mary swallowed past the lump in her throat. "When I know, you'll know." She leaned against the back of the sofa, and held out her arms. "Thanks for coming. I'll talk to you soon."

Squeezing Mary hard, Claire nodded. "I'll text you when I get in."

Though frigid Kansas air billowed into the house, Mary stood at the door, and watched until Claire turned the corner. Gratitude mixed with sadness, the way it did every time she said goodbye to her friend these days. She missed having Claire close by. Mary had promised to keep Claire in the loop, but how she hated the idea of burdening her friends and family. Instead of sharing information, she vowed to share time. As soon as she could, with every bit of energy she could muster, Mary would visit Claire in Wichita. That was a trip way overdue.

A few days later, a padded envelope came in the mail from Claire. The adhesive was too strong – or Mary's fingers were too weak – to rip it open, so she trudged to the kitchen for scissors. Sinking into a chair at the table, Mary pulled the contents from the package, and laughed out loud. Several small carnival-type trinkets landed on the table, along with a blue first-place ribbon and a pair of soft, slip-free fuzzy socks that matched her cane. A small notecard read "Grand Prize." The laughter turned to tears as a wave of nostalgia washed over her. Claire was right. She couldn't do "this" without her.

## Chapter Sixteen

Realizing she was too old for an all-out public hissy fit, Sara took a deep breath. *Two thousand dollars?* That was not in the budget. She hitched her purse on her shoulder, and addressed the mechanic, hoping that direct eye-to-eye contact would show she wasn't one to be taken advantage of. "Wow. That's a lot," she said.

The man shrugged. "It's a major part, and involves a lot of labor."

"I see. Is there any way we could fix the problem in stages? Do part of the work now, and the rest later?"

"I'm afraid not, Ma'am. You'll have to replace the entire transmission."

"What about a warranty?"

"Most cars have a five-year warranty on something like this. Looks like you just missed it."

Was this guy trying to get himself clobbered over the head or what? That information only made it worse. Her parents had given her the car as a combination 21st-birthday and early graduation present – about five and a half years ago. "Any idea how urgent this is? Could I get by for a few more months?" Until she had a steady pay-check again?

Paul pursed his lips, while a hand slid over his chin. "I sure couldn't say about that, Ma'am. It's hard to tell. Might have a few months, might have a few weeks."

She forced an 'I'm-trying-not-to-kill-you' smile. "Could you write up the details for me? And break down the amounts for labor and parts?"

"Sure. Why don't you have a seat? It'll take a couple of minutes."

Sara plopped into a threadbare metal frame chair, fuming over this unexpected expense. She'd have to get a second opinion. But where? She'd already asked for recommendations from everyone she knew in Dallas, which had landed her at Parkside Automotive. They had a good rating from Better Business Bureau, and several good online reviews. Of course she could take it to the nearest Ford dealer, but dealerships were notoriously more expensive. Maybe her dad's mechanic could do the work in Whitfield while she was there for Christmas. If it could make the seven-hour drive. It'd be risky.

Paul got up from the grimy desk, and handed her a piece of paper. "Here you go. Give us a call if you want to schedule the work and maybe we can squeeze you in before Christmas. Gets kind of short-handed around here for a couple of weeks, you know."

Sara took the estimate, and folded it, though she wanted to smash it into a tight ball and dunk it into the nearest trash can. "Thanks," she said. "I'll let you know." Her steps slowed as she approached her traitorous Focus. "Why are you doing this to me?" she wailed. "I've taken good care of you."

The car problem added insult to injury. Just that morning, she'd turned down the only job offer she'd received so far. A large fashion company invited her to join their market research library. That meant not being on the product development or PR teams, but being stuck in a library simply collecting data all day. In her mind, it would be a step backward from where she'd been. Not the way she wanted to go. At all.

She slipped into the car, and sat for a moment, trying to collect her thoughts and calm down. Things happened, and getting upset didn't help. As her college algebra teacher had said 'all problems have solutions.'

Unfortunately, she'd learned that in the real world, the solution was almost always money. She'd have to dip into savings for this one.

Driving back to the apartment, Sara passed the park she and Evan had claimed as a favorite hangout. Making a quick decision, she turned in at the next entrance, and made her way to a bench near the playground. Although it was cold enough to need a jacket, mothers and young children were out in full force. Several moms carried a baby in a front pack while spotting older kids on the climbing equipment. Or kept an eye on a preschooler while they pushed a toddler on the swings.

She watched the children all vying for their mom's attention, heard the constant shouts of "Mommy," "Mommy, look at me!" And she felt the niggling in her brain telling her to reconsider motherhood. More and more lately, Sara questioned whether she was doing the right thing, or whether adoption made more sense. It wasn't as if her biological clock was ticking – she still had a good ten to fifteen years to have kids.

The question that loomed largest now was how Evan would take the news. As much as she wished they could blot everything else out and just enjoy spending time together, she was starting to feel deceitful. At this point, he probably had a right to know. It had to be soon – or at least before New Year's. Her heart fluttered at the thought. Evan had suggested she visit him in Tulsa for New Year's weekend. There wasn't a doubt in her mind how that would play out. No roommates. No hotel. It'd be a huge step, not just in their relationship, but because of the implications for family drama. What if they dated for a while, slept together, then broke up? It could be awkward for the families. Aside from those issues, she absolutely couldn't stay with him without telling him about the baby.

A fierce shout broke Sara's thoughts, and her eyes tracked a little boy all decked out in gray and denim hollering from the top of the slide, brandishing a stick in each hand. God, what would she do with a boy? She knew nothing about boys. Would adoption make more sense if the baby was a boy? What if he looked like Todd? Would she be able to love him? And what about the possibility of a stepdad? It seemed to her that a man could more easily love a stepdaughter, but would want his son to have his genes.

With her elbows on her knees, Sara rubbed her temples. Next week she might know for sure. Her first sonogram. It'd be nice to know something definite. She sure as hell didn't know why she wasn't getting the jobs that interested her. Still no word from Imagine. Her follow-up email had been answered politely, but missing the enthusiasm from her interview. They needed a little more time. The other agencies seemed like sweat shops where people were stressed out and worked long hours. Not an option for someone with a new baby.

**

The call Sara wanted came Wednesday morning just as she stepped inside the McDugall Communications office building. No way would she let the call go to voicemail even if it meant being late for her interview. In fact, if the offer was right, she'd apologize but walk right back out the door.

"Sara, this is Carolyn from Imagine Studio. Is this a good time to talk?"

Her heart pounded. "Hi, Carolyn. Absolutely." Looking around the lobby, she headed for a corner near a window. She had a few minutes to spare.

"Great. Well, first of all, you already know we were impressed with your résumé and attitude in the interview process. And I want you to know you're our number one candidate."

Sara gave a breathless laugh. "Thank you so much. I'm honored." *Yes!* She squealed inside, doing a mental happy dance. She'd be back on track soon.

"So we're extremely disappointed that we can't offer you the position."

What? Sara's stomach dropped, and the air whooshed out of her lungs. She faltered, trying to respond while her brain went numb. "I– I'm sorry. I don't understand."

"It's been a tough few weeks around here. We unexpectedly lost an account. A significant one. Not only can we no longer fill the marketing position, we may face layoffs. I'm very sorry. You'll receive an official letter, but I wanted to call you first."

"I see. That's– Wow. I'm sorry to hear that."

"You're a talented young lady, and we're truly sorry to miss this opportunity. Another agency or company will be lucky to get you."

Uh-huh, Sara thought. Or not.

"If at any time in the future you find yourself in the job market again, please let us know. Or if you ever decide to work freelance. We sometimes hire out for special projects."

Freelance. Of course they would. Especially now. They wouldn't have to pay benefits and health insurance. Sara dropped onto a bench, willing her voice not to tremble, fighting the tears that threatened to spill out.

"Definitely," Sara assured her. "I've considered freelance as a way to get some new experience and work with a company before making a commitment." *Liar.* "In fact, Carolyn, please keep me in mind for that. I'm still getting my bearings in Dallas, and project work might be a great opportunity for me." The fake platitudes spewed out. Blah, blah, blah. Save face. Move on. Sara glanced at her watch. She should be greeting Allison Murdoch, marketing director at McDugall Communications.

"You'll be first on our call list," Carolyn told her.

"Excellent," Sara said. "I'm disappointed, but I understand. Best wishes for a quick turnaround."

"Thank you, Sara. All the best to you, too."

Sara ended the call, and pressed the phone to her chest. Damn, damn, damn. Now what? Was it better to show up late or not at all? She had no choice. She needed a job. Hitching her purse onto her shoulder, she pushed aside the frustration that was beginning to border on panic, and sprinted toward the elevators.

Despite the cool greeting from the Human Resources receptionist, Sara kept a smile plastered on her face. At least starting in HR meant Allison might not even know Sara had been late for the appointment. In the end, it probably didn't matter. Sara's head pounded as she muddled her way through both interviews, answering the same questions she'd answered over and over for the past five weeks. It wasn't her best performance, but at least she'd finished it. She didn't expect a call back.

She shook hands with Allison, and left the office on wobbly legs.

Carolyn's timing really couldn't have been worse. Sara climbed into her car and grimaced at the granola bar waiting in the passenger's seat. For the first time in three months, the thought of food turned her stomach. She drove to her apartment on autopilot. Inside, Sara slammed her purse onto the coffee table and flung herself onto the sofa. Wow. The hits just kept coming. Why was everything going wrong?

Okay, one thing wasn't going wrong – yet. A half-hearted smile lifted her lips as her thoughts went to Evan. She sat upright, needing to talk. Maybe she could catch him at lunch. She reached for her phone and found a text from Evan waiting for her. Sudden tears burned her eyes.

*How'd it go?*

Of course he was talking about her morning interview.

She swallowed past the lump in her throat, and began typing. *Not well. Had just found out I didn't get Imagine.*

A second later, her phone buzzed in her hand. She picked up immediately.

"Hey," came the deep voice.

That one word, low and concerned was all it took. Sara's heart clenched, and she burst into tears.

"Shhhh. Sara, come on. It's okay. Everything's going to be fine."

Holding a tissue to her eyes to stem the flood, Sara tried to catch her breath, but she couldn't speak.

"Sara? Sweetheart, calm down."

The endearment smacked her in the chest, and she cried harder.

"Sorry it didn't come through," Evan said.

"I just–" Sara shuddered and hiccupped. "I really wanted that one."

"I know. I wish I was there."

"Me, too," she murmured through her sniffles.

"Damn. This is my Saturday to work, so I can't get there Friday."

"Oh. Right." Well, shoot. She'd forgotten about that. "Maybe it's not even worth it, Evan. That's a lot of driving for what, twenty-four hours?"

"Not a problem. I want to see you. Tell me what Imagine said."

"Lost an account, not hiring after all. I was the number one candidate. Maybe I can do some freelance. Like that's some consolation."

"Could you? Do freelance until something else comes through? Think you could stay busy enough?"

She let out a heavy sigh. "I don't know. Haven't thought about it. Freelance is tough. It's running a business, pounding the pavement to get work, doing my own billing and accounting. And no benefits."

"We could work up a business plan if you're interested. At least take a look at the numbers, what it would take. You might like the flexibility."

Her ears perked up at that. Flexibility might be good if she had a baby. But it might make daycare more difficult. She couldn't pay for full-time care if she wasn't making full-time pay. Maybe it was something to consider, though. Especially since her interviewing days were about to run out.

Sara raked a hand through her hair, thinking a couple of Tylenol would go down nicely about now. "I'll give it some thought," she said, trying to keep the discouragement out of her voice.

"Same," Evan said. "We can talk about it this weekend."

Her breath caught in her throat. Oh, boy. He'd just handed her a perfect opening, but she couldn't bring herself to give him advance warning. That wasn't all they'd be talking about this weekend.

**

Over and over, Sara rehearsed her lines until she fell asleep Friday night – only to get Evan's call mid-morning on Saturday that changed everything. Not only had he awoken with a sore and scratchy throat, someone at the bank had called in sick, making a hectic morning for everyone.

"I hate to do this," he told her. "Really hate to do this. But I should probably stay put. I feel like crap, and wouldn't be good company."

The words hit Sara's stomach with a dull thud. So much wasted mental energy. She'd psyched herself up, braced herself for his reaction – all for nothing. But he was right. The last thing she needed now was to get sick. Fine. She'd tell him next weekend. If they had some time alone before Christmas Day, he'd still be the first to know aside from her parents.

"You sound wiped out," she told him. "Why don't you take it easy and get some rest? I know Mom wants me and Annie to help with some baking on Saturday, but I bet I can sneak away for a couple of hours. I'll see you then."

"Sounds like a plan. I'll give you a call later."

Sara talked to Evan six or seven times before the weekend was finally over. From what she could tell, the down time had been good for him. By Sunday night his voice sounded stronger, as if there were more energy behind it. Even better, she managed to talk with him and text back and forth all day without accidentally mentioning her sonogram appointment, which weighed heavily on her mind.

Anticipation mixed with fear and excitement Monday morning as Sara attempted to down yet another glass of water. Her instructions were to arrive at her appointment with a full bladder. She hoped all parties involved were aware of this fact, and would act accordingly – a long wait would be miserable.

Sara signed in and took a seat in the waiting area along with several obviously pregnant women. A few had spouses or significant others with them. One couple must've just come from a sonogram – with a bright smile, the woman looked from a stack of photos to her husband's face. So happy. So excited. When the woman's eyes met Sara's, Sara returned the smile. It cheered and hurt her heart at the same time. She quickly picked up a magazine and began flipping through the pages. It was fine, she told herself. Doing this alone was something she'd have to get used to. Thankfully, a nurse opened the side door a moment later, and called for Sara.

After the nurse checked Sara's vitals, and confirmed she was having no physical problems with the pregnancy, she delivered Sara to the sonogram technician. Sara settled into the chair while Amy chatted about the procedure, explaining all of the steps as she went through them.

"All right, let's take a look at this little angel," Amy said, moving the wand over Sara's abdomen. She pointed out each body part, snapping pictures as she went. "Looks good," she said. "Just perfect." Then she let out a long "oooooo."

"What?" Sara asked. Balancing on her elbows, she looked from the screen to Amy.

"Oh, hon. I've got a great view. We don't always get this. Do you want to know whether it's a boy or girl?"

Sara sucked in a deep breath, and nodded.

Amy flashed a grin and pushed the camera button in quick succession.

Thirty minutes later, Sara sank into her car, staring at the fuzzy black-and-white images Amy had given her.

And now Sara faced another decision. Should she tell her mother? She said she would. They'd agreed that a stocking on the mantel would be a fun way to make the announcement. But did it matter? If she decided on adoption it might be best if everyone didn't know. She could make a case for either path at this point.

It was odd that she hadn't received a call from her mother last night or this morning. After all of her initial excitement about becoming a grandmother, she seemed to have detached a little, seemed preoccupied in their last couple of conversations. Hmm. Perhaps she was exercising some restraint. Sara smiled at her own joke. Doubtful. Probably just the whirlwind of Christmas.

Heart pounding, Sara punched in her mother's number.

After five rings, Sara was about to hang up when her mother's voice finally came on the line. "Hey, Sarie." She cleared her throat.

"Hey, Mom. Am I interrupting anything?"

"Not at all. What's up?"

Her question gave Sara pause. Had she really forgotten? "Well, I thought you might want to know–"

"Oh, my gosh! Sara, your appointment. What did the doctor say?"

There was the excitement Sara had been expecting, and it sent a wave of guilt crashing through her. If she opted for adoption, it'd be hard on her mother.

"What did–"

She swallowed hard, hoping not to regret her announcement. "Make that a pink stocking, Mom."

## Chapter Seventeen

*Incoming,* Mary thought, feeling like an open target while she talked on the phone with Annie. Much as she'd love to take evasive action, she didn't see how she could duck this one. All of her children were on their way home for Christmas. She had no choice but to give them the news, at least a watered down version. She still had the cast, and there were the obvious signs of whatever "illness" had settled inside her, plus, they'd see the hideous walker. They'd see her creeping around the house like an old woman, and nodding off every time she sat down. Much as she'd tried to make everything seem normal, it wasn't. They all knew about the fall and broken wrist, and the girls knew about the fatigue and some testing. They didn't — and wouldn't — know that the doctors were tossing around terms such as "quality of life."

Thank God for Rita. Mary's housekeeper had earned every penny of her holiday bonus, and more. Mary took a deep breath, and smiled into the phone, determined to keep her mood and attitude upbeat with Annie and all the kids. Mary couldn't be happier that Sara had decided to share her news this weekend as well. That's what she would focus on. A new baby would upstage her problems.

"Dad and Jason are on their way. Sara should be here any minute, so come on over. Can't wait to see you, sweetie."

When she heard a car door shut a few minutes later, Mary shoved the walker out of sight, and made her way to

215

the front door following the path of furniture. She and Grant had reconfigured the rooms so that she could easily have support, if needed, from a chair, wall or table as she moved from one room to the other. It'd take a keen eye to even notice.

With any luck they also wouldn't notice other things as well – like the number of pills she was popping to get through the day or the slight drooping of the right side of her mouth. Mary had discovered the new symptom while applying make-up only two days earlier. The terror of that tiny difference had almost sent her to her knees. At first, she thought she'd imagined it, but she spent an entire day constantly checking the mirror, smiling and not smiling at herself like some kind of clown rehearsing a pantomime routine. It was subtle, but the change was there – more noticeable when she smiled. Talking made it less apparent, and she vowed to chat or hold a cup to her lips every waking second she spent in her kids' presence.

Still, her grin was automatic as Sara stepped into the house. Mary wrapped her arms around her daughter and squeezed. "Oh, sweetie, it's so good to see you. I'm glad you're here first," she spoke almost in a whisper even though no one else was in the house to possibly hear. Hanging onto the door, Mary took a small step back, and surveyed Sara. "You look great. How are you feeling?"

"Good. Just kind of tired sometimes."

"Completely normal. Aren't you glad it's almost out in the open so you don't have to keep a secret or worry about slipping up?"

"Oh, not sure about that, Mom."

And still not exactly excited, Mary thought. Even after learning the baby was a girl? Something seemed off. "Well, why don't you take your things to your room, then we can talk. Annie and Blake will be here soon."

"Okay," Sara said, tapping on her cell phone.

At least she'd waited until she got out of the car. "Important messages?" Mary asked.

"Just letting Evan know I made it."

"Really?"

"Yeah. We might try to get together."

216

With that, she disappeared up the stairs. Interesting. Apparently they'd reconnected at Annie's wedding. Normally, Mary would've followed her, fished for details or helped her get settled, but these days the stairs were too much effort. In fact, they scared her. She hadn't been upstairs since she'd broken her wrist. With Sara out of sight, Mary turned and slowly made her way to the kitchen.

"Mom!"

Mary swiveled quickly, grabbing for the kitchen island to steady herself, at the unexpected sharp sound of Sara's voice behind her. So much for unpacking. "What?"

Sara's eyes were wide as she stared, then pointed. "You– You're walking funny. What's the matter?"

"Yes. I'm still having some trouble with that foot, and of course, it's harder to get around with this ridiculous cast. But we can talk about that later."

Frowning, Sara moved forward. "What does the doctor say?"

Mary waved a dismissive hand, and dropped into a chair. "I'll tell you about it, but I'd rather wait until Jason and Annie are here and so I don't have to go through it three separate times, okay? Come on in here. Let's–"

The sound of the garage door interrupted her, and Mary groaned inside. There went her private time with Sara. Seconds later, Grant and Jason bustled in, and voices filled the air. Mary stood, but waited for Jason to come to her. She folded him into her arms while Grant reached for Sara, everyone talking at once.

"Hey, Mom."

"Hey, you. How was the trip?"

Jason shrugged. "Fine. Airports are busy, though."

"I'm sure. So glad the weather's cooperated."

"Just in time," Grant said. "They're saying a storm is heading our way, up through Oklahoma."

Sara grimaced.

"Oh, now, Miss-I-don't-want-to-own-a-coat, a white Christmas might be kind of fun, after all the travel happens," Mary said. She hoped every traveler got home safely. But after that, if a couple of kids got stranded at home, well, that was all right with her. Maybe she'd get some private time with Sara *after* Christmas.

**

Mary glanced around the room. Such a familiar scene. The whole family perched on bar stools at the kitchen island or curled into chairs at the table, laughing and talking. With a smile in her heart, she took it all in, listening to the banter and the friendly teasing, each voice a distinct and cherished melody to her ears. The best sound ever.

If any of the kids noticed that Mary wasn't jumping up to refill drinks or check something in the oven, they kept it to themselves. They all seemed perfectly content to catch up and enjoy each other's company. Oh, how she didn't want to spoil this moment. Her eyes met Grant's, and the little flicker of sadness there told her he felt the same way. But it was probably time. "Hey, y'all grab your drinks, and let's go in the fam–"

She broke off when the doorbell chimed. "I'll get it," Grant said, already heading toward the door. The kids gathered their things, and began shuffling around.

"Someone bring the snacks," Mary said, reaching behind her for the cane. Annie picked up a platter of cheese and crackers, and Jason lifted the bowl of trail mix. He looked back at Mary – and stopped in his tracks.

"Mom? What is this–"

Mary shooed him ahead of her. "We'll get to it." She smiled as Grant ushered Pamela Shore, Whitfield mayor, into the entryway.

"Well, hi there," Mary said.

"Merry Christmas," Pamela said. "Hey, I don't want to interrupt, but wanted to drop this by. I made shepherd's pies this morning, and figured I might as well make an extra."

"Oh, Pamela. That is so sweet. Thank you. It won't last long around here, for sure."

Grant stepped behind her and placed the bag on the counter.

"And here's something else." She held out a yellow folder. "But this is strictly for after Christmas."

Mary gave a little laugh. "That's good." She knew the contents of the yellow folder. Reading material. Bids, proposals, ordinances, complaints – council business she needed to catch up on. Even without opening the folder, the papers swam in her jumbled brain. How would she ever get to all of that? Swallowing hard, she smiled at Pamela. "Thanks for running it by."

"No problem at all. Give me a call if you have any questions. The agenda's on top, so you'll know what's most critical." She inched her way back toward the front door, and Mary followed behind. "You take care, and we'll see you on January fourth," Pamela told her.

Maybe, Mary thought. The next meeting was only a few days before she and Grant left for Minnesota. But she nodded to Pamela. "Yes, ma'am. I'll be there. You have a merry Christmas." Grant held the door open and Pamela disappeared.

"Thanks, again!" Mary called. When she turned back to the family room, four sets of eyes stared at her.

"Mom," Annie drew the word out to about five syllables.

Grant cleared his throat, and put a hand on Mary's back. "Let's all sit down. Your mother and I want to talk to you."

Those four sets of eyes looked back and forth from Mary to Grant. Blake took hold of Annie's hand.

*Here goes.* Mary took a deep breath, her insides churning. "Okay, remember how I said I'd need some help with Christmas cooking?"

Annie and Sara nodded.

"Well, I don't mean just baking a few cookies. I need help with everything because I can hardly peel a potato or carry a plate to the table. I can only be up and around for a few hours before I'm exhausted and need to lie down. I can't put weight on my left foot, so I have to hang onto something or use a cane or walker."

She held up a hand when they each opened their mouth to speak. "I've had some tests done, and I seem to

219

have some kind of neuromuscular problem. The doctors haven't given an actual diagnosis, but it could be something bad." She moistened her lips, then forced herself to continue. "I'm going to Mayo Clinic in January."

Stunned silence met her announcement.

"Holy hell, Mom," Jason finally blurted out.

Sara simply stared, and Annie put a hand to her mouth, tears glistening in her wide, shell-shocked eyes.

Damn it. She hated this. Hated those stunned, hurt expressions. Hated causing her kids to worry. That was supposed to be her role, not theirs. She reached out and patted Annie's knee. "Nothing to cry about," Mary said softly.

"Don't worry," Grant said, his voice sure and strong. "We're going to do everything we can to figure out what's wrong, and get Mom well. We just thought you ought to know. And we all need to pitch in a little more so she can take it easy."

"I get this cast off next week, so that will help a lot," Mary added. She remembered to hold her mouth as though she were about to speak when Grant perched on the arm of her chair, and slid an arm around her shoulders. "So let's don't let this ruin Christmas, or spoil your appetites. I've got chili and all the fixin's, and now we have shepherd's pie, too."

"We'll take care of getting all that set up, Mom," Sara said. "What else can we do now?"

"Absolutely nothing. I mean it. We can cook tomorrow. Tonight, I just want to have fun. I'll probably go to bed early, but I want all of you to stay up half the night playing games, watching movies, getting silly or whatever."

"Mom." Jason rested his forearms on his knees and leveled his eyes on Mary. "Tell me about these tests. What are they looking for?"

Mary shook her head. "I'll talk to you later." She figured her med-school student would want more details, and maybe he'd have some ideas, but she didn't want to inundate the others with all the jargon and scary stuff.

"No way, Mom." Standing, Annie almost shrieked. "You've been hiding enough. If there's more, I want to know, too."

Mary also stood, and ran her hands up and down Annie's arms. "Honey, calm down. It's just a bunch of medical mumbo-jumbo. When we know more next month, I'll give you an update. I promise." Pushing away the feeling of guilt, she drew Annie into a hug. As soon as she stepped back, Sara was there. And then Jason. And the lump in Mary's throat ballooned. These kids. These awesome, amazing kids. She clung tight for a good long time, but when she loosened her grip on her son, she saw the concern in his eyes, and knew that later they would, indeed, talk privately.

**

Sara closed the door as Evan's voice came on the line. "Oh, my gosh, Evan. Something's wrong with my mom." Nearly eleven o'clock, and it was the first opportunity she'd had to call him. Before she and the others started the next round of gin rummy, she'd escaped on the pretense of changing into pajamas.

"What do you mean?"

"She can hardly walk. She's using a cane and a walker. Dad's taking her to Mayo Clinic in a couple of weeks. She's been to doctors in Kansas City, and they can't figure out what's wrong. Can you even imagine my mom with a cane?"

Sara swiped at the tears escaping down her cheeks, and let out a choked laugh. "Of course, it's my mom, so the cane is hot pink leopard print."

"Um, yeah. I'm having some trouble with that visual on a lot of levels. Wow. That's crazy."

Sara sniffled. "I know. And she wants me and Annie to go grocery shopping tomorrow, and help cook and get everything ready for Christmas dinner. I don't know when I'm going to be able to get away."

"No worries," he said in that smooth, calm voice. "We've got a few days. I'm pretty good at carrying groceries if you want another pair of hands."

Oh, right, Sara thought, her chest heaving. Maybe he should go shopping with them, and she could toss in some pickles and ice cream *because I'm pregnant*, she wanted to shout. She shook her head, trying to keep hysterical laughter at bay. Her emotions were careening all over the place. How could she tell her mother that she was considering giving her grandchild up for adoption when she just announced that she was sick?

"I'm serious. I could come to your place and hang out or you could put me to work."

And never have a private moment with him the entire time they were in Whitfield. She wanted to beat her head against a wall.

"I'll text you tomorrow when I see how things are going, okay?" Sara tiptoed into the hallway and listened. She wanted to talk to Evan, but she also didn't want to miss any conversation between Annie and Jason.

Back downstairs, Sara picked up her cards and curled into an armchair, tugging a blanket around her shoulders. Her mother was right. They stayed up way too late, playing cards and talking. But it wasn't quite laughing and having fun. They talked about their mother and her illness. They told stories about her, and remembered childhood days and past Christmases. They talked, and talked, but avoided the question of what if? What if it was serious? What if she didn't recover, if she ended up confined to a wheelchair? Or worse. By the time they went to bed, Sara's stomach was in knots. Never had she dreamed her life would be so complicated. Her head ached with the questions hammering inside it.

**

Mary wanted to get up early the next morning to be with the kids. She wanted to fix coffee and put out a big spread of fruit and rolls. But she couldn't do it. Couldn't force herself out of bed. At eight o'clock, she attempted to sit up, and then it dawned on her. Who was she kidding? It was a holiday. There was no way any of her kids would be up before nine o'clock. And ten or eleven wouldn't be a surprise. She rolled over snuggled back into her covers.

At nine-thirty, she slowly made her way to the kitchen and found Jason and Sara talking in hushed tones with Grant.

"Morning, everyone," she called out.

"Morning, Mom. How are you doing?"

"Good." She caught the flicker of guilt in Grant's eyes, and had no doubt she'd been the topic of their conversation.

Jason got up and poured her a cup of coffee.

"Thanks, sweetie." Her eyes tracked Grant as he pushed back from the table and walked toward her.

"I've got a few errands to run," he said. Leaning down, he pecked her cheek, and whispered, "They cornered me, but I was strong." Mary cracked a smile. Maybe they hadn't gotten to water torture yet.

"Annie and Blake still asleep?" she asked.

"No," Sara said. "They went downtown. A couple of last minute things to pick up. She'll be back to get the groceries, though. Do you have a list ready?"

"Yeah. It's in the top drawer."

"Okay. I'll go ahead and get dressed."

Mary watched as Sara bounced up the stairs, and couldn't help feeling once again that something was off. Here she was, alone with Jason, and the last thing she wanted to talk about, to think about, was her condition. Her eyes strayed up the stairs. What was going on with Sara? The distance Mary felt wasn't simply from Sara retreating to her room. There was something else. Mary wavered. She wanted to be supportive, to be a sounding board, but she didn't want to push. She considered her options. Was there any chance she could make it up the stairs without falling and breaking her neck?

She met Jason's eyes.

"Mom, you want to talk?"

"Not really. Can you do me a favor?"

He made a face. "Yeah, I think I could."

"Help me up the stairs."

Mary peeked around the door to Sara's room, and realized she was in the bathroom. Glancing around, it was also obvious Sara hadn't unpacked her suitcase. Mary pushed some papers out of the way, and sank onto the bed. She gasped as her eyes focused on the papers. *What You Need To Know About Adoption* was the title on one page. Another was a blank 'interest' form.

"Mom?"

Sara stood in the doorway.

Mary tidied the papers in her hands. "What are these?" she asked softly.

"Mom, really? What are you doing up here?"

"I'm sorry. I didn't mean to snoop."

"You climbed up the stairs. That's crazy."

"Jason helped me. I figured you hadn't unpacked, and thought I'd give you a hand. Then I saw these. Are you–" She clutched the papers to her chest. "Have you changed your mind?" She couldn't bring herself to say the actual word.

Sara looked at the floor while Mary waited, holding her breath as silent seconds ticked by. Finally, Sara met her eyes. "I'm still thinking."

"Why?" Mary cried. "What's changed?"

"Changed? Everything! I'm seeing Evan. I don't have a job, and now you're sick. It might be too much for everyone."

"Oh, no. Do not even think about including my situation in this scenario. You didn't know about my illness when you printed out these papers, right?"

"That's true. But now it matters more. I mean, even though I'm in Dallas, we talked about you being an involved grandma, spending weekends here or there. Mom, you're walking with a cane now. You say you're tired and foggy and achy. And it could get worse. How could you even hold a baby?"

"Of course I can hold a baby. My hands are fine. I'll have this cast off in a week." She supposed Sara did have a point, though. Carry a baby with one hand while tottering around with a cane or walker? The other part of her daughter's comment rang in Mary's head. "What do you mean you're seeing Evan? As in dating? More than hanging out with a friend?" That would explain Dana's hunch that Evan had a girlfriend he wasn't talking about.

224

"Yeah. We're dating. I thought you'd be happy about that."

Mary shook her head. Maybe she wouldn't be so foggy if people would stop springing seismic announcements on her. "Is this influencing your decision? Six weeks ago you weren't even speaking to him."

"I know. But a lot has happened in six weeks. He's been to Dallas a couple of times, and we're in a relationship, you could say. And yes, that weighs into it."

"Does he know about the baby?"

"Not yet. I'm going to tell him tomorrow, before everyone else finds out. A baby could be a serious complication. I mean, how many guys really want to raise someone else's kid? Or date someone who's pregnant?"

Sara slumped against the dresser, and Mary registered the pinched face, and dark circles under her daughter's eyes. Looked as if the decision was keeping her up at night. Was she just talking, or did she want an answer to her questions? Did she actually want Mary's advice or input? Sometimes it was hard to tell with Sara.

"Maybe it would be best to give the baby to a couple who's desperate for one, more ready for one than I am," Sara said.

"Oh, Sarie." Mary closed her eyes, trying to get her bearings. This wasn't the conversation she'd expected. It took her a moment to process Sara's words – and the fact that she could be losing her first grandchild. Her throat clogged. She'd been so excited about the thought of announcing it. Anticipation of that baby was the bright spot in her life right now. She blinked back the tears that threatened. Oh, man, she needed to get out of there before she fell apart. Fighting to stay calm and cool, Mary straightened. "Only you can make the final decision," she told Sara, her voice hoarse and weary. She pushed off from the bed, and took a few steps forward. "But take some time. I know you're disappointed about the job, and things aren't going the way you'd planned. Don't rush into anything. And please promise you won't make a final decision without talking to me first."

When she reached the doorway, Mary called for Jason.

Sara rested a hand on Mary's arm. "I'm sorry, Mom. I'm just struggling with it right now."

"I know you'll do what's best," Mary said. And in her heart, she wondered what that meant. She turned back as another thought occurred to her. "What about the stocking? It's ready to go, but would you rather wait?"

Chewing her lip, Sara looked at the floor. Slowly, she shook her head. "Time's just about up," she said. "We might as well just do it."

## Chapter Eighteen

When her phone rang, Sara picked it up and made for the hallway – away from listening ears.

"Hey," Evan said. "Looks like I'm in a time crunch today. Mom's freaking out about this storm that's supposed to hit tonight. She wants to move Christmas to late this afternoon so I can get on the road and get home before anything starts. Guess it looks like ice for Tulsa."

No way. He was leaving Whitfield early? Sara went numb. Apparently the forces of nature were working against her, too. She squeezed her eyes shut. It was so hard to act mature in the face of constant opposition. Of course she wanted him to be safe on the road. She'd see him next weekend. And it would just be the two of them. With a heavy sigh, she conceded that might be a better scenario for a deep conversation, anyway. She didn't want to ruin his family's Christmas or have him driving while distracted. Pushing the hair back from her face, she attempted to sound understanding.

"Well, that sucks," she said. "But it makes sense. If it's half as bad as the hysterical weather people are forecasting, you shouldn't be on the roads."

"Can you get away for a few minutes?"

"I think so. Why don't we go to the park? Mom mentioned that she never had a chance to pick up pinecones for centerpieces this year. I could get some for her." The weather in Whitfield was overcast, but still not bad for late December. Hopefully, they wouldn't get the leftovers from the Oklahoma storm.

"Sure. I'll pick you up in a few."

He arrived within a few minutes, as promised, but it was several more before they could escape. The entire family came running at the sound of the doorbell. You'd think they'd never had visitors before. Sara hovered near the door while Evan good-naturedly chatted with everyone. He shook her father's hand, and gave her mother a hug. Sara kept a smile on her face, but avoided her mother's eyes.

"Sorry about that," Sara told him when they finally climbed inside his Element. "I had no idea they were so desperate for company."

"I don't mind," he told her. "I like your family. Always have."

"They obviously adore you," she said. It was true. And it was nice to be able to skip the introductions. Her family already knew him, already had a history. With Evan, there was no awkward probing and vetting stage.

"Hey, if you want pinecones, I know a better place to find them."

Sara swiveled. "You do?"

"Yeah. There are a lot of big pines at the cemetery."

She stared at him. "Okay, that's weird. How would you know that?"

"I go there sometimes with Mom. My grandma and aunt are buried there."

"Oh. Of course. I'm sorry."

"No big deal. I never would've noticed if Mom hadn't gathered some up one time."

"Really? You mean you're not always on the lookout for pinecones?"

Evan shot her a smile, and turned the car into the entrance of the Whitfield Cemetery, winding along the outside road to a thick row of pines that stretched the length of the northern side.

"Oh, shoot!" Sara said, flopping back against the headrest.

228

"What?"

"I didn't bring a bag or anything to put them in."

Evan opened his car door. "I'm sure I have something. But first—" He leaned toward her, and his lips met hers. "You okay? You sounded kind of frazzled on the phone."

She blew out her breath. "I'm fine. I needed a break, though. Haven't had a minute to myself. Things have been crazy at the house with people in and out and Mom needing so much help." Sara climbed out of the car and surveyed the grounds while Evan rummaged around the backseat of his car.

"How's this?" He held up a brown paper bag.

"Perfect." She dropped the first pinecone in the bag. "Wow. There are tons. Do you think your mom would like some, too?"

Evan tossed in a few more. "Maybe."

"So, first Christmas in the new house. Is it all done?"

"Pretty much."

"Is your mom excited?"

A grin spread across Evan's face. "Would giddy count?"

Pausing, Sara sucked in her breath. She envied Dana's joy. Giddy sounded wonderful. She wouldn't mind a dose of that. Maybe they should go hang out at Dana's place, get away from the nervous faces and somber atmosphere at home, and interrupt the tense war inside her own brain.

"Absolutely," Sara said. "That's the way it should be. I'm happy for her. It's too bad you have to rush through Christmas."

"I know."

"Does everyone at your place know you were coming to mine?"

Straightening, he looked at her. "They do. Hope that's okay. It raised a few eyebrows. Are your ears burning?"

"Probably no more than yours are." She glanced around, taking in the quiet stillness around them. You could almost hear the silence.

"Ben's grave is just across the road," Evan said, nodding that direction.

Sara's hand flew to her chest. "It is? I don't remember exactly." Her eyes locked with Evan's. "We should go over." Thoughts and feelings hit in rapid succession. She hadn't been to their friend's grave since the day he was buried. Leaving the bag of pinecones behind, they stepped carefully around gravesites and crossed the worn gravel road. As far as Sara could see, they were the only visitors in the cemetery. Together, they studied the engraved words on Ben's dark granite headstone.

Benjamin Douglas Stapleton

Beloved Son and Brother.

In Our Hearts Forever.

When Evan reached for her hand, Sara twined her fingers into his. His phone buzzed with a message, but he ignored it.

What would Ben think of the two of them together, Sara wondered. He'd probably think it was cool. She hoped he was grinning down at them that very moment. She swiped at the tears that blurred her vision, then let Evan turn her around and into his chest. The tears came harder, and his arms tightened around her. His body warmed her, and after a few minutes, she wound her arms around his neck. As soon as she did, he pushed back her hat and buried his face in her hair, pulling her even closer. When they separated a bit, Evan adjusted her hat. His hands lingered at her face, and he brushed a thumb across her cheek.

"Missed you," he told her.

Her eyes met his, but her throat clogged. She couldn't even whisper a response.

Slowly, he lowered his head, and his lips settled on hers.

"Mmmm," she murmured. Sara closed her eyes and let herself enjoy the moment. The warmth of his lips sent heat spreading through her veins. A delicious dizziness stole over her, and she tightened her grip, letting one hand reach into the thick hair at his collar.

"Do you remember the first time I kissed you?"

Puzzled, she cocked her head.

"I mean the very first time," he said.

Oh. Smiling, Sara looked away as a crazy flush heated her face. She gave a little laugh, remembering the scene. So long ago, and tucked so far back in her memory she hadn't thought of it in years. Finally, she looked at him. "Yeah. I remember." She covered her mouth with her hand as tears welled in her eyes again. "Oh, my gosh, Evan. You gave me my first kiss."

The boyish smile on his face tugged at her heart.

"Valentine's Day."

She nodded. "Yeah. Fifth grade. Sitting on the porch at our old house." The memory came alive front and center. He'd hidden a pink carnation and a valentine card in his lunch bag. As soon as her mother went inside the house, Evan held the items out to her. When she took them, he grabbed her arm, pressed a feather-light kiss to her lips, then turned and ran away. They'd never spoken of it.

She shook her head. "That was so sweet."

Evan's brows shot up. "Sweet?" His fist went to his heart. "Angel, please. Have a little consideration for my man card." He took a step closer. "Let me see if I can do better than that." With a hand at the back of her neck, he bent his head again. Warm lips slanted over hers, and he was a long time coming up for air.

Head spinning, Sara took a deep, shuddered breath. It was so easy to fall into Evan's arms. It'd be so easy to let things escalate. Her heart pounded as her thoughts went to next weekend. She realized she was already anticipating an intimate weekend. Suddenly feeling overwhelmed, Sara took a step back.

"Let's make some kind of arrangement to leave on Ben's grave." She took off toward the pines, and began gathering fallen branches from the ground. "Maybe some from that other tree?" she asked when Evan caught up to her. The cemetery had all kinds of evergreen trees, the branches in varying shades of blue and green. "I don't suppose you have any clippers in your car?"

He shot her a curious look, but didn't mention her abrupt move. "'Fraid not, but I've got a pocket knife." He pulled it from his jeans, and cut a small branch from a blue spruce.

"If we tie some of these together, maybe they won't blow away." Sara dug into her pocket and retrieved a ponytail tie that she kept on hand to deal with her hair. She twisted the boughs together and wrapped the tie at the end. "Look at that. I've seen people put this kind of thing on their doors. It's pretty."

"It is," Evan agreed.

"Just needs a few pinecones."

"Got 'em."

Sara gently placed the greenery on Ben's grave so that it rested part way across the base of the headstone, then placed three pinecones in the center. It was a nice effect. Taking a step back, she met Evan's solid chest. His arms came around her shoulders, and she grabbed hold of them, leaning against him.

"It's so sad," Sara said.

"Still hard to believe."

The shrill peal of Evan's phone broke the stillness of the cemetery. Evan looked at the phone and frowned. "Mom again."

"Maybe you'd better see what's up."

He answered the call, and did more listening than speaking. A few um-hmms, then he grimaced and pulled Sara to him again. "Okay," he said into the phone.

Sara knew before he ended the call that their time was up. "She wants you home."

"Yeah. I'm sorry."

"It's okay. You have to have Christmas."

"But first . . . I have something for you." He pulled a small square package from his coat pocket. "This wasn't how I'd planned to give it to you, though. Want it now or should we wait until next weekend?"

Sara bounced her fists together. "I have something for you, too, but it's in my car." Unsure when or where they'd be together, she'd left his gifts out of sight. Would he even want them next weekend?

He waved the package in front of her. "Waiting then?" he asked, his voice teasing her.

Laughing, she grabbed for his hand. "You can't make me wait now."

Evan hid the package behind his back, and steered her to one of the small cement benches dotted around the cemetery. A gust of wind swelled around them as if to confirm winter was about to descend, and they were out of time.

Quickly, Sara tugged on the gold bow wrapped around the box, then lifted the lid to find a necklace of sparkling red and coral stones nestled in the tissue paper. She held it up. "Oh, Evan, it's gorgeous." The semi-precious stones were linked with delicate, intricately hand-painted stones. She was amazed that he could know her tastes so well. "Did you pick this out yourself?"

"I did. It's good?"

It was perfect. "Oh, my gosh. It's so cool. I absolutely love it." She leaned in for a kiss. "Thank you."

"You're welcome."

"Guess we better get going."

Reluctantly, they wound their way back to the car. They'd go their separate ways and try to enjoy their altered Christmas celebrations. She'd spend the week thinking about Evan, and her mother, and the baby growing inside her, wondering if another storm was coming.

**

In the house, Sara found her mom and sister laughing hysterically, Annie taking a photo with her cell phone. Apparently the atmosphere had improved since she'd left. "What's so funny?" Sara demanded.

When Annie turned around, Sara could see her mother's face – and her wide, silly grin.

233

"Got frosting?" she whooped. She had a butter knife full of creamy white frosting in her hand, and a frosting mustache above her lips.

"Nice," Sara told her, reaching for the knife. "I can see you two got a lot done while I was gone."

"We did, as a matter of fact. We made cookies."

"And pecan pie," Annie added.

"And frosting," her mother said, waving a bowl in the air. Her tongue waggled out, and she licked the icing from her upper lip.

Sara shook her head. But her mother's laughter was infectious, and she couldn't help smiling. "Uh, Mom? Do we need to check your meds?"

"Possibly." She shoved the bowl at Sara. "Here. I think you need some of this."

"Thanks, but I prefer chocolate."

"Too bad. Annie, you too. And bring your phone. We need a group shot."

They smeared the frosting on their upper lips, then, giggling like teenagers, huddled together for a selfie.

A sharp pang hit Sara in the chest as she admired her mom's silly smiling face in the picture. No one would ever guess anything was wrong. She was still happy and positive and fun. Memories crashed in and she thought of the times she'd stood on a chair and "helped" her mother make cookies or brownies – her mother dancing around the kitchen, letting Sara lick the spoon or cram a handful of chocolate chips into her mouth. Another thought hit deep inside. Her mother was going to be an awesome grandmother. If she got the chance.

## Chapter Nineteen

Mary set her alarm early for Christmas morning, knowing it'd take a couple of hits on the snooze button before she could drag herself out of bed.

At the first ringing, she rolled over, and heard Grant groan.

"It can wait," Mary whispered, her voice still thick with sleep.

He pulled her against his chest. "Merry Christmas, darlin'. I'll start coffee."

The kitchen buzzed with laugher and conversation by the time Mary pulled on her robe and shuffled down the hallway. Mornings were the worst. Every part of her body ached and creaked. She leaned heavily on the cane. Grant stepped forward with a steaming mug as soon as he saw her.

"Thanks, hon." She braced herself against the granite island.

"Last one up," Annie teased.

"Did I miss Christmas?" Mary asked.

"Nah. We saved a little for you," Jason told her. He ran a hand along her shoulders. "Merry Christmas, Mom. How you feeling?"

Mary set the mug down, and grabbed his hand. "Happy," she told him. And so fortunate to have all the people she loved the most together under one roof. "Very happy." She tried to catch Sara's eye, but failed amid the chorus of "awwws" and "Merry Christmases" that broke out.

Sara hadn't communicated any change in plans to Mary, so the "big news" was waiting. "Should we get this party started?" she asked, hoping she didn't sound as nervous as she felt. Even though she had to put on a neutral front, she hoped seeing the baby items and feeling the support of the entire family would have a positive effect on Sara. Going this alone so far had to contribute to her indecision and fears. The family's support should bolster her confidence.

Annie tugged on Blake's arm, and started toward the family room with everyone else tagging behind.

"Jason, cue the Christmas music, please, but keep it kind of low," Mary said.

"What is *that?*" Annie pointed to the fireplace, and cast a puzzled look at Mary.

Mary knew immediately that Annie had spotted the adorable pink stocking hanging among all the others. Two days ago, Mary would've been grinning, jumping up and down, figuratively, at least. But now, faced with the possibility of losing her first grandchild, she could hardly muster a smile. She looked at Sara then back to Annie. "It's an announcement."

"And a gender reveal," Sara said softly.

"What? For who?" Annie put a hand on her hips and stared at Sara. When realization dawned, the hand went to her chest. "Oh, my God. Are you pregnant?"

"I am. Due around mid-May."

Mary's heart sank when Annie looked around the room, hurt in her eyes, and no smile on her face.

"Wow. All these secrets. Anything else? Jason, what about you? Leaving the country? Joining a monastery? Getting married?" Annie's voice pitched up.

Jason spread his hands. "I got nothing, Sis."

"Annie," Mary said softly. Maybe this hadn't been the best idea. Well, good idea, bad timing. She hadn't expected Annie to have hurt feelings.

"It's not a conspiracy against you," Sara said. "I wanted to wait. I'm still deciding what to do."

236

"What does that mean?"

Sara flashed a glance at Mary, before answering. "I'm considering adoption."

Annie's mouth fell open again. "Giving the baby up? But, why?"

"Lots of reasons." Sara looked away, clearly not wanting to get into that conversation.

Mary figured she was going to have to step in and manage the situation before Christmas morning completely derailed. But Annie spoke up first.

"So, you're not with the dad? Is it Todd?"

"It doesn't matter," Sara told her. "Anyway, I'm seeing someone else."

Annie shook her head. "Wow," she said again. "I feel like I walked into the wrong house – or a soap opera. Did you meet this someone else in Dallas, or is he the reason you broke up with Todd?"

"Neither," Sara said, without further enlightenment.

Annie set her mug on the coffee table, and dropped onto the sofa beside Blake, still shaking her head.

Sara stood, and reached for Mary's cup. "I need a refill. You, too?"

"That would be lovely, thanks. But why don't you go ahead and bring the pot?"

When Sara was out of hearing distance, Mary turned toward her eldest daughter. "Annie, let's try to be supportive, okay? Sarie's got a tough decision to make that will affect her life forever."

"I don't understand, Mom. You're okay with her giving away your granddaughter?"

The words stung like a slap in the face. Of course I'm not, Mary wanted to scream. She let out a heavy sigh. "I can give her information and help her see the pros and cons, but it's not my decision," she said. It was good to keep reminding herself, so if that happened, she'd be prepared. Or at least not fall apart completely.

Sara returned with the coffee carafe and offered refills all around in an uncomfortable silence.

Mary turned to Jason. "Who wants presents? Jason, do you want to do the honors?"

"Sure."

"Don't you want to do stockings first?" Annie asked.

Oh, right. That was the usual order of things. Mary gave a sharp clap of her hands. "Absolutely. Why don't you hand them out? But take a picture first."

"But don't you dare post anything on Facebook!" Sara hollered from the kitchen. "My news stays in this room only. No exceptions."

Grant suddenly perked up and lifted the camera from the table. "Let me get some before everything's ripped to pieces." Mary smiled. The frenzy didn't take long.

Sara returned and glared around the room, her eyes resting on Annie. "I mean it."

"Let's get the girls," Mary said. Annie and Sara dutifully flanked her and, hopefully, smiled. Grant snapped a shot, then several more of the kids in every possible combination.

Then Annie reached for the pink stocking and held it out to Sara. "So I guess this is for you."

Mary had filled and hung the pink stocking after everyone else had taken turns dropping surprises into the others last night. With a lump in her throat, she watched Sara take the baby's gifts from "Santa."

"I'd already bought these things before I knew you were having second thoughts," Mary said, her voice barely above a whisper.

Sara nodded. "I know."

Normally, this was the time everyone would turn their attention to the goodies inside their own stocking, but all eyes were on Sara as she began pulling out tiny baby items. There were darling baby booties, a pink pacifier, a headband with a flower bow, a teething toy and various other small things – all girlie and every shade of pink.

"I had a lot of fun," she told Sara. "And no matter what you decide, the baby will need these things." She'd seen so many cute things at the local drug store that she'd wanted to pick up, but knew there was no way of being discreet about it. She'd had to settle for online shopping, and rush delivery, instead.

"Oh, that's adorable," Annie cooed when Sara picked up the headband.

"It's very sweet, Mom," Sara said. "Thank you."

"Do you really think you can give up your little girl?" Annie asked.

Mary's heart stopped.

Sara ran her fingers across the baby girl sweetness in her lap, touching the soft fabrics and ribbons. A moment later, she scooped them up and left them in the chair as she vacated it. "I don't know," she said, her voice breaking as she turned away.

"Sara, wait." Damn this foot. No way could Mary right herself, get the cane and get to Sara before she ran out of the room.

But Grant was amazingly fast, and had been paying attention. He stepped in front of Sara, and pulled her into his arms. Her muffled sobs into his chest were the only sound in the room.

When Mary managed a glance at Annie, her face was stricken.

"I'm sorry. I just– I didn't know she couldn't talk about it."

"It's all right," Mary told her. Annie's question may have been on the insensitive side, but Sara was going to have to deal with the tough questions.

"I wish I knew how to help her make the decision," Mary said, her voice hushed.

"Do you know anything about this new guy?"

"I do, but it's not my place to share."

Annie's eyes widened. "Oh, nice. Another secret?"

Damn. Mary hadn't thought about how that would sound before she answered. She wasn't getting anything right. At the rate it was going, this Christmas would go down as the worst ever.

She caught Grant's eye as he rejoined them, and Sara slipped quietly up the stairs. Probably needed time to regroup. But how long? Should they wait? Was she expecting Mary to follow her?

"Need anything?" Grant asked. Mary heard the weariness in his voice. It'd been a tough couple of months,

239

and his least favorite thing was drama. She held out her bum hand. "I'm good, love." She forced a smile.

He leaned down and gave her a firm, quick kiss. "Want to put this on hold?"

"How about rewind?"

"Good idea. You got an app for that?"

Wishful thinking. She glanced around the group. Not the festive morning she was accustomed to by a long shot. Even the tower of gifts that Jason had been stacking at each person's seat seemed lackluster.

Mary drew in a deep breath. "Why don't you all get started? Maybe we can–"

"Mom, wait," Annie broke in. "I'm sorry. Why don't we take a time out? Let me go up and talk to Sara. It's not right to start without her."

Quick tears burned Mary's eyes, and she nodded. "That would be nice." They had all day, all night, if needed.

**

"Hey, you okay?"

Sara picked at her comforter as Annie walked into the room. Had she come on her own, or at her mother's request? "I'm fine."

Annie sank onto the bed. "Hey. I'm sorry I upset you."

"Not your fault."

"Wow. I can't believe you're pregnant. And you ditched Todd."

Sara gave her a wry smile. "Wasn't exactly like that. Turns out he's married."

Annie sprang off the bed as though she'd been goosed. "What?!"

With a heavy sigh, Sara gave her the condensed version of the story.

"Oh, my gosh. That rat bastard."

Nodding, Sara looked away. She didn't miss him, but the truth of it still stung. "Pretty much."

Annie moved in close, and wrapped her arms around Sara. "Well, screw him."

240

"Uh, yeah, that turned out to be a problem."

Annie covered her mouth with her hand, but Sara could see the laughter in her eyes. And then her shoulders began shaking. Then they were both laughing uncontrollably and rolling into each other on the bed.

When they finally sobered, Annie rolled off the bed and stared at Sara. "Do Mom and Dad know all this?"

"Yep."

"Wow," she said again. "How'd Dad take it?"

"As you would think. Support with a dose of disappointment."

"Right. Well, he'll get over it. In fact, looks to me like he already has." She sat next to Sara again, and put a big-sister arm around her shoulder. "Look, it's your decision, but I'd love to be an auntie. Think how much fun we'd have. Next year, we could all be sitting around watching an adorable little girl opening her Christmas presents, and sticking bows on her head."

"I know. I want kids. This just wasn't what I'd planned, and now there's Evan."

"What do you mean?" She jumped up again, her mouth gaping. "No way. Are you serious? Evan is the new guy? Not just an old friend?"

Sara couldn't help laughing at Annie's reaction. To her, Evan was still just the corny kid next door. "He's still a friend. But a little bit more."

"He did turn out to be kind of a hunk, didn't he? I hardly recognized him at the wedding."

She flopped onto the bed again, her face inches from Sara's. "Don't make your decision based on any of these guys. Personally, I think I'd go crazy always wondering where she was, if she was happy, what she looked like. And you know if you give her up, she'll track you down one of these days and want to know you."

She paused, and took Sara's hand. "Besides, you'll be an awesome mom."

By Thursday, the house was quiet. Sara was the only one left, and she enjoyed the solitude and slower pace. Her dad was taking Jason to the airport in Kansas City, and her mother was sleeping in – her new norm even without the craziness of Christmas.

Sara made decaf coffee then wandered into the family room with her mug to curl up in front of the Christmas tree. She gasped when she saw her baby album on top of the coffee table. Sara whirled around as if to find her mother or some explanation. What the heck? Did her mother leave this for her to find, or had she been leafing through it? Either one begged the question of why. Thinking about a grandbaby? Advocating for one, trying to influence Sara?

Setting her mug on the table, Sara slowly sank onto a chair and pulled the album onto her lap. She hadn't turned more than three pages before tears welled in her eyes. That she was loved and happy couldn't be questioned. The evidence was there in every photo, every smile, in her mother's eyes. No doubt this is what her mother had wanted Sara to see. Yes, the cuddling and playing was adorable, but the photos didn't show the other side – the dark side – the round-the-clock feedings, crying fits and sleepless nights.

The sound of her mother's cane against the floor snapped Sara's head around. That was a sound she'd never get used to. She stood quickly. "Morning, Mom. I made coffee, but it's not your kind. Let me start a fresh pot for you. I wasn't sure when you'd be up."

"No, honey, this is fine. What are you–" Her eyes strayed to the album. "Oh." She moved in close, resting her head against Sara's. "You're not mad, are you?"

"No, Mom. It's okay."

Her mother smiled. "Good. I love looking at those pictures."

Coffee in hand, they headed back to the family room, but when Sara started to resume her place in the chair, her mother patted the cushion beside her on the couch.

"Sit over here by me."

Sara curled up, facing her mom.

"So, here's the deal, toots, I think you're over-thinking this. You're pregnant. You're going to have a baby. Those are the facts. I feel like you went off to Dallas

242

and haven't had a chance to be excited because you haven't told anyone. You haven't let yourself get excited about it." She leaned in close. "A baby is a happy thing. Look at Annie. She was surprised at first, but now she'd love to be your little girl's auntie."

It was true. After her Christmas morning blow-up, Annie had spent the rest of the day being sweet and sympathetic and encouraging. Now she was on Mom's team of lobbyists. "Just call me Aunt Annie," she'd whispered in Sara's ear Monday morning before heading home.

"It's okay if you aren't ready to make a decision," her mother said. "You've got some time. Don't rush into something you aren't sure of."

Sara let out a long sigh. "It wouldn't be as big an issue if I had a job. But, that's kind of a problem."

"You know we'll help out."

"I won't come crawling home pregnant with no means of supporting myself, Mom. That's— that's humiliating. It's not who I am."

"Shhh. I understand. But there are no rules on this. Nothing says you can't take some time off, have the baby and then go back to work."

Sara sipped her coffee, and relaxed against her mother's arm. "We'll see." She glanced over. "No pressure, right?"

"Absolutely not. Can I change the subject?"

Sara arched her brows. "To?"

"Evan Gerard."

Sara rolled her eyes, but it took only the mention of him to make her smile.

"Did you tell him?"

"No. Since he left early because of the storm, I never had a chance."

"Sure didn't take long for that to develop."

"I know. Honestly, Mom I'm just as surprised as you are. But I feel like we . . . we click. We have fun together, and he's cool. It's comfortable between us whether we're going out or doing nothing. He's thoughtful and smart.

We have the same ideas and opinions on things." She met her mother's eyes. "He seems like someone I can trust."

"Wow. Those are all excellent qualities. Does he make your heart go pitter patter?"

Sara's grin returned as a deep flush spread over her. Could she really tell her mother that his steel blue eyes took her breath away, that a little rush of heat shot up her spine every time he kissed her, and when he pressed against her . . . well, just thinking about it sent her pulse skyrocketing. "Yeah," she said, finally. "Yeah, he does."

Her mother laughed, and pulled her into a hug. "That's all I need to know. So, remember, you aren't a worrier, right? Everything will work itself out."

## Chapter Twenty

"You sure you don't mind?" Evan asked when he called Sara Thursday night.

"Of course not. It sounds fun," Sara told him. She recalculated the timing in her head. It was another delay, but a small one. The change of plans might actually be better. Going into Tulsa Saturday morning, she could watch his buddy basketball game then spill her news. If things went south, she'd still have plenty of daylight to get back on the road to Dallas.

She spent another day lounging around the house and watching movies with her parents, then packed her car. After Saturday morning brunch, Sara climbed into her car and slipped her sunglasses into place. She hoped the sunny skies were a good omen. The Christmas storm had passed, the roads were clear, and she felt better. Spending time with her mom could be exhausting, but also energizing. Sara was approaching the heart-to-heart with Evan with a more positive outlook. Yes, she was dealing with huge life issues, but it didn't have to mean a storm. There could be a little sprinkle, a few dark clouds, and then blue skies. Evan was level-headed. Once he got over the shock, he might be the person to help her see things clearly. Doom and gloom wasn't her style. Her mother was right. Maybe Sara had let the job rejections get to her and skew her perspective.

She was looking forward to watching Evan's game, and meeting some of his friends. She'd never thought of him as an athlete, but it seemed he enjoyed several sports.

At least he participated, staying in shape, rather than simply watching them from his living room sofa.

Sara pulled up to Evan's apartment only minutes before they needed to leave for the game. She'd cut it close on purpose, needing to avoid any spare time alone with him. But it was closer than she'd planned. The drive took longer, and she'd lingered at the rest stop, her stomach churning. By the time she arrived in Tulsa, her head and back ached. If she remembered anything she planned to say, it'd be a miracle. At this point, she just wanted it done.

Evan opened the door with concern etched in his features. "Hey, I was starting to worry. You okay?"

"Yeah. Sorry. Just running a little late. Do I have time for a quick pit stop before we leave?"

"Sure." He steered her down the hallway. "First door on the right."

When she returned to the living area, Evan pulled her into his arms. "I don't think I gave you a proper greeting," he said, his breath warm against her ear.

She kissed him back, but was careful not to press her body too closely to his. At four-and-a-half months, her baby bump was harder to disguise.

"Did you get a chance to eat anything?" Evan asked.

"Oh, yeah. Mom wouldn't send me off without breakfast and a bag full of snacks." Sara wasn't sure whether it was nerves or something she ate that had her stomach feeling unsettled. She hadn't eaten that much. "I'm good."

"Great. When we get back, we can look at the stuff I got from marketing on what they pay freelancers and what kind of work they do for the bank."

"Really? They gave you that information?"

"Sure." He ushered her toward the door. "Looks like there's some potential, especially if you can get a couple of steady clients. Carolyn, our client services VP, says a lot of companies are outsourcing like that now."

"Client services?"

He shot her a wry smile. "Yeah, that's what we call marketing these days. Sounds better, not so much like sales and promotion."

"Right." She hadn't done any research on the freelance market in Dallas. Maybe there were options, but she wasn't pinning her hopes on that. If so many people were looking for jobs, then there was probably a glut of freelance professionals – *i.e. desperate people*. And that meant companies could pay lower wages. Still, she should at least look into it and know the standards within the industry. "Thanks for doing that," she told Evan. "I haven't had a chance to look into it in Dallas."

"Well, like I said, Tulsa would be happy to have you."

Ugh. Why did everything he said remind her that he was seeing a different future than she was?

She was relieved when Evan pulled into the fitness center parking lot a few moments later. Inside the gym, he introduced Sara to some of his teammates, then she took a seat on the bleachers along with other spectators. Girlfriends and wives, she guessed. She pressed a hand to her back, thinking bleachers were about the worst invention ever. Looking across the gym, Sara caught her breath when a man dressed in the same jersey as Evan entered the gym with a young boy on his shoulders. Evan was the first to give the grinning toddler a high-five. He ruffled the child's hair, and handed him a basketball when his dad lowered him to the floor. Of course Evan had already told her that he liked kids, but it touched her heart to see him engaging with – and enjoying – someone else's child. It occurred to her that Evan Gerard might be too good to be true. He had so many positive attributes, was such a nice guy. But no one was perfect. There had to be flaws. Was she about to expose them?

As the game got under way, Sara tried to concentrate on the action, but her thoughts kept wandering, and her discomfort made it hard to pay attention. When Evan glanced her direction, she smiled. She remembered to clap when he made a basket. In her admittedly biased opinion, he was one of the best players on the team – and definitely the most fit. While other players left the court practically panting, in search of their water bottles, Evan sauntered off, took a few sips of water and was ready to play again. Sara reached for the bottle of water Evan had given her, but found nothing. Damn. Must've left it in the car. Glancing around, she took a small notepad from her purse and began fanning her face, wondering if she was the only one melting. The gymnasium was stifling. The only air flow appeared to be about ten feet up.

She swiped a hand across her brow when the final whistle blew. Ready for a blast of cold Oklahoma air, she stood too quickly, and grabbed for the handrail when a wave of dizziness washed over her. She took a moment, then made her way down the stairs. She had to get out of there.

Sara crossed the polished wood floor toward Evan.

Evan did a double-take, and his smile disappeared. He was at her side in a flash. "Sara? You okay? Angel, you look really pale."

Sara put a hand to her forehead. "I'm sorry. I don't feel very well."

"Don't be sorry. What can I do?"

"Where's the restroom?"

He steered her to the women's room. "I'll be right here. Holler if you need anything. I can send someone in."

She slipped past him, and nearly collapsed against the door of the stall. What the heck was going on? She considered lying down on the dirty cold floor, but sat on the toilet seat instead. Maybe something just needed to–

Oh, God. Panic rose in her chest and her head swam at the sight of blood on her panties. Only a few drops, but enough to tell her that something was wrong. She'd have to get to a doctor. But how– What would she tell Evan? She screamed inside. *No, no, no. Not like this.*

Barely standing, she stumbled to the door. Evan must've heard her bang against it because he opened it from his side.

He reached out to steady her. "Jesus, Sara. We need to find you a place to lie down."

"I– I think I need to go to the hospital."

His brow furrowed, but he didn't miss a beat. "Okay. Come on, let's get you to the car." With one arm around her waist and the other holding her arm, he helped her out of the building and into his car.

248

"Is it close by?"

He squeezed her hand. "Sit tight, angel, I'll get you there."

Sara sat perfectly still, willing her body not to betray her. Was this a sign of miscarriage? Was she about to lose the baby? Could she be in danger herself? And what the hell was going through Evan's mind? He probably thought she had the flu and was seriously over-reacting. What a nightmare.

She put a hand on her abdomen.

"You feel sick?" Evan asked.

Yes, she felt more than a little sick. Truth be told, passing out sounded like a good option. "I'm okay," she managed.

"Almost there."

He pulled into the emergency entrance and parked under the canopy. "Stay there." He dashed inside the building. When he returned, a woman pushing a wheelchair scurried behind him. Evan helped Sara into the chair then proceeded through the sliding glass doors while the woman pushing the chair bombarded Sara with questions.

"Well, I . . ." She gulped for air, her voice quaking. "I– I'm spotting. My back hurts, and I'm four and a half months pregnant." Fists clenched, Sara looked back at Evan, her eyes pleading with him to wait, to understand.

"Oh, dear. Let's get you to a room, and see what's going on." Turning to Evan, she smacked her hand on the counter. "Dad, might need you to answer some questions."

Sara's face flashed white hot. *Oh, no.* Just before the woman whisked her through another set of doors, Sara got a last look at Evan – and the shock that was frozen on his face.

**

Sara lost track of time, and the number of people who went in and out of the room. She had no idea who they all were or what role they played. They descended on her like a swarm of bees. The one thing she knew for sure

249

was that she was on the verge of losing her baby. She couldn't explain the tremor of fear – or the heart-wrenching regret that stole over her. Her baby girl was going to die before she even had a chance to live. That thought filled Sara with a deep sadness, and sent tears flowing down her cheeks.

Someone brushed them away.

"There now, you take it easy, sweetie. Everything's going to be fine," a soothing voice told her. Sara's eyes fluttered open, but she wasn't sure who had spoken the soft words. "Just breathe," the voice said.

She closed her eyes, but opened them again at the now-familiar squirt of liquid over her abdomen.

"Sara?"

A woman took her hand and leaned in close. "Sara, I'm Doctor Anderson. I'm going to do a physical exam now, and we're looking at your baby through a sonogram. Okay?"

Sara nodded, tensing as soon as the doctor began her examination.

"Just relax."

As if that was possible.

The doctor and technician murmured to each other as the wand roved over her baby bump. It took Sara a moment to realize they didn't seem panicked. After a little more poking, the doctor stood, and snapped off her gloves while a nurse covered Sara's legs with a sheet.

Sara gasped when another nurse entered the room with Evan. Apparently he hadn't corrected them after the first woman assumed he was 'dad.' Dr. Anderson approached the bed, and one of the nurses nudged Evan forward.

"Is– is the baby all right?" she asked, her voice strained.

"Placenta and baby look fine," the doctor said without hesitation. "I'd like to do some lab work. You may have an infection, and we'll start a saline drip for dehydration."

Keeping her eyes focused on the doctor, Sara nodded.

Dr. Anderson squeezed Sara's hand, then turned and began issuing instructions.

**

Sara awoke to a quiet, darkened room. Blinking, it took a minute to get her bearings. Where were all the people? Had she– She put a hand on her stomach. Had she lost the baby? What even happened? Her eyes tracked across the dim room, and she froze when they focused on Evan only a few steps away. She sank farther into her pillow as he came toward her.

Evan stood beside the bed, hands shoved in his pockets. "Hey."

Sara was almost afraid to look at him. She pressed a hand to her head, willing it to clear. With a sigh of relief, she remembered the doctor's words. She hadn't lost the baby. Tears welled in her eyes, and she stared at Evan, trying to read his face. His eyes were clouded, his expression serious. Not angry, but not smiling. Not encouraging.

She swallowed hard and asked the next agonizing question, her voice barely a whisper. "Did I lose you?"

He held her gaze, then looked somewhere behind her, his lips moving, but forming no words. Obviously, he was struggling with what to say. Regret settled in her chest, like a heavy weight, crushing her, stealing her breath.

Finally, he reached out and touched her hair, his hand brushing against her cheek. "Of course not."

She choked on a cry, her face crumpling as the tears spilled over. Evan handed her a tissue. But he didn't hold her or kiss her. Doubt lingered in his eyes.

"How are you feeling? Do you want me to get a nurse?"

Sara shook her head. She felt raw and exposed. Nothing a nurse could help with. "I've just been asleep?"

"Yeah. They gave you something to help you relax. That's probably why you feel groggy. You just have to take it easy for a while."

"Oh." Her eyes met his again. "I'm sorry– sorry they put you on the spot like that. I know they thought–"

251

He shook his head. "It's fine. I'm glad I was here. I do have a couple of questions, though."

Sara clenched the sheet in her fists. "Yeah, I'm sure you do."

His hands went back in his pockets, and he faced her. "Why the hell didn't you tell me?"

A nurse breezed into the room. "Thought I heard voices in here." She moved forward and lifted Sara's wrist to take her pulse, then checked the various equipment in the room, tapping on her keyboard. "How do you feel?"

Sara figured overwhelmed and exhausted wasn't what the nurse was looking for.

"I'm okay, I think. A little tired."

"Normal. What about dinner? I can put in an order."

Dinner? Sara pushed the hair away from her face, wondering what time it was. It'd been a long time since she'd eaten, for sure. "Yes, thank you. But, does that mean—"

The nurse handed Sara a menu. "Looks like you'll be spending the night with us. Dr. Anderson wants to keep you overnight – just a precaution. She wants to be sure this doesn't develop into pre-term labor."

She took Sara's order, then headed for the door. "This'll just take a little while."

Sara turned her attention back to Evan who was still waiting for an answer to his question. She drew in a deep breath.

"I'm sorry. I wanted to tell you earlier. I was going to tell you the weekend you got sick and couldn't come to Dallas. Then I was going to tell you over Christmas, and we had no time. Other than my parents, no one knew. I only told Annie and Jason Christmas morning. I wanted to get it out in the open this afternoon, but not this way."

She crossed her arms, and studied him. "So now you know. I'm going to get big and fat. And I'm going to have a baby. Not ideal dating material."

Evan brushed her comment off with a shake of his head. "That doesn't matter. I'm guessing this had something to do with the sudden move to Dallas, right? Where's the dad?"

That apparently mattered. She gave him the brief lowlights. "So the 'dad' is not in the picture. And, yeah, that's how I ended up in Dallas. Lately, I've been thinking about putting the baby– It's a girl. Putting her up for adoption."

"What?" His eyes widened as he stared at her. "Why would you do that?"

Sara hesitated. Repeating herself over and over was getting a little tiresome. Wasn't it obvious? She took a deep breath. "Well, I– I'm not sure I'm ready for a baby. Not sure about the whole single-mom thing. Not sure it's fair to the baby."

"Sara, I have to tell you that sounds a lot like running away from responsibility. Besides, you could've married the guy and still ended up a single mom. It's not always a choice."

Okay then. Here we go. Maybe this is where they part ways. High moral ground, and judgment.

"A lot of people have babies and aren't sure they're ready for them," Evan continued. "Hell, is anyone ever really ready? The way I hear it, you jump in and swim."

Her defenses rose. "And that's what I'd planned to do," she cried.

"This is why you've been so interested in my mom and my family life."

"I admire your mom, Evan. I've thought about her a lot since I first decided to do this on my own. She– She's my role model."

"Ah. She'd be a good one. Is that–" His eyes pinned her to the pillow. "Is that what this thing between you and me is all about?"

"What?!" Sara's voice pitched. Did he really think that? "Of course not. This, this thing. You and me . . . God, Evan, I never expected this to happen. How could I know that we'd reconnect after Annie's wedding? Or that we'd start– have a relationship?" Tears burned in her throat. "I honestly thought I *would* be a single mom. And then you happened, and it's been so much harder than I thought to find a new job. Now my mom is sick. So many things seem to be working against me that I– I'm having second thoughts."

A charged silence hung in the air, and Sara waited.

Evan leaned against the railing of her bed, and lifted her hand, toying with her fingers.

At least he was touching her. Hadn't stormed out of the room.

"What do you want me to do?" he asked, his voice low and husky.

The question sent tremors through Sara's body. Love me, she thought instantly. Love me, and stay with me. Her heart pounded. Could she say it out loud? "Just– just stick with me, okay? I totally understand if you want some time, if you want to back off. Most of all . . . most of all I want you to know that I never meant to hurt you or hide anything from you. It all happened so fast . . ."

A nurse interrupted, and Sara offered a terse smile. Less than an hour later she was being released, and told to "go home" and rest. They hadn't specifically told her not to drive, and she wasn't about to ask clearance for a four-hour road trip. She was stuck in Tulsa, temporarily. Evan had withdrawn into polite conversation – speaking only as necessary. It was obvious he needed some time to process the news. She couldn't impose on him any more. Things were awkward enough already. As soon as she picked up her car from his place, she'd locate the hotel where she'd reserved a room, and then crash.

She touched his arm. "I just need to pick up my car. I've got a place to stay lined up."

"Sara, you can stay at my place," Evan said when the nurse turned away. "You take the bed. I'll sleep on the couch. Not a big deal. Then you can go on to Dallas when you feel up to it." He leaned closer, and cleared his throat. "Or, I can drive you to Whitfield in your car, then catch a ride back here with Chase or Kent. I'm sure one of them could do that."

She twisted her hands, trying to think fast. Is that what he would prefer? Then he'd only have to spend two more hours in her company. He'd been calm and concerned and helpful. But that wasn't the same as warm and loving.

"That would be a huge inconvenience," Sara said, her voice wavering only a little. "I could call my dad." It was an option she hadn't thought of, but she had to admit it wouldn't be her first choice. Her dad already had his hands full with her mother. Not to mention that it was New Year's Eve, and they might have plans. "No." She gave a quick glance toward the door to make sure no nurses were within hearing range. "Honestly, I think I could go on to Dallas. I feel fine. They're just being overly cautious."

"Sara. No way. You'd be by yourself."

"I have a roommate."

"Not on the road, and not someone who's going to look after you like your parents will."

She noted he didn't add 'or like I will.' Sara sucked in her breath. He was right about the driving, but it wasn't her style to involve everyone else in her problems. If she took a couple of days to rest once she got to Dallas, she wouldn't need anyone looking after her at all. "I don't know, Evan. If I go to Whitfield, everyone will know what happened and that I've been here with you."

Hands on his hips, he slowly nodded. "Yep. Just like everyone's going to know you're pregnant." The look he shot her held sympathy, but his words were firm. "Might be time to own that, angel."

\*\*

The car ride back to Evan's was silent, and Sara stewed in her thoughts. When she chanced a sideways glance at Evan, his eyes were fixed firmly on the road, both hands on the steering wheel. In the parking lot outside Evan's apartment, he switched off the ignition and swiveled toward her. "If you don't want to go to Whitfield, I'd like you to stay here. I'll worry if you don't have someone with you. Besides, we need to talk."

Ugh. She wasn't looking forward to that conversation. Could she handle such an emotionally charged discussion right now? "Evan, are you sure? Maybe we watch a movie tonight and let things go for a little while."

After a short silence, he nodded. "Sure. Unlock your car, and I'll get your bag."

Inside, she dropped onto the brown leather sofa and took out her cell phone. "I guess I'll cancel my reservation," she said softly.

"Right. That reminds me, I'd better cancel our dinner reservations, too."

"Oh, Evan. I'm sorry."

He put up a hand. "Stop apologizing. Please."

Sara swallowed the lump in her throat. She'd day-dreamed of ringing in the new year with him, but this wasn't how she'd envisioned it.

He sat on the coffee table, facing her. "We could still go out if you feel up to it."

She could tell by the flat tone of his voice that his heart wasn't into it. A quiet evening at his place would be best. "Let's just stay in," she said.

"Okay by me as long as you don't mind carry-out or pizza delivery. I don't have much in the fridge because I thought we'd be eating out."

She thought of the little black dress rolled up in her bag. Boy, she had royally screwed up those plans. "If you know a good pizza place that'll deliver on New Year's Eve, let's do that."

"I'll call now. It might take a while." Pushing off from the table, he left her.

When he returned a few minutes later, he set a glass of water on the side table and placed a throw blanket on the cushion beside her.

"Thank you," she murmured.

"Can I get you anything else?"

She drew in a deep breath. "Evan, please sit down. You don't have to wait on me."

He picked up the TV remote and perched on the edge of the chair next to her, leaving her the entire sofa, which suddenly felt like a deserted island.

"Let's see what's on Netflix."

256

Fine by her. She kicked off her shoes and drew her legs up, watching the selections flip by. "Wait, what's that one with Bill Murray?"

Evan flipped back. "St. Vincent. No idea what it's about." He clicked to the movie description.

"Oh, it has that McCarthy gal, too," Sara said. "I think I've heard of this one. Might be worth a try." Something light and funny would be perfect.

"Works for me," he said. He clicked play, and sat back.

Within the first ten minutes they became engrossed in the movie, and, Sara noted, both laughed at the same lines. A few moments later, she gasped when a bikini-clad pregnant pole dancer sashayed across the screen. Sara's face warmed, and she quickly looked at Evan. "Oh, my–"

"What the hell?" Evan said simultaneously.

Could they possibly have chosen anything more inappropriate?

Evan reached for the remote, mumbling under his breath. "Jesus Christ, it didn't say anything about–"

Sara held up her hands. "Evan, calm down. It's all right." At any other time, the ludicrous image might have been amusing. But the damage was done. Evan hit pause – after the dancing scene had ended, thankfully – and practically slammed the remote down on the table.

Sara jumped, and her eyes met his. Standing, she made a referee's signal with her hands. "Okay, time out," she said. "Tell me what you're feeling, Evan."

He looked at her for a long moment, then sank back into the chair, his elbows resting on his knees.

"I'd like to know," she pressed. She knew confrontation wasn't his style, but she needed to know where she stood, to break through the awkwardness. "I get that it was a huge shock, but what else? What's making you uncomfortable? Is it that I didn't announce that I was pregnant on our first date? That I've had sex with someone else? That you don't want to be with someone who has a kid? Is this a choice for me? I can't be with you and have this baby? Is it one or the other?"

He sprang from the chair. "Absolutely not. You have to decide whether to keep the baby on your own. I can't be part of that equation."

Sara held his gaze. "But you already are," she whispered.

He raked a hand through his hair, his deep blue eyes troubled. "Look, Sara, I care about you. I always have. You know that. I honestly—"

The doorbell interrupted him, and they both froze. The pizza delivery driver's timing couldn't have been worse. She glanced around for her purse, but Evan was already heading toward the door as he pulled his wallet from his pocket.

At the table, Sara chewed slowly in the charged silence, taking frequent sips of water. She was into her second slice of pizza when Evan spoke again.

"I guess I feel cheated."

"Cheated?" Sara echoed. She dropped the pizza, and stared at him.

"Yeah. Cheated out of time alone with you. Just the two of us spending time together, figuring things out. If you keep this baby, everything will change. She'll be the focus of your life."

"Well, that will for sure be true if she's the only thing *in* my life," Sara said, her voice quivering. "But it doesn't have to be that way. A lot of people have kids and still manage to have an adult relationship, Evan."

He got up and pulled a bottle of beer from the fridge. Sara's eyes strayed to the bottle of champagne there as well. Chilled and ready for a celebratory evening that wasn't going to happen.

"I think I just need some time and space," Evan said, resuming his seat at the table. "Like you said, it's all happened pretty fast."

Sara swallowed hard. She nodded, but words stuck in her throat.

The rest of the evening passed with little conversation. They continued to watch the movie, which, in the end, Sara found entertaining, though she could have done without the breastfeeding scene at the end – while

258

everyone else began eating, the new mom was focused on the baby. That's just the way it was, Sara figured. A phase that you got through and laughed about later.

"Want to choose another one?" Evan asked as the credits rolled on the screen.

Sara shook her head. "There's no way I'm going to make it to midnight. I'm kind of tired." Fading fast, and more than ready to put the night behind them.

"Right. Let me get a few things out of my room."

She watched him retreat down the hall, then took her glass to the kitchen and finished tidying up.

"It's all yours," Evan told her from the living room. He tossed a pillow on the sofa.

"Thanks," Sara said, her voice weary. She slipped into Evan's room, and closed the door behind her. She took the opportunity to look around, not snooping, but taking in her surroundings and satisfying her curiosity. The dark wood furniture was clean and simple, the platform bed sporting a heathered gray comforter. Not much other decoration. Very Evan.

Disappointment washed over her as she dug through her bag and pulled out the lacy cami and matching satin shorts she'd brought. What a waste. She quickly changed and slid under the covers.

She pulled them up with her when she heard Evan's light tap on the door.

"Come in," she said.

Evan opened the door a crack. "You doing all right? Got everything you need?"

The polite questions of a host. She didn't have the one thing she wanted most. "I'm good, thanks," she said, sending a polite smile.

"Okay, goodnight, then."

"Evan?"

The door opened wider. "Yeah?"

Sara's heart pounded. "You– You could stay in here with me."

He leaned against the door casing, presumably considering her suggestion, and she held her breath. Slowly he straightened. "Don't think I haven't thought about it, or wouldn't like to," he said. "But it's probably not a good idea right now. Get some rest." He quietly clicked the door into place.

Alone, Sara switched off the bedside lamp and lay still. Here she was in Evan's bed – exactly where she'd hoped to be tonight. But no Evan. Funny how things worked out.

She tried not to be disappointed the next morning when he walked her to her car, loaded her suitcase into the hatch, then turned and pressed a kiss to her cheek.

"Text me when you get there," he told her.

She forced a shaky smile. "I will."

Four hours of open road stretched before her. A lot of time to think, or more likely, to play the weekend over and over in her head. At least he said he still cared for her. That was something. But their future was clouded and uncertain. He needed time and space. The question was, how much and for how long?

## Chapter Twenty-One

The lines of text blurred before Mary's eyes, and she finally closed the folder. Squeezing her eyes shut, she rested her head on the table. She'd struggled through about two-thirds of the material in the packet, reading a little each day for more than a week, but there was no way she'd get it all read in time for the seven o'clock council meeting. If a vote came up and she didn't know enough to give an opinion confidently, she'd just have to abstain. She'd given it her best shot.

Mary pushed her chair back and reached for the new claw-foot cane to stand. It wasn't as fun or lightweight as the leopard print, but it gave her more stability. Her goal now was to simply make it to the meeting on time. That included getting dinner ready, and putting herself together. Moving at the pace of a slug, it wouldn't be easy.

She flexed her fingers. At least the cast was gone. She didn't look like such an invalid. And she could manage to get a meal on the table again.

An hour later, she called Grant to the kitchen. "Just grab those rolls out of the oven, love, then we're all set." She admitted the oven had her spooked a bit.

"All ready for the meeting?" Grant asked when they sat down.

"Well, I didn't get through all the material, but close enough."

Grant glanced at his watch. "Where's the packet? Show me what you didn't get to, and I'll read it out loud."

261

Mary's fork hit the table, and her throat clogged. Would he soon be spoon-feeding her, too? She took a sip of water before answering. "Thanks, love. That's a great idea. I may take you up on that next time, but let's don't worry about it for tonight."

At ten minutes to seven, she hoisted herself out of the car. She tossed her purse over her shoulder and picked up her packet, then made her way to the council chambers.

With impeccable timing, she arrived at the entrance along with Steve Unruh who stepped ahead and opened the heavy glass door.

"Good to see you, Mary. We missed you last time."

"Thanks, Steve."

"Good holidays?"

"Absolutely. And you?"

"Had a nice break."

Mary smiled, grateful for the mundane, ordinary conversation. Made her feel normal.

When she started up the small step to the elevated tables where the council members sat, Phil Matthews nearly leaped out of his seat and rushed to her side. "Here, Mary, let me help you with that," he said, grabbing her arm.

She swayed a bit. "Thanks, Phil, but I've got it." People yanking on her arm was the worst. It threw her off balance.

Mary sank into her padded chair, and glanced around the room, nodding at the city attorney and other council members there. A moment later, Pamela Shore placed a bottle of water on the table in front of Mary.

"Can I get you anything else, Mary? Would you like coffee?"

"No, thanks, Pam. This is great."

"How are you doing?"

Mary sensed heads turning their direction. Maybe if she spoke loudly enough, everyone could hear, get the scoop, and not ask again. "Taking a little longer for me to haul myself around, but I'm doing well, thanks."

"Have you got a diagnosis yet?"

She forced an upbeat tone to her voice. "Still testing. Apparently I'm something of a mystery. 'Stump The Doctors' . . . just a little game I like to play."

Pamela patted her arm. "All right. Keep us posted. Glad you're here."

Mary turned her attention to the agenda on the table, but her head snapped up again at the sound of Kent Donovan's voice. When she caught his eye, she smiled and waved. Didn't remember seeing him on the agenda. Must be library business – something she'd let fall by the wayside knowing that Claire and Kent were on top of it. Kent appeared to be heading her direction when Pamela called the meeting to order. Instead, he took a seat in the front row.

He stood and approached the podium when Pamela announced the public forum open.

"Evening, everyone. Sorry I didn't contact the office in time to get on the agenda. Just wanted to give you all a quick update on the library opening."

"Thanks for coming, Mr. Donovan," Pamela said. "We're eager to hear about it."

"Ribbon cutting and grand opening will be at ten o'clock on Saturday morning, March twenty-seventh. Of course you're all invited. We'd love for you to join the library board to help cut the ribbon."

Mary made a note in her calendar. Claire would be in town. The thought made her smile so she added an exclamation point and a happy face to her note. Something good to look forward to.

"Interior work should be finished in a few weeks. Books on the shelves and computer system up and running two weeks prior to opening. Marketing and advertising campaign will start end of February."

Mary's ears perked up at that. She hadn't considered marketing needs for the library, but she just happened to have a daughter experienced in that field who needed a job.

"Excellent," Pamela told Kent. "Thank you for the update. It's exciting to see the new facility coming together. You can be sure we'll be there."

Kent nodded, and instead of returning to his seat, headed for the door. As discreetly as she could, Mary pulled her cell phone into her lap. She sent a text message, hoping she wasn't too late to put Sara's name on the table.

For the next thirty minutes, the council listened to people unhappy about the new traffic flow around their neighborhood, complaints about shoddy sidewalks and assorted problems that made Mary's head hurt. They hadn't even come to the real agenda yet.

Trying not to space out, she sipped her bottled water, and forced herself to make eye contact with members of the audience, nodding when appropriate – she hoped. By the time they got to the first voting item, Mary was considering excusing herself and bailing out. Without comment, she voted in favor of the zoning change allowing a multi-family development as a buffer between a residential area and the highway. Mary didn't see a big demand for that kind of housing in Whitfield, but the tornado had brought change, and maybe it was needed. There didn't seem to be any opposition. *Thank God.*

She flipped back through her packet to see if there was controversy over the next item. Park benches. Hmmm. Why would anyone object to new park benches? She re-read some of the comments. Too much noise? Wait. Oh, that was the play equipment. No, the bids for the play equipment were coming in over budget. That was a money issue.

"And to plant some of her rose bushes, which the garden club will care for. No obligation from the city."

Mary glanced up and saw Cynthia Schroeder at the podium. What did rose bushes have to do with anything? She looked around the room, but no one else seemed confused.

"All in favor?" Pamela asked.

Mary held up a hand. "Wait. I'm sorry. I think I've missed something. We're voting on rose bushes?"

264

Cynthia stared at her. "We– We're talking about Mother's memorial bench."

Mary's face flashed hot. *A memorial.* Cynthia's mother had been killed in the tornado.

All eyes turned to Mary.

"We thought it would be nice to plant some of the rose bushes we salvaged around her bench at the park," Cynthia explained.

The papers in front of Mary blurred. How had she missed that? "Right. Of course. Yes, of course. That's a lovely idea. I vote yes." Her heart sank as she registered the hurt in Cynthia's eyes. Her mother, Adele, had been a delightful woman with the greenest thumb in town. That they still had some of her prize roses was a blessing. She made a note to call Cynthia tomorrow.

Mary muddled her way through the rest of the meeting, abstaining from the final vote on cell service providers and a tower. She hadn't read the supporting background material, though she knew people were eager for better service. She'd trust her colleagues on this one.

As soon as Pamela's gavel hit the table, Mary gathered her things, ready to bolt. She pushed back her chair to find Pamela behind her.

Leaning close to Mary, she whispered, "Stay put for a few minutes. I'm driving you home."

Mary stayed where she was. Standing, she rested her knee on the chair, and chatted with the other council members as they came by. She'd hang around to avoid a scene. Besides, she didn't need an audience while she trudged to her car. But she didn't need a ride, either.

"Whew. That was a long one," Pamela said when she returned to Mary's side. "An awful lot to take in for your first meeting back."

"It's fine," Mary told her. "I'm sorry I didn't get through everything. With all–"

Pamela cut her off. "Not a problem. You ready to go?"

"Definitely."

Pamela kept pace beside Mary, making her self-conscious. She'd be better on her own. Outside the building, Mary took a deep breath, hoping the blast of cold air would make her more alert. Then she tried to brush off her pesky sidekick. "Thanks, Pam. I appreciate—"

"Let me run you home, Mary. My car's right here. You can get yours tomorrow."

Pamela's car was closer. Mayor's spot. First one next to the handicap spot. Not for the first time, Mary wondered if she ought to apply for one of those handicap tags, but the idea made her grimace.

In the end, she didn't have the energy to fight it. Pamela unlocked the door and hovered while Mary maneuvered inside. Thankfully, Pamela didn't insist on chipper conversation during the drive.

Sagging against the front door, Mary dug in her purse for house keys. She rarely used them since she kept her car in the garage. Before she could find them, the porch light snapped on, and Grant opened the door.

Grant caught hold of her as she tumbled into his arms. "Hey, what's going on? You all right?"

Apparently not. She blew out a heavy breath. "That may have been my last council meeting. It was awful."

Grant offered his arm, and helped into a chair by the fireplace. He returned a moment later, handed her a glass of wine and sat facing her, his eyes full of concern.

"What happened?"

She took a sip before launching into the details. They talked until Mary couldn't keep her eyes open or think coherently. "I've got to get this figured out," she told Grant, rubbing her temples.

"Well, not tonight, you don't. Sleep on it." He held out his hand to help her from the chair.

"No, I mean what's going on inside me. I have to get some answers. I—" Hearing the high pitch in her own voice, she stopped short, and took a deep breath.

Grant tipped her chin. "Hang in there, darlin'. We're going to find the best doctors in the country. And we're going to get our answers."

266

**

The meeting was still on Mary's mind the next morning, but she hadn't come to any conclusions. Except that she'd made a fool of herself. She let out a snort. The word on the street would probably be that she was losing her mind. Maybe no one would be surprised. She glanced at the clock as she poured a cup of coffee. She'd wait until mid-morning to call Cynthia and apologize for her behavior.

"Hey, babe?" Grant suddenly hollered at her from the family room. "I forgot to tell you last night, Dana called while you were gone."

"Okay, thanks."

At this rate, she'd spend the entire day on the phone. There were worse ways to spend the day, she supposed. She'd put off calling Dana for too long. She wanted to know what, if anything, Dana had heard from Evan, but there was a fine line between catching up with her friend and gossiping about her daughter. Mary didn't want to be on the wrong side of the line. Sara was also on her list of people to check in with. Looked like the call to Kent was going to pay off. Hooray for that. He'd practically pounced on her suggestion last night. Hopefully, Sara would agree to take the job, and the work would charge her batteries and revive her spirits – possibly bring her to Whitfield.

She sent a text to Dana. *Hey, give me a call if this is a good time to talk.*

Mary's phone rang within a minute, and Dana's voice came on the line. "Hey, stranger. How are you? How you feeling?"

"Made it through the holidays," Mary said, ignoring the question that sounded as though it came from *Nurse* Dana. She didn't want to talk about her health. "Missed you New Year's Eve."

"We just decided we wanted to ring in the new year at the new house."

"Sounds very cozy."

Dana gave a light laugh. "It was. I'm so glad I didn't skip the fireplace."

Mary decided to test the waters. "It was great to see Evan at Christmas."

"I wish the weather had been better and we could've seen Sara, too. Sounds like we'll be seeing more of her, though. You do realize she and Evan have something going on, right?"

"I know." Mary couldn't contain the grin that spread across her face. "Isn't that fun? I sure do like that guy. I'd love to see this go somewhere."

"Oh, Mare, I'd love it, too. I don't want to get way ahead of ourselves, but he sure did seem happy."

"I haven't heard anything about New Year's Eve, have you?"

"No, why?"

"Just wondered if he'd said anything. They were supposed to be together for the weekend, you know."

"Actually, I didn't know. He didn't mention going to Dallas."

Hmm. Entering gray area here. "I think Sara was visiting him this time," Mary hedged.

"Oh." Dana's voice lowered, and Mary knew the direction her thoughts had turned. Of course there was that other thing she didn't know. Mary cringed, feeling a little guilt about keeping that news from Dana. On further consideration, she probably should've called Sara first.

"Interesting," Dana said.

"Well, like you said, we're probably getting ahead of ourselves." A change of subject was in order. "You all set for the big day?"

"Oh, I am so ready."

The conversation turned to Dana's upcoming wedding. Two more weeks and she'd be in Hawaii, getting married. And Mary would be home from her appointment at Mayo. In her mind, everything revolved around that. She tried not to dwell on it, but–

"Listen, Mare, I need to get back to work. I'll give you a call later." Dana's words snapped Mary back to the present.

"Sounds good," she said. Mary ended the call, and turned her gaze to the light flurries dancing in the gray skies outside. The frosty weather reminded her of Sara, and memories of playing in the snow. For a moment, Mary let herself imagine the possibility of making snow angels with her granddaughter – something a little girl couldn't do in Dallas. But that line of thinking brought her right back to wondering what had happened last weekend and whether it had affected Sara's decision. That Sara hadn't called didn't seem like a good sign. Taking a deep breath, Mary punched Sara's number.

"Hi, Mom."

"Hi there. Do you have time to talk?"

"Yeah. I just got off the phone with Kent Gerard. I think it's going to work out for me to do the library marketing. Thanks for the tip."

Mary squelched an outright squeal. "That's fantastic. I wish I'd thought of it earlier."

"Yeah, it is kind of short turn-around. Guess they were so focused on getting it built and stocked, they forgot about telling people about it."

"You think you can accomplish what they need?"

"Sure. Might be a little more expensive if we run into any rush charges, though. Kent thought the budget would be okay. He has to check with a couple of committee members first. He said they're trying to do things locally as much as possible, and I still qualify."

"Good. I'm–"

"My only concern is, well, whether it could be awkward. Working with Kent, I mean."

Mary held her breath a moment. "Why would it be?"

Silence greeted her question.

"Do you mean because of you and Evan?" she asked cautiously.

"Yeah. I– I don't know what he's told his mom, and I'm definitely showing."

"You told Evan?"

"Yeah."

"And?"

"Oh, Mom. He– he was surprised, of course."

"What did he say?"

"Well, he didn't say 'hey, that's great. Congrats.'"

Mary's heart sank. She could hear the disappointment in Sara's voice. "Did you stay the weekend?"

"I stayed at his place one night, then came back to Dallas."

"Oh, sweetie. I'm sorry. Was he angry? Did you break up?" Another rejection? Mary wondered how many her daughter could handle in such a short amount of time. She couldn't imagine Evan being ugly or hateful, though.

"Not exactly, but, he, um, wants some time."

Mary blew out her breath, careful to keep her tone neutral. "I suppose that's understandable. How are you doing?" Time was no big deal. A few years apart obviously hadn't eroded their relationship before. No reason to assume it would now – once he got over the shock. Mary sensed that the bond between these two went deeper than they even realized.

"I'm okay. If I can start working, that'll help."

"Definitely. Keeping busy will keep your mind occupied. Can you do it all from there?"

"No. If they want to use local talent and print shops, I'll probably have to come to Whitfield at least for a few days."

"That makes sense." And was exactly what Mary had hoped. She was tempted to offer to meet in the middle, but she knew Sara would roll her eyes at the idea. "Listen, sweetie, I just got off the phone with Dana before I called you. Evan hasn't told her anything. She didn't even know you were there for New Year's." Mary paused a moment, weighing the options. Who should be the one to drop the bomb? "Do you want me to tell her? Or should it come from Evan?" And could it possibly wait until after Dana's wedding? The last thing Mary wanted to do was cause her friend any worry. Perhaps blissful ignorance would be best on this one. "Can you text Evan and get his opinion?"

"Maybe I should."

"Might get some dialogue going."

"I'll think about it. Don't do anything for now, okay?"

"Okay. Keep us posted." Mary retrieved her mug and sank into the chair behind her. Doing nothing sounded like the perfect plan for the moment.

**

The last call of the day was to Jason. After supper, Mary curled up on the bed and opened her laptop. It'd been two days since her son had sent her a list of questions and discussion points for her appointment at Mayo. She'd read through them once, but wanted to make sure she understood them. Normally, she had no problem asking direct questions, but she had to admit that the thought of questioning doctors at Mayo Clinic was a little intimidating.

"The main thing is to know all the tests they're doing, and make sure you understand the meaning of the results," Jason told her. "If they take blood, find out exactly what they're testing for. And get your own copy of the results."

"Sure, but, honey, I won't be able to make any sense of it. It'll be like trying to read Greek to me."

"I want to see it, Mom. Also, I've talked to some people around here. Make sure they check for Lyme disease."

"Yeah, they already did. It was negative."

"Tell them to check again. It can be hard to detect."

Mary drew in a deep breath. She was beginning to lose focus. Asking questions was one thing, telling these top doctors to re-check something could get her labeled as annoying right off the bat. Rubbing her temples, she tried to infuse her voice with a light teasing. "Sounds like you're telling me to be bossy and demanding," she said.

Jason chuckled. "Mom, come on. That's not going to be a problem for you, is it?"

Mary let out a whoop. It was her first real laugh of the day. "All, right. All, right. I've got this."

It felt good to laugh, but as she ended the call, reality hit hard. She had appointments to see some of the most renowned doctors in the world — because whatever was going on inside her was serious.

**Chapter Twenty-Two**

Grant reached across the table inside the small bistro that had been recommended by one of the nurses at Mayo, twining his fingers through Mary's. It was a quiet place with a low fire burning between the main seating areas. Something noisier might have been better to cover their silence. They couldn't talk about it. Not yet. For now, they were going through the motions.

He ordered a burger, and Mary ordered soup and salad. He figured neither one of them had much appetite. Eating was just one of the things they had to do. At least it offered a diversion.

With her free hand, Mary lifted her hot tea, and their eyes met over the mug. The pain in her beautiful eyes tightened his chest, and he looked away. He stared into the fire, the anger and frustration inside him burning every bit as hot.

"What are we going to tell the kids?" Mary's soft words snapped Grant's head around.

He looked at her for a moment, wondering if there was a right answer, if she already had an opinion. In a split second, he formed one. "The truth." His words were firm. Their children were his wife's greatest joy, and by God, if her days were numbered, he'd see to it that they spent as much time – quality time – with her as possible. If she tried to hide the facts, they'd check in as they were doing now, but they'd go about their regular routines. That was not acceptable.

With a quick squeeze, she withdrew her hand. Lifting the mug again, she turned to stare at the fire. "Just trying to think it through."

"Mary," his voice softened. "The kids will want to know. You can't cheat them out of spending time with you."

The waitress delivered their food, and they ate in silence. Grant chewed, swallowed, got the food down, but tasted nothing. Enjoyed none of it. He couldn't shake the heavy cloud that had settled over him. His heart ached.

"Dessert, folks?" Their waitress appeared at the table. "We have excellent peach cobbler, apple pie, chocolate cake." She smiled expectantly.

Grant watched Mary, gracious as always, smile at the waitress as if it was an ordinary dinner out, as if their world hadn't been turned upside down. "It all sounds lovely, thank you. But I couldn't eat another bite. Dinner was delicious."

"Just the check," Grant added. When she returned, he quickly calculated a tip and left cash to avoid waiting any longer.

In the car, Mary's phone buzzed, indicating she had a text message. Grant glanced over as she pulled the phone from her purse. A moment later, she pressed the phone to her chest. "I've got three text messages." He heard the quiver in her voice and willed her to stem the tears until he could pull her into his arms. He took her hand.

They drove the short distance to their hotel, and he helped Mary from the car. The five-minute walk to their room was slow and arduous. Inside, he snapped the deadbolt into place, helped Mary out of her coat, and then pulled her against him.

"Oh, Grant." She clung to him as sobs wracked her body. He held her close, rocking her, rubbing his hand across her back, pressing kisses into her hair, desperate to reassure her, but knowing there was nothing he could do to take away the hurt.

This woman was his life, his joy. He simply could not imagine living without her.

But the words of the doctors hammered in his head. Signs indicated ALS, a disease that robs its victims of mobility and, eventually, the ability to breathe. The lucky ones might live five years, but most people succumbed within a few.

He'd never known a greater fear in his entire life.

Belatedly realizing it might be hard for Mary to stand even though he was holding onto her, he scooped her up and lowered them both to the edge of the bed. For a long time, he cradled Mary on his lap, letting her cry, his own tears wet on his face. "I love you so much, Mary-me," he whispered near her ear. He felt her nod as she burrowed into his shoulder, fresh tears flowing.

"We're going to fight this," he told her. "We're going to do everything we can."

In addition to her physical therapy, that meant occupational therapy, finding ways to help her function and move around. He'd gut the whole damned house if necessary. She'd also start taking Riluzole, the only medication FDA-approved for ALS – a medication that *may* slow the progression, but would not cure the disease. Mary had tucked the prescription into her purse without looking at it. There were other meds, too. Something for muscle spasms, one to help boost her energy level, and now one for depression. He couldn't imagine his help-others, take-charge, get-things-done Mary needing an anti-depressant, but he understood that the disease would take a mental toll as well as physical.

Mary shifted, and Grant smoothed her hair. "You want something to drink? Water? More tea?"

"No," she whispered. "I think I just want to go to sleep." She lifted her head and met Grant's eyes, then placed her palms against his face. "I'm so thankful for you."

Grant's chest tightened, and with a groan, he pulled her close once again. They sat quietly, lost in their own thoughts until Mary raised her head again.

"I should probably respond to the kids."

"Let me set you up a group text." When she'd changed into her pajamas, Grant handed her the phone.

"Just say things went well, we're heading home in the morning, and we'll call tomorrow night. How's that sound?"

She raised her brows.

"We can't tell them in a text." And even when they gave the news he knew she'd try to put a positive spin on it. He didn't see how that was going to work this time.

He turned down the covers, and helped her into bed. A few minutes later, he switched off the light, and spooned up behind her. As exhausting as the day had been, he knew sleep would be a long time coming – if it came at all. How could he shut out the what-ifs and mental images of a future he didn't want to see?

The sense of failure and complete helplessness nearly strangled him. He'd always taken pride in providing for and protecting his family. He could make money to build a solid house, pay for a high-tech security system, install sprinklers and smoke detectors and carbon monoxide sensors. But he could not protect his wife from the disease that was attacking her, an unseen enemy that had kidnapped her and was threatening to take her from him.

He thought of the trips they'd planned, and wondered if they would take any of them. People traveled in wheelchairs all the time. But it was more than that – there was the fog and listlessness. If she could get some strength and energy back, maybe they could still manage a few of them.

Not intending to disturb her, he pressed a kiss to her bare shoulder.

Turning to him, she twined her arms around his neck. And sleep didn't matter.

\*\*

Sara gripped the steering wheel hard. She wished she could go faster, but she'd set the cruise control to keep her speed from getting out of hand. Getting to her parents' house a few minutes earlier wasn't going to make a difference – wouldn't change the diagnosis or make it any easier to accept. But she had to get there.

She was still numb from the shock of the phone call her parents had made last night to her and her siblings. She'd been expecting the doctors to figure out what was wrong with her mother – and *fix* it. That her mother could be issued a death sentence had never crossed Sara's mind. *Mind blown.* A few minutes online were enough to understand this was the worst possible outcome. Sara swiped a hand across her eyes to catch the tears that welled again. She wanted to scream and cry. Wanted to call Evan and tell him. Tell him life was too short. That they shouldn't stop seeing each other, or slow down, but spend more time together. Every possible minute.

But she couldn't tell Evan about her mother's disease. Her mother had specifically forbidden it. "I refuse to say a word until after Dana's wedding," she told them in her 'I mean business' voice. "I'm holding the four of you accountable to make sure there's no leaking." That meant at least another week of secrecy. God, Sara hoped Kent had a crap-ton of work for her to do.

The upcoming meeting with Kent weighed on her mind as well. Was she still hiding her pregnancy, or did Evan's family know? When she'd texted Evan and explained that she'd be working with Kent, Evan's response was that "he'd take care of it." What the hell did that mean? Would he, too, want to protect his mom from any stress or worries? Did that mean Sara needed to wear a bulky sweater and coat to meet with Kent? Or was it, to quote Evan, "time to own" the pregnancy?

She rested a hand on her protruding abdomen. Unexpectedly, the name Heather floated into Sara's head. Again. The name had come to her when she picked up a home and gardening magazine at her last OB-GYN appointment. Thinking about a name gave her goose bumps, but she liked Heather. It seemed like the kind of name that would go with someone sweet and calm and thoughtful. Someone who would enjoy nature and music and be curious about the world around her – the kind of traits she'd wish for in a little girl.

Sara shook her head, trying to erase that train of thought. Most days, she maintained her conviction to keep the baby. Other times, doubts crept in – times when she worried about money and Evan. And now, her mother. Thankfully, her GPS interrupted with a route notification. Her heart bounced as she merged onto the state highway that would take her into Whitfield.

Annie's car already sat in the drive when Sara pulled in. She scrambled into the house and found her mother and sister at the kitchen table. Her mother stood immediately, a smile lighting her face, even though it drooped slightly on one side. She held out an arm, and Sara rushed forward, wrapping her mother close. This time, she couldn't stem the flow of tears. Soon, Annie joined in, and the three of them held each other in a long three-way hug.

"My girls. I'm so glad you're here," her mother murmured. *Her girls.* Sara choked on a sob, and corrected her earlier thought. No, it was a four-way hug. Her daughter would be one of "the girls."

Her mother pulled back, and pushed Sara's hair away from her face. "Let me look at you," she said, her hand resting gently on Sara's bump. "You are finding the cutest tunic tops and sweaters."

Sara swiped an arm across her eyes then squeezed her mother's hand. "Mom, come on, I don't want to talk about maternity fashions. I want to know how you're doing. How do you feel?"

Her mother heaved an audible sigh. "Not too bad today. A little tired and achy, but that seems to be the norm these days. We don't know any more than we told you on the phone. And I really do want to talk about something else. I want to talk about you two. Dwelling on this damned disease is only going to make me cranky and miserable. So, please, let's don't go there."

Sara exchanged glances with Annie in silent agreement. They could talk later. But at the same time, Sara's heart pounded. She could give them something to talk about. It was in her power right now to bring her mother joy and happiness. Was this the right time? Once she confirmed, there was no going back.

"Sara, grab something to drink, and let's go find the comfy chairs."

While her mother and sister headed for the family room, Sara reached into the fridge and pulled out a carton of orange juice. With shaking hands, she poured the drink, then followed. When she started to sink into an armchair facing them, her mother gestured. "Come over here. We can all fit on the couch."

Sara perched on the edge so that she could see her mother's face.

Her mother's brows pulled together. "What's the matter?"

Sara drew in a deep breath. "I– I've got something to tell you."

Folding her hands in her lap, she gave Sara her full attention, but her reply was hesitant. "Okay."

"I've made a decision," Sara said quietly, noting her sister's wide eyes. "I'm keeping the baby."

Her mother's mouth dropped open. Taking Sara's hands, she looked deeply into her eyes. "Are you sure?"

Blinking back tears, Sara nodded.

Her mother's warm hands cupped Sara's chin. "Three weeks ago you were considering adoption. What changed? This isn't because of my diagnosis, is it? Because that–"

"No. No, Mom. This is what I want. On New Year's weekend, I ended up in the hospital in Tulsa. I had some spotting that turned out to be nothing serious, but it was scary. I was so afraid of losing her. And I realized I didn't want that to happen."

"What?" Her mother gasped. "You were in the hospital?"

Sara launched into the story, recounting everything that had happened – except for the aftermath with Evan, which she already knew, anyway. Sara leaned forward. "So, it's not because of your diagnosis, but I do want this little girl to have the chance to know you. You're going to be the best grandmother ever."

Her mother's face crumpled, and she pulled Sara into a fierce hug. "I cannot wait to meet this baby girl," she whispered, her voice thick with tears.

Sara squeezed her eyes shut, and let her mother's hug envelope her. For better or worse, this was the trajectory of her future.

**

The following day, even under the shroud of her mother's diagnosis, Sara felt as though a weight had been lifted from her shoulders. Having made her decision once and for all, she felt more in control – ready to move forward.

Still dressed in a bulky sweater, but with renewed confidence, she headed to Hannah's Café to meet Kent Donovan. Inside, she greeted a couple of familiar faces, and ordered a protein smoothie, though her mouth watered at the sight of the decadent pies lining the glass case at the counter. Hopefully the mango-strawberry drink would provide a sugar fix. Drink in hand, she settled at a large table where she and Kent could spread out materials.

She'd done her homework, and had a long list of ideas and potential costs. And, thanks to Evan, she had what she considered reasonable, competitive rates for her own hours and efforts.

It was only moments before Kent arrived. He scooted into the booth across from her and extended his hand. She didn't have to stand, keeping her secret safely out of view.

"Great to see you again, Sara. And really happy to have you on board."

"Thanks, I'm looking forward to it." And she meant it, more than she'd realized until now. It felt good to be working, contributing, doing something productive.

"I did some research on bookstore openings and other library openings, the kinds of activities they feature and what we might be able to do in Whitfield," Sara told him. "But first, why don't you tell me your essentials. What are the main points you want to make about the new library?"

For an hour, they discussed the features of the library and publicity points.

"This is awesome," Sara told him. "Sounds like it's going to be a great place for Whitfield kids." Growing up,

280

the library had always been one of her favorite places, and that was without all the new reading nooks and computer stations for kids. Visions of fun outings with her little girl flitted through Sara's mind. She'd have to find a local library in Dallas. Now that she thought about it, she couldn't recall spotting a single library in her area.

"That's the idea," Kent said, pulling Sara's thoughts back to the present.

She smiled at the excitement in his eyes. "All right. Let's get them in there. What about the grand opening?"

Sara had big visions of activities and events – appearances by authors, story time with the mayor or local police and firefighters, buttons, banners, bookmarks and other giveaways. Her list was long. She stopped recounting her ideas when she realized Kent was staring at her with wide eyes.

"Wow," he said, shaking his head. "You're way ahead of me. Love the idea of getting some local celebs involved." Kent made checkmarks by some of the items on her list. "Why don't you get started on these, and let me run a few of the others past the committee?"

"No problem," Sara said. "I'll write this up and send you an email that you can print and sign." Even though she preferred working the creative side of things, she knew enough about the business side to want a signed contract.

She told Kent good-bye, and practically skipped toward the door. Hopefully by the time she contacted the local businesses and nailed down a designer, Kent would have a green light on all the items he wanted.

**

Sara spent the next four days talking to local businesses and working on plans for the library opening. The evenings, she spent with her mother, sometimes her parents, curled up in front of the fire. It seemed to her that they'd slipped into a silent agreement not to talk about her mother's health. Sara wasn't sure that was the best approach, but she wanted to respect her mother's wishes. Alone in her bedroom at night, Sara checked and rechecked her cell phone for messages from Evan.

Finally, on her next-to-last night in Whitfield, one popped up.

*Mom said Kent was singing your praises. Glad to hear the meeting went well*, he wrote. Short and sweet. Well, sweet was questionable. But that didn't stop her from obsessing over the tone of the message. Was it meant to be terse? A conversation starter?

*It's a fun project*, she wrote back. *And I really like Kent.*

*Great. You still in Whitfield?*

*Leaving tomorrow.*

*How are you feeling?*

Sara blew out her breath. He probably thought he was being nice and showing concern, but she wished he would stop asking how she was feeling. It only served as a reminder that her pregnancy was front-and-center in his mind. And she wished he'd call. She'd much rather hear his voice. But at this point she was still taking cues from him, and he seemed to prefer texting. Probably because it felt less personal.

*Hey, getting ready to board the plane. Safe travels back.*

*Thanks. Bon voyage. Hope Hawaii is wonderful.* With a sigh, she plugged in her phone to charge and set it on the bedside table. It'd be a long travel day, and she doubted she'd hear from him again for a while.

The following day, she met with the graphic artist she'd hired in Paxton, had lunch with Annie and made about a dozen phone calls. So far, people seemed genuinely interested in participating. Good thing, since she didn't have much time.

When she got back to her parents' house, she found her mother napping. Four o'clock seemed awfully late for a nap. Leaning against the wall, Sara watched her mother sleeping, and frustration welled inside her. Surely she wouldn't spend all her days either sleeping or going to doctor's appointments. As far as Sara could tell, the medicine her mother had started was only making her feel worse.

She tiptoed to the kitchen to start peeling potatoes.

"Wow, look at you," her mother said behind her a few minutes later. "Handling that knife like some kind of ninja."

Sara let out a sharp laugh, and turned. "Glad it looks like that, anyway." She gestured toward the table. "But for your own safety, you might want to step back. How 'bout some tea?"

"Sounds lovely. Seems a little drafty in here. How did your appointments go?"

"Good." Sara poured two cups of tea then dropped into a chair across from her mother and filled her in on the library opening.

At six, the garage door went up, signaling her dad's arrival. She wasn't sure whether he was really that busy in retirement, or whether he was deliberately trying to stay out of the way and give her and her mother some girl time.

"Hey, Daddy," Sara said when he came into the kitchen from the mudroom.

"Hey."

Getting up from the table, she peeked inside the crockpot, and jabbed a fork at the roast. Shredding perfectly. She rinsed the fork, checked the potatoes roasting in the oven, then slipped past him into the combination laundry/mud room and moved the load of clothes to the dryer.

"Supper will be ready in about ten minutes," she announced, returning to the kitchen and pulling plates from the cupboard. "Just need to finish up the salad."

Her dad stood in the middle of the kitchen. "You did all this?"

"She did everything," her mother piped up. "While I just sat here on my tush like some kind of princess."

"A princess exiled from her throne," her dad said, humor in his voice. "How are you feeling?"

Sara smiled as her father leaned down to kiss her mother full on the mouth. She didn't hear her mother's murmured response. A pang of envy swept through Sara. Her parents had been in love a long time. Sadness quickly replaced the envy. She couldn't imagine the hell her dad was going through. She swallowed hard. "Daddy, what would you like to drink?"

Tired eyes met hers. "Got any coffee?"

With an ache in her chest, she turned quickly. "I'll make some."

They lingered over dinner long after their plates had grown cold. Sara enjoyed hearing her mother chat and laugh. When they finally fell into a comfortable silence, Sara refilled her mother's wine glass then began clearing plates." I'll clean up. You guys take your time finishing your drinks."

Sara jumped a few minutes later when her father moved close beside her. "Thanks for helping Mom," he said quietly. "I appreciate it."

An instant lump clogged her throat, and Sara simply nodded. Tears sprang to her eyes when he planted a quick kiss on the top of her head.

"I told her she didn't have to," her mother said. "Rita has offered to help cook. Plus, we've still got some casseroles and soup in the freezer."

"You can save those for when . . . when you need something quick and easy." Sara stopped herself from saying when you don't feel well or when no one's here to help, but a wave of guilt washed over anyway. It didn't make sense. She hadn't lived in Whitfield since college days, but going back to Dallas somehow seemed as though she were abandoning her mother. In truth, there weren't that many casseroles in the freezer. Then again, most people didn't know yet that her mom had been diagnosed with ALS. When they did, would they come through to help? She thought of her earlier conversation with Lindsey. Surely the people of Whitfield would put that behind them and rally to her mother's aid.

It wasn't as if she'd be alone. Her dad was there. Dana would be home soon. Annie was less than an hour away. After more than a week in Whitfield, Sara was beginning to feel a little too familiar in her surroundings. Her apartment in Dallas seemed like a distant memory.

## Chapter Twenty-Three

Sara saved the edits she'd made to the press release for the Whitfield Library grand opening, then opened a new tab in her browser. Time for a little social media break. She began gathering her notes, then glanced back at the computer screen. In the next second she gasped as Evan's face popped up on her monitor – and hand collided with the glass of water on the table.

Lurching out of her chair, she grabbed her laptop and reached for a towel to mop up the mess. "Damn it," she hissed under her breath. Fortunately, the glass had been almost empty. She'd been hoping to see some photos from his mother's wedding, but the reality of that one took her breath away. The guy was spine-tingling handsome in his dark tux and white dress shirt unbuttoned at the collar. There must've been a breeze because his hair was nicely rumpled. That smile was delicious and genuine. *Wow.*

Heart pounding, she set the computer back down and scrolled through the few photos Evan's sister had posted – the close-up of Evan and his mother, one of the ceremony, and one of the whole family. Tears pricked Sara's eyes. Dana looked stunning in her ankle-length dress, and her curly hair swept into a loose up-do. Sara couldn't help but smile at the family photo on the beach. Dressed in wedding attire, except for their bare feet, every one of them radiated joy and happiness.

She eyed her phone, quickly calculating the time in Hawaii. Middle of the day, they were probably doing some time on the beach. That visual warmed her cheeks. Shaking her head, she picked up the phone and punched in her mother's number instead, hoping it was past her naptime.

"Hey, Mom."

"Hi, sweetie." Her mother answered too quickly to have been asleep.

"How are you feeling?"

"Fine. What's up with you?"

Sara figured that was a lie, but she let it go. Her mother had probably answered that question a hundred times in the last week. "Have you looked at Facebook today? Maddie posted a few pictures of the wedding."

Her mother let out a low squeal infused with excitement. "I didn't see anything from Dana. Bet she's been a little busy."

"You think? Try Maddie's page. Not sure whether you can see anything without being friends, though."

"Oh, we're friends. Give me a minute to get to my computer."

"Sure. Where is it?"

"In the bedroom."

If her mother was at her usual spot in the kitchen, Sara knew that was going to be a long, slow walk. "Mom. It's okay. You can look later."

"No, I want to see them. I'm sure they're gorgeous. Dana has such a flair."

Sara tried not to visualize her mother's progress down the hallway, the tedious lift of her foot with each step. She kept talking to cover the time. "You're right. They're amazing. Dana's dress is beautiful."

"I know. I saw it. She ordered it from a place in Chicago then had it altered here."

"Looks like the weather was perfect, too."

"Oh, good. I hope the whole thing was perfect. Okay, hang on."

Sara waited. Then she heard the gasp on the other end of the phone.

286

"Oh, my. They should sell the rights to these to a travel company. They look like something you'd see in a brochure."

"I know, right?"

"The bare feet are cute."

"Yeah, pretty fun."

"Wow. Look at Evan. He should take up modeling. Oh, Sarie, he's–" Sara heard her mother's voice thicken. "I sure wish–"

"Mom, we can't go there. I've made my decision, and Evan will have to decide for himself what he wants."

"Have you talked to him since he's been in Hawaii?"

Sara squeezed her eyes closed. "No. I haven't. Listen, you sound tired. You all right?"

"Oh, I'm feeling melancholy, I suppose. I look at these beautiful pictures, and see so much happiness and I– I can't help but wonder about the future. It's a hard thing to get my head wrapped around."

"I know."

Her mother let out a heavy sigh. "Okay, enough of that. I'm kicking melancholy to the curb, and better start thinking about what I can throw together for supper."

"All right. I'll talk to you later." Sara glanced at the photos again, grazing her hand across the screen. And she'd better start thinking about Evan as a friend again. The way they used to be . . .

He was the only friend she had from that far back. Though Sara had plenty of friends from college, she didn't have a best friend. No one to whom she told her deepest fears and feelings. No one who had her back the way her mom's friends did. No one outside of the family, anyway. She and Annie were closer than they used to be, but somehow, that was different. Morgan was probably her best buddy, but Sara wondered if they could stay close as their paths diverged, as she took a sharp turn down the "mommy track." Maybe through motherhood she could acquire the kind of close-knit friends her mother had.

Sara slumped into the chair, and glanced around the apartment, her thoughts churning as doubt crept in. With everything going on, she was starting to question whether

Dallas was the right place for her. Did it make more sense to be closer to her mom and sister now? Her dad might not love the idea, even though he'd been appreciative of her help while she was there. But maybe he'd be okay with it if she got her own place. She let out a frustrated groan. How would she pay for that? Once the library opened, that account would dry up, and she couldn't imagine many other career opportunities would knock at her door. Then again, Dallas hadn't been exactly lucrative, either. The cost of living would certainly be cheaper in Whitfield. Evan's words came back to her – Whitfield was a great place to grow up. Could it be for her daughter, too?

**

Mary shoved the phone in her pocket and rubbed her temples, trying to think. She was sure she'd taken all her meds today, but the muscle spasms were driving her crazy. This might be a good day for one of those frozen soups. She doubted she could stand long enough for meal preparation. A few things she could do sitting down, but it didn't feel right. Lately she'd taken to pulling a kitchen chair to the counter and propping her bum knee against it for support. That gave her a little extra time upright.

She forced herself to do ten minutes of exercises, hoping that would help, then headed back toward the kitchen. About halfway down the hall, her leg buckled. Her stomach lurched as though she'd just taken the first dive of a roller coaster, and she grabbed at the door casing to the hall bathroom to catch herself. Chest pounding, she stood still for a moment to balance herself, and listened for Grant's footsteps – hoping he hadn't heard anything. Thankfully, she'd managed not to land on the floor. Grasping the cane, she gingerly tested her weight before taking the next step.

Grant met her in the kitchen a few minutes later. "What can I do?"

Pasting on a smile, Mary leaned against the counter and gestured toward the fridge. "Want to poke your head in the freezer and make a decision?"

He looked from her to the appliance and back again without opening it. "How about I take you out to dinner instead, darlin'?"

Myriad thoughts collided in her brain. She'd become such a homebody since it turned cold and going out was such an effort. Since the anger over the layoffs had made chance encounters touchy. Since she'd become dependent on an ugly claw-foot cane and sported a droopy smile. Mary sucked in her breath. Was it vanity keeping her at home? Was it fair to Grant to make him a recluse as well?

And the biggest question – could she rally and get herself put together for a public appearance?

Mary reached out and took hold of Grant's arm. "Well, that's the nicest invitation I've had all day. But don't plan on eating any time soon. It's going to take a while to make this happen."

He opened the fridge, took out a beer and held it up to her. "Take all the time you need."

An hour later, she debated between Grant dropping her off at Hannah's door and wrestling it open herself or going with Grant to park the car and walking in the cold. She chose wrestling the door. She stepped carefully over the threshold, and started toward the hostess station, but stopped when she saw the Kellers at a table nearby. Gail Keller, longtime leader of the children's choir, stood and wrapped Mary in a hug. "How are you getting along, hon? We sure do miss you at church."

"Oh, I'm a little shy of sunny-side-up, Gail." They were still going to Sunday morning services as regularly as possible, but had given up some of the more social activities. Going to church was part of her faith, and she wanted to be there. She just didn't like feeling as though her attendance was part of a plan to try and curry favors with God. And while she believed in the power of prayer, she was uncomfortable being on the prayer list. What stung a little bit was giving up her time slot in the nursery. She was perfectly able to sit and rock a baby, but she'd sensed some concern from the parents. Trying not to dwell on all the things she was missing, Mary shook the cane. "Look out, y'all. I'm like a bull in a china store with this thing."

Gail laughed, and squeezed Mary's shoulder. "Good to see you. Enjoy your dinner."

"Thanks. You, too."

Mary managed an awkward slide into the booth, and tucked the cane underneath, resting it against the seat. At least it was small enough to still be discreet. If the progression was true to form, she'd need a full-fledged walker eventually. And then a wheelchair. At that point, getting out would probably be more work than it was worth – at least for her.

She looked up from the menu when Grant slid in across from her.

"You all right?" he asked.

"Of course. I didn't even hurt anyone on my way in."

"I'm just worried about you hurting you."

"Stop worrying. This was a good idea." Hannah's dinner menu offered pure comfort food. "I think a good old-fashioned chicken pot pie is what I need."

After they placed their order, Grant turned to her. "Hey, I heard some good news today."

"Yeah? Well, do tell."

"Dave Henderson got on at the co-op."

A whoosh of relief swept through Mary. "Did he really? Oh, thank goodness. I'm so glad people are getting jobs and bouncing back."

"Yeah. It's good. Also talked to Doug about hiring a couple of guys to do maintenance at the strip center. We're about ready to open."

"Right. That would be great. Who'd you have in mind?"

Her brow furrowed as Grant toyed with his straw, avoiding her eyes. "Tough question?"

With a lopsided smile, he reached over and squeezed her hand. "Thinking about Billy Jordan. He's looking for part-time work. And maybe Rob Daniels."

"*Rob Daniels?* Are you serious?" Now she understood his hesitation. Bobby and Regina's son – the vandal. Oh, boy. "Why?"

290

"He needs something to do in his spare time to keep himself out of trouble. He's a decent kid."

Mary sat back as their dinner was delivered. Good timing. She could use a minute to think about this one.

"I don't know, Grant. I'm not sure Regina and Bobby would love it. On one hand, it might seem like charity. On the other hand – and this is worse – it might seem like you want to influence their kid."

"I do."

"Um, Grant, parents don't generally appreciate other people interfering with their parenting. Or their kids."

He fell silent, and they both concentrated on chewing their food. Mary considered his proposal. She was reluctant to get involved, having been told by the boy's mother to butt out and buzz off. But, if they could do something good, if they could help a kid get back on the right track . . .

She leaned forward. "You think you can trust him?"

"I'm willing to find out. He's done a good job on the community service. Showed up every place he was supposed to, and on time. Seems pretty responsible."

Heaving a sigh, Mary met Grant's eyes and the sincerity there. Maybe he needed a new project, and this would give him something to do other than worry about her. "It's not a bad idea," she consented.

"Might take some of the pressure off if the kid had his own money."

Mary gave a reluctant smile, and shook her head. "God, Grant, we are such suckers."

Grant chuckled. "Call it what you want. I'd go with Mr. Nice Guy."

The title reminded Mary of Kent Donovan, and she pulled her cell phone from her purse. "Speaking of nice guys, you have to see these pictures of Dana's wedding." She held the phone out to him. "Doesn't that look heavenly? I'm so happy for her."

"Me, too." His eyes searched hers. "So, about Hawaii . . ."

Uh-oh. She knew what was coming.

"What do you think?"

The long drink of water she took was strictly a stall tactic. Slowly setting the glass on the table, Mary shook her head. "I don't know," she said, her voice barely more than a whisper.

"We'll need to cancel soon if we aren't going."

"I know." Their trip was only a month away. They'd planned it over the summer when Grant's retirement was getting close. "I'd love to go," she told him. "But what if I can't do anything? What if it's like Phoenix? That would be a huge waste of money and just no fun." Her throat constricted as she envisioned her cane sinking into the soft grains of sand and herself following soon after. "I can't walk on the beach or do any hiking. Can you see me trying to stay upright on a boat?"

"Maybe not, but I can see you lounging at the pool or the beach. It's about relaxing in the sunshine, right?" He reached across and ran a thumb over her hand. "It's up to you."

Yeah, she knew that. And she knew he'd support her decision, whatever it was. But she didn't miss the flicker of hope in his eyes. Traveling had been at the top of their to-do list for the new year. If they didn't go now, would they ever?

**

The next morning dawned cloudy and gray. The wind howling against the windows offered no motivation for Mary to leave her warm blankets. She rolled over and burrowed deeper into the covers.

When she woke again, she glanced at the bedside clock. Already ten o'clock. If she didn't find the energy to get up now, she'd miss her therapy appointment – and lunch with Annie. It took all the effort she could muster to swing her legs to the side of the bed and sit up. In the next second, she clutched her right hand. Then let out a sharp scream as panic seized her. She shook her hand as though someone had spilled acid on it.

*No!* Oh, God, no. She squeezed it into a fist, then shook it some more. A second later, Grant burst into the room.

"What's the matter?" He knelt beside her.

"Oh, God, Grant, I can't feel my hand."

He took her flailing hand in both of his and began kneading. "Shh, baby. Let's see."

His voice was calm, but the flicker of fear in his eyes told her he knew the significance immediately. Progression of the disease. Limbs were affected first. Often legs, and then hands.

Slowly, the feeling returned. As relief rushed through her, Mary sagged against Grant. "Oh, God, I thought– What if–?"

He rocked her, pulling her close. "I know, sweetheart. I know. You probably just slept on it funny and it fell asleep."

She nodded, but didn't let go. She took in some deep breaths, trying to calm her shaking hands and the queasiness brought on by the sudden onslaught of fear and adrenaline.

"I feel sick," she whispered.

"You need to get to the bathroom?" he asked.

"No. Just let me sit here a minute."

"Would some tea help? Maybe some toast or crackers? I've got coffee made, but–"

Mary shook her head. "I don't think so." The thought of food turned her stomach. "I don't think I'm ready to get up."

Grant pulled back, but held on to her arms, looking into her eyes. "Mary, are you sure? You've been in bed for twelve hours. You've got the therapy appointment."

She fell back against the pillow. "I'll have to miss." All she wanted to do was curl into a ball.

"Well, you have to eat something."

"In a little while." She closed her eyes, and didn't open them as Grant pulled the blanket over her then kissed her cheek.

Grant studied her a moment. Looked like it'd be lunchtime before she was up, and then she'd have to take her medication. Which might make her feel worse. He ran a hand over his jaw, wondering if he should call her doctor. Of course he knew the answer already. *People react differently to the drug. Some people don't tolerate it well. Not a lot they can do, blah, blah, blah.* Bottom line was, the drugs might not help – and she might never get better. He clenched his fists. Sometimes the thoughts slammed into him so hard they took his breath away.

He quietly left the room. He wouldn't call the doctor, but he'd better let the therapist and Annie know they weren't coming.

At lunchtime, Grant watched Mary pick at her grilled cheese sandwich and take a few sips of tomato soup. By the time he cleared away the dishes and got her a fresh cup of tea, she looked as if she was about to doze off again.

He began kneading her shoulders. "Hey, babe, how about I read some of the materials for the next council meeting to you? Get a little jump on things."

Swiveling, she looked up at him, and he saw the uncertainty in her eyes.

Turning away again, she lifted the mug. "I'm wondering if it would be better to help me write a letter of resignation."

Grant went cold, and in a flash he pulled out the chair beside her, and faced her. "Are you serious?" He took her hand. "Mary-me, you can't give up. Come on, you're just having a reaction to the medicine. You've got to give it some time."

She pushed her hair back and met his eyes. "Even so, I'm not sure that's the best use of the time I have–" She glanced away. "–my time now." With a hollow laugh, she gave him a smile. "It's not like I was planning an intense political career, you know."

"It's good for you to stay active, though," Grant countered. Wasn't it? He wished he'd asked more questions. Hell, he was starting to think a visit to a shrink might not be a bad idea after all. Just to talk things through.

"Good in theory," she said, her voice taking on a weary tone. Her gaze shifted somewhere behind him, and he could almost feel her withdrawal. How could he keep her engaged? Lift her spirits? Maybe it was the meds or she was simply tired. Or could she be giving up?

"Tell you what, I'll get the folder and we can see what's coming up. You don't have to commit to anything yet."

"Sure," she murmured.

He helped her to an armchair by the fire then went to retrieve the folder, stopping by the kitchen to grab the bowl of chocolate-covered almonds she kept on the counter.

She lasted less than an hour.

"That's enough for now," Mary told him. "I can't think any more."

Standing, he kissed the top of her head. "How about some mind-numbing TV?"

"Perfect."

As they watched, or more accurately, he watched and Mary dozed on and off, a couple of ideas began buzzing in Grant's head. By the time he tucked the blankets around Mary that night, he'd made up his mind.

He picked up the phone and punched in Claire's number.

"Grant?"

Claire's voice came on the line, tentative, laced with concern. Grant swallowed hard. "Hey, Claire."

"Hey. What's up?"

Right or wrong, he'd face the consequences later. "Mary needs you," he blurted out.

"What?" Claire's voice turned sharp. "What do you mean?"

"She's really sick, Claire. She doesn't want to make a big deal of it, but you—"

"What does sick mean, Grant? Tell me."

He took a deep, shuddered breath. "I don't know how much she's told you. Did you know the doctors are treating her for ALS?"

"Oh, God." Claire's voice was barely a whisper.

"The medicine is making her sick. Today she was so weak she could hardly get out of bed. The thing is— I think she's—" He swallowed hard, hating to say the words. "She's scared, Claire."

"I'm packing a bag now. I'll be there first thing in the morning."

Before Grant could respond, the line went silent. His head dropped to his hands as relief washed over him. He needed the back-up.

## Chapter Twenty-Four

Mary opened her eyes. And blinked. Twice. Was she still dreaming, or was her best friend sitting not three feet away from her with a silly smirk on her face?

"Hey, stranger," Claire said, confirming her presence. "It's about time you came around. Watching you sleep has been a blast, but I'm ready for the next act."

Mary pushed herself upright, and ran a hand through her hair knowing she must look like something out of The Walking Dead. "What are you doing here?" she croaked.

Claire leaned forward and took her hand. "Do you happen to remember a little conversation we had a while back when I said you weren't doing this sick thing without me? Did you think I was kidding?" Her gruff tone matched the concern clouding her eyes. "Well, I wasn't."

Mary's lips trembled, and she was immediately pulled into Claire's arms. The tears came swift and hard. Half laughing, half crying, Mary clung to Claire like a woman drowning. It was a long few minutes before Claire pulled back and handed Mary a wad of tissues.

Mary pressed them to her face. "I'm sure I blubbered all over you," she said.

Claire shrugged. "I'm completely wash and wear." She ran a hand up Mary's arm. "Let's talk."

A thousand thoughts raced through Mary's mind in about a second. Of course Claire was here because she'd already heard the news. Drawing in a shuddering breath,

Mary met Claire's eyes again. "Let me guess. You've talked to Grant."

Claire bit her lip, nodding. "I did. He called me. Now don't get mad at him for doing the right thing. He's worried."

"I know," Mary told her. "I'm not mad. I'm–" She searched for the rights words, unsure which emotion was the strongest at the moment. "I guess I'm stunned. And heartbroken. I want to see my kids get married, and I want to know my grandkids. I just can't believe it's real. Sometimes when I think about it, I have anxiety attacks. I can hardly breathe."

It was the first time she'd mentioned the panic attacks. Now that she'd started, she couldn't seem to stop talking. She could always spill her guts to Claire. Mary's voice broke as she slammed a fist into the palm of her other hand. "It's so frustrating. I want to go places and do things. I want to make the most of whatever time I have. You know me, I'm used to juggling and running and–"

"Yes, I'm familiar with your Wonder Woman syndrome."

Mary gave a snort. "Looks like that bitch left me high and dry. I feel so tired and foggy I can hardly get out of bed and get myself dressed." She blinked back the tears that welled again. "Damn it, I missed lunch with Annie yesterday." Her voice pitched higher as she filled Claire in on the details of the past few days.

"When's your next doctor's appointment?"

"I see my regular doctor next week. We'll assess the medication. We can change the dosage, or I can switch to an IV instead of a pill, but honestly–" she met Claire's eyes, and took a deep breath. "This is it. This is the only medicine there is, and it's not always effective."

Claire pushed up from the bed and began to pace the room. "Okay, look. It's the middle of winter. It's cold and crummy, so this is the perfect time to get the medication figured out, and take a break. Lighten up. Don't be so hard on yourself. You don't have to do anything. This is your chance to try out hibernation."

She stopped and shot Mary a pointed look. "Seriously, think about how much you'd be complaining if you had to get out in the cold and snow, right? So relax. Listen to some music or books on CD. Let Grant wait on you. Look at this way – you can opt out of winter. Think how many people would kill to do that."

Mary couldn't help but chuckle. "True that." Somehow, Claire managed to put things in perspective, or at least offer a different view. "Audio books are a good idea," Mary agreed. Why hadn't she thought of that? "I can't read more than a few minutes at a time. My brain turns to mush and I zone out."

"So zone out. Doesn't matter. What's the next read for book club?"

Mary rubbed her temples. "Hmm. Not sure."

"Never mind. I'll look it up. I'm still getting the emails."

While she did that, Mary took a minute to count her blessings. Claire was good for her. Mary had always imagined them as crazy old ladies, still best friends, causing trouble with their nursing home antics. Maybe they wouldn't get to that point, but she refused to be angry and bitter. They'd had so many good times – thirty-some years of watching each other's backs. Each additional day was a gift. Same went for Grant, and her kids. She wanted more. She desperately wanted more, but the truth was, she was a lucky woman. Whether she had two more years or twenty, or more, her life was so full.

"I've got this," Claire said, interrupting Mary's thoughts. "Let's order several. Some funny ones, too."

"Please, God," Mary said.

Thirty minutes later, they'd ordered six books. It might take her a year to get through them, but at least it felt like she was doing something proactive. Maybe she'd even make it to a book club meeting. "That was fun," Mary said.

"Oh, hey, I have some magazines for you, and . . ." Claire lifted a canvas bag. "Chocolate, of course."

"You're talking my language," Mary told her. "That's–" She broke off at the sound of her phone buzzing, and lifted the pillow beside her. "Where the heck did I leave my phone? Oh, who cares? I don't want to talk to anyone, anyway."

"Here. It's on your dresser. Want me to get it?"

Mary waved her off, but Claire picked up the phone. "It's Dana."

"Oh, she must be home. Yes, yes. Answer!"

"Why, hello, Mrs. Donovan. How's life?"

With a grin on her face, Mary listened to Claire's side of the conversation.

"Just down for a visit. Yes, she is. Sure thing." Claire held the phone away from her face. "Hey, can Dana come over and play, too?"

"Absolutely. And tell her to step on it. I want to hear all about Hawaii and the wedding." Of course there was more than Dana's wedding to talk about. Mary was sure Dana didn't know the results of the Mayo visit, but she might know that her son was backing away from the romantic relationship that had been blooming with Sara. And she might know why.

**

Mary considered getting out of bed and getting dressed. It'd be the proper thing to do. But proper had gone the way of normal and pretty much ceased to exist. "I should probably get up," she said, anyway.

"For what?" Claire asked. "Dana's seen your bedroom before."

"Food," Mary said, remembering she hadn't eaten breakfast. "I should at least get some sustenance for us if it's going to be a pajama party."

"Well, hey, I happen to know the guy who runs the joint, and he says there's a cheese and cracker tray ready to go, and some fresh fruit. I'll just run down and get that. What do you want to drink?"

Mary shook her head. "This must be a dream. You're waiting on me?"

"Haha." Claire tipped an imaginary hat. "As you wish," she said, quoting a favorite line from The Princess Bride. "Just don't get used to it."

300

"Right. I'll have coffee if it's made. Otherwise tea will work. With caffeine."

As Claire retreated from the room, Mary remembered a time not long ago when their roles had been reversed, when she'd feared for Claire's life as she struggled through grief, depression and alcoholism. Mary, along with Claire's daughter, had been there to hold her up and help her get back on solid ground. A new worry crashed in. How strong was Claire now? How would she deal with Mary's absence? Could it send her spiraling into a relapse? Oh, how Mary didn't want to be responsible for that. She wanted to be around to see her friend thrive in her new life and newfound freedom. And, yes, to push her when necessary. That's what friends were for.

And then she remembered how her friend happened to be at her bedside. Today's turn of events had started with her amazing husband. She picked up the phone and sent Grant a text. *Thanks, love. I needed this. XOXO*

Mary closed her eyes and let her head fall back against the pillow. She had to take advantage of every opportunity to recharge. Hopefully some food and caffeine would help, too.

It seemed only a second had passed when Claire announced her re-entry. Mary's eyes fluttered open as Claire placed a steaming mug on the bedside table.

"Here you go, your Highness." She jerked her head. "Found this one loitering in the hallway, so I put her to work."

Mary's gaze strayed past Claire to find Dana also carrying a tray. Mary pushed herself upright again, and held her hand out to Dana. "Just put that on the bed. Wow. Look at you. You look fantastic."

Dana's face was tanned, and lovely as ever, but her eyes conveyed her shock. Claire had apparently spilled the beans. Dana ditched the tray and pulled Mary into a tight squeeze. "Oh, Mare."

Mary clung to Dana, and tears welled again. "I am so, so sorry," Dana said, her words muffled against Mary's hair. She pulled back, and watery eyes met Mary's. "I can't believe it. This can't be right."

Mary heaved a deep, shaky sigh, unsure whether she was speaking to Dana-the-friend or Dana-the-nurse. "Well, I've been poked and tested and bled dry for two months now. And that's what they say."

Dana's face pressed closer, her eyes wide. "Tell me everything. What exactly are they saying?"

Ah. The nurse. Mary shook her head. "Not now. Really. My head is spinning, and my heart hurts. Can we not go there right now?" She refused to indulge in or subject her friends to a pity party. What she needed was a distraction from the doctor's words beating inside her brain.

Claire's arm and a plate came between them. "Here. You need food. You need to get some strength back, because we are fighting this."

Mary offered a shallow smile, and took the plate. She wasn't sure how much she could get down, but at least looking at it didn't turn her stomach.

"That's right," Dana chimed in. "Go for the protein and carbs. The more, the better."

Reaching for a chunk of cheese, Mary nodded. "Thanks, team. Listen, if I doze off between bites, talk among yourselves until I come-to."

The company definitely improved her appetite, and a social occasion made nibbling much more pleasant. Once Mary felt as though she could follow a conversation, she nudged Dana. "You. Start talking. I want to hear all about the wedding."

Dana's eyes suddenly sparkled like the diamond solitaire on her finger. "It was perfect. Absolutely magical. I couldn't have asked for anything better."

For the next twenty minutes, Mary listened to the lilt of happiness in her friend's voice as much as the details of the trip. That's what mattered most.

"So no travel snafus?" Claire asked. "All the kids get back to their places all right?"

And with a thud, reality hit. Mary's glance met Dana's in the same instant. Evan. The silent question hung between them for a moment until Mary found her voice. "Did you have a chance to talk to Evan?"

Dana took a sip from her mug then slowly nodded. "I did. He told me about– about Sara." Brows raised, Dana's eyes darted toward Claire.

"It's okay. She knows," Mary said. "How's Evan doing? What did he say?"

"Well. It wasn't a long conversation. He's surprised, of course. And I have to admit I was caught off guard, so I don't know if I said anything helpful or intelligent."

"Was he asking your advice?"

"Not really. Said he just thought I should know."

Her voice trailed off, and Mary waited for more, hoping to get some insight on Evan's intentions. When no more information came, she leaned forward, blurting out the question that weighed heavily on her heart. "Do you think he still wants a relationship with her?"

Dana's face twisted. "Oh, Mare. I don't know. I think he truly loves her. But he's hurt. Evan has always been my rule-follower, the one who wants to do things the right way. It's not that he couldn't love a baby. He's good with kids, but . . ."

"But?" Mary prodded.

"I think he has some doubts."

"Doubts?" Mary echoed. "About what?" She could see Dana's deep intake of breath before she spoke again.

"Whether their relationship was partly her wanting to find a dad for her baby."

Mary let that digest. She could see how that would be a man's initial reaction, of course. But Evan – and Dana – knew Sara. Knew her character. Knew she wasn't dishonest or devious. Still, there were those years of distance. And they left plenty of room for doubt, she supposed. She, too, took a deep breath. They had to get through this with everyone's feelings and respect intact.

"Listen, I'm not criticizing Evan. That reaction is understandable, but I can tell you the baby had nothing to do with it. Sara agonized over telling him about the baby. Her real fear was that it would ruin what was developing between the two of them. I also know that she made the decision to keep the baby fully expecting to be a single mother. You, in fact, are her role model."

When Dana shot her a 'yeah, right' look, Mary stared at her. "You don't believe me?"

Dana turned away. After a moment of silence, she looked back at Mary with a soft smile, and a shrug. "I've made some mistakes."

"So, you married the wrong guy. Personally, I'm glad Sara's not doing that. But everything else? Hell, you're an excellent role model. You've raised three terrific kids on your own. You're a success in your career. You're creative, and generous. You care about people–"

Dana put up a hand. "All right, already. You'll have this going to my head, and bust my halo."

Mary squeezed Dana's arm. "Hey, whatever happens, we're not letting this come between us."

"Of course not," Dana agreed, shaking her head. "We can't interfere, either. We'll just have to wait and see what happens with Evan and Sara. And you know what? It's been ages since I had a knitting project. My fingers are itching to do something, and I think some baby blankets and booties are just the thing."

Mary's lips trembled as tears threatened again. "Thank you," she whispered.

"For what?"

"For understanding and not judging her. For not being angry."

Claire, who'd been silent but listening, stepped forward. "They'll work it out," she said. "It's out of your control, and you don't need another thing to worry about."

"Group hug," Dana said, moving closer. "Claire's right. You just need to focus on your health."

"And that baby," Claire added. "Think about that sweet baby, and how much fun you're going to have being grandmamma."

"That's right, Mare," Dana said. Mary choked back a sob as her friends surrounded her. "She's going to bring so much love and be loved by all of us."

Gratitude swelled inside Mary, and she knew without a doubt that whatever happened, her daughter would not be alone, and her granddaughter would have the love and support of these incredible surrogate grannies.

## Chapter Twenty-Five

Almost an hour before her alarm clock was set to wake her, Sara gave up on the idea of sleeping, and climbed out of bed, her checklist running on an endless loop in her head. Somewhere in the past two months marketing coordination had turned into project management and event planning. She was set to meet Kent and other library committee members at nine. The mayor would lead the ribbon-cutting at ten. After that, the doors would open to the public for children's story time, tours and talks with librarians, and author appearances throughout the afternoon. It'd be a full day. With posters plastered all over town and some advance publicity from local and surrounding newspapers, she expected a good crowd.

She slipped into the kitchen, not surprised to find it dark and quiet. Her mother slept until at least nine o'clock most days, even though she was starting to come out of her winter hibernation. In the five weeks that Sara had been back home, living in Whitfield, they'd fallen into a routine with her and her dad up first, making coffee, and then taking turns helping her mother get ready for the day. That would be her dad's job today.

After making some adjustments to her mother's meds, they'd established that late morning was her peak time for energy level and attention span – and the best time to get her out of the house and engaged in regular activities. She'd participate in the ribbon-cutting, and then take the eleven o'clock shift at the library card sign-up table. She and Claire had been on the library board long before the tornado destroyed the facility, and she deserved to be part of today's celebration.

Sara glanced out the kitchen window at the high pink clouds just beginning to glow in the morning sunrise. Daylight Saving Time meant mornings were a little later for now, but she didn't mind. She welcomed the longer days and the arrival of spring. Giving up Dallas meant a longer wait for warm, sunny days. Still, she'd lucked out today. The forecast of 63 degrees would allow her to wear her gray "business" dress and black boots. There was no disguising seven months pregnant, but she'd look professional.

A light breeze greeted Sara when she hoisted herself out of her car across the street from the gleaming new Whitfield library. Considering it was March in Kansas, she appreciated the absence of gale-force winds.

Inside, she took a last look around the library to make sure all tables and stations were in place. Volunteers would begin arriving soon to set up drinks and snacks. Cookies and popcorn would be available all day. She'd snagged the old-fashioned popcorn machine from the VFW hall plus a couple of guys to run it. She wondered now if the smell of popcorn would forever permeate the books on the shelves. There could be worse problems, she supposed.

She lingered a bit in the children's section, taking in the bright colors, computer stations and cozy reading nooks. Named the Andy Donovan Youth Center in memory of Kent's son, Sara had no doubt it would be a huge hit. She already looked forward to the day when she and Heather would snuggle up with a book in one of the big window seats with pillows.

"Sara!"

She turned to see Kent striding toward her, a huge smile on his handsome face. "You ready for this? It's going to be big. I can feel it."

She returned the grin. He was like a little boy who'd just scored a winning touchdown. "I think you're right.

And I'm sure we're all set to go." She knew because she'd taken care of every detail. Checked and double-checked. "Really, Kent, the community is going to be blown away. It's fabulous."

"What do you say we get this party started?"

"I'm in."

Near the main entrance, board members and community leaders were beginning to gather. "You enjoy," Sara told Kent. "Call me if you need anything. I'm going to check–" The buzzing of her cell phone interrupted, and Sara gave a quick thumbs-up. "It's the Paxton news station," she whispered before moving aside. Adrenaline shot through her as she took the call. One thing she'd learned on this job was she enjoyed being the go-to person, seeing the whole picture rather than a small part of it. The news crew was setting up outside, getting ready for the ribbon-cutting.

Sara ended the call, but before she made it to the front doors, Claire stepped in front her. "Hey, you!" She wrapped Sara in a hug. "Wow, you look fabulous. Now, listen, don't tire yourself out. We've got lots of volunteers." She lowered her voice and added conspiratorially, "And a lot of people who do nothing but stand around who we could put to work."

Sara patted Claire's arm. That was another lesson from this project – how blurred the line between personal and professional relationships could be. In this case, she wanted to stand out in a professional manner. Still, she loved Claire and the rest of her mother's friends, and couldn't help but smile. "Don't worry. I'm fine."

Just before ten o'clock, Sara located the photographer she'd hired to document the event, and they shuffled outside along with everyone else. News crews and a crowd she estimated at more than a hundred people milled around the entrance. Sara stopped to make sure the scissors for the cutting were in place, and that the mayor's lapel microphone was turned on. Then she stepped back and let the board members take their places. Her mother moved to the entrance with her chunky cane and Claire for support. Sara hoped her mother could stand for the duration of the short ceremony.

Movement on the other side of the line-up caught her eye. Her heart flip-flopped as Evan slipped through the people to stand beside his mother. She quickly looked away as questions hammered her. What was he doing here? Surely he didn't come to Whitfield just to support his mother's new husband's pet project. Of course he knew she'd be here. Did he come to see her? With blood pounding in her ears, she barely registered Kent stepping forward, and had no idea what he'd said before he announced her name. Her head snapped around, and the crowd began to clap.

"Couldn't have pulled off today's event without her."

Oh. A public thank-you had not been on the agenda. Nor was it expected. She belatedly thought to smile at the audience. Almost against her will, she glanced Evan's direction. For a second, her smile faltered – until her eyes met his, and she realized they held . . . pride? Admiration? Heat washed over her, and relief almost buckled her knees. But what was he thinking? To show up here in a public place in front of curious eyes, where both of their mothers were in attendance? Not to mention that she was on the clock and would be all day.

Maybe he felt a public meeting would take some of the intimacy out of the situation. Or, he could simply be satisfying some curiosity. One thing he would see front-and-center was her protruding abdomen. Several locals had commented on her pregnancy in the last few days, and she accepted congratulations, engaged politely, but gave away no personal information. Today, all conversations would be redirected to the new library. There was no way she'd have time for any real discussion with Evan. Maybe that was best.

Her eyes were drawn his direction again, and she acknowledged that she wouldn't mind resting her head against his solid chest for a moment, or feeling his strong hands knead her shoulders. At the end of the day, that'd be heaven. Her daydream came to an abrupt end when she realized Dana was sending her what seemed to be an encouraging smile. Had Dana known Evan was coming? More importantly, had she influenced his decision? Sara had warned her mother weeks ago that she was to be Switzerland – neutral territory with silent opinions. Or none at all. She'd prefer the same from Dana.

Sara glanced at her watch, and turned her attention back to Pamela Sharp, mayor of Whitfield. If the woman stuck to her script, they'd all be inside soon, and scattered throughout the library. Finally, Pamela lifted the scissors for all to see, and then sliced the wide red ribbon in half. As the doors opened, and people filtered in, Sara was thrilled to see the news reporter who'd been standing next to her make a beeline for the mayor. Interviews and airtime would be tallied and added to her event report – and her portfolio.

She'd already picked up another job from the connection she'd made with a designer in Paxton. And she had an appointment next week with the director of the community center. Over time, she just might be able to eek out a living doing what she enjoyed even in Whitfield. For now, this is where she needed to be. This where her head needed to be, too, but that didn't keep her from scanning the area for a certain familiar face a few minutes later, though. Just knowing Evan was in town was a huge distraction.

She handed the reporter her business card and then headed inside to make sure everything was off to a smooth start. In the foyer was the library card sign-up station. Her mother waved frantically.

"Hey, Mom, how's it going?" she asked in the most neutral voice she could muster.

"Busy," she said. Standing, she moved close to Sara, and whispered, "Sarie, did you see Evan's here?"

As if she could miss the fact.

"I did, Mom. How are you holding up?"

"Hanging in there for now. Did you talk to him?"

"No. I don't have time. Does anyone have questions out here? No technical issues, I hope?" Their conversation was like a game of ping-pong.

"No. Everything's fine. Evan stopped–"

"Mom . . ." Sara gave the warning tone.

"All right, all right. I'm so proud of you. I always knew you were talented, but this is outstanding, sweetie. You're really good at this."

"Thanks. Let me know if you need anything." Sara turned away before her mother could switch topics again.

For an hour, she wandered the premises, touching base with volunteers and Marcia Hurst, the head librarian – and keeping one eye on high alert. After confirming there were no fires to put out, and no sign of Evan, Sara made her way to the break room, wondering if he'd actually left without speaking to her. Sure, there was a good crowd, but the building was certainly not big enough for him to get lost in. Why come just to avoid her? She sat for a moment, nearly inhaling the protein bar and small carton of milk she'd stashed in the refrigerator. Lingering would only give her mind more time to wander and stew. When her cell phone buzzed, she stood quickly, ready to get back to work. But a glance at the device stopped her. Evan had sent a text message. Holding her breath, she opened it. *Nice job*, he'd written.

Nice job? Well, that was personal and heartfelt. She groaned inside. With a shake of her head, she tossed the milk carton in the trash and practically marched to the far corner of the building – the quietest area – where authors were doing readings. Of course, she'd have to respond to his text, but it would have to wait. She had no idea what to say. He hadn't exactly done a ghost-out on her, but their communication had become polite and distant.

Sara slipped behind a group of people listening to the author from Paxton. Leaning against a bar-height bookcase, she unzipped a boot and wiggled her aching foot, almost sighing out loud. A few minutes later, a different kind of tension filled her as she felt a presence behind her. Slowly she turned, and Evan slid a book toward her.

"This is a good one," he said, his voice low and close beside her.

Sara looked at the title, and caught her breath. "In a World of Crazy, Be the Love." What was that supposed to mean? Her world had turned crazy, for sure. But the rest of that . . . Be the Love?

"You've read that book?" Finally, she found her voice and glanced up.

Nodding, he shoved his hands into his pockets. "I have. A gal at work was reading it. Said it was helping her through a rough time with her daughter."

Sara frowned, unsure what point he was trying to make. It was hard to think at all with him so close. She stared at the book for a long moment while questions jumbled her brain like a tangled mass of wires about to short circuit. Was he sending her a message? Could he want to be part of her life again? She wiped clammy hands against her dress then met his eyes.

The tender sincerity there sent a surge of hope rushing through her. She gripped the bookcase hard.

"There's a chapter about the rewards of unselfish love," he continued. "Loving someone without thinking about what you'd get out of it yourself." He looked behind her, and paused, as if deliberating his words. Then deep blue eyes rested on hers again. "I read that chapter three times. And knew I had to be here today."

She held his gaze. "Why?"

A hint of a smile turned his lips, and he caught her free hand. "What time are you done here?"

Her heart pounded, and she fought to keep her voice steady. "It's over at four, so I should be done by four-thirty probably."

He cocked his head. "Can we talk?"

Tongue-tied again, all she could do was nod.

"I'll pick you up."

\*\*

Sara leaned against the door and watched the last volunteers load the popcorn machine into a waiting van. She glanced at her watch. Evan could already be on his way, but her leggings and sweater called to her. Wherever they ended up for their "talk," she'd be more comfortable in a change of clothes. She said a quick good-bye to Marcia, who'd lock the place up, then headed for her car.

Inside, Sara pulled out her phone and sent Evan a text to meet her at home instead.

In a lucky break, she discovered her mother was napping. Still, she'd have to let her dad know she was going out. Maybe she could avoid any details, though. Not that she had many. Where would they go? On a Saturday evening all the bars and restaurants – public places – would be full. Their other options, their parents' houses, offered no privacy, either. It was as if they were back in high school, with no places of their own. Nowhere to get away from curious, prying eyes and ears.

When she heard Evan's car pull into the drive, Sara reached for her purse and jacket.

"Hey, Dad, I'm going out."

"Celebrating the big event?" he asked.

Not exactly, Sara thought, though she admitted the positive vibes she'd picked up made her feel optimistic. Maybe celebrating *something*. She smiled. "Probably won't be around for dinner. You two okay on your own?"

"I think we'll manage. Have fun, Sunshine."

She dashed to the door before Evan could get there.

He greeted her and opened the car door.

She managed a breathless, "hi," and climbed inside. "Where to?" she asked when he slid into the driver's seat.

"It's still early enough I was thinking we could get one of the corner booths at Bailey's."

That might work. Bailey's would be busy and noisy, but if they got a table in the back corner, they'd be away from the main crowd. "Sure. Let's try it."

Inside, most people were lingering at the bar. A few people glanced their direction, and Sara couldn't help wondering if Evan would feel uncomfortable under their gaze. Would people speculate she was pregnant with his child? And would it matter? Though he'd silently conveyed support and encouragement, nerves fluttered in her stomach. She needed to hear what he had to say.

"Did you get lunch?" he asked when they were seated.

"Not really. I mostly snacked."

"Let's order food then."

312

First things, first, she supposed. Sara ordered house chips and a turkey Panini, though nothing sounded particularly good. She took a sip of the water their waiter had left, then lifted her eyes to Evan's.

Hands folded, he leaned forward. "So, here's the deal."

Watching him, she waited.

"I miss you."

Tears flooded her eyes, and she swiped at her cheeks. Smiling, she nodded, too emotional to speak. She chalked up the emotional outburst to being pregnant. Or nerves. He'd had her on edge all day. Plus, she'd been on her feet and hadn't eaten a real meal. The combination of those things hit harder than she expected. The next thing she knew, Evan was beside her. He offered his napkin, and pulled her into his arms.

Yeah, she's missed this. Missed his smooth, sexy voice and his soothing serious voice. Missed his late-night calls and the feel of his arms around her. That they held her now mattered more than she'd even realized. To bear the disappointment, she'd told herself she had to accept his withdrawal, that it was only natural. But the truth was, she wanted him in her life.

Sniffling, she pulled back and took a deep breath. "I miss you, too."

That familiar slow, boyish grin spread across his face. "I was hoping you'd say that."

Somewhere between laughing and crying, she let her head fall against his arm.

He kissed the top of her head. "I've been tracking you, you know."

"What?"

"I knew all about today. I can't have a five-second conversation with Kent or my mom without them mentioning your name. Singing your praises. I know you've run into Mom and Chase around town. Seems like I know when you've been to the grocery store or the bank, or post office."

Sitting up, Sara shook her head. "Wow. Stalker much? Like big brother watching me."

313

With a sudden light in his eyes, Evan shook his head. "Not quite," he said just before his lips met hers. The long, slow kiss left her feeling drugged. And warm. And happy.

He pushed the hair back from her face, and gently twisted a strand around his finger. "Can we start over?"

## Chapter Twenty-Six

Mary turned from the refrigerator when Grant walked in from the garage.

"Hey, love."

He leaned in for a kiss. "Morning," he said, running a hand across her back. "Looks like you got some good sleep."

"Yeah?" That was encouraging. Early mornings these days weren't pretty. It was probably best if he didn't see her until closer to noon – by then she usually managed to get dressed and put on a little make-up. She gave him a long, speculative look. If she didn't look like hell, perhaps she should take advantage of the situation. At night, she was too wiped out to do anything but sleep.

"What's going on today?" he asked.

"Not a lot. I was just thinking about supper." Among other things, she added to herself. "I may need to run over to the grocery store."

Grant frowned. "Why can't Rita or Sara go for you?"

"I can still manage to get myself to the store," she told him. "Besides, Rita is off, and Sara went to Tulsa." She cocked her head, waiting for a response. "No appointments, either."

He took a seat at the bar and picked up the newspaper, then turned toward her, apparently missing the invitation in her voice. "Oh. You need something? Got a honey-do list for me?"

Clearly, she was a bit rusty. Disappointed, Mary swallowed the lump in her throat. She'd never had to hint this hard with her husband, and it made her feel needy – if not invisible. He was so polite. Very accommodating. Which wasn't bad, but it worried her. She couldn't help but wonder if her sickness had made her more of a patient than a wife. So often she looked tired and pale, and felt lethargic. And had the drooping lip. Maybe it was all just a huge turnoff.

She bit her lip when dumb tears sprang to her eyes. With a hand on her hip, she stared at him.

His eyes widened. "What?"

"Grant, I just told you I'm free all day, and no one else is here. And a honey-do list is what comes to mind?" Glancing away, she choked out a forced laugh. "Where is your imagination?"

She looked at him then, and saw the surprise on his face change to something else. A slow smile spread across his face.

"We haven't taken advantage of certain retirement benefits in a long time," she said softly.

He pushed back the chair, and came toward her. "Now that's a problem I can fix."

\*\*

Mary ran a hand over the heavy arm that circled her waist. "That was nice," she murmured.

Grant scooped her closer to his chest, and she snuggled in, happily sated and glad she'd made the suggestion – and had the energy to follow through.

"Very," he whispered against her hair. He held her a few moments longer, then stirred. "I should probably get up and get some things done. Want to make me a grocery list?"

She stretched her legs, and smiled up at him. "No. I feel like getting out. I'll take a rain check on that, though."

"You got it." He gave her one last squeeze, then pushed back the covers.

Mary freshened up, then dressed slowly, not because she had to, but because she could, and she wanted to enjoy

316

the feeling of warm contentment as long as possible. No need to rush, anyway. She eyed the comfortable black leggings dangling from one of the chairs, but decided against them, and reached for jeans instead. The form-fitting leggings might reveal too much. And she didn't mean her tush. She had plenty of tasteful long sweaters to cover that. But her left leg was beginning to show signs of atrophy. Though they worked it in therapy, she was losing muscle. It probably wasn't noticeable to anyone else, but it made her self-conscious.

She let Grant help her into the car then drove the short distance without incident. Driving was no problem. It was getting in and out of the car that challenged her. She'd figured out a system, though, and pulled the cane across her lap and out the open door.

Inside, she hooked the cane onto a cart and made her way to the meat counter, arriving just in time to hear Regina Daniels request a pound of ground beef. Mary lingered a few feet away, pretending to look at another display. But when Joe, one of the butchers, spotted her, he hollered. "Be right with you Mrs. Logan. I've got those fillets ready for you."

Mary groaned inside, sure that Regina would make some connection between their meat selections and feel marginalized. That was confirmed with a hostile glance from Regina. "Figures," she muttered, just loud enough for Mary to hear.

Take the high road, Mary reminded herself. She pasted on a smile. "Hello, Regina. How are you?"

Without making eye contact, Regina returned a stiff "fine."

Mary could not comprehend the woman's attitude. After all, it was her son who'd vandalized Mary's home. And then Grant had given the little hoodlum a job. "I understand Bobby landed a nice management position. That's wonderful."

Regina took the package Joe offered, then turned to Mary.

"That's right. Bobby and I are leaving, and the way I hear it, you won't be around much longer, either. I guess Whitfield is going to have to survive without both of us."

The air whooshed out of Mary's lungs, Regina's cruel words hitting like a sharp slap in the face. The warm comfort of the day shattered in an instant against such toxic spite and animosity.

"I guess bad things just happen, don't they?" Regina snapped.

"Yes." Mary whispered. "They do." With a heavy heart, she searched Regina's face, and registered the dark circles under her eyes, and fine lines around her mouth. It'd obviously been a difficult six months. They'd taken their toll on her spirit and her appearance.

Mary considered lashing out. Telling this miserable woman good riddance. It might be fun to make a scene in the grocery store. To release her own anger and frustration over her terminal diagnosis. Give folks something new to talk about. But she couldn't muster the energy. Couldn't shake the frost that had settled over her. Instead, she spoke evenly, holding her emotions in check. "I hope your new place makes you happy."

Regina stared hard, as if suspecting something other than sincerity in Mary's words. "Thanks." Then she sucked in a deep breath. "I'm sorry for your family. I– It's–" She stuttered over her words. "Well, I've got to be going."

Mary stood rooted in place.

"Mrs. Logan?" Joe called her name.

With shaking hands, Mary slowly pushed the cart forward.

"Can I get you anything else?" he asked.

Mary looked at the display and her mind went blank. What else had she come for? "Oh, um, let's see," she stammered. She shook her head. "No. I think this is good. Thank you." She tucked the package of steaks into the cart and moved on.

After wandering the aisles in a fog, she mumbled a greeting to the cashier and handed over her credit card. As Gary loaded her groceries, she hoped whatever was in those bags would be enough to create a decent meal.

318

Mary started the car, but didn't budge. Regina's words haunted her. How long before she was forgotten in Whitfield? Had she done anything worthy of remembering? Did all the little things she'd done over the years, the volunteering, casseroles, and committee work amount to anything? She wanted to believe it did, that she'd made a difference in people's lives if only in a small way. As a member of the Library Board, her name was now on a plaque in the new library. Even if people didn't remember her, they'd enjoy the new facility for years to come.

Her greatest contribution to the world, of course, was three caring and intelligent children who'd grown up to be good, productive citizens. Feeling better, Mary reversed, then pulled out of the parking lot. Still, she drove slowly as she continued to process the disturbing encounter with Regina. Facing her mortality in such a real way made everything she did – or didn't do – so much bigger. Every minute more important.

By the time she turned onto her street, Mary was determined to stay involved in the community. It was the only way to stay useful and true to herself. Maybe no one would remember ten or fifty years from now, but she'd go out on a high, knowing she'd done everything she could in the time that was allotted to her. There was pride and courage and satisfaction in that.

In her head, she mapped out a plan. Working around therapy and doctor's appointments, she'd schedule one thing per day up until the week before Sara's due date. That gave her all of April, and the first week of May.

Grant must've heard the garage door go up. He was out of the house before she could even open her car door. He helped her out, and grabbed a paper bag. "You go on in. I'll take care of these."

"Thanks, love." Inside, she put a cup of water in the microwave for tea, and waited for him. As soon as the groceries were put away, she took the cup and headed for the office.

"Nap time?" Grant asked.

She had to admit, it didn't sound half-bad. But she was determined to put her plan into action first. Or at least get started. If she nodded off and did a face-plant on her keyboard, so be it. "No. I think I'll try to do a couple of things on my computer. Maybe I'll just go to bed a little early tonight."

"Okay. Let me know if you need anything."

With a smile on her face, she simply nodded. He didn't need to know all the details, and he would never know about her run-in with Regina.

Mary settled into the padded desk chair, and opened her laptop, then reached for her calendar. Hopefully, she'd remember how to access all the online schedules. A wave of guilt rolled over her as she looked at the blank pages of her calendar. The hibernation had been good for her, but it had also been self-indulgent. Now it was time to do her share. To give those people who'd stepped up and filled in a break. As long as this damned disease would allow it. She said a silent prayer for more good days and began typing her name on shift openings at the food pantry, carefully cross-checking with her personal calendar.

The one thing on her calendar that she didn't need to be reminded of was Sara's baby shower. Two weeks to go. They were cutting it close, but Sara had insisted it be after the library opening. Dana and Claire were teaming up as hostesses with input from Annie and Elise. And a couple of Sara's friends from Dallas were driving up Friday night. With Annie home, too, it'd be a full house.

Mary glanced toward the closet where she'd hidden her stash of gifts for the shower. Her primary activity for tomorrow would be getting those wrapped up while Sara was away. It'd take some time since she'd naturally gone overboard buying gifts for her first grandchild. *Whew.* Hibernation had been good for her, but hard on her credit card. Online shopping was a wonderful, dangerous thing, even for a sluggish woman with a short attention span.

**

By the time baby-shower weekend rolled around, the packages sat like a towering centerpiece on the dining room table.

"Mom, I think you might have gotten a little carried away," Sara said Friday night as Mary set the last bag on the table and fluffed the tissue paper.

"Oh, dear, you might be right," Mary teased. "Which ones should I return?"

Annie laughed, and gave Sara a nudge. "We can take them to the church if it's too much of a burden for you," she told Sara.

"Yeah, yeah," Sara said, breezing out of the room.

Mary stifled a yawn as she slid an arm around Annie's shoulder and gave her a squeeze.

"How you holding up, Mom?"

Though she was fading fast, her smile was automatic. "Hanging in there, sweetheart. I'm so glad you could come and spend the night." She cherished every minute with her daughters – and was also grateful for the extra set of hands, and the unconditional support in making this a special time for Sara. "Be sure to tell Blake we appreciate him fending for himself this weekend so that you could have some girl time," Mary said as they headed for the family room.

"Not a problem, Mom. He gets it."

Mary glanced around the room at the tables laden with snacks and drinks. Seems like old times, she thought. Like days past when her house was full of kids and their friends. That had always given her so much satisfaction. She got pleasure just watching Sara and her friends having fun. After dinner, Elise had gone back to Claire's house, to spend some one-on-one time with her mother, but Annie and Sara and her two friends from Dallas were still going strong.

Of course eleven o'clock looked a lot different from Mary's point of view. She should probably give the girls some time alone, anyway, and make sure she got a decent night's sleep. It was possible she'd over-extended this week. She'd spent a couple of hours at Claire's place helping to decorate for Sara's shower. And she'd taken a few more ibuprofen tablets than she had any other day that week. Her joints ached, but she refused to miss out on any of the festivities. Having both girls home and the chance to get to know Sara's friends was a rare treat worth a little extra discomfort.

Still, she wanted to be alert and functioning tomorrow. Claire had confirmed attendance from fifteen people. Since the furnishings in her house had been pared down to bare bones, she had plenty of room to bring in rented tables and chairs. It promised to be a fun day.

**

Pink balloons greeted them at Claire's front porch the following day. And inside, there was pink everything – pink tulle around the chairs, flowers and booties on the tables, a beautiful sparkling punch, and a sideboard candy station with evidently every kind of pink candy Claire could get her hands on.

Sara's wide grin extended beyond the hand at her mouth as she took in the pink fairy's handiwork. "Oh, my gosh. This is beautiful."

Mary pulled her into a quick hug. "Enjoy, sweetie."

Claire greeted them and also pulled Sara into a hug. "Wow, Claire, thank you so much. I can't believe how fabulous this looks."

"It's been a ton of fun," Claire told her.

Other guests moved in behind them, and Mary pushed forward. She needed to get out of the way before she got run over. She dropped her purse onto the sofa and pulled out her camera. Her plan was to find a good vantage point and snap as many photos as possible.

"I've already taken a ton of pictures of the cake and decorations," Claire told her. "I want to get some of you and the girls before things get crazy."

"Okay," Mary told her. "But give me a head start before you round up the girls. There's a lot to maneuver around."

Claire shot her a quick look, frowning. "You feeling all right?"

322

"Just a little stiff." Mary waved her off. "Sitting cross-legged on the floor for children's reading hour at the library on Thursday may not have been the best idea."

"You were doing children's hour?" Claire's voice went up a notch or two.

"Yeah, is that a problem?"

"Maybe not if you sit in a proper chair. How the hell did you get off the floor?"

Mary laughed out loud. Trust Claire to be real. "Climbing bookcases. It's my superpower."

Claire shook her head. "Come on. Let's start the fun and games."

Claire and Dana took photos in combination after combination of guests and family. Then Claire nudged Dana. "Let's get one of the two of you." Mary's throat tightened as she realized this might be the first photo of Sara with the woman who could potentially become her mother-in-law. She couldn't ask for a better one.

Sara beckoned to Maddie, and then Mary. "Come on. You guys get in here, too. One more, Mom." One turned into several as they added Annie, and then Claire and Elise. Finally, Mary sank into an armchair, and turned her attention to Claire, who was banging a spoon against a glass, attempting to begin the activities.

When the games were over, and the prizes distributed, everyone began making their way to the luncheon tables, and regrouped. Penny Archer, director of the food pantry, sidled up to Mary. "Sure is nice to have you back, Mary. I hope we didn't work you too hard this week."

Claire turned, eyebrows arched. "You were at the library *and* the pantry this week?"

"And, she's helping us get organized for the Spring Fling," Jane chimed in.

Mary wanted to muzzle her. The Spring Fling was the annual local arts and crafts event at the church. Mary's only role was calling artists and vendors to double-check their attendance and requirements. Easy to do from a sitting – or lounging – position. She didn't miss the look Claire exchanged with Dana.

"Wow," Claire said. "You're keeping yourself busy."

"Making calls. I can't run but I can still run my mouth. Imagine that."

Dana leaned across and squeezed Mary's arm. "I'm glad you feel up to it."

A few minutes later, when the guests were seated and ready to enjoy the sesame chicken salad and fruit Claire and Dana had prepared, Claire flopped down beside Mary. "You trying to kill yourself, or what?" she whispered.

"I'm trying to be normal."

"Ha! That'll be the day." Claire gave her a light nudge. "Sounds like you might be overdoing it a bit."

Mary knew her friend was concerned. Still, the criticism rankled. "I know what I can handle, Mother."

"What happened to hibernation?"

Mary shrugged. "Hawaii." She raised her brows. "Seemed like a pretty good reason to come up for air, don't you think?" She pushed up her sleeve. "Unfortunately, my golden tan has disappeared. Thank you, Kansas."

"Ah, the magic of vitamin *SEA*. All right, then. I'd better get back to my hostessing duties."

Mary grinned. "Because, speaking of overdoing it . . ."

Mary considered joining her in the kitchen and attempting to help out. That would be normal. But she decided not to risk it. She might be more hindrance than help. Instead, she joined the conversation about baby names and nurseries.

"I have a name picked out, but since I've already told everyone it's a girl, I'm keeping the name a secret," Sara told them.

Mary was dying to know, but she hadn't pushed. She agreed that a secret was more fun.

"And the nursery is almost finished." Sara glanced at Mary. "I think my dad is putting the crib together today."

Mary nodded. "I believe that was the plan." It would be the finishing piece. The small playroom that had later become the kids' study room was now transforming to a nursery. Since it was upstairs across the hall from Sara's room, Mary wouldn't spend much time there, but they'd have plenty of baby gear in the main living space as well. Her own rocking chair was on order.

Dana clapped her hands. "Okay, ladies, grab your drinks, get a refill, and let's see what's in all these gorgeous packages."

Looking around, Mary debated whether to head to the powder room or try to discreetly fish her Advil out of her purse – until she realized she'd left the purse in the living room. Asking Annie to get it would just alert her that Mary needed something. *Suck it up, Buttercup*, she told herself. She flexed her knees under the table before standing. Three steps later, she let out a sharp yelp as her cane caught on a chair leg, and her knee buckled.

"Mom!" Annie gasped.

"Mare!" Claire caught her arm as Mary grasped the chair to steady herself. Only one knee connected with the floor. But every head swiveled her direction.

Embarrassment heated Mary's face. The last thing she wanted was to be center of attention. Hanging on to the chair, she stood as straight as possible, willing her legs to stop trembling. She forced a smile. "I'm fine. Just got tangled up. Annie, could you grab my purse off the sofa, please?" Mary jerked her head at Claire. "Go start."

Dana quickly changed places with Claire. "You sure you're all right?"

"Just a bruised ego," Mary told her. "Really. You go on in." Mary swallowed the pill, and took a moment to regain her composure, then quietly joined the group. A chorus of oohs and ahs broke out as each gift was unveiled. So many adorable outfits, bibs, blankets, books and toys. So much fun only weeks away now. Her eyes met Sara's, and she grinned. Looked like the shower was meeting expectations – not only to make sure Sara had the necessary equipment for a baby, but to heighten the excitement and anticipation of her arrival.

Sara stood to pull some pink fluff from a long, flat box. She held it against her face. Eyes shining, she looked at Dana. "Oh, my gosh. It's so soft. Did you make it?"

"I did. I'm glad you like it."

The hand-knitted blanket was cotton-candy pink with matching satin edging. "Oh, that's a keepsake for sure," Mary said. She was constantly amazed at the range of Dana's talents. And her patience. Mary silently thanked her friend, once again, for being so loving and supportive toward Sara and this baby.

"Last one," Claire said as she deposited a huge box next to Sara. "This one is a group effort."

With her stomach in the way, Sara stood sideways to rip the paper and reveal a snazzy car seat.

"Wow, that looks like the Maserati model," Mary said. "Very nice."

"Only the best for this munchkin," Dana told her.

"This is much nicer than the one we got for my car," Mary added.

"You're still driving?" asked Marcia Hurst, their new librarian. She'd been a late addition to the guest list, having become acquainted with Sara during the planning for the grand opening.

"Oh, yes." Mary caught the surprise in Marcia's eyes. "Don't worry. I've still got my license. And if my legs give out on me, I'm getting a car with hand controls."

"Really?"

There was no mistaking the doubt in her voice. "Absolutely," Mary countered, glancing around the room. "We've been looking online. It's amazing what they can do. I'm not going to spend the rest of my days sitting around the house." She glanced at Sara. "Oh, the places we'll go with this little sweetheart," she said, borrowing a line from Dr. Seuss. So they might not make in any farther than the city park, or the backyard, but damn it, she wasn't ready to admit defeat.

It took Mary a moment to realize that an uncomfortable silence had settled over the group. Having just witnessed her clumsiness they probably thought she was unstable and about to put her granddaughter in danger – a thing she would never do.

Sara, bless her, broke the tension. "We might even want to put this seat in your car, Mom, since it's bigger and easier to get in and out of."

For once, Mary cheered the fact that Sara wasn't a worrier.

"It's good to have two, anyway," Dana added. "It's a hassle to switch them out."

Mary shot her friend a grateful smile. "Exactly. Who needs that aggravation?"

With the mood restored, Mary took a long drink of her pink raspberry punch, glad to turn the stage back over to Sara, where it belonged. Looking around, her heart warmed as she realized how far Sara had assimilated into the Whitfield community. Sure, some of the guests were Mary's friends, but the mayor and the new librarian were there because of their new relationship with Sara. She'd become acquainted with them and other business leaders. She'd become personal friends with the cute gal she'd hired as a graphic designer, and reconnected with a high school classmate.

Truth was, she fit right in. Mary knew Sara didn't really want to be back in Whitfield, but it seemed to be growing on her. Or maybe she'd just accepted the situation for now and would high-tail it back to Dallas when Mary— when she no longer needed to help her. Or Tulsa? Mary doubted Sara had a burning desire to live in Tulsa, either.

Was it possible that her daughter could be part of a new generation of Whitfield women? Young women who raise their children, form lasting friendships over school events and volunteering and hold the community together?

The only thing that would make Mary happier was if she were around to see it.

## Chapter Twenty-Seven

Mary squinted at the bedside clock. Two in the morning. Unsure what had woken her, she listened for a sound before readjusting her pillow and covers. A moment later, though, she bolted upright at a tap on the door.

"Mom?"

The door opened, and Sara was silhouetted in the hallway.

"Sara? You all right, honey?" Mary swung her legs over the bed.

"I– I think my water broke."

The quiver in her voice sent Mary surging into action. "Oh, my gosh." Mary nudged Grant. "Wake up, love, we've got to get Sarie to the hospital."

Thirty minutes later, they checked into the Whitfield Community Hospital. Heart pounding, Mary held Sara's hand, and pushed away the natural worries and fears. Her goal was to be a calming, encouraging presence. She so wanted an easy time for her daughter.

Once Sara was comfortable in the hospital's birthing room, Mary sent a brief text to Jason and Annie to let them know Sara'd gone into labor, and she checked her watch again. Three o'clock. Let the waiting begin.

"I hope Annie can be here in the morning," Mary told Sara, trying to keep up a conversation to help take her mind off the contractions. "I don't know if she has any important appointments today."

"Neither do I," Sara said, blowing out her breath. "Hey, Mom. Could you grab my phone for me? I need to text Evan."

"Sure, sweetie." Mary kept her smile inside. She hadn't wanted to bring it up. Sara and Evan had obviously decided to maintain a relationship, but she didn't know the details of how it was going to work with the new baby. Knowing Sara, there might not be a plan. But the fact that she was texting him so early in the process was encouraging.

They spent the next couple of hours alternately walking the halls and resting. By, six o'clock, contractions came more frequently, and Sara opted to stay in bed. It was also when Annie discovered the text Mary had sent. *Be there in an hour*, she texted back.

Mary stepped out of the way when the nurse entered the room to check Sara's progress again.

"Ah, we're seeing some movement," she said. "Up to four centimeters. A little more and we'll start the epidural."

"Thank you," Mary said, when Sara nodded. Mary caught the nervous glance, and smoothed Sara's hair away from her face. "You're doing great, sweetie. That means you're about half-way."

"I hope so. I just want it to be done."

"I know." It was how they all felt at that stage. And that was good. It put getting to the end above the pain and fear. Mary turned when she heard voices outside the room. Surprise jolted through her a moment later when Evan appeared in the doorway.

"Evan's here," she whispered to Sara.

Sara let out something between a squeal and a gasp. "He is?"

Mary headed toward the door, and Evan stepped inside. Smiling, she wrapped him in a one-armed hug. "Evan. It's good to see you."

"Hey, Mary. She doing all right?"

Mary wanted to sing and dance. This adorable young man obviously cared very much for her daughter. "Yes, doing fine. Things are starting to get a little more intense, though."

"Can I see her?"

"Of course. You sit with her for a while, and I'll take a break."

Sara's mouth went dry. She'd hoped he would come, but had tried not to expect it. "Hi," she said softly as Evan approached the bed.

He took her hand, then leaned over for a kiss. "Hi. How are you feeling?"

"So far, so good. You're missing work?"

Brows pulled together, Evan's look said no-duh. "Absolutely."

"What are you going to tell them?"

"Sent a couple of emails before I left, angel. Told them my girlfriend is having a baby."

"You did not!"

"Did too."

"Oh, Evan, they'll think . . ."

His eyes held her gaze. "I know what they'll think."

The implication in his words took her breath away. She squeezed his hand, about ready to throw her arms around him, but then tensed all over as a contraction hit. They were getting stronger.

Evan rubbed her back. "What can I do?"

Gripping the bed railing, Sara shook her head. She could hear the concern – maybe bordering on nervousness – in his voice. There had been no childbirth coaching classes for him. "Can I get you anything?" he asked as she relaxed again. "The nurse or your mom?"

She offered a tight smile. "Yeah. Do you mind? They said it might be about time for some drugs."

"Be right back."

Sara watched him go, her thoughts returning to his earlier comment. He was being so incredibly cool and supportive. They'd agreed to stay in the here and now with no firm expectations for the future. But things were about to get real. She was anxious to see his reaction when her daughter was finally a part of their lives.

Only a couple of short minutes later, her mother and a nurse bustled into the room – without Evan. Her mother quickly clarified. "I didn't think you'd want Evan in here for the visual check or the epidural," she said. "Sometimes men freak out, and it's best if they just do the waiting."

Sara nodded. She figured her mother was right. Even though Evan had seen her ugly cry, had seen her with morning bed hair and no make-up, they hadn't shared the intimacy of daily living. She wasn't quite sure how much he could take at one time.

Taking her mother's hand, Sara curled into a ball as instructed, and held still knowing that a large needle was being inserted into her spine. She'd gone around and around in her head over doing natural childbirth but ultimately decided that the end result was all that mattered. Why make the process more difficult? She wanted to meet her daughter.

"There, sweetie. All done. You just relax now," her mother told her.

Sara let out her breath. "Okay, Mom. Why don't you sit for a while? You're going to wear out your leg."

"Oh, I've got it propped up on this chair. I'm–" She broke off when Annie stepped into the room with wide eyes and a smile tentative.

"Hey, hey, how's it going in here?" she asked in a loud whisper. "Can I come in?"

Sara motioned her inside, and was quickly smothered with a hug. As much as Sara appreciated the enthusiasm, the room was beginning to feel suffocating. She just wanted to concentrate on the task at hand. The next two hours were a blur of activity that culminated in a much faster and easier delivery than Sara could've asked for.

"Here she is," a nurse sang out. Almost immediately, Sara heard the first cry of her child, and then got her first glimpse as the nurse placed the baby on Sara's chest. Half laughing, half crying, she pressed her close.

Without warning, Sara's body began to tremble, and her teeth chattered. "Perfectly normal," the nurse assured her, tucking a warm blanket around Sara and the baby. "Your body's just been through a traumatic experience."

When the shaking subsided, Sara relaxed, relief flowing through her. For a little while, it was just the two of them, except for her mother. At Sara's side, a soft smile lit her mother's face. "It's all done, sweetheart. You did it."

The nurse reached toward Sara. "Give us a few minutes then you'll have your sweet baby back." Moments later, she returned cradling a little pink bundle. "Here you go, Mommy."

Sara gasped as she stared at her. "Oh, Mom. Look at her. She's beautiful."

"Of course she is."

She had a full shock of light brown hair, and a clear pink face. Sara brushed a finger against her satin-soft cheek, love swelling inside for this tiny human she'd created. She met her mother's eyes again. "I love her already."

Her mother moved in and hugged them both. "So do I. Now, tell me, what's this little sweetheart's name?"

"Mimi, meet Heather Rose."

Her mother smiled, and squeezed Sara's hand. "That's beautiful. Shall we introduce her to the rest of the crew?"

Swiping at the tears, Sara nodded.

It was only seconds until the room was full of people crowding around the bed to get a first glimpse of Heather, all taking turns hugging Sara and the baby, and snapping photos. Sara looked over Annie's head to see that Dana had joined the party, and was hovering in the background with Evan, who looked uncertain. Understandable, since his role was uncertain. Had he been her husband and the baby's father, he would've been first in line. Probably would've been with her the whole time. Sara held out her hand, beckoning them over. She kept her eyes focused on Evan. She didn't want him to feel awkward or out of place.

The others parted like the Red Sea. Beside her, he gave a private, tender smile, then leaned in to plant a kiss on her cheek. "You look happy," he whispered in her ear. "You made the right choice."

And she mostly had him to thank for that. If he'd asked her to choose between them, she may have done the wrong thing. Her head bobbed up and down.

His eyes dropped to the baby in her arms. "She's gorgeous. Just like her mom. Can I hold her?"

"Of course," Sara murmured, her throat tight.

She watched as he carefully lifted the baby from her arms, and cradled her as if it were the most natural thing in the world. He winked at her, then turned to his mother, who was tugging on his shirt sleeve.

"I want to see," Dana said. Her eyes were bright as she looked from Evan to Sara. "Oh, my goodness. She is just precious." She held out her hands. "My turn." Dana rocked Heather for a few minutes, then nudged Evan out of the way. "How are you feeling, honey?"

Sara pushed back a stray strand of hair. "Good." She figured she was riding an adrenaline high, though, and would crash soon.

"You're a lucky lady. I've helped deliver a lot of babies around here, and that was a perfect textbook delivery. I'm thinking the nurses will be in soon to help you feed her, and we'll all get out of here so you can rest."

"Okay."

Sure enough, only moments later, Jeanie, one of the nurses, came in and suggested exactly that. The visitors began moving toward the door, but "Mimi" wasn't leaving without giving them both one last squeeze. Evan lingered also, and when it was just the nurse left, he leaned over the bed, and gave Sara a real kiss. "Mmmm." Her eyes fluttered shut.

"I'll be back in a little while."

The task of teaching Sara to nurse and Heather to latch on was more difficult and nerve-wracking than Sara expected. Heather's high-pitched cries echoed in Sara's ears. The poor thing was equally frustrated before she finally got the hang of it and began swallowing.

It may have been only twenty minutes, but it seemed like hours. Sara blew out her breath and sank into the pillow behind her. *Whew*, she hoped they didn't have to go through that again.

When she opened her eyes, the room was dim, though it had to be mid-day. She glanced around and found Heather's hospital crib beside the bed. She leaned over to peek inside, and was startled to meet Evan's eyes across the room.

"Hey," she said.

Evan rose and came toward her. "Hey." Taking her hand, he propped a thigh against the bed. His smile sent rays of sunshine through her. Then her eyes locked with his, and her dad's question tumbled through her mind. Did she feel loved? Did she feel beautiful? She couldn't keep the smile from her lips. That was exactly how she felt.

Breaking the spell, Heather let out a soft whimper, and they both looked toward the crib.

"Want me to get her out?"

Sara nodded. "Yeah. Where is everyone?"

"Out in the lounge. Your dad was going to bring some lunch."

"Oh, good. I hope he's bringing something for me, too. I'm starving."

"Definitely, but I could get something out of the vending machine, or run over to the cafeteria to tide you over."

"No. I can wait." They weren't likely to have much time alone.

Evan lifted the tightly wrapped pink bundle and placed her in Sara's arms. She scooted over so that he could perch beside her. In the quiet room, Heather claimed their undivided attention.

Until Evan broke the silence. "Hey, since we've entered the era of full disclosure, there's something I should tell you."

Sara registered the teasing note in his voice, and tried to relax. "Okay."

Straightening, he shoved his hands in his pockets, and faced her. "Do you know why I went to Annie's wedding?"

She remembered clearly. "Yeah, you said it was like a wedding in the family."

Evan shot her a sheepish smile. "Well, that's true, but not the whole story. I wanted to see you. Once I did, I couldn't take my eyes off of you. And then I couldn't stop thinking about you. Then we started spending time together, and I wanted more." He paused, and ran a thumb over her hand. "I admit the pregnancy threw me a curve. But over the past few months, I've seen everything you've gone through – helping your mom, stepping up and giving your all to the library opening, having a baby. You're strong and amazing, and– this may sound dumb, but I'm proud of you." He leaned closer. "And I love you. I always have."

Hot tears sprung to Sara's eyes. Could this day get any better? Grinning, she held out her free hand. "That's wonderful news," she told him. "Because I happen to be in love with my best friend."

"That also is excellent news," he said against her lips.

Sara closed her eyes, basking in overwhelming happiness.

"Oh, I have something else to tell you, too," Evan whispered.

She opened heavy lids. "Okay."

He shrugged his shoulders. "I've been keeping something from you."

Well, she could hardly fault him on that score. She swallowed hard, meeting his eyes. "I'm all ears."

"I've been talking to the board of directors at Community United. They're looking for someone to come in, work the bank a couple of years and take Bill Carson's place when he retires. I, uh, I guess I'd like to know if you're interested in sticking around Whitfield. Long term."

Sara's mouth dropped open, her ears practically on fire with the blood pounding inside. "Evan, are you—" Tongue-tied, she stopped and tried to gather her thoughts. "What do you mean?"

He tilted her chin. "Here's what I'm wondering. Other than the fact that Whitfield is my hometown and my family lives here, is there any other reason I should consider moving back and taking this job?"

Sara held his gaze, and with a catch in her voice, whispered, "Take the job."

## Chapter Twenty-Eight

Mary watched the paper slide out of the printer, ready to put indecision behind her. At least this was one thing she could control. She picked up the paper, gave it a quick proofread, and was about to sign it when Grant appeared in the doorway.

"What are you up to?" he asked.

"I'm signing my council resignation."

Grant pushed off from the doorframe. "Why?"

She placed the paper on her desk. "It's time. I opened the packet this morning, and realized I just don't care about most of the things on the agenda – code violations and park improvements . . . permits. It's–" She sank into the chair. "I care about Whitfield, but I have more important things to do – like spending every minute I have left on this earth rocking that baby."

Slowly, Grant nodded. "I agree."

"You do?" His response both surprised and cheered her. Good. Maybe she could stop the back-and-forth battle going on in her head. On one hand it felt like admitting defeat, but it also felt . . . right.

He perched a hip on her desk. "Yes. Staying active is good, but you were overdoing it. But I do object to you spending every minute rocking Heather. Maybe you could spare the rest of us a crumb of your time."

She reached for his hand. "Aw, are you jealous of your sweet little granddaughter?"

In the two weeks that Heather had been in their home, she had, of course, taken center stage – and taken

337

over their lives. Mary was helping as much as she could, allowing Sara to get some sleep between the three-hour feeding intervals. Grant had run errands and done more than his share of cooking and cleaning up. And he was just as smitten with their granddaughter as Mary was. He couldn't walk past her without a peek or a touch.

"Nah. I've got a pretty good handle on who's in charge around here now," Grant told her.

"Well, by the time you get back from Bolivia, she won't be quite so needy. Oh, but before you go, I need your help with something."

"Yeah? What's that?"

"Do you think you can find someone to put a ramp from the back door down to the patio for me? Or maybe you and Doug could do it? I– I went ahead and ordered one of those motorized wheelchairs the OT people mentioned."

Grant's eyes widened, and she'd swear his face paled. "You think you need a wheelchair? Your leg– your other leg is weakening?"

"No, it's not that. So far, my right leg is okay, but the weather's so nice, and I'd love to be able to take Heather outside. I think operating a wheelchair and holding her in my lap might be safer than gimping around with a cane. I'd hate to risk a fall with her in my arms. Just as a precaution," she added, trying to reassure him. "Besides, I don't want Sara to feel like she has to be here every second or can't even take a nap."

His Adam's apple bobbed. "Sure. I'll figure it out. If we have to hire someone, though, might not get done before I leave." Standing, he raked a hand through his hair. "Jesus, Mary, you talk about needing a wheelchair and me leaving for six weeks practically in the same sentence. I'm not sure I should even go."

Her heart sank at his words. She didn't want to hear that. She did not want to be the reason he missed this opportunity. Mary pushed off from the chair and leaned against the desk, facing him. "Don't say that. Of course you should go. You've been planning this for more than a year. Sara and I can fend for ourselves. And you know Rita and Annie and Dana will pitch in. It'll probably be like a three-ring circus around here."

He stared hard. "Sounds like you want me to go." His voice took on the slightest edge.

"I do. I want you to go on this trip, Grant." With a weary sigh, she stepped away from him, and dropped into the armchair near the window, letting her gaze drift. "You have no idea how heavy the weight of disappointing you is. Some days it crushes me." She looked up to see irritation turn to disbelief. "Come on, Grant. You retired. I got sick. All those events we've missed? All those vacations we'd planned? We aren't going anywhere. You can't tell me you aren't disappointed about that."

Grant shoved his hands in his pockets. "Sure. It hurts like hell. But I'm not disappointed in you. I can go next year."

Mary held up a hand. "Let's don't kid ourselves. Things will likely be worse next year. This is your chance. Please don't miss it, too." She didn't bother to state the obvious, but it hammered in her brain, anyway. He *could* wait. It could be a cathartic trip for him after she was gone – when he didn't have to worry about leaving her behind. But then she'd miss seeing him accomplish something he'd talked about for years. She'd miss the joy of that. She'd miss hearing his stories. Her lips trembled, and Grant took her hand.

"I haven't cancelled Alaska yet."

"Alaska! Oh, love. How on earth could I possibly go to Alaska?"

"You went to Hawaii. That worked out all right."

"But all I did was sit."

Grant shrugged. "The ship will have a pool."

"Hawaii was lovely, but it wasn't what we had in mind. No hikes or walks, no climbing around on lava rocks. I guess it's my perverse nature. The more I can't do something, the more I want to do it. Alaska is supposed to be so much more than sitting on a boat. We're supposed to go see the grizzlies. We can't do that from the boat."

He crouched beside her. "So, we'll scale back."

And once again, she'd be holding him back, keeping him from doing the things he'd looked forward to. She hated that more than she hated the idea of missing the trip. Maybe they could look into modifying it. She sucked in a deep breath. "Don't cancel yet."

Grant leaned forward and kissed her forehead. "If it doesn't work this year, we'll try for next year. And if we don't? It doesn't matter." He gently pulled her out of the chair and down to his lap as he stretched out on the floor. Mary rested her head against his chest. They sat quietly, Mary lost in thought, until Sara shrieked from the hallway.

"Mom!"

In the doorway, Sara stopped and sagged against the framework. "Oh, my gosh. I saw your legs . . . I thought you fell or something."

"Sorry, sweetie. I'm fine." Mary scooted from Grant's lap onto the rug.

"What are you guys doing on the floor?" Sara demanded.

Laughter bubbled up inside Mary. She supposed they did look a little ridiculous. Grant stood, and helped her up, then handed her the cane. "We were just talking," Mary said. As if that explained anything.

Sara shook her head. "On the floor."

Mary caught Grant's eye, and the laughter froze as her heart clenched. Little moments like this, private just-between-you-and-me moments were the fabric of their lives. Private jokes, I-know-what-you-mean smiles, secret eye messages, memories that meant nothing to anyone but them . . . in bed, on the floor, in a car surrounded by the relentless chatter of three kids. Woven around the big stuff were a million quiet connections.

**

After two full days of banging and sawing, Mary had her ramp. At the back door, Grant and Doug built a wide platform to accommodate a wheelchair and then a long, very gradual slope to the patio, complete with a railing to ensure she couldn't veer off the sides.

When Grant declared it finished, Mary and Sara assessed their handiwork. "This looks very sturdy," Mary said.

"Want to give it a go?" Doug asked.

Grant crossed his arms. "Better start practicing," he told her. "I'm not leaving until I know you can do this without breaking your neck."

"Fine. Let me get my wheels." Fortunately, the chair was easy to maneuver with one hand. Holding a bag to simulate holding her granddaughter, Mary fixed the stay on the door without Grant's help, then closed it once she got outside. She settled into the chair and with only a tiny bump, eased onto the ramp. She grinned all the way down, and stepped into Grant's arms. He twirled her around, and landed a quick peck on her lips. "Nice moves. But you gotta get back up to the house, too."

"All right, all right. Such a task master." The chair seemed to work a little harder going back up, but it did the job. Mary applied the brakes, pushed herself out of the chair, and turned to her audience. "Satisfied?"

Sara started the applause, and Doug and Grant chimed in.

Mary considered herself proficient at the maneuver by the time Grant deposited his bags near the front door Saturday morning. Only one duffle and a backpack. For six weeks. Definitely a man's trip.

At eight o'clock, Blake's car pulled into the drive. He was dropping Annie off to spend the day in Whitfield while he took Grant to the airport in Kansas City. Sara tiptoed down the stairs, baby monitor in hand. The girls hugged their dad goodbye then draped themselves across the sofa while Grant loaded his bag. Mary lingered at the door, and a moment later, he jogged back up to the house. They'd already said their private goodbyes, but she'd take one more kiss. "Be careful," she whispered when he drew her against him.

"Yes, Ma'am. I'll call you when I get there."

"I sure hope that international service works."

"Only one way to find out, darlin'. You girls take care of your mom." His lips met Mary's one more time. "I love you, Mary-me."

Mary stood just inside until the car lights went out of sight. Slowly, she closed the door and turned to the girls. "I hope it's a grand adventure. You girls staying up or want to go back to bed?"

"I can't go back to sleep now," Annie said.

"I'm good," Sara added.

"All right then, who wants coffee?"

They both answered with a strong "me."

"But first I'm going up to poke my niece," Annie said.

"*Not*," Sara objected, putting out a hand to restrain her sister. "Don't you worry, she'll be awake soon enough."

Annie made a face. "Okay, grouch."

The girls meandered into the kitchen, helped themselves to coffee, and curled into chairs at the table. "What are we doing today?" Annie asked.

"Well, we could hang out in our pajamas and watch a movie," Mary suggested. "But I bet we'll spend most of our time watching Heather Rose."

As if on cue, the monitor sprang to life with a soft whimper.

"No way." Pushing back her chair, Sara turned to Annie. "See that? I took one sip of my coffee. That's how this works."

Smiling, Mary enjoyed a drink of her own robust brew. "Ahhh. Look at that. What goes around, comes around."

"Can I get her?" Annie asked. "Will she scream if it's not you?"

Sara hesitated a moment before sitting back down. "Let's find out."

Mary and Sara listened through the monitor as Annie cooed to Heather upstairs.

"Sounds like she's got another one wrapped around her finger," Mary said. "You might want to take advantage of that today."

Sara grinned behind her mug. "Oh, I plan to. And I think I'll start with a lesson on diaper changing," she added loudly as Annie came down the stairs.

After Heather had been changed and fed, Sara handed her to Annie, who had taken a seat in the new rocking chair. "Let's try to keep her awake for a little while," Sara said. "Let her look at your face and the lights."

The women followed the baby's lead and spent the day napping and eating between intervals of conversation and baby-watching.

Blake arrived back at the house around three-thirty, and stayed for dinner.

"We grabbed some lunch, then he went through security. Looked like everything was on time," Blake told them.

Mary glanced at the clock. With the hour and a half layover in Atlanta, Grant was due to arrive in Bolivia around ten. She'd have to remember to take her cell phone to bed with her.

At eight, Annie reluctantly turned Heather over to her mother, and Mary wondered how long before Annie would want one of her own. It'd be so much fun if her daughter's children were close enough in age to be friends.

"Remember, next week I'm coming to Paxton," Mary said as they moved toward the front door. "I have my six-month appointment. I think that's at ten, so we can go to lunch afterward."

"What will they do, Mom?"

"Basic stuff. And blood tests, of course."

Annie glanced at Sara. "Are you bringing her?"

They hadn't discussed it yet, and Mary didn't want to assume. "Oh, she's got her hands full. I can get there on my own." She probably should've made the appointment for Whitfield instead of Paxton, but hadn't been thinking about the timing when she scheduled it.

"Well, let me know," Annie said. "Maybe I can meet you at the doctor's office. I hate for you to go alone, Mom."

Mary smiled and nodded. "We'll see," she said. "But either way, I'll take you to lunch." Unless Sara really wanted to pack Heather up and meet Annie for lunch, she wouldn't be imposing on her daughters. Not if she didn't have to.

## Chapter Twenty-Nine

Mary looked at the caller ID and took a second to brace herself before answering. She would never get used to seeing the word Mayo pop up on her phone. Never wanted to get used to it. Truth be told, never wanted to see it. Period. She could practically feel her blood pressure rise. So far, no one from Mayo or her primary care office had called to follow up on last week's lab work, and she'd been operating under the premise that no news was good news.

"Mary, it's Julia from Dr. Corbin's office."

"Hi, Julia." She held her breath, waiting for the nurse to confirm that there was nothing of significance in the lab report.

"Dr. Corbin wanted me to call you. He's found something in your blood work that he wants to double check. You don't have to come to the clinic. He's sending an order to your primary care doctor there."

Mary dropped into a chair, and let her head fall into her hand. Now what? "I don't understand. An order for what?"

"Lab work. We need another blood sample."

More blood? They'd taken so much over the past six months Mary wondered how she could possibly have any left. She blew out her breath, and absently opened her calendar. "Sure. What are they checking for?"

"A second positive on Borrelia burgdorferi, the bacteria that causes Lyme disease."

Mary's heart stopped. Second? That didn't make sense. "What? A positive for Lyme? But all the tests have been negative. That's why–"

"The most recent one appears to be positive. Dr. Corbin is–"

"What does that mean?"

"Testing needs to be confirmed, which is why I'm calling. We need–"

"Is Dr. Corbin there?" Mary interrupted again. Her heart pounded as a rush of adrenaline surged through her. "May I speak with him?"

"I'll see if he can take a call. One moment, please."

One moment seemed more like ten minutes while Mary raced through the possible implications in her head.

"I'm sorry, Mrs. Logan," Julia announced, back on the line. "Dr. Corbin is with a patient. I'll let him know you'd like to speak with him."

But now she wanted to scream at the nurse, wanted to insist that she track him down and get him on the phone immediately. She needed some answers. With great effort, she forced herself to speak calmly. "Yes, thank you," Mary said. "Do you happen to know when–"

"I'm sure he'll contact you at his earliest opportunity."

Mary understood she was being politely dismissed. "Thank you," she murmured, swallowing hard. She ended the call, and glanced around the kitchen wondering what she could do to keep her mind occupied while she waited. She reached for a nail file, and realized her hands were shaking. Tossing it down, she grabbed the claw-foot and made her way to the office in the fastest limp she could manage, and opened her laptop. Staring at the computer keys, she hesitated. Was this just an exercise in getting her hopes up? A force she couldn't name compelled her to keep going. Call her stupid, but she typed Lyme disease in the search bar, her heart pounding.

An hour later she nearly jumped from the chair when the landline pealed beside her.

The doctor came on the line with a brisk, "Corbin here."

346

"Hello, Dr. Corbin. Thanks so much for calling. I– I understand my latest tests showed positive for Lyme."

"That's correct. As we discussed, this is not uncommon. It's often difficult to detect."

"But it means I don't have ALS?"

Dr. Corbin sighed. "I honestly don't know, Mary. I don't want to promise something I can't deliver. It's too early to change the diagnosis. We'll need to duplicate the result, make sure it's not a false positive. I have to caution you. I've seen this go both ways."

Mary gulped air. He didn't sound optimistic. "But if it *is* positive again?" she persisted, her heart hammering.

"Then we'll start a new treatment plan. But let's cross that bridge when we get there. We need to take it one step at a time. First, a new blood sample."

"Right. Yes, I'll get that done right away." For once, Mary couldn't wait to offer up her veins.

Ending the call, she let go of the walker and dropped to her knees. Her hands shook, and she whispered a prayer. Oh, please, let it be true.

The call had Mary tossing and turning all night. Her euphoric bubble from the day had burst – leaving her in purgatory. There was no point telling anyone about the blood tests, not until there was something conclusive. No sense getting everyone's hopes up.

Unrested and anxious, she finally got out of bed. This time, she was simply having blood drawn at the clinic in Whitfield. Wandering into the kitchen, she spotted the mug on the counter – a sure sign that Sara had been up earlier. She must've gone back up to get in a little more sleep. Good. Mary left a note – *going out for coffee* – then quietly slipped out the garage door.

Once inside the clinic at the Whitfield Hospital, Mary's bravado failed. When the woman at the check-in counter told her to have a seat, she hesitated. Unless Dana had a meeting this morning, she was probably in the building. "Excuse me, could you contact Dana Donovan and let her know I'm here, please?"

The woman raised her brows, but didn't question the request. "Sure."

Good thing they weren't checking blood pressure. Her nerves were so frazzled Mary figured cardiac arrest was not out of the question. At least she was at the hospital.

Mary had just been called in, and was doing her best to make idle chit-chat with the lab technician when Dana appeared at the door of the tiny room.

"Hey, lady, what are you in for?"

Mary blinked back quick tears.

"Mare? What's going on?"

"Can we– do you have a minute to talk when I'm done with this?"

"Absolutely."

Ten minutes later, Dana ushered Mary into her office. "Have a seat, and drink this." She handed Mary a cup of orange juice, and pulled a chair around to face her.

"Tell me what's going on, hon. And why are you here alone?"

Mary shot her a wry smile. "I had to sneak out of the house, because I don't want anyone else to know I'm here."

"Uh-huh. Spill."

Hardly daring to say the words out loud, Mary took Dana's hand. "This blood draw is for a retest. They got a positive on Lyme."

The concern on Dana's face immediately changed to surprise, then delight, just before she lunged out of her chair and wrapped Mary in a tight squeeze. Pulling back, she searched Mary's face. "So you're keeping this information under wraps?"

"Until I know for sure. I'd like to think I'm being cautiously optimistic, but I'm actually a basket case. And I'm sure I will be until I get these lab results. I might– I could get my life back."

"Oh, Mare, that is the best news ever. Now I'll be a basket case, too. How long did they say it would take?"

"Couple of days. They're sending to two different labs."

"Okay, you call me any time day or night if you need to talk. I won't tell a soul, but I'm hoping, hoping, hoping it's true." She cocked her head. "So, how are you getting back into the house?"

"Left a note that I was out for coffee. Guess that makes you my alibi."

**

By day three, Mary was having a hard time hiding her anxiety. Her stomach was so unsettled, she picked at her food more than she ate it. And every buzz of her phone gave her heart palpitations.

She was rocking Heather when a call came on her cell phone from Dr. Bates's office.

"Sara, come get Heather."

Sara, working on her computer at the kitchen island, looked up in surprise.

"Quick!" With shaking hands, Mary turned the baby over to Sara, and picked up the call. Was Dr. Bates finally getting old news, or could she be the bearer of the new lab results? Mary's heart pounded. Would the people at Mayo leave it up to her primary care to give her bad news?

"Hello?" Mary asked tentatively, aware that Sara was watching her with a puzzled look on her face.

"Mary Logan, it's Dr. Bates. Listen, I only have a minute. I've got patients waiting, but I couldn't let you wait another second. We got lab results from Mayo this morning, and they've got a second positive on Lyme disease. They want to start a new treatment plan."

Mary let out a sharp scream, and threw her head back, which sent Sara to her side.

"Mom! What is it?"

Still trying to catch her breath, Mary hugged Sara's arm, then put a finger to her lips. She didn't want to miss a single one of the doctor's words.

"I'm calling in a prescription for you. We'll get started right away on a 21-day course of doxycycline. I'll want to see you in the office as soon as we can get it scheduled. Keep taking the meds for fatigue and aches as you need them. This would be the time to get online and do some research. You need to know that this could take a while, and your symptoms may get worse before they get better,

349

as the antibiotic pulls the bacteria from your tissue. It can be pretty stubborn."

Oh, she'd been doing research whenever she had a chance to open her computer in private. She knew about the treatment, learned about chronic Lyme, and read a dozen personal stories from people who'd dealt with the disease. Talk about stubborn. She was ready to do battle. "Okay, so is Mayo out of the picture?"

"For now, yes. If we need specialists, they recommend the infectious disease center at KU Med in Kansas City. Let's see how we do with the doxycycline first."

"I'll go get the script today."

"Perfect. I'm so excited about this news."

"Me, too," she said with a catch in her throat. *Understatement of the century.*

"I'll transfer you to the front desk now. Call if you need anything or have questions."

Mary waited impatiently for a scheduler, and took the first available appointment. With a flourish, she ended the call, and threw her arms around Sara and Heather, unspeakable joy bubbling in her chest. She felt as though the tectonic plates of her life had done a course correction and shifted back into place.

"Mom, what the heck is going on?"

Mary grinned. "It looks like I have Lyme disease."

Sara's forehead wrinkled. "On top of everything else?"

"No. *Instead* of everything else. Instead of ALS."

Sara's mouth dropped open as her eyes widened. "Are you serious?"

"Two labs. Two positives."

"Oh, my gosh, Mom." She moved in for another hug, tears spilling down her cheeks.

Mary rubbed Sara's back as they rocked together. "Hey, is Heather good to go for an hour or so?"

Sara sniffled. "Should be, why?"

"I need to pick up a new prescription, and I'm thinking ice cream."

"Don't need to ask me twice," Sara said on a choked laugh. "Let's do it."

Of course the new diagnosis didn't mean she could move any faster – not yet. Mary painstakingly made her way to the car while Sara grabbed her baby bag, and buckled Heather in.

Mary ordered a turtle sundae, and smiled around every bite. One indulgence led to another, and she let herself daydream about the future. Maybe Alaska could happen. She had the chance once again of seeing her kids married and her grandkids grow up. Of growing old with the love of her life. Glancing at her watch, she calculated the time in Bolivia. Only two hours ahead, Grant would still be working. As soon as they got home, though, she'd send a text, and hope her head didn't explode before she could spill her news.

She couldn't wait to tell Jason, either. Her son had suspected Lyme was the culprit all along. And she'd have to tell Annie, and Dana, and Claire, and – *everyone.*

At home, Mary pressed a soft kiss to her granddaughter's cheek. "The best thing is getting more time with this angel," she told Sara. "I've got some calls to make."

She retreated to her bedroom to send the text to Grant, on the off chance that he might respond right away. She was careful to craft the message so as not to alarm him. *Hi, love. No worries, but call me as soon as you can. I have some news.* She lingered, running her hand over the photos on her dresser – photos of the two of them. Picking up the wedding photo, she let her thoughts wander. They'd started this journey together so long ago. Even without a lot of travel, the journey had taken them on an amazing adventure. They'd gone through some twists and turns and some scary moments, but they'd weathered them, and would continue–

Mary jumped when her phone rang. She pressed it against her chest then answered, tears already clogging her throat.

"Grant."

"Hey, darlin' what's up?"

"Oh, Grant. You won't believe it." Her words spilled out in a rush about the blood tests, the days of waiting, keeping the secret, the new diagnosis. "I didn't want to tell before I knew for sure. And now–" She broke off, realizing he'd gone completely silent.

"Grant? Hey, you there?"

"I'm here, Mary-me. I'm here," his voice was low and thick. "But I wish like hell I was there."

She smiled softly into the phone. "Me, too, love. But it's only a few more weeks. And then Jason will be home, too. We'll celebrate."

"I'm celebrating already."

Her heart thumped. In all the craziness she'd forgotten how much she missed him. "Me, too."

"Tell me everything."

"Well, it's not like I'm cured. That might take a while." Mary launched into the details of the conversations with the doctors. Finally, she caught her breath. "So, I'm starting the antibiotics right away. With a little luck, I won't need all this equipment much longer, or the– Oh, the ramp." She paused, feeling a little sorry about the amount of work that had taken. "You and Doug did such a great job, and I might not need–"

"Mary, it doesn't matter. I'd love to tear the thing out."

"And I'd love to help. Speaking of building things, how's it going there?"

"Making progress. Poured some concrete today. It's a good bunch of men. How are the girls?"

"Everyone's fine. Little Heather is so much fun to watch. We've been having morning coffee outside."

"When I got your message, I figured you were going to tell me Annie's pregnant or Sara's engaged."

Mary gave a light chuckle. They were on the same page there. "Either of those things would be worthy of announcing, for sure. And they'd both be a safe bet, I think. Just give it a little more time."

More time. She swallowed hard as tears threatened again. Those words held so much meaning now.

## Chapter Thirty

Mary let her head fall back, enjoying the cool shade on her face while she curled her bare toes into the grass and let them soak up the sunshine. She was careful to adjust as the sun moved so that she kept Heather out of the bright rays.

They'd settled into a routine of spending mornings and early afternoons outside, until it got too hot, or one of them needed a nap. They had to enjoy the moderate temperatures while they could. A few more weeks, and they'd be retreating into the air conditioning for sure. Some mornings Sara took Heather to the park. Other times, she left the baby with Mary while she caught up on some sleep or went to yoga class.

Today, Mary guessed she'd be the one who needed the nap most. Only three days into the new meds, and she'd developed afternoon headaches. The first of the new side effects. She tried to take it one day at a time, but couldn't help wondering what would be next and how long before she'd start showing some improvement.

Heather flinched and Mary looked down, waiting to see if she was on the verge of waking before she spoke. It was so hard to resist cooing to her or running a finger across her cheeks. And those sweet baby toes – it was all she could do to stop herself from playing with those toes.

Mary adjusted the pillow under her arm and closed her eyes, hoping for a few more minutes to enjoy the sunshine and soft breeze.

A sound from the house startled her a moment later, and her eyes flew open. Peering toward the patio, she squinted. Then her heart bounced. Grant stood in the doorway. What in the world? Remaining as still as possible, Mary beckoned Grant out, then put a finger to her lips.

"What are you doing here?" she asked, trying not to shriek.

"Change of plans."

Her face fell. "Oh, no. What happened?"

The lazy smile he sent her didn't make sense.

Grant shook his head. "Nothing happened. We made a lot of progress, and the project's in good hands. Things change, and sometimes you just have to roll with it."

Her head fell back, and she nearly laughed out loud. Oh, boy. Wasn't that the truth? She couldn't remember the last time she'd made a plan and actually stuck to it.

His eyes locked onto hers when he knelt beside her chair. "I missed you, darlin' and I figured out this is the only place I want to be right now."

Mary blinked back hot tears. With her granddaughter tucked snuggly into the crook of her arm, she reached her other one out to Grant. "I think I can roll with that."

THE END

If you enjoyed Barefoot Days, please take a moment to write a brief review at www.Amazon.com.
Thank you, in advance. Reviews are much appreciated.
You can also find Books One and Two of the Women of Whitfield series there.

## Acknowledgments

Many thanks to my fans and supporters who encouraged me to make The Storm Within into the Women of Whitfield series. I so appreciate your input. As always, I'm indebted to my beta readers and critique partners who read and read, and offer invaluable feedback, and to my editor, Toni Ferro.

Special thanks to the amazing women who shared their experiences with ALS and Lyme with me.

1

Darlene Deluca writes contemporary romance and women's fiction from her suburban home in the Midwest. You can visit her author pages at Facebook, Amazon or Goodreads, and her website at www.darlenedeluca.com. Find her Women of Whitfield storyboards on Pinterest.

48114390R00206

Made in the USA
San Bernardino, CA
18 April 2017